The Toymakers

Also by Robert Dinsdale:

The Harrowing
Little Exiles
Gingerbread

The Toymakers

ROBERT DINSDALE

1 3 5 7 9 10 8 6 4 2

Del Rey, an imprint of Ebury Publishing
20 Vauxhall Bridge Road,
London SW1V 2SA

Penguin
Random House
UK

Del Rey is part of the Penguin Random House group of companies
whose addresses can be found at global.penguinrandomhouse.com

www.penguin.co.uk

A CIP catalogue record for this book is available
from the British Library

Hardback ISBN 9781785036347
Trade Paperback ISBN 9781785038129

Typeset in India by Integra Software Services Pvt. Ltd, Pondicherry

Printed and bound in Great Britain by Clays Ltd, St Ives PLC

Penguin Random House is committed to a sustainable future
for our business, our readers and our planet. This book is
made from Forest Stewardship Council® certified paper.

MIX
Paper from
responsible sources
FSC
www.fsc.org   FSC® C018179

For Esther, who was there
in the toyshop

ACKNOWLEDGEMENTS

I extend my sincere thanks to all of this novel's early readers and champions: Maggie Traugott, Celia Hayley, Euan Thorneycroft, Elliott Hall, Geoffrey Dinsdale, Sophie Lambert, and of course Kirstie Imber; thanks too to all of those who provided moral support along the way, especially James Clegg and Susan Armstrong.

Last but not least – no book is written in isolation, and I am indebted to Gillian Green and her team at Del Rey for steering the good ship Toymakers on, and for all the enthusiasm and editorial support along the way.

SURRENDER!

PAPA JACK'S EMPORIUM, LONDON 1917

The Emporium opens with the first frost of winter. It is the same every year. Across the city, when children wake to see ferns of white stretched across their windows, or walk to school to hear ice crackling underfoot, the whispers begin: the Emporium is open! Christmas is coming, and the goose is getting fat ...

If, at a certain hour on a certain winter night, you too had been wandering the warren between New Bond Street and Avery Row, you might have seen it for yourself. One moment there would be darkness, only the silence of shops shuttered up and closed for business. The next, the rippling snowflakes would part to reveal a mews you had not noticed before – and, along that mews, a storefront garlanded in lights. Those lights might be but pinpricks of white, no different to the snowflakes, but still they would draw your eye. Lights like these captivate and refract the darkness. Lights like these can bewitch the most cynical of souls.

Watch out, because here one such soul comes, hurrying out of the night.

He is a barrel of a man, portly to those who would look on him kindly, corpulent to those who would not. Outside the Emporium, he stops and gazes up, but this is not the first time he has been enchanted by these lights, so he steps through the door to be met by the whirlwind smells of cinnamon and star anise. Ribbons of navy blue stream apart and, in the vaulted ceiling above, miniature bells tinkle, spiriting up memories he has tried hard to forget: sleigh rides through parks too painful to remember, wassailing on the village green, Christmases in better, more innocent times.

Come, go in after him. You would not be the first. Children are already tugging on their parents' hands; a pair of young lovers hurry to make secrets of their gifts to one another; an old man unwinds his scarf as he hobbles in, if only to feel like a boy again. If you follow after, there will be much to see.

He is already disappearing into the throng when you come through the doors. What had seemed a tiny shop from without reveals itself to be a grand labyrinth within. At your feet a miniature locomotive glides past on rails set into the floor and, beyond that, each aisle explodes into a dozen others, floors stacked upon floors like the illusion of a master mathematician. Shoppers disappear along one aisle, only to reappear, bewildered, on the galleries above.

It would be easy to get lost in a place like this, but the man we are following knows the way. Alone among the shoppers, he does not stand to gawk at the displays – and nor must we. There will be time for lingering later. For now, do not let yourself get distracted by the bears whose eyes follow you from every shelf, nor the tin soldier who stands to attention as you pass (he is only playing a parlour trick to tempt you into taking him home). Forget, for a moment, the whinnying of the hobby horses eager to be ridden. If you see a doorway through which there lies a wintry grove bedecked in lights, do not give it a second glance. Keep your eyes on the man in front, for he is almost at his destination. Come closer now, that we might listen.

The man, let us think of him as a friend, queues at the counter. Before his turn comes there is a family laden down with a nest of silver satin mice, and a lady who must keep the Russian dolls in her basket from clambering out of one another in their haste to be bought. By the time our friend reaches the counter he is purpling with impatience.

'Madam,' he begins, 'you may recall me. I have been coming here more Christmases than I remember. I came here not one week ago, to find a present for my sons.'

The storekeeper may or may not have been the one to serve the gentleman. The Emporium has been a maelstrom of activity since before this century was born; its storekeepers are many, and increasing year on year. Every new toy demands a new assistant; new atriums and playhouses are being discovered with every exploration.

She does not remember, but she nods all the same. All are welcome at Papa Jack's Emporium, for everyone was once a child, no matter what they've done or whom they've grown up to be.

'How are your boys enjoying those toys?'

Our friend is incandescent. He sets his leather briefcase upon the counter and opens it to reveal a battalion of toy soldiers, wrapped carefully in the crêpe paper in which they were bought. Upon bringing them out, he lines them up in formation, sparkling creations of varnish and wood.

'Well,' he says, and here he pauses, as if he is himself confounded by the thing he is about to say, 'picture it, if you would. It is Christmas morning, and two boys are

3

tearing open their presents. Imagine how thrilled they were to see these. So noble and proud, so lifelike! Well, they wanted to play their battles there and then – but it is Christmas, and first there must be church, and then there must be dinner, and then, only then, can the boys set out to play. I tell you this so that you can see – they had waited all day for their battle. So when the time came and they lined up their soldiers across the parlour floor, you can imagine how excited they were.'

'And what happened?'

'It is, perhaps, better if I show you.'

The customer takes three soldiers and positions them at one end of the counter. With great care he places an opposing force at the other end. 'If you would,' he says to the storekeeper, and as he winds the first soldiers up, she winds up the second.

At opposing ends of the countertop, the soldiers start to march.

'You can quite imagine their excitement. Noah was crying out for victory. Arthur could barely contain his delight. Which one would win out? they started asking. Father! Arthur cried. Come and see! So I did. And what do you think I found?'

On the countertop, the fronts have advanced. Some other customers have drawn near, lured by the commotion. See the woman with the cage of pipe-cleaner birds, the vagrant soldier marvelling at the stuffed dogs lounging in their baskets? Keep a careful eye on them; you will see them again. But, for the moment, bring your gaze back to the battle. The soldiers are almost on top of one another. Three more paces and the fronts will collide; according to the rules of boyhood battles, the last soldier standing will reign supreme.

One pace, and rifles still drawn. Two paces, and the barrels of those rifles hang so closely that the opposing soldiers can see into their beady black eyes. Now, at last, is the moment all have come to see.

Then – the soldiers stop. On each side the soldiers spin their rifles, holding them aloft.

And, on the end of those rifles, hang rippling white flags.

Each figurine lifts a hand to grasp the hand of the soldier it was sworn to kill.

'Well?' our friend demands. 'What is the meaning of it?'

The storekeeper has stooped down to study the soldiers, the forces so interwoven that only a boy of the keenest eye could separate his own from his playmate's. Our friend is telling her how it happens every time, how Christmas morning has been ruined and reparations must be made – but the storekeeper is silent, and none could miss the beatific look she is trying hard to keep out of her eyes.

These simple toy soldiers, these lifelike recreations on which the Emporium has built its Empire, these playthings that have sat upon the shelves for as long as the store has existed, who have provided generations of boys with untold delights, have, for the very first time, lain down their arms.

'They have surrendered,' she whispers – and she doesn't care at all for the outrage of our friend, for the money she must pluck from the till and return to his hands. The soldiers she is staring at are happy now, and it is the most incredible thing.

IN THE BEGINNING . . .

SITUATIONS VACANT

DOVERCOURT TO LEIGH-ON-SEA, NOVEMBER 1906

They brought her down to Dovercourt to sell her unborn child.

Mrs Albemarle's Home For Moral Welfare did not have a sign to proclaim itself outside the door. A wandering eye might have caught the curtains closed during the day, and the neighbours could not overlook the steady stream of girls who passed through its doors, but to passers-by it was just another palatial home off the seafront, a double-breasted affair of Georgian design with whitewashed walls and balconies garlanding its bedrooms. To Cathy, who had known nothing of it even as she was bundled on to the omnibus this morning, the door had a magical effect: by filling her body with dread, it somehow quelled the nausea she had been feeling for days.

They stood in silence outside the door, with seabirds wheeling overhead. Cathy's mother flicked her finger, and Cathy knew without asking that this was an instruction to knock. She did so tentatively, hopeful she might not be heard. But such good fortune had been in short supply this winter. After some time, the door drew back, revealing a hallway bedecked in floral designs. The woman in the frame was wearing a bright gingham house dress. Her square shoulders and significant chin gave the appearance of a woman unused to idleness – and, indeed, her sleeves were rolled up, her forearms dusted in flour and shreds of dough.

'You must be Catherine,' she said, acknowledging Cathy's mother with barely a flutter of her eyes.

'Cathy,' Cathy began. It was the most defiant thing she had said all day.

'When the time comes for you to reside with us, you'll be Catherine,' the woman returned. 'We deal in propriety here.' At this, she stepped aside. 'Come in, Catherine. We'll have this sorted in a trice.'

The Home had once been a minor hotel, and in the common room the décor had not been changed. Cathy sat alone in the bay while her mother and Mrs Albemarle (for so the woman had introduced herself) spoke about the essentials of Cathy's future stay. As they were speaking, other sounds drifted through the common room, past the little table with its pile of dog-eared *Reader's Digest*s and *Lilliput* magazines. Somewhere, in this building, babies were squalling. There were no words, only shrieks of glee, the bleating of a creature still growing used to the sound of its own voice. Cathy was listening to them so intently that she did not hear Mrs Albemarle calling her name. It was only when her mother added her flinty tones that she turned.

'This way, Catherine.'

There was no choice but to follow. Mrs Albemarle led her along a back hall and into the cramped office at its end. Here, behind a desk on which sat a tarnished typewriter, Mrs Albemarle took a chair. She had produced a form with black boxes and now she ferreted in a drawer for an ink pot and pen. When none was forthcoming, she settled on a pencil, using it to direct Cathy into a seat.

'How old are you, Catherine?'

Catherine. That had been what her mother called her as well. Her father had been unable to utter a word.

'She'll be sixteen by the time you take her,' interjected her mother, but Mrs Albemarle lifted an admonishing finger. 'She must speak for herself, Mrs Wray. If she's old enough to be in this position, she is old enough to do that.' She paused. 'Perhaps you had better ...' Out came the pencil again, to indicate the door. Flushing crimson, Cathy's mother retreated into the hall.

'There, that's better. We can speak freely now, can't we, Catherine?'

'I'm fifteen,' Cathy said. 'And my name is Cathy, not—'

'And the date of your birth.'

'The twenty-fourth of May, 1891.'

Mrs Albemarle made notes, stopping intermittently to press her tongue to the end of her pencil. 'And how far along are you?'

For the first time, Cathy's skin darkened.

'Catherine, dear. It isn't a test. Do you know how far along you are?'

'No.'

'But you *have* visited a doctor.'

She had, because her mother had taken her. His fingers had been gnarled and cold; she had felt his wedding band icy against her inner thigh.

Deciding to take a different approach, Mrs Albemarle asked, 'How did you know you were carrying a baby, Cathy?'

ROBERT DINSDALE

By God, but she hadn't. It was her mother who'd come to her, because it was her mother who brought fresh linens each month. She had been feeling unsettled for days, hardly wanted to eat, even when her sister was baking rye cakes on the range, but only when her mother crept into her bedroom at night had the pieces fallen into place. You're late, she'd said, in hushed but virulent tones. By the look of her, she'd been brooding on it for days. She'd even waited until Cathy's father was away, drinking in that squalid little hole down by the cockle sheds, just in case she was wrong. But no: the moment she said it, something broke inside Cathy, something made sense. There was a chasm inside her – she wanted to call it an emptiness, only that was the opposite of what it was. Something was growing; a seed had sprouted shoots. In that moment she knew that there were the buds of arms and legs, the four tiny valves of a heart. She had sensed it beating as she tried to embrace her mother, but her mother had staggered backwards, refusing to be held. She'd probably said things after that, but sitting here now, Cathy couldn't remember. After her mother was gone, she had turned around and been sick into her bedsheets. Strange how you could keep hold of it when the sensations were without explanation. As soon as she knew, it came out of her in floods.

'And the father?'

Those were the words which jolted her back into this cold, stark room.

'I'm presuming you do know who the father is.'

'Now, look here—'

'Understand, Catherine, that we need to know these things. They're the sorts of questions people ask. Why, nobody wants to bring a cuckoo into the nest. They want to know where their baby comes from. They want to know about the mother and the father, if they've got *breeding*.'

'He's a local boy,' she admitted. 'He's my—'

'You're courting.'

No, she wanted to say. It wasn't like that. Daniel lived in the house at the head of the lane, the house with the big gables and the grounds and the wrought-iron gates she had stopped to peer in every day on her way to school. By rights they should not have been friends. And yet they had been friends since they were small, and that summer her mother worked in the grounds. Theirs was the purest form of friendship: the one that begins even before you can talk; a friendship of gestures and grunts, toys quietly offered and toys eagerly snatched away. They had walked to school together and caught first trains together. They had gone carolling, picked dandelions, eaten pastries at the harvest festivals (held in the grounds of his home, such a lavish affair) – and when, one afternoon, she had met him by the back gate and they had done other things together, well, it didn't feel unusual and it didn't feel like courting at all. Even afterwards, when she had decided it was a thing they would not do again, it did not feel so very strange. She did not know, even now, why a thing like that had to change the world.

She realised she had tears in her eyes. That wasn't Cathy's way, but there was another creature inside her; possibly these were *its* tears, and Cathy merely the conduit.

'Has he taken responsibility?'

'His father wouldn't allow for it, not with a girl like me.'

'A girl like you?'

'You mustn't marry down, Mrs Albemarle.'

'Yes,' said Mrs Albemarle. 'They won't marry down but, when it comes to the rest, they wouldn't care if you were scullery maid or debutante. What about the boy himself? This ... *friend* of yours. Put up a protest, has he? Cast off his considerable inheritance to look after his bastard born?'

'Oh,' Cathy said, and for the first time allowed herself the merest bitterness, 'Daniel's a good boy. He'll do what his father says. They're to send him to Derby. Their cousins own a mill.'

For a moment Mrs Albemarle was silent. Then, reaching across the table as if to take Cathy's hand, she said, 'Catherine, understand that, what we do here, we do for the very best. Your baby will rise from the shame of its beginnings and find a new, better life.'

The way Mrs Albemarle was smiling returned the nausea to Cathy's stomach. She was too late to excuse herself; in Mrs Albemarle's office, the smell would linger for days.

Her mother barely said a word as they waited for the omnibus home. Shame had compounded yet more shame (the stains on Cathy's dress didn't help), and perhaps she would have taken a different seat altogether if only the vehicle hadn't been so crowded.

Back in Leigh, where the smell of seaweed cast up on the estuary sands stirred such vivid recollections, Cathy followed her mother through the door. Caught in a whirlwind of memory and scent, she took off her shoes and ventured further in. How many times had she come through that same door, laden down with shopping and heaving on her mother's hand? How many times had she scurried in unbridled excitement along this hall, having spied her father tramping home from work? And now, there he was, eating his dinner of pork and beans, steadfastly refusing to look up as Cathy hovered at the dining-room door.

'Upstairs,' said Cathy's mother. She had already closed the door, and the last thing Cathy saw was her father studying the marbling of marrow from a bone on his plate. He still hadn't looked up.

An onlooker might have thought pregnancy was catching, that if she stayed around a second longer, Cathy's sister – now locked in that room with their father – might suddenly issue forth some progeny of her own. Wordlessly, Cathy followed her mother upstairs. In the bedroom that she shared with Lizzy, the shelves had been denuded of her books. The toy chest and doll's house were both gone, and the rabbit figurines that ordinarily lined up so prettily on the window ledge had been spirited away.

'Don't start with me, Catherine. It was your father's decision, but I'll brook no nonsense from you. If you're old enough to be a mother, you're not a little girl any more.'

'I'm sorry, Mama.'

She felt sick after she said it, but at least that complemented the nausea already bubbling in her gut. It was a pointless gesture anyway; the words did not penetrate her mother's resolve. Instead, she began to reel off a list of instructions: Catherine was no longer to go beyond the front door – a letter would be sent to her schoolmistress instructing that she had taken work – and into the back garden only with the express permission of her mother; Catherine was to dress only in clothes that might hide her swelling stomach. 'It's only for three months,' her mother concluded. 'Then you can go where you need to go and come back to us afresh, our own little girl.'

After she had gone, Cathy took in the room. How big it looked, emptied of all the tokens of her childhood. She tried to make herself comfortable on the bed, but conversely it seemed too small; too small for two, at any rate. She was still lying there, curled up like a question mark, when the door opened again. Expecting her mother, Cathy turned against the wall, but in the corner of her eye she saw Lizzy sidling through.

Lizzy was the taller of the two. Her hair was blond where Cathy's was dark, but they had the same grey eyes, the same high cheekbones. Common knowledge (the knowledge of the neighbours) held that Lizzy was the prettier, and she held herself that way too. Only once had she ever climbed a tree, and even then Cathy had to scramble up to help her down.

'Cathy, it's me. I—'

Cathy crumpled. She opened her arms and Lizzy dropped beside her on the bed, and then they were clinging to each other as they had done when they were small, waking together in the night to hear the sea making war against the coast.

For a time, neither said a thing; for Cathy, it was enough that she was here. There was a look on Lizzy's face that might even have been excitement. Her eyes kept flitting to Cathy's stomach, as if she might see a little face there, pressed up against the cotton of her blouse.

'What does it ... feel like? Does it feel special, Cathy?'

As a matter of fact, it did. It felt hot and righteous, like none of the scorn nor shame mattered, like nobody else on the planet had ever done it before. That was how special it felt. And yet all Cathy said was, 'You shouldn't be in here. Mother will explode if she knows.'

Chastened, Lizzy whispered, 'I wanted to bring you this.'

She had produced a newspaper, a day-old copy of the local gazette their father trawled through each night. It would be something to while away the sleepless hours, Cathy supposed, that or something else to throw up into when the feeling next came. Yet, as she took it, she felt something hidden inside. She laid it on the bed and opened it up, and inside was the same dog-eared copy of *Gulliver's Travels* that had sat, for so long, on the cabinet between their beds.

'Do you remember it?'

Cathy clasped Lizzy's hands.

'Hide it. Take it with you when you go. Oh, we loved it so, Cathy! Maybe you'll have a chance to read it to the little thing, before they ...'

Lizzy could not bring herself to finish the sentence. Instead, she kissed Cathy full on the lips and vanished through the bedroom door.

After she was gone, Cathy picked up the book, smelled its pages; that scent was the scent of being five, six, seven years old. Funny how quickly it could transport her back there. For some time, she savoured old sentences, until finally the sweetness turned to bitterness and she buried it beneath her pillow.

She was drying her tears, the room coming back into focus, when she saw the newspaper lying on the bed. It had fallen open at the situations vacant. There she saw the calls for tinkers and joiners, for shipwrights and salesmen, all the usual fare that her father entertained and dismissed as a daily rite. She was still staring at those adverts when her eyes were drawn to a smudge of black on the opposite page. Between a notice for a removals firm and an advertisement for the bonfire celebrations to be held on the Point, another notice had been circled in ink.

~

Help Wanted
Are you lost? Are you afraid? Are you a child at heart?
So are we.
The Emporium opens with the first frost of winter.
Sales and stocktaking, no experience required. Bed and board
included.
Apply in person at London's premier merchant of toys and
childhood paraphernalia
Papa Jack's Emporium
Iron Duke Mews, London

~

There was a different quality to the letters, something that made them appear to float an infinitesimally small level above the page. How her eyes had glanced over it before, she did not know.

Cathy ran her hand across her belly, pretending she could sense the tiny kicks that would one day come. Though she felt nothing, she could still imagine it – the he, the she, the unformed promise of days and years to come – tumbling in unrestrained delight within her. How could something so beautiful be the worst thing in all of the world?

Something drew her eyes back to the advert, refusing to let them go. Because an idea was blossoming inside her. An advert like that had to be circled for a reason. Certainly it had not been for her father. A message, then, from Lizzy to her sister, compelling her to run?

Yes, she thought, *run*.

She was still staring at the newspaper as the soft autumn darkness descended. In the house around her, time was slowing down. She heard the familiar rattle of doors being bolted and the fire being stifled in the grate. Once upon a time, there would have come a tapping at the door and her mother would have peeped in to whisper her goodnights. Tonight, there was only the long silence. The lamp on the landing fizzled into blackness, and Cathy was left, still staring at the advert by the silvery light of the stars.

Sales and stocktaking – that sounded simple enough. No experience required – that seemed an invitation too good to be true. And, if she wondered why there was an advert for a store in London so far outside the city itself, her bewilderment did not last long. London, she thought. Yes, she could disappear in a place like that. People went missing in London all of the time.

THE GIRL IN THE TOYSHOP

LEIGH-ON-SEA TO LONDON, NOVEMBER 1906

Running away was not like it was in the stories. People did not try and stop you. They did not give chase. The thing people didn't understand was that you had to decide what you were running away from. Most of the time it wasn't mothers or fathers or monsters or villains; most of the time you were running away from that little voice inside your head, the one telling you to *stay where you are*, that *everything will turn out all right.*

That voice kept Cathy up almost all of the night. In the darkest hour she sat in the window, one hand cupped around her belly, the other holding the advert up to the starlight that cascaded through. 'And what do *you* think we should do?' she whispered. 'It isn't just me, little thing. It would be you running too.'

The answer came in a rush of feeling, of love and nausea and imaginary kicks.

Her mind made up, she was awake before dawn. She could hear the house coming to life, the fire being stoked in the grate. She watched from the window as her father set out into the dark. She watched, some time later, as Lizzy disappeared for school: just another ordinary day. Later still, her mother brought her toast, depositing it without a word. Even then there was that little voice in the back of her mind.

Stay where you are, it was telling her. *Everything will be all right.*

But everything wouldn't be all right. She knew it, with the same sinking inevitability that she knew she would not keep the toast down this morning. Even her stomach was mutinying against her.

There was so little to take with her: three clean dresses meant for school, socks from the drawer, the copy of *Gulliver* Lizzy had meant for her to have. The few pennies she had saved were meant for Christmas gifts, but she pocketed them all the same.

Goodbyes would be in short order today. She did not want to make one to her room – it would only lead to tears, and tears would only keep her here – so without looking back she went out on to the landing and hovered at the top of the stair. Down there, her mother was lost in a clattering of buckets and mops, pots and pans.

Cathy paused once at the bottom of the stairs. But it was not a second thought holding her here. It was only the realisation that this place where she had been raised, where she had squabbled and sobbed and sought comfort in her mother's arms, wasn't hers. It was already changed – so, without a moment of regret, she stepped out into the bracing November air.

After that, all she had to do was walk.

The station sat on the seafront, only a short walk along the estuary sands. If anyone looked at her on the way, they saw only simple, smiling Cathy Wray. They did not see the baby she brought with her. If they noticed the way she kept glancing over her shoulder, fearful of being followed by some fisherman friend of her father's, they did not try to stop her. And when she finally stood on the platform, ticket in hand, she understood why: the world cared nothing for a single runaway daughter. It had seen the story so many times.

Alone, she boarded the train and watched the seafront sailing past. Cathy had ridden the train before, but never with this same sense of freedom. Was there a word for having done something wrong and yet so terribly *right* at the same time? If not, she would have to make one, a word for only her and her child. She pressed her face up against the window as the towns and rags of country flickered by. London was stealing up on her by degrees, the railway sidings and towns becoming a city only in those moments when she looked the other way. One moment she was passing through the shadows of Upminster, the next the platforms at Stepney East. By the time she stepped off the train, all the other passengers fanning out into the streets, she had quite forgotten the exhilaration of escape. It was a revelation to know that, after all the pious staring of the last six weeks, she was a nobody again.

She had been to London once before, but that had been in the Distant Past, and all she remembered of that trip was a café with chequered table cloths, sausages and chips and ice cream. A holy dinner, if ever there was one. Now, she found herself coming down the steps into a city she could not understand. A horse-drawn bus was sitting in front of the station, while the pavement heaved with office clerks. It was best to keep her head down, to barrel on, even though she had only the faintest idea in which direction to head. By instinct, she picked her way to the tramline and watched as one, two, three trams rolled past. When the fourth came she found courage enough to ask the driver if he knew where Iron Duke Mews might be. Somewhere up west, he said, and invited her aboard.

Soon, the driver summoned her up and set her back down. Regent Street was dizzying, and no place for a girl whose nausea was growing by the minute; all she could do now was hurry on, putting her trust in whatever lay at the other end.

Fortunately, Iron Duke Mews was not far away, though it took her some hours, weaving in her own wake, to find it. She had circumvented the overwhelming opulence of Claridge's Hotel three times before she saw a regiment of children bullying their nursemaid along the row. Though the nursemaid looked harassed beyond measure, a smile was playing in the corner of her lips. Soon, Cathy began to see others – a father with his son tugging on his hand; a Kensington couple, carefully controlling the chaos as their three daughters cavorted around them – all heading in the same direction. But it wasn't until she saw others returning that she knew she was right. A grandmother, dressed as if expecting a night at the opera, was leading her grandson out of the alley, and in his hands was a wooden sled harnessed to tiny woollen dogs. They seemed to scrabble in his palms while the sled floated on air behind.

Iron Duke Mews opened in front of her – and there, in the kaleidoscope of lights at its end, she saw Papa Jack's Emporium for the very first time.

It was a double-fronted building, dominating the dead-end where the alley turned in on itself and forbade further passage; Papa Jack's Emporium, it seemed, was a destination, not some place to be discovered by pedestrians idling by.

The entrance was a gothic archway, around which heart-shaped leaves of the most fearsome red had been trained. On either side stood windows of frosted glass, obscuring the myriad colours within. The edifice of the building was speckled in lights, like snowflakes rendered in fire. Cathy had never seen electricity used like this, had not imagined it could be so giddy or enchanting. Smells were calling out to her too, gingerbreads and cinnamon that plucked her out of this November night and cast her down in a Christmas ten years ago.

She was still staring as a family emerged, trailing behind them a dirigible balloon. As long as a motorcar, it bobbed along at the height of their heads, while in the gondola below their two toddlers turned and gaped. One of them caught Cathy's eye as he was borne past.

'I'm going to have to talk to you, little thing,' she whispered, with her hand on her belly. 'If I don't talk to somebody, I'm bound to go mad, and you're the only one there is. So … what do you think?'

What the baby thought was: cinnamon! And gingerbread! And – where are we sleeping tonight, Mama? It called out to her through sinew and bone.

The way into Papa Jack's Emporium was narrow, but soon she stepped into tassels of navy blue – and, through a prickling veil of heat, she entered the shopfloor. It was big in here, bigger than it had seemed from the street – impossibly big, Cathy might have noticed, if she wasn't so fixed on keeping her nerves at bay. Her eyes were drawn, momentarily, to the serpents of fabric and lace that swooped in the vaulted dome above the aisles. The mannequin of a woodcutter at her side bowed ostentatiously. A pyramid of porcelain ballerinas turned *en pointe* to display themselves at their best.

The aisles were alive. She took a step, stumbled when her foot caught the locomotive of some steam train chugging past. She was turning to miss it when wooden horses cantered past in their jagged rhythms, their Cossack riders reaching out as if to threaten the train gliding by.

The aisle that she chose was lined with castles at siege. Some of the dioramas were frozen, with siege towers rolled into place, but others clicked into gear at Cathy's footfall. Knights errant ran sorties with loyal companions across tabletops and shelves. On one shelf, a party of pikemen held the defence against a warband of troglodytes plucked from some Scandinavian saga.

Around the corner, where more dirigible balloons were tethered, a queue was forming at a countertop. Cathy joined it and waited until the shoppers in front had finished having their mammoths wrapped up in paper, or the pieces of their pirate galleons slotted together by expert hands. Then, finally, she reached the head of the queue. At the counter, a boy no older than she was battling to keep the lid of a tiny box stamped EMPORIUM INSTANT TREES from springing open, while simultaneously attending to the spinning tops making a symphony on the shelves behind.

'I'll be with you in one moment,' he said as he finally snapped the box shut. Then he reared up. He was a good-looking young man, with eyes of mountain blue and black hair growing frenzied around his shoulders. He had been attempting a first beard, but the shadow on his chin was pitiful compared to the black thatches that were his eyebrows, and there was chubbiness to his face that gave him the air of a boy much younger.

'Forgive me,' said Cathy, 'but I'm here about the job.'

The boy's mountain eyes narrowed to ravines, and when he took hold of the gazette that Cathy was holding, they narrowed yet further. 'Where did you get this?'

Cathy was fumbling a reply when the boy lost himself in a clamour of pages. The newspaper positively exploded around him as he searched for its front page. 'Leigh-on-Sea? I'm sure we get seashells from ... Look,' he said, stopping dead, 'you've caught us on the hop. It was first frost this morning, which you probably know. *Opening night!* That means – chaos and plunder, catastrophe and clamour! If you'd wanted a position, if you'd *truly* wanted a position, you'd have been here ...' The boy seemed to be fighting a battle against himself. Which side won, Cathy could not tell. Stepping back, he fiddled with a latch and the counter groaned open, panels in the wood revolving out of one another at the command of pulleys and gears. As the unit came apart, and only for the briefest of moments, it froze in the air, depicting the perfect image of a snowflake. Then the snowflake fractured to reveal a way through. 'You'll have to stay near. If you go wandering, there's a chance I won't find you.'

'I'm sorry?'

'Well, you want a position, do you? Then you'll have to be interviewed. He's in his workshop, where he always is. You'll have to come this way.'

Cathy watched him disappear into a doorway barnacled in yet more perfect crystals of snow and pressed her hand to her belly. 'I'm sorry, little thing. Not much further now.'

And then, with the cries of some pretend battle exploding behind her, she wandered on.

Behind the counter a set of stairs spiralled up to the galleries above. The boy was already puffing his way around the first bend by the time Cathy reached its bottom. Swiftly, she followed after.

The way was narrow. At the first landing he took her out on to a gallery, from which they could look down across the bustling shopfloor. From here: another door, and another stair, a passageway lined with storerooms in between. Each gallery grew into the next, one door opened into an antechamber from which several other halls sprouted – and, though she could have sworn they had not climbed as far, soon Cathy emerged on to a balcony at the very height of the Emporium's dome. The shop must have grown into the others around it, one of those tricks of London geography that marked it out as a city much older than most, or perhaps it was a trick of perspective – for, from up here, Cathy believed it almost as big as the cathedral at St Paul's.

The boy was waiting for her at a single heavy door, oak with rivets of grey-black steel. He had already knocked when Cathy arrived, breathless from her travels. Here the walls were banked in hooks and, from those hooks, there dangled the detritus of a hundred unfinished toys. A jack, uprooted from its box, stared at them with delirium in its eyes.

From beyond the door a voice beckoned the boy to enter and, with an almost apologetic look, he tumbled through. From the hall, Cathy peered in. The workshop was illuminated in the oranges and reds of a great hearthfire, its walls banked in aquariums and shelves where the toys of past Christmases peered out.

Nervously she waited, the silence punctured only by the tolling of the boy's feet. Finally, the footsteps came to an end. She heard something landing, the newspaper being thrown down, and the boy piped up, 'I didn't know we still had this thing out.'

And a gravelly voice, as of a bear still sluggish from hibernation, said, 'It's always there when we need it there, Emil. You know that. Why, do you not think we need more help?'

'We always need more help.'

'Then show her in. Let's see if she's Emporium, through and through.'

Soon after, the boy named Emil reappeared. The look on his face was either panic or exasperation. 'You'll have to forgive me. They'll need me on the shopfloor. It's not as if Kaspar would rush to the helm when the deluge comes. No, he just preens up in his tower, lording it over the rest – and on opening night as well!' He ran a hand through his hair, as tangled as briars. 'I'm Emil, by the way.'

He lingered longer, so that Cathy had no option but to say, 'I'm … Cathy.'

At this he clapped a heavy paw on her shoulder. 'Good luck, Cathy. And remember, he isn't as awful as he sounds. He's … only my father.'

As Cathy stepped through, her eyes took in the bellows and tools, the bundles of dried fabric that hung from the rafters like the herbs of an apothecary. It was only now, her feet crunching through wood shavings and shreds of felt, startled at a family of wind-up mice who scattered as she accidentally upended their nest, that she wondered if she had done the right thing. Running was easy, she decided; but every runaway had to *arrive*, and arriving seemed the most difficult thing of all.

The workshop was long and narrow, swollen like an hourglass at either end. At its apex, Emil's father sat in a chair whose arms had been hewn off, so that he could overhang each side. He was a mountain of man – his square head framed by curls of white and grey, his face an atlas of fissures and cracks – but by his eyes he was undeniably Emil's father. They had paled with age, but across the workshop's length Cathy could see they had once been as vivid and blue. Now that she saw him, he seemed more like grandfather than he did father. He was old enough, at any rate – or else seemed it. The only thing about him that had any youth were his hands. They were delicately threading ruby feathers into what at first seemed the carcass of a bird. Only as she got closer did she take it for a toy, its hessian hide already thick with crimson down.

Her nerves grew the closer she got. At once the workshop seemed impossibly long; the toymaker at its end shrank further and further away, while behind her the way she had walked stretched out, as in a fairground hall of mirrors. She had reached the second hearth when something picked itself up from the bails of wool that covered the floor. A framework of branches and wires rose jaggedly up, enclosing cam shafts and wooden pistons within. Half of the frame had been covered in muslin, threaded with hair; there was enough for Cathy to take it for a model of a deer, but so incomplete it could not rise to its feet. It turned its sightless face to her, a blind foal reaching for its mother.

Finally, she stood before the toymaker.

'Please, sir, I've caught you on your opening night. I'm sorry it's so late. I didn't mean to—'

The man shook his head, because evidently this was a preposterous notion. 'It's never too late.' His voice was like snowfall, ghostly and soft, and the way his eyes tightened suggested some double meaning. 'Did my Emil take you through the questions?'

'What questions?'

Bewildered, the man lifted a single finger and gestured to the gazette that had fallen at his feet. 'They were right here, in the vacancy.' He intoned them slowly, rolling his whiskers around each one. 'Are you lost? Are you afraid?' He fixed her with his eyes, as if descrying one in her silence. 'Are you a child at heart?'

'Yes,' Cathy found herself saying, resisting the temptation to turn it into a question of her own.

'That's good enough for me. I have an ear for a liar. Do you remember being small, how you could tell if your mama or papa were trying to outfox you? Something in the back of their voice always gave them away. Well, I never lost the knack.' The man rose from the chair, giving the impression of a fallen tree being hauled back on to its roots. With one hand in the small of his back, he levered around to extend the other for Cathy. 'My name is Jekabs. But you might call me ... Papa Jack' – and, when she shook his hand, his fingers were not gnarled like she had expected, but smooth and soft: a painter's hands, the hands of a child.

It was important to be brave. She had been brave when she stepped out of the back door, brave when she took the train and knew there was no going back, but bravery, she supposed, could not end there. Now that there was somebody else lurking inside her, she would have to be brave every day. Brave in the little things, as well as the big.

'You'll need showing to your room. Allow me.'

There was a small bell by the workshop lathe. He lifted it in an outsized hand and its chimes echoed all around. In the rafters above, the chimes were answered by pipe-cleaner birds.

'My room?'

'Bed and board, remember?'

'You mean I'm hired?'

'It was the first frost of winter this morning. We don't turn folk away, not on first frost.'

With those words, Papa Jack sank back into his chair. In moments, the phoenix was in his lap. His fingers danced along its seams, and in their wake sprang up more feathers, crimson and vermilion and burgundy red.

'You can come this way, dear.'

Cathy turned. A figure was standing in the workshop door, no doubt summoned by Papa Jack's bell. She set off that way, careful not to crunch the wind-up mice still milling at her feet. Only halfway along the workshop hall did she dare to turn back. 'Sir,' she ventured, 'don't you even want to know my name?'

Papa Jack looked up, airily. She had not noticed, until now, the way his white locks fell about his head, like an avalanche. His eyes had the faraway look of the fishermen she had known, those who had fought in foreign wars and come home wanting only to fish. In reply he breathed no words, only opened his hands, and the phoenix, whose feathers he had been darning, took flight.

The lady waiting in the door was not as old as Cathy supposed. She might have been no older than Cathy's own mother, and wore a look similarly severe. 'You'll let me carry your bag?' she said as Cathy joined her. Her house dress was a simple starched cotton, and on top of this she wore a holland apron.

'If it's all the same, I'll carry my own.'

The lady led her along the hall, back to the galleries that overlooked the shopfloor.

'The master might not want your name, but I'll have it soon enough.'

'It's . . . Cathy,' she replied, her eyes drawn by the confetti snowfall coalescing into clouds above the aisles.

'And you came off one of them adverts, did you?'

'I did.'

'That's how I found myself here as well, but that was twelve years gone, when his boys was just bairns. You'll call me Hornung. Mrs Hornung, though the first name's Eva.'

Together they wound their way along a crooked servants' passage to the foot of a crooked servants' stair. Along the way, Mrs Hornung trilled and whispered under her breath but Cathy could not make out a word.

The way was steep, each step uneven, but there was light at the top of the stairs. The landing was cramped, barely big enough for them both to stand there together, with a door hanging open on either side. Through one lay a simple washroom with toilet bowl and tub. Cathy was about to step through the other when Mrs Hornung touched her hand and whispered, 'Are you sure about this, girl?'

The question caught her off guard.

'It wouldn't be too late for you to go back ... wherever it is you came from. You could make up a story. Whoever it is, they'd understand.'

She stiffened. 'I'm sure I don't know what you mean. All of these others are here, aren't they? I can work like the best of them.'

Mrs Hornung considered her oddly. Then, something shifted in her appearance. She seemed to have acquiesced to some unvoiced demand. 'You'll find Sally-Anne on the shopfloor come sun up. She's been with the Emporium too many Christmases to mention. She'll show you the ropes. Get your rest, Cathy. There's much you'll have to learn.'

It wasn't until Mrs Hornung had disappeared that Cathy's heart was stilled. She wondered if the other heart was beating as rapidly. Perhaps it could sense her trepidation, and beat in unison with her own. Quickly, she slammed the door shut and scrabbled to find a bolt. Only once she was sealed within did she look around. There was a bed in the corner, where the pitched roof met the wall. A steepled window looked out across black rooftops and streetlights, half a moon hanging between towers rising up on the other side of the city. Apart from that, there was nothing.

'Are you still there?' she whispered, with her hand on her belly. She prowled around the room, until she reached the window. She had not known she was so high, but there was a clarity to the air, the taste of winter's first frost. It was strange not to smell the sea. London had odours of its own. 'It can't be so bad. We might have turned up at a den of thieves. They could have killed us already. No reason why they'd wait until the dead of night, creep up here and smother us with a pillow ...' Her eyes revolved, until they landed on the door. 'No reason at all.'

The thought propelled her to heave her bed against the door, but that revealed black holes in the floorboards that had been gnawed away to reveal the pitted darkness underneath. In the end, she heaved the bed back into place. It was better to be afraid of what she knew than what she didn't. She lay down and closed her eyes; her body was ready for sleep, but her mind was not. It kept erupting with images of Lizzy a victim of their father's inquisition, with the idea of their mother storming to Daniel's house and demanding to search every cupboard and crawlspace.

'How long before they call the police?' she whispered, but the baby fluttered inside her and, to Cathy, its inference was clear: they won't call the police; they couldn't stand the shame. 'So it's only me and you. And hang them,' she uttered. 'They would rather you never existed.'

Such thoughts could turn self-righteousness to self-pity, so she concentrated on other things. She whispered, instead, about all the things they would do together in this, their new home. She had not thought about it when she slipped through the back door this afternoon, but now it seemed startlingly clear: this was not about a week, a month, or even a year; this was about a new existence. 'Perhaps we'll stay. What better place to grow up than in a toyshop? Why, you'd have everything you'd ever want ...'

After she had lain out what few things she had, she climbed to the window ledge and looked out. Oh, but life was a strange and terrifying thing! She was still there, hours later, when the last shoppers flocked out into the winter dark, bound for the horse-drawn buses lined up against the

Regent Street arcades. In their hands were bags in which confetti fireworks were already erupting; ballerinas so impatient to get home they were already turning their *tours en l'air*. Behind one gaggle of shoppers a reindeer in hessian and felt, no doubt the ancestor to whatever half-finished contraption had been resting in Papa Jack's workshop, trotted out, only for a group of shop hands to hurry after and corral it back on to the Emporium floor.

Cathy cupped her hand to her belly. 'Funny to think how close we are. An hour on a train, nothing more. And yet ...' This was a different world, though it seemed so guileless to say it. She was not a child, she had to remind herself. She could not be, not with a child of her own budding inside her. 'It's hardly like home, is it, little thing?'

No, it didn't feel like home at all – and yet, as she hummed lullabies to soothe herself to sleep that night, one thought was knocking at the door, determined to be let in: Papa Jack's Emporium did not feel like home, but home it would have to be.

. . . .

PAPA JACK'S EMPORIUM, CHRISTMAS 1906

There are a hundred different clocks in the Emporium. Some keep time with the comings and goings of London seasons. Others tick out of sync, counting down the hours of that faraway coastline the Godman brothers once called home. Still more keep erratic and uncontrollable times: one counts each third second backwards, the better to extend the time between chores; another elongates the evening, all the better to keep bedtime at bay. These are the times that children keep, and which adults are forbidden from remembering. Only a child could understand how one day might last an eternity, while another pass in the flicker of an eye.

Yes, Papa Jack's Emporium is a place out of step with the world outside. Come here day or night and you will find a place marching to the beat of its own drum. Listen and you might hear it, even now ...

Emil Godman was up with the Baltic dawn, for such was the habit of his father's lifetime, and, above all other things, Emil wanted to impress his father. Consequently, a full three hours before sunlight touched Iron Duke Mews, when it was shedding its pale winter light over the countries of the frozen East, Emil was already out of bed and in his workshop. A miniature of his father's own, its tables were lined with wooden soldiers in various states of undress. Emil walked among them, trailing his fingers over faces half-etched, oblongs of wood waiting for the workshop lathe. According to the shop ledgers, a full three legions of soldiers had left the Emporium doors in the two weeks since opening night; shelves that had been eighteen thousand strong were now depleted, and the knowledge gave Emil one of the greatest thrills of his life. Most of those soldiers were his summer's work, or else the work of last winter's craftsmen, but all of them were Emil's design. He settled into his chair, rolled up sleeves around his meaty forearms (they had his papa's girth, though he was some years away from sprouting the same wiry hair), and set to work. Simple infantrymen and cavalry he allowed the shop hands to sculpt and paint, but the Emporium's most prized pieces were for Emil alone.

By the flick of a wrist, the deft twirl of a brush and a misting of lacquer, the faces of the soldiers became known. Emil worked by rote but he worked as if in a trance, his fingers crafting expressions that astonished him when he set each soldier down to dry. This first was of noble bearing; this second had waged too many battles before; this third carried the scars of some prior campaign and wore a look that revealed his innermost dream: to return to the sweetheart he had left behind. In this way, an hour passed in Emil's workshop, then two and then three. Not a window here looked out upon the outside world but he knew when dawn was breaking by the rattling in the pipes, the echo of distant footsteps which told him the shop hands were up, about, and preparing for the chaos of the day.

His morning's work would have to end here, with the final soldier in his hand. With a flurry of paint and varnish he crafted a face, dipped him in lacquer to create jackboots of sparkling green, adorned him with tiny brass medals and a sash of crimson red. It was only when he set the soldier down among the others that he realised what he had created – for this figurine was quite the most venerable of all. This soldier bore the many campaigns he had waged with a quiet dignity; this soldier had a single scar above his left eye, a line in the wood caused by some enemy soldier's sabre; this soldier had known triumph and disaster and treated those impostors exactly the same. He was, Emil decided, quite extraordinary; any boy would be proud to have him among his collection.

A tingle he had not felt in many months was lighting up every nerve of his body. He would have to set the shop hands to replicating it soon. Their copies would be imperfect, but they would still be toys to shout about, toys to draw the customers back. Thinking of the stories his papa once told, he decided to give it a name like no other. This, he decided, would be the first: the Imperial Kapitan.

The great bell in the Emporium dome was tolling, bringing the rest of the shop hands out from their roosts. Emil hurried out of his workshop and on to the shop floor. While he had been sleeping, the night hands had transformed the displays. Theirs was a job coveted by all the rest: to come out after dark and work wonders along the atriums and aisles. This morning an Oriental dragon snaked from one end of the store to another. The atrium at the Emporium's heart had become the wilderness lair of two enormous black bears.

The doors would not open for another two hours but the first-shift shop hands were already at work. Emil trod among them, eager to show the Imperial Kapitan to everyone he passed, but most were too engrossed in their tasks to stop. Kesey and Dunmore, who had first come to the Emporium as astonished customers and signed up as shop hands the winter they came of age, were corralling a herd of runnerless rocking horses, painted up as if they had cantered down from the Siberian steppes. Sally-Anne was repopulating the princess aisle, decimated in last night's deluge, while John Horwood, the Emporium caretaker, was patching holes in the floorboards caused by some boys' pitched battle. Even the new girl, the one who had arrived on opening night and barely spoken a word ever since, was emerging from the storerooms, heaving a sled spilling over with fresh stock.

Emil fingered the Imperial Kapitan in his pocket. It occurred to him that there was only one person he really wanted to show, and that was the one person who hadn't even deigned to get out of bed.

Kaspar.

Emil took the short cut to the Godmans' quarters, high in the Emporium eaves. Mrs Hornung was serving Papa Jack his salt fish for breakfast, but Emil's brother Kaspar was nowhere to be found. His bed had the air of one that had not been slept in for days, its covers heaped high in a kind of vagabond's nest (Mrs Hornung had long since forsaken cleaning the Godman boys' rooms on account of the clockwork spiders she had once caught nesting there). Kaspar's notebook was open at the side of his bed but Emil was proud enough to resist peeking inside; whatever designs had been scribbled here were Kaspar's alone and he had no desire to betray him. When the Emporium one day belonged to Emil, he wanted the victory to be *clean*.

There was another place his brother would be – and sure enough, there he was, bent over the worktable in the attic workshop above their father's own. Bigger than Emil's only because they had once shared it (Emil had left three winters ago and built a workshop of his own, a private place where their secrets need not be shared), it was cluttered with more debris than Emil thought possible. A disorderly workshop, Emil knew, meant a disorderly mind. He allowed himself the slightest of all smiles.

Kaspar was at the hearth in the hourglass's end, though no fire had been kindled in the grate. One year Emil's senior, he had shed the puppy fat both boys had once had and which Emil's body stubbornly refused to lose, and crouched over his work table with the same intensity with which Emil had worked on his soldiers. His hair was swept back in an ostentatious peak, revealing eyes more shrill and blue than Emil's, and a nose that might have befitted a Roman legionnaire. Emil saw, with a sinking feeling, that the Imperial Kapitan had features almost wholly the same, and the thought brought him great displeasure.

Nevertheless, 'Kaspar,' he called out, 'I've something to … Wait until you …'

'One moment, little brother. *I've* something to show *you.*'

On the worktop in front of Kaspar sat a simple glass jar, etched in sygils and lines. Kaspar took a small candle from the mantel on top of the hearth, struck a match against the wick and dropped it into the jar. Moments later he screwed the lid shut – and reclined as the dark workshop walls turned into a theatre of shadows and lights.

The walls were a kaleidoscope, animals and men picked out in different gradations of shadow and all of them spinning a synchronised *arabesque*. A princess appeared, blew a kiss at Emil, and vanished in a whirlwind of dancing girls. An armada of galleons manifested, and beneath them there arose a great whale, which devoured each ship in turn. Stick men sailors tossed themselves overboard, lost to the shadowy sea.

'A night light!' Kaspar exclaimed. 'For boys and girls too excitable to go to sleep. Can you imagine it, Emil? Your nursemaid comes, reads you some dull-as-ditch water story – probably with a nice *moral* at its end – and expects you to roll over and sleep. But – *bang!* – they close the door, you light your light, and ...'

Emil barely heard the rest. On the walls, a swarm of fairies were dancing in pirouette as a vast, fire-breathing serpent struggled to fight them off. A knight on a fierce destrier dropped his lance and cantered in, skewering the dreaded beast in the same moment that his horse revealed itself a pegasus, spread its wings and took flight.

In the jar the candle guttered and died. The shadow spell vanished, leaving behind only naked walls – naked walls and a familiar, obliterated feeling in Emil's stomach. He had been fingering the Imperial Kapitan all the while, but now he slipped it back into his pocket.

'Well? What was it you wanted to show me, little brother?'

Kaspar had kicked back, a satisfied grin on his face.

'I'll show you a fist full of my knuckles if you aren't on the shopfloor when those doors open. You've had all summer for trying new things, Kaspar. It isn't fair to shirk all the hard work ...'

Kaspar skipped through the detritus of the workshop floor and put an arm around his brother. 'You're being a scoundrel. Don't you think it took hard work, my night light?'

Emil was about to reply when the workshop door blew open, as if under the fist of a blizzard, and there hunched their father. The great bear had to stoop to come into the workshop, for it had been built to the design of a twelve-year-old boy.

'Papa,' Kaspar exclaimed, always swift to the attack, 'might I ...'

In a second he had lit a new candle in the jar. This time, the shadow dance was different. Emil tried to resist his delight as a damsel-in-distress fled from the wolf pack of a spidery forest, as a castle made out of clouds descended from on high, as mermaids danced and swam in formation.

All the while, Papa Jack's glacial eyes flitted between the shadow dance and Emil. Then, when the performance was in full flight, he tramped across the workshop, took Kaspar's place at the worktop and snuffed the candlelight. A moment later he was pressing a minuscule blade to the jar. A magnifying glass was in his eye and he was scratching particles away, opening up infinitesimal chasms, prompting a billion tiny fractures in the glass.

When he was done, he set the jar back down, relit the candle and fastened the lid.

Fireworks exploded across the walls. What started as shadows turned into blooms of glittering colour. The fairies that fought with the dragon fluttered wings of silver, cyan and gold. The dragon's scales were emerald green, and the pegasus was white as the world's most dazzling pearl.

Unicorns cantered across rolling dells, castles sat stark while briars rose up around them, burst open with ruby-red roses, and withered away again. A rainbow burst out of the masonry and cascaded from one wall to the next, erupting in gold in every place that it landed.

Papa Jack picked himself up. 'I don't want you two fighting today. There's an example needs setting. It's well understood.' Then he pressed a piece of parchment into Emil's hands and disappeared.

Emil made as if to follow, but Kaspar remained still.

'Yours was magical, Kaspar. It was.'

More magical than my soldiers, thought Emil, though he said not a word.

'How does he do it?'

If I knew that, thought Emil, *I'd be doing it too. And then – then the Emporium would come to me …*

Kaspar raised his hand, as if to swat the jar on to the floor – but something, perhaps his sense of wonder, perhaps his ambition, stayed his hand. 'Come on, little brother,' he said, 'haven't we got work to do?'

And that was how another day at Papa Jack's Emporium began.

The paper Papa Jack had passed to them was a list of chores only the Godman brothers were entrusted to undertake. The reindeer which had starred in the opening night extravaganza had wandered into one of the storerooms and set to grazing on the bales of felt warehoused there; their motors needed neutering for they were literally eating the winter's profits. By the time that was done the shop was open, the first customers swarming the aisles. Emil tramped (and Kaspar sashayed) to the atrium at the centre of the aisles and set to work on the diorama waiting there.

An hour later they were still hard at work, grappling after a nuance that always seemed out of reach. While Emil worked on the landscape of papier mâché and clay, Kaspar crouched between the jaws of the two enormous bears, positioning their teeth to provide just the right amount of horror (fear had to be leavened by joy, or a toy had no appeal at all). It was an operation that was taking the brothers much longer than it ought, because Kaspar kept rising on to his haunches to peer through the stacks at the new girl working in the alcove of paper trees. There was something about her that kept drawing his eye, though Emil would have pointed out that *every* new girl drew Kaspar's eye. It was one of the many things that exasperated him about his brother.

'She's called Cathy. Cathy Wray.'

'There's something about her.' Kaspar slid the final tooth into place. Perhaps the effect caught even him off guard, for suddenly he could feel the moist breath of the bear across his cheek – and all the terror that came with it. That was when he knew he had the diorama just right; that was the kind of thrill little boys would want. 'How long has it been since she came?'

'Two weeks,' said Emil. 'Three?'

'And you're only just telling me now?'

'Kaspar, I'm really not telling you a thing ...'

Emil stared. This girl, this Cathy Wray, was filling shelves with more EMPORIUM INSTANT TREES. They were a new toy for this winter, and it pained him to remember that they were one of Kaspar's inventions. Their papa hadn't even seen any need to tweak them himself, and this pained him most of all. The toy over which Emil had spent all summer labouring – the pipe-cleaner birds who, released from their nests, would explode forth and find roosts on top of cupboards and bedposts and picture rails – were selling in pitiful numbers compared to the trees. When customers bought them at all, it was only so that they had something to roost in one of Kaspar's Scots pines.

'Do we know where she came from?'

'She answered one of Papa's adverts.'

'So do they all,' sighed Kaspar, and, picking himself up, he vaulted the first black bear and took off through the aisles.

Emil watched him go. There was a time when he used to think: when I'm Kaspar's age, I'll be just like him; I'll be making the toys they all clamour for, and I'll be vaulting bears; I'll be talking to the shop girls whenever Papa's looking the other way. But the thing he'd been thinking recently was: I'm already Kaspar's age. I'm the age he was last year, and last year I was the age he was the year before that. That was the fate of being a younger brother. Sometimes he wished there was some way he might catch up, overtake him somehow – if, only for a moment, Kaspar might have been the one looking up to *him*, cooing over the toys *he* had made, sloping off to his workshop at night and thinking (no, *dreaming*) that one day he'd be as close to achieving the feats their papa could in his most marvellous toys. But that was a terrible thing to think about his own flesh and blood. He and Kaspar had played in these halls for so many years, built labyrinthine dens together, spent whole weeks running wild with the rocking horses. There was not a memory in Emil's head in which Kaspar did not sit at his left-hand side – so why was it that, in recent seasons, things had started to feel so strained?

He thought, suddenly, of the feat of magic in the workshop above, how Kaspar's night light had cast those enchantments, even before their papa's tinkering had magnified it a thousandfold. There was a time only their father was capable of such things. He might have brooded further, but small hands were tugging at his sleeve, and when he looked down there was a girl, bearing up one of his father's Russian horses and begging him to show her how to make it canter. He settled down, cross-legged, right there in the middle of the aisle. Let Kaspar talk to the shop girls all he wanted. Let him chase real magic, let him devise the most fanciful, flamboyant toys his imagination would allow. Emil (or so he told himself) needed nothing of that. He set the little horse to canter and placed by its side the Imperial Kapitan. Once wound up, the Kapitan marched off to war at the side of his trusty steed. The little girl beamed and clapped her hands at their dainty movements, and out of the aisles poured more boys, more girls, all desperate to see.

Yes, let Kaspar dream up anything he cared to dream; this was where the true joy of the Emporium existed – in the ordinary magic of children at play.

Cathy was concentrating so deeply on building her pyramid of boxed-up trees that she did not notice Kaspar's approach. It was the middle of the afternoon and across the Emporium the shopkeeps were tending to their aisles. Seventeen days had passed since the night she stepped through the Emporium doors. There had been much to learn, and had it not been for the moments when nausea got the better of her and she had to bolt for a secluded corner or washroom, those first Emporium days might have passed in a blur. As it was, fixing her mind and trying to commit all its many corners to memory gave Cathy a focus that helped her ride each crest and wave.

It was important to do a good job. She made it her litany as she set about her tasks. 'If we do a good job, they'll want us to stay, even after Christmas.' That seemed important. Get to Christmas, get to New Year, and things could begin afresh. By then, they'd like her. By then, she'd be indispensable. She'd done it before. That summer in the raspberry fields, they'd begged her to come back next season, said she did the work of ten other girls (and didn't even shovel the berries into her face all day as well). 'We'll make it so this place can't go on without us, little thing ...'

She placed another box on the shelf. This one, or so the simple stencilling declared, was a black larch. The one she was placing on top of it was Bosnian pine. Most of the trees in the pyramid were hawthorn and horse chestnut, and a separate stack were simple firs, of the kind draped in tinsel outside the Emporium doors. People had been buying them instead of Christmas trees; there had even been a letter from the Forestry Commission instructing them to desist. Each box had a tiny image etched into it with a burnt match-head, and under that were the words 'WARNING: DO NOT SHAKE'.

'Watch how you go with those. Open them wrong and they'll put down roots.'

She turned. There, propped against a pillar, was the boy they called Kaspar. She had seen him often enough, striding across the shopfloor with his black hair flowing behind him, dressed in a waistcoat more ostentatious than she had ever seen on a boy of his age. Like his brother Emil, he had eyes of the shrillest blue, but Kaspar was lean and angular where his brother was given to fat. The way he held himself, he almost seemed to be reclining, even while he stood upright. Sally-Anne, who lodged in a room in the same attic as Cathy and had been with the Emporium every winter since opening night, said he was the one you had to watch out for; his tongue was loose, but his hands were looser. 'And him,' she said, 'just nineteen years of age ...'

'They're mine, don't you know?'

He said it with the same pride Cathy's sister had when she was but two and three years old. Every last thing – be it a toy, a spoon, a seashell – had been *mine mine mine*.

'These trees?'

'You wouldn't think it, but that's three months of my life you're putting on those shelves. Papa says it's as good as any toy he ever made, and he wouldn't say that lightly.' At this point, a dog of cotton wadding and patchwork paws crossed the mouth of the alcove, stopped at one of the paper trees to cock a leg, and drifted on. Cathy followed it with her eyes, then looked at Kaspar as if to say: *as good as that?* But Kaspar was not deterred. 'It really is a marvel of engineering. Shall I show you?'

It was on the tip of her tongue to excuse herself, but Kaspar was already lifting a boxed-up black larch from the pyramid and turning it in his hands.

'You see, it's all about perspective. You can do the most extraordinary things if you keep the perspective of a child. That's how our papa's training us – to never lose that perspective. To make a toy, you've got to burrow into that little part of you that never stopped being a boy. Because, hidden down there, are all the ideas you would have had, if only you'd never grown up.'

Cathy had not lived such a sheltered life that she had never been buttered up by a boy before. Boys talked to Lizzy all of the time, but there had been moments when it had been Cathy forced to listen to some simpleton prattle on about how his father was getting a motorcar, or the crabs he'd hauled in from the traps that morning. She looked at Kaspar with the same glassy expression as she had with those boys, but she was ashamed to admit there was a little corner of her that *wanted* him to go on. The idea that one of the paper trees decorating the alcove could spring from a box so small seemed absurd. She looked up at one now. The display was ringed by yews of crêpe paper and corrugated card, a hazel tree with catkins of newspaper curls. Even the smallest of them stood twice as tall as Cathy. The biggest, whose canopy stretched across the rest, reached as far as the gallery above, its branches rimed in hoarfrost of confetti.

'I don't know where the idea of trees in boxes came from. Only – I can still remember the little village where we Godmans used to live, and how big the trees seemed there. I was barely a boy when we left, but those images always stayed with me. And, at the end of the day, that's what toys *do*, isn't it? They take you back there, where a part of you always remains. And I knew – if I could only fix that memory in my mind, I could make the paper do anything I desired. Well, it took me a thousand-and-one attempts to make it work. One wrong fold, you see, and the magic just collapses. Some of the early ones opened up into great shredded nests. One became this gnarled archway of branches and bones – it looked just like a ruined temple. But then ...'

He had been toying with the boxed-up black larch all along, and now he cast it at the ground. Where it hit the hard Emporium floor, the varnished box cracked. As soon as the seal was open, whatever forces pinned the tree within grew frenzied and wild. The box whirled on the spot like a spinning top as the paper fought to break free. Then, it erupted forth. The box stopped dead, anchoring the paper as it tore upwards. In fits and bursts of unfolding, the trunk revolved and filled out. Low boughs sprang outwards, with yet more branches and twigs unfolding from them, and a myriad of brown paper leaves unfurled at their ends. Higher up, the pressure exploded and out rolled a canopy of interlocking branches and vines, a bird's nest of shredded paper. From a hole in the trunk, the stencilled eyes of an owl gazed watchfully out.

All of this had happened in seconds, but for long minutes afterwards the tremors worked in the tree and all of its details fell into place. The sound of the paper leaves settling was like the rustling of an autumn wind, even though the Emporium was already in the grip of deepest winter.

'It's ... magical,' breathed Cathy.

'Would that it were,' Kaspar replied, gazing into the branches above. 'But some things aren't magic at all. Some things are only mathematics.' He stopped. 'Cathy, I have to apologise. Ordinarily, when new shop hands enlist, I'm the first to welcome them. But you must understand, the night you arrived, it was ...'

'Opening night,' finished Cathy.

'And you arrived not a moment too soon. We're understaffed this year, as every year. We never know how busy things are going to—'

A cry went up, somewhere on the Emporium floor. Kaspar cut short whatever he was about to say and whirled around just in time to see two boys hurtling out of the aisle, their faces contorted in terror. Immediately, he knew what he had done. The bears between the bookshelves, they had been too real. He had aligned the eyes and teeth *too* well, taken his work too far again. It was not the first time. Probably one of those boys had dared to put his hand in the bear's mouth, and when he had, he had felt the deep rumble from inside its belly, seen the gleeful malevolence sparkling in its eyes. It was all make believe, but to boys that didn't matter. Once his father found out, the lecturing would last long into the night: until Kaspar knew what he was doing, until he properly knew his craft, he should contain himself. Things could go drastically wrong with a toy ill made; games turned sour on an instant. No doubt Emil would watch gleefully from the corner of their quarters, because any black mark against Kaspar was a golden star for Emil.

Kaspar held up his hands. The boys were rampaging toward him, looking desperately for a place to hide. Some of the shoppers had noticed the commotion now; all eyes along the aisle revolved until they stared into the copse of paper trees.

Clawing at each other to get ahead, the boys scrambled into the alcove. As they breached the first line of trees, Cathy felt Kaspar's hand close over her own. Then he was wrenching her out of their path. Not a moment later, the boys came cartwheeling past, no longer in control of their own arms and legs. Tangled together, they plunged headlong into the pyramid of boxes.

Kaspar's hand was like a claw over Cathy's own. She had been trying to tease hers away (this is what boys always did) but now he was straining in the other direction, and when she caught his eyes they too were open in horror. Only, unlike the boys spread-eagled in the boxes, this horror was tinged with glee. 'Run!' he mouthed. It took Cathy too long to understand what he meant. By then, the first paper tree was already sprouting.

Beneath the prostrate boys, one of the boxes had started to unravel. Paper burst upwards like a geyser, forceful enough to send one boy flying and carry the other up high on a tide of unfolding boughs. Other boxes, their seals already broken, were pulsing as the paper tried to force its way into the light. More had been snagged in the branches of the first tree as it rocketed upwards, but when that tree's growth suddenly stopped, they continued their flight, arcing up past the galleries and into the Emporium dome, where one of the serpents of fabric and lace looped the loop to avoid being hit. Through the branches still budding newsprint leaves, Kaspar saw the flying boxes open. One tree was exploding mid-flight; uncertain which way was down, it became an orb of latticed branches before crashing to earth, somewhere among the doll's houses of the neighbouring aisle. Other boxes remained intact as they flew. They seemed to hang in the air, if only to tease, but in a second they would come down like hailstones.

'This way!' cried Kaspar. 'New girl, now!'

He took her by the hand and darted along the aisle. Behind them, one of the boxes crashed down and, seconds later, a Douglas fir erupted. Up ahead, a row of hawthorns ascended, battling against each other as they curled into the vault above the aisles. Kaspar steered her left, heard the panicked cries as other shoppers ditched their baskets and fled for the entrance. Somewhere, the patchwork dog was setting up the kind of bark only it could, with a sound like wet laundry.

Cathy risked a glance upwards. Boxes were raining down. One had lodged in the rails of the gallery above, and the rowan tree that had sprouted out was teetering, ready to tumble. Instinctively, she cowered. That was when she felt Kaspar's arm about her shoulder. 'Here!' he cried, and steered her into a dead end of an aisle. At its apex sat a Wendy House, ringed with a perfect picket fence.

Kaspar was harrying her towards it when one of the boxes landed at her feet. She reeled back, just in time to feel the rush of paper leaves roaring across her face. Kaspar put his arms around her, pirouetting through the branches of yet more trees springing up around them. To Cathy, the Emporium was a whirlwind of whites and yellows, crêpe paper and card. Half blind, she let Kaspar usher her over the picket fence, and in through the Wendy House door.

For the first time, the world felt still. Kaspar still had his arms around her, but now she tore herself out of the embrace. She was ready to barrack him, but the pained expression on his face made her pause. That was when she saw where she was standing.

Inside the Wendy House, what had promised to be a cramped corner revealed itself to be a living room of preposterous size. Three armchairs gathered around an open hearth, and in between them was a table with board games piled high. There was a shelf full of books and a deep-pile rug, and in the corner a basket in which a toy tiger lounged. As they had approached, the Wendy House had barely reached the line of her shoulder. She closed her eyes, but they had not been deceiving her. Inside, the room was big enough to perform a cartwheel – and she would have done exactly that, if only her insides had not been cartwheeling of their own accord all morning. She stretched a hand upwards but her fingers could not even grace the rafters overhead.

She was about to step outside and check the veracity of her own vision, but Kaspar reached out for her again. 'Not yet ...'

Outside, the Emporium floor was groaning as the new trees settled. Cathy and Kaspar gazed out across a paper forest. Some enterprising customer had opened a box of Emil's pipe-cleaner birds and they were now fluttering up high, their wings spinning vainly as they searched for a roost.

'It will be safe soon,' said Kaspar. 'Just wait to make sure they haven't—'

The words had barely left his lips when there was a rustling in the boughs of the nearest tree, and from its uppermost branches another varnished box crashed down, fracturing in front of the Wendy House door. Kaspar staggered back, taking Cathy with him, just as the tree exploded upwards, bulbous trunk and overhanging branches blocking their view. Moments later, when the tree was fully grown, Kaspar picked himself up and ran his hands across the bark. There was no way through.

Half of him was already counting the cost of putting this right, imagining the grave look on his father's face, but the other half was grinning inanely, overjoyed to behold this wonderland his toys had made. The customers who had seen this (those without concussions, at any rate) would make sure this story was told for Christmases to come. There would be a rush on EMPORIUM INSTANT TREES tomorrow; this he could say with every inch of merchant's instinct that lay within him. Papa, he would say when the old man began his rebuke, don't you see what I've done? I've done better than make us a fortune – I've made us a *spectacle.* My toys, they'll outsell Emil's soldiers for certain ...

He was about to impart all of this to the new girl – yet, when he looked around, she was still agape, exploring every recess of the Wendy House, running her fingers over every surface as if to make certain it was real.

'What is this place?'

'This, Miss Wray, is my papa's pride and joy. He loves it so much he can't bear to sell it, so we keep it just for show. Last Christmas, a man waltzed in here with a Gladstone bag stuffed full of pound notes, but Papa wouldn't even come out of his workshop to see him. I had to send him away with a flea in his ear.'

'But ... how?'

It pained Kaspar to admit that he did not yet fully comprehend what his father had done to stretch out the space inside the playhouse. 'Papa ... does things. Emil or I, we'll make a toy and along comes Papa and ... he's *better,* don't you see? The things he does – why, there are toys, and then there are Papa Jack's toys. And this Wendy House, well ... I'll get to the truth of the matter soon enough. Didn't you ever have a lair when you were small? Somewhere secret only you knew about? A place in the bushes, or a corner of an attic, or ...'

'Well, yes,' said Cathy, 'but never like this.'

'When Emil and I were just boys, we must have had a dozen different dens hidden around the shopfloor. They still show up from time to time, never where you'd think to look.'

'We had a treehouse,' Cathy remembered. 'Lizzy – that's my sister – used to sneak up cups and saucers and old china.'

'Well, there you have it. And didn't that treehouse seem huge when you were small? It might have been a castle itself when you were five years old. You probably thought it had an east and west wing, different antechambers, a gatehouse and a bailey and a curtain wall. Only, if you went back to it now, you'd find it tiny, just a few lengths of stick and a cramped little cubby. Do you see?'

Cathy really didn't.

'That's the secret, I think. Papa won't tell me because he says I'll only really understand if I discover it myself, just like he did. But it's got to be the *perspectives*. When you're making toys, you've got to have the perspective of a child. Get that right and I would think you can do almost anything with space.'

Cathy had finished walking the circumference of the room and, for the first time, returned to the door where the paper tree sprawled.

'We'll just have to wait it out,' said Kaspar, still hardly masking his glee. 'They'll dig us out soon. But ...' He paused, for there was a pained expression on Cathy's face. She was cupping her belly with one hand and, with the other, bracing herself against the Wendy House wall. 'New girl, what's wrong?'

She opened her mouth to tell him it was nothing, but when no words came, Kaspar was already at her side. 'New girl?' He might have been shouting, but to Cathy the voice was as distant as the Emporium doors.

'It's nothing,' she said, but this time she did not resist as Kaspar put an arm around her and helped her into the armchair at the hearth.

It had been happening too often, these moments when even the dizziness grew so acute she could feel the Emporium spinning. Normally it was in the mornings, when she woke in the small hours and had to creep to the washroom. On those occasions the dizziness could be stifled with tea and dry toast, but more and more often it was coming in the middle of the day. Only yesterday, she had been resting in the stacks when Sally-Anne had wandered past and made some remark about her shirking. Secrets, it seemed, always wanted to be shared.

Kaspar had found water from somewhere. She put the mug to her lips and felt rejuvenated, if only for a second. It was only now, when she was at her weakest, that her thoughts flickered back to that little strip along the estuary sands and all the people she had left behind. And: is my mother still knotted with fear? she wondered. Is Lizzy worried for me, or does she secretly smile when our parents look the other way?

Now that the room had come back into focus, she could see that Kaspar was considering her like she was some puzzle he had to unpick, all his glee at the paper forest suddenly drained away.

'It's nothing,' she promised. 'I haven't been eating properly, that's all.'

Kaspar's eyes dropped from her face to her belly, before drifting back up. There was no doubt what he was thinking, for Cathy had felt her body straining at her clothes too often in the past days. It was foolish not to have brought more. New life was not the sort of thing you could overlook for ever. The baby had been tumbling all day; she could feel it as a new kind of nausea rippling across her insides.

'Cathy,' he whispered, 'how old are you?'

'I'm nineteen,' she said, tensing beneath his touch.

'You're sixteen if you're a day.'

She held his stare. His eyes had pierced her, but she held it still.

'You answered one of Papa's adverts. That means you had to be running away from something. You can't keep a secret in the Emporium, Cathy. Along these aisles, a secret's never safe.'

It seemed important to go on looking into his eyes. They were not eyes you could get lost in; they were open and empty as the oceans, blue threaded with grey like the breakers of waves. The more she stared, the deeper that ocean seemed. And yet she went on staring.

He was on the verge of saying something, but she would never know what – for, at that moment, the paper trunk blocking the door began to buckle and crease. Kaspar leapt to his feet. Without exchanging another word, they watched as the glint of an axe appeared through the bark. It drew back, swung again, and at last the paper monstrosity began to list, revealing the Emporium floor.

In the doorway, showered in scraps of paper and card, stood Emil. His eyes were alive with the joy of discovery.

'Kaspar,' he said, shaking shreds of paper bark out of his hair, 'I just knew it would be you.'

'Who else?'

'Papa knows it too. He's looking for you.'

'I'll bet he is,' beamed Kaspar – and Cathy saw the look they exchanged, the one that said: there'll be stern words, brother, but every one of them worth it. Because – just look at all this! Look at all this beautiful chaos!

'You're a bona-fide Bedlamite,' Emil laughed. And, with a conspiratorial whisper, 'Kaspar, we should go up high, after hours, up to the highest gallery and just throw them all down. It would be like that time with Papa's snow clouds. He'll know it was us, but it will be—'

Kaspar was poised to revel in the idea when Emil's face suddenly soured. For the first time, he had looked beyond his brother – and there stood Cathy, plain as day and with no place to hide. Suddenly, all temptations vanished; whatever they had been scheming evaporated into thin air.

'It isn't what you think, Emil.'

'No?' the younger man breathed. 'Then what is it?'

Kaspar marched on, kicking the detritus of paper tree aside, and passed Emil. From the aisle, he looked back, his eyes taking in Cathy again: her face, her hair, the curves of her body that she knew, for the first time, were no longer invisible. He mouthed three words – 'We'll speak soon' – and then he disappeared.

Left behind, Emil looked her up and down. 'I'm sorry,' he stuttered, 'but you really can't be here. If my papa were to ...' He stopped. 'My brother isn't a bad man, but ... Back to work,' he said, abandoning the thought. 'The evening stampede is about to begin.'

And then he too was gone, leaving Cathy to pick her own way out of the ruin. In the aisles outside, the shopkeeps were already descending on the accidental forest. Some of them had hacksaws and more axes; some of them had brought shovels to lever up stumps. Yet more had decided to leave a tree in place and were rushing out boxes of baubles and other decorations.

Ignoring the complaints of the baby putting up a protest inside her, she rolled up her sleeves and returned to her work.

WARGAMES

PAPA JACK'S EMPORIUM, CHRISTMAS 1906

That moment in the Wendy House had frightened her. She had to admit that. The way Kaspar Godman had looked at her – not admiringly, not possessively, as those fishermen's sons used to do, but *curiously*. She had thought she was being careful. At the end of every shift she took toast and biscuits and stewed apples from Mrs Hornung's trolley and retired to her room, just her and her baby to while away the long winter nights. She was keeping her head down, keeping out of sight, keeping herself to herself – and yet ... *I'm coiled*, she admitted. *Coiled too tight. Hiding away doesn't keep you hidden, not in a place like this. Hiding away only gets you seen.*

'We haven't been thinking straight, little thing. Running away was never just running. It was *keeping* running, even when you're standing still. It's all your fault, you know. When I'm not nauseous I'm dog-tired, and when I'm not dog-tired I've moods you wouldn't believe. I'm up one minute and rock bottom the next, and it's *all your doing*.'

Cathy had found her way through the lower storerooms, where the toys of past Christmases waited patiently to revisit the shopfloor. Now she stood outside what seemed a forgotten wardrobe, its door half-hanging from its hinge. Sally-Anne had tried to tempt her here on more than one occasion, but this time, it was a little voice inside her head tempting her on.

'People with secrets hide away. People with nothing to hide? They make friends. They laugh and they dance and they ... live life. Nobody ever came to the Emporium to bury themselves. So ... in plain sight,' she whispered, and was thrilled to feel the flutters of her baby's response, 'that's the only place worth hiding.'

With those words, she opened the wardrobe door.

They called this place the Palace, because that was what Kaspar and Emil had called it when they were just boys and this place one of their secret dens. Now the long hall on to which the wardrobe door opened, decked out like the lodge of some medieval Viking jarl – with thrones carved out of the trunks of great oaks and a dais upon which three of the shop hands were playing fiddles (or more properly being *played* by those fiddles, for it was the instruments leading the way) – was a retreat for exhausted shop hands to drink and eat and make merry. Cathy stepped through a fug of smoke to find the evening's banquet already half-devoured. Shop hands were lounging around the long table, or in the corners playing at cards. Some had opened up copies of other Emporium games. Little Douglas Flood was playing a game of backgammon, himself against the board. The West Country boy named Kesey was battling through a game of chess; black had already beaten him to a retreat, the pieces gliding of their own volition across the chequerboard squares.

Cathy might have let her nerves get the better of her and fled there and then, if only Sally-Anne – tall, with flaming red hair and fiery eyes to match – hadn't appeared out of the haze and thrown her arms around her shoulder. 'Rapunzel is out of her tower!' she announced. 'Make room!'

Sally-Anne's laughter was infectious. Soon Cathy was being swept across the room and deposited in a seat, where Joe Horner (who worked the production line, replicating Emil's toy soldiers) and Ted Jacobs (who once trained hounds for the shooting at Sandringham, but now put patchwork dogs through their paces before they could be sold) provided her with food and wine and meringues of the most intricate design. Too used to a diet of toast and stewed apple, the baby inside her started to turn cartwheels of delight. Cathy had to take her first bite just to barter its silence, for she was certain the shop hands would notice the way her body squirmed in response.

'I'm sorry I've been so ... locked up. You'll know how it is. First season nerves.'

'No apology needed,' Sally-Anne declared, 'but you have catching up to do. This,' she declared, urging an older man, comprised almost entirely of beard, to the table, 'is Pat Field. He's one of Papa Jack's first woodworkers. He prunes and prepares all of the logs from the Forestry Commission. And *this* is Vera Larkin. She's a seamstress, touching up the ragdolls. And this – well, this is Ted. He's with the patchwork dogs.'

'Blithering things they are as well,' Ted said as, around him, the rest made their hellos. 'It's as well you weren't here last Christmas. Papa Jack, he can make almost anything with his hands, but you just can't get loyalty in a patchwork dog.'

'There were *complaints*,' Sally-Anne butted in, as if laying a taunt at Ted.

'Little boys upset their new toy would only play with their sister. A patchwork Dalmatian, of all things, who took a shining to some old fella's next-door neighbour and wouldn't stop howling at the walls. Why, three Christmases ago, I was up and roaming Battersea on Christmas Eve itself – one of his hounds had gone feral, started running with a pack of street dogs down there.'

'Ted,' Sally-Anne interjected once more, 'isn't good enough at his job, you see.'

Ted looked as if he might summon up a spirited reply, but instead he slumped into a seat, pulled the stopper from a decanter of what Cathy took for brandy, and poured himself a generous measure. Moments later, as he stared into the fire, a bundle of velvet and rags unfolded itself from a basket and scrabbled to get into his lap. 'And these cats aren't up to much either!'

'How are you finding our little Emporium, Cathy?'

'Little?' she exclaimed. Her eyes had already taken in the extent of the Palace; perhaps she was mistaken, but it seemed another trick of perspective, or whatever it was that opened up the Wendy House down in the paper trees. 'Why, I don't think I've seen a fraction of it ...'

'And you won't,' Ted chipped in, 'not this season at any rate. Midwinter's barely a week away and how long will we have after that?'

'How long?'

'Until the thaw,' Sally-Anne explained.

'Then it's drawbridge up and us shop hands out on our ears.'

Cathy froze; even the baby had stopped tumbling inside her. 'You don't mean to say ...'

'What is it Papa Jack always says? A toy shop's trade is in the dark winter months ... Yes,' Sally-Anne went on, 'it'll be back to the boring life soon. Reckon I'll find myself cleaning dishes in Bethnal Green. Douglas Flood can go back to – what is it, Douglas? Understudying at the Old Vic?'

Up on the dais, the boy named Douglas set down his fiddle (though it played on without him) and said, 'Vaudeville. I've a mind I'll chance my arm in the music halls.'

'Well you'd best be taking that fiddle with you. I've heard you try and play a—' Sally-Anne stopped, for a shocking paleness had spread across Cathy's face. 'Cathy, are you ... Is it the food?'

'No,' she said, 'not the food,' though the way her stomach was revolting made her certain she was going to be side. 'If I may ... Might I be excused?'

'Excused?' somebody baulked. 'Lor', girl, you're not at mama's table any more!'

Just as well, thought Cathy, and reeled as she got to her feet.

'Oh Cathy, come on, you've hardly eaten ...'

She was unsteady. She caught herself as she made for the wardrobe door. Sally-Anne was at her side, but Cathy pulled herself through alone. Halfway through the storerooms she stopped to catch her breath, looking back to see Sally-Anne standing, a question given form, in the wardrobe door.

Lives turn on an instant, just as they are made. There was no going back. There never had been, not since the moment she set foot out of the back door. But if there was no staying – if there was no long summer in the Emporium, no place for a mother and child, well, what then?

*

The approach of Christmas only intensified Cathy's terror of what might happen when the Emporium closed, but the invitation that came on Midwinter's Eve pushed those thoughts to the back of her mind. It had been lying in an envelope slipped beneath the attic door when she returned at the end of the day, and Sally-Anne – who had followed her up from the Palace, soliloquising on the Herculean good looks of Jon Mosby, brought in this winter to wrangle the runnerless rocking horses – was already perched on the end of the bed, pontificating over its contents. There was so little privacy to the room that Cathy could not stop her from seeing. The envelope was sealed with scarlet wax, imprinted with the emblem of Papa Jack's Emporium – a single tin soldier of unquantifiable rank – and inside was a piece of golden card:

~

An Invitation to a Midwinter's Supper
Your confidant, Kaspar
9pm

~

Sally-Anne was either disgusted or beset with jealousy. Cathy could not tell which. She tossed her hair and leapt to her feet, brandishing one of those romantic penny novels she so loved. 'He just wants to know what's under your skirts.' Well, thought Cathy, that was probably true – but not in the way Sally-Anne was thinking. And what was this about *confidant*? Cathy felt quite certain Kaspar Godman was not the kind of man who could keep any sort of secret, let alone one as revelatory as this.

The clock on the wall was inching towards eight. Cathy folded the invitation and slipped it beneath her pillow. Then, 'Sally-Anne, have you any clothes I can borrow?' she asked.

The Godmans had quarters on the highest gallery above the shopfloor, up a servants' stair that spiralled out of their workshops. Winter staff only rarely ventured up here, no matter how long their standing, and, like so many corners of the Emporium, this was virgin ground to Cathy. As it was, the great oaken door that led to Papa Jack's workshop was barricaded shut (Cathy had heard tales of one assistant who had gained a position here only so that he could deliver secrets back to his overseers at Hamley's; the workshop had been a fortress ever since) but the stairs grew out of a narrow passageway just beyond. Cathy was halfway up before she saw the movement on the top step and watched as something unfolded, sniffed the air and stood up. The dog she had first seen among the paper trees lumbered forward on patchwork paws, its stuffing bulging where it had been pressed out of shape while it slept. Its fur was of velvet, cut up by seams as if somebody had taken it apart and stitched it back together. In patches it was grey, in others purple and blue. The insides of its ears were pieces of tartan, and the tongue that lolled from its snout had a heel in it, like a dangling sock. Its nose was nothing more than a crosshatch of black thread.

When it realised Cathy was near, it set up a bark. For a moment, Cathy was stilled. Then, judging that what teeth it had were only scraps of felt, she knelt down to pet it. Soon, the creature – if creature it could be called – rolled over, imploring her to knead it back into shape. Unable to refuse the doleful look in its black button eyes, Cathy sank to her haunches and began. Her fingers found the little wind-up mechanism buried in its tummy and she turned it once, giving the dog even more vigour. After that it lolled in ecstasy, its contented noises like the swishing of cotton against cotton.

Finally, Cathy gathered herself and knocked at the door.

She was expecting Kaspar, or Emil, or Papa Jack himself, but instead Mrs Hornung opened the door and battled back the patchwork dog with a broom. 'Sirius!' she exclaimed. 'I've a set of shears in here just right for a pest like you ...'

The dog's whimper was the sound of wet laundry being slapped.

Mrs Hornung had never seemed as sour as she had on the night Cathy arrived at the Emporium doors. The way she looked now, Cathy might even describe her as *genial*. Her official position was Emporium Mistress, a title that made her seem more matronly than it ought. Sally-Anne said she used to be the nursemaid, a job that had predominantly comprised of tracking Kaspar and Emil down to whatever hiding place they had made on the Emporium floor and delivering a series of improbable punishments for their cheek. She had even been the one to teach them the King's English, but whatever they had done had aged her prematurely; their misadventures could be read in the wrinkles latticing her face. Now that the Godman brothers were grown, her role had transformed: a better title might have been Emporium Housekeeper, responsible for making sure the shop assistants were watered and fed.

'I'll help you off with those. These carpets are a nightmare to clean.'

Cathy had to brace herself as Mrs Hornung levered off her shoes. Then she was ushered onwards, into a palatial hall where glass capsules set between the rafters revealed snow clouds strewn across the London sky. Steps couched in thick burgundy dropped into a living room bedecked in Emporium Instant Trees, colourful streamers hanging around each. A huge hearth dominated half of the room, flames licking high into the chimney, and on a raised level close to the door a table was already laid for supper. Somewhere, a piano was playing a concerto to itself, ebony and ivory rippling up and down without the touch of human hands.

Mrs Hornung meant to whisk her on, but the carpeted expanse in the middle of the room was occupied by a hundred toy soldiers. Some of them were in static regiments on the fringes of the carpet, but others were either marching at each other with rifles raised, or lying prostrate on the ground. On one side of the room, Emil was hunched over a regiment, winding them up madly; on the opposite side, Kaspar was mirroring the action, but spreading his soldiers along a much vaster front.

As Mrs Hornung hopped through, her foot caught one of the marching soldiers, knocking him back into his brethren. 'Forfeit!' Emil piped up, leaping to his feet. 'I call it null and void!'

'Act of God,' Kaspar announced. 'We've accounted for them before.'

'Act of God? It's outside the rules of the game.'

'It's *warfare*, little brother. There are no rules.'

'That's demonstrably untrue! Don't you remember your Deuteronomy?'

Kaspar grinned, 'You'd do better to remember your Sun Tzu.'

Just as the battle seemed about to escalate from the minions on the carpet to the deities above it, Mrs Hornung returned – and beside her, Papa Jack. Cathy had only rarely seen him since that first night. The toymaker, Sally-Anne said, stayed in his natural habitat, and that was his workshop. He was holding himself on two wooden canes, their bulbs carved into the visages of bears, and looked even more mountainous like this than he had in his workshop chair. His hair was a waterfall frozen over the crags of his body.

'Let there be an armistice,' he announced, with a voice full of whispers. 'Boys, your guest has arrived.'

Kaspar's eyes had already found her, but it took some time before Emil could tear himself away from the calamity on the battlefield. Whatever had happened here was so unjust he had tears pricking in his eyes – him, an eighteen-year-old man, crying over toy soldiers. 'This doesn't count, Kaspar.'

'We'll talk it through later, little brother.'

'I tell you, *it doesn't count.*'

Kaspar met Cathy on the step. 'You came,' he said, taking her hand.

'I did.'

'I wondered whether you might have another engagement.'

He was needling at her, but with what purpose Cathy was not sure. 'When your employers invite you to dinner,' she began, 'it's customary to accept.'

'I'm glad that you did. When two people have been in true danger, as we have, it engenders a bond.' He paused. 'Hungry, are you?'

Perhaps that was it, Cathy thought. Perhaps he was trying to catch her out somehow, trying to trick her into revealing her secret. His eyes had not lingered on her bump yet, but the night was young. And why was he still holding on to her hand?

'Dinner is served,' came Papa Jack's fraying voice, and at once Kaspar took her to the table.

It was not food Cathy had ever imagined before, though she was no less grateful for that. Mrs Hornung had spent years perfecting the dishes of the Old Country, Kaspar explained, putting a particular emphasis on the words so that it seemed to Cathy to be some faerie kingdom, not quite real. The dumplings were called *vareniki*. The gingerbreads had a warmth she was not expecting; the soup was of beetroot and to be eaten cold, alongside slabs of dark rye bread. She started tentatively, but soon the baby was demanding more.

'So,' said Kaspar, 'you are hungry, after all ...'

At the head of the table, Papa Jack lay down his spoon. 'I think what my firstborn means to say, Miss Wray, is that he apologises earnestly for jeopardising your safety as he did the other day. Kaspar, have you anything to add?'

'Papa, I've explained – Miss Wray was positively thrilled to see the paper forest. And so were the customers. Do you know how many EMPORIUM INSTANT TREES we sold last week?'

Papa Jack returned to his food.

'*All of them ...*'

It was true; Cathy had sold many of them herself, in her first afternoons working the register. Kaspar had put two of the Emporium's most trusted shop hands on to night shifts so that more could be made, but no sooner did they go on to the shop floor than they were taken again. Somebody, some duchess or minor baronet, was reputed to have lain a forest of them in her hall for the village children to explore. Somebody else had thought to line the trails of Regent's Park.

'Nevertheless,' said Papa Jack, and for the first time his eyes fell entirely on Cathy, 'you came to this shop not only as our assistant, but as our guest. There are laws of hospitality we would be fools to overlook. We are supposed to honour those responsibilities. Aren't we, boy?'

Kaspar lifted his eyes to meet hers. 'My apologies given, Miss Wray.'

'And accepted,' said Cathy, though the whole thing seemed preposterous.

'I hope it has not diminished what you think of us. Tell me – what do you make of our little Emporium?'

There were too many traps in this conversation, and it was too difficult to know which ones were being knowingly laid. So, honesty being the best policy, Cathy said, 'I don't want to leave.'

'There are some weeks yet before winter's end. You may think differently before then ...'

He was making a joke, of sorts, and Cathy found that she didn't have to force a smile. Papa Jack's voice was as placid as the snowfall she could now see plastering itself against the window panes beyond the paper trees. High above London, the clouds were giving up their gifts, decorating the rooftops in white. What would it be like to be tramping those streets now, a baby swaddled up against her breast? 'Do you really open at first frost and close when the snowdrops flower?'

'Every year,' said Papa Jack. 'A toyshop's trade is in the dark winter months, Miss Wray. It's only then the magic can truly be conjured. Our summers are given over to … creating. The Emporium would not be what it is today were it not for those months. Yes, while the rest of the world is out there lounging in the long grass, the three of us are here, in our workshops, waiting for winter …'

He made them sound like a family of bears – and, now that she thought of it, there was something peculiarly ursine about Papa Jack. Emil had something of the same look about him. She looked his way and found him with his head down, concentrating on dinner. Surely he couldn't still be brooding on whatever game they had been playing as she walked in? Her eyes danced across the table and found Kaspar instead.

'This summer was when I made my trees,' he said. 'The dirigibles too. Somewhere, out there, there's a family floating in one of my dirigibles through a forest of paper trees. Tell me – can you think of anything more perfect?' He stopped and turned on Emil. 'Emil, what did you make this summer?'

'You know what I made, Kaspar.'

'Tell Miss Wray, Emil. There's no need to be ashamed.'

Pointedly, Emil dropped his fork. 'I'm *not* ashamed.'

'Good, because there's really no need to be. Your birds are something quite special. The way they explode and flutter up – you'd think they were almost real. And remember last year? What was it? Your picnic hampers. Yes, you'd really believe you were in a park on a lazy summer's day … Did we ever go through the ledgers for them, little brother? Did we see how they sold? Only, I don't see the hampers on the shelves this year – and there are still so many boxes of birds in the storerooms, I wonder if we ought to be letting them go, out into the wild? You never know, it might draw some customers in, to see your pipe-cleaner birds in Hyde Park. A spectacle like that – just think of what it did for my trees!'

Cathy had thought Emil had the same ursine look as his father and it intensified now. Every muscle of his face tightened, as if preparing to snarl. Then, quashing whatever had been bubbling up inside him, he stood up. 'You'd do well to pay attention to the ledgers, Kaspar. It might be your trees, Papa's patchwork dogs, they write about in the *Chronicle*, but what is it that boys come back for time and time again? *My* soldiers. *My* infantry and cavalry and ...' Cathy could see he was fingering a wooden soldier even now, just beneath the line of the table. This one was so much more striking than any she had seen: noble and distinguished, Imperial somehow. 'Take all the attention you like, you scoundrel, because if it wasn't for all those weeks and months I spent with my soldiers, why, there'd hardly be a roof above our head.'

'You overestimate things, little brother. Your soldiers, they're commendable little things, but it's hardly an act of *toymaking*, is it? No, it's rather a form of ... carpentry, wouldn't you say?'

He said *toymaking* like another man might *enchantment;* he said *carpentry* like another man might describe his morning ablutions. Cathy saw the way it made Emil shudder. The younger Godman brother brought his fist up from beneath the table and planted this new soldier on the surface, to stand proudly among the dumplings and dishes.

'We'll begin again, Kaspar. Victor takes all, Act of God or no.'

Kaspar was still reclining as he weighed up the challenge. 'That's the spirit, little brother!' He stood. 'Miss Wray. You'll have to excuse me. My brother has asked for a flogging.' He was gesturing for Emil to lead the way (Kaspar Godman was nothing if not a gentleman) when he had a sudden thought. 'Or perhaps you might like to watch?'

Moments later, she was looking over a battlefield in a bedroom above. She took it for Kaspar's, because a single paper tree stood in the corner, and she doubted this was something to which Emil wanted to wake each morning. The bed had been pushed against the outer wall, candles had been lit, and hillsides and forests, sculpted perfectly in sponge and clay, were being arranged according to rules only Kaspar and Emil seemed to know. Next, each brother took a turn to line up his soldiers. Kaspar's, Cathy saw, did not have the polish that belonged to Emil's; some of them were replicas, made by shop hands and sold across the shopfloor, but even those that Kaspar had evidently crafted himself did not live up to Emil's designs. Their faces betrayed little emotion; their eyes did not glimmer with the story of a life hard-lived, a war being desperately fought. They were mere playthings next to the Imperial Kapitan that Emil so proudly placed at the head of his phalanx.

Between each deployment, the silence stretched out. Once, Cathy tried to venture a word – but Kaspar gave her a grin and begged her to remain quiet, so her eyes wandered instead. She was standing beside a tall glass cabinet and in it stood toy soldiers very different from the ones Kaspar and Emil were winding up. These only looked like soldiers at all in a certain light. They were made out of pinecone and pieces of bark, bound up with bootlaces and string and dead grass.

She was still staring at them while Kaspar and Emil's game got underway. Through the glass, those little faces, etched and burnt into the bark, gave the impression that they too were watching the battle. She could see the conflict being reflected in miniature. Kaspar's expeditionary force had already been routed. Emil had wind-up cavalry poised to shatter his flanks. She turned, just in time to see them rolling down one of the hills. The joy on Emil's face reached a zenith – but then exploded, for he had not seen Kaspar's reserves marching in from beneath the first bed. With his cavalry divided, Emil's soldiers were easily scattered. Those who survived the onslaught walked on, only to be upended when they reached the skirting board that ran around the edges of the room, a pile of pillows in place of a mountain. Finally, only the Imperial Kapitan – weighted more heavily than the rest – remained.

'Do you concede?'

With his bottom lip bulging, Emil strode out of the room.

For a moment Kaspar held himself as if victorious. Then the cost of the victory appeared to him – and, heaving a sigh, he loped to the door. 'Emil!' For a moment, he disappeared into the hall and Cathy listened out for the clattering of footsteps. 'Emil, I didn't mean to ...' But the words petered out, and then Kaspar was back in the room. His face was missing its customary smile.

'I'm sorry,' he said. 'That's just ... Emil.'

'Oh, I wouldn't be so sure. I think you may have had a little to do with it.'

Kaspar had got to his knees to sweep the battlefield clear, lining up Emil's fallen soldiers with his own. Most had wound down; only one or two still kicked feebly in their death throes. 'I'll admit it. I've been being sore with him. But he takes his soldiers so seriously! You most likely think me frightful. And yet ... he's my little brother. He pains me, but it doesn't mean I don't ...'

'It was a rotten trick, Kaspar. The way you baited him back at the table. It wasn't ... honourable.'

'No?'

'It isn't how a family treats itself.'

Kaspar appeared to find this sentiment intriguing. 'Well, what about your family, Miss Wray? How did they treat you, that you should run away to live in our Emporium?'

'I never said I ran away.'

'Oh, Cathy, you say it every time you close your mouth. You say it every time you try so hard not to say it.' He stopped. 'You'll tell me soon enough. I don't see why you try so hard to keep a secret you're so desperate to tell.'

But Cathy was practised at silences, and when this one went on too long, Kaspar had to find another way to fill it. 'You think we're fools, don't you? To care so much about a game of soldiers?'

'No,' said Cathy, and something drew her eyes back to the pinecone figurines trapped behind the cabinet glass.

'No?'

'Because I think there's something more to it than a game.' She paused, as if willing Kaspar to enter the silence.

'I'm right, aren't I? With you and Emil, it isn't just a game. It's ... life, of a sort.'

Kaspar breathed out, as if trying to form a word, but no word came. It was, Cathy decided, the first unrehearsed reaction she had seen in him since the moment they'd met.

'You oughtn't to grind your brother into the dirt like that.'

'Miss Wray, you misunderstand. You might not believe it, but there was a time before all this, before the aisles and atriums, before any toys at all. You look at it now, and you imagine the Emporium our entire world. Well, before the Emporium, it was just us, the Brothers Godman, without even our papa to call our own. *We* were each other's world back then. I'd do anything for Emil, and Emil for me too – though ...' And here Kaspar could not stop himself from smirking, for the joke was too perfect to resist. '... that was generally because I'd have told him to do it. When you see Emil get upset, it's only because he cares so much about this ... Long War of ours. It's true what you say, Cathy. It isn't just a game. It's ... who we are.' He went to the door and peered out. When he was certain that the coast was clear, he looked back – and only then did he say, 'The Long War has been going on since the very first day we met our papa. Back then, if you can picture it, we weren't the sorts of boys who had toys. That came much later, once our papa started to teach us all of the things that he'd learned. No, don't look at me like that. It's *you* who wanted to know.' He paused. 'You do want to know, don't you?'

Cathy nodded. It was a long story, he said, but he would tell it, if that was what she wanted. 'And it started with these.' He took her back to the cabinet, where the pinecone figurines had been watching, unmoved. 'I was eight years old the day I first saw these. They came flurrying out of the backwoods, a thin column carried by the wind – and my papa walking behind them, like they were his guards. That was the first time I'd seen him, in anything other than a picture. That was the day the Emporium was born.'

Picture it, if you would: Kaspar Godman is eight years old, dishevelled as all the village children with whom he spends his days. Most of them are simple, certainly too simple for Kaspar, who has had an inkling, ever since he can remember, that he is more intelligent than them, a supposition borne out by the way he can ordinarily get them to do whatever he pleases, whether that be stealing hens' eggs, raiding the rock pools for crabs, or else taking a beating more properly meant for Kaspar himself. Yes, Kaspar has had the village children trained since before most of them could talk. He runs rings around them like a sheepdog to its sheep, and the only one who ever resists is the one they call Emil. Which is a terrible shame, because Emil is Kaspar's brother, and has been Kaspar's to look after ever since the day he was born.

On this particular day, Kaspar has grown bored and is following one of the lesser trails to the headland overlooking the village. From here he can see every house in Carnikava, all of the trails that converge out of the woods, the way the river Gauja broadens and deepens in colour as it joins with the sea. As he comes between the trees, he hears noises in the roots around him. Determined that it can only be Emil following in his footfall, he finds a hiding place beneath an overhang of earth. There, squatting with the woodlice and worms, he waits. But it is not Emil who has been following him out of the undergrowth. Instead there come a procession of little figures, carried along on the wind. At first they are formless, but then he sees: the twigs as arms, the briars that bind them, ringlets of leaves and pinecones for heads. These are stick soldiers and the wind gives them the appearance of marching.

Temptation is a terrible thing for an eight-year-old boy. Before Kaspar has any thought to deny himself, he darts out to scoop up a soldier. And he is standing there, turning that bundle in his hands, when a heavier tread comes along the track. He looks up, into encroaching shadow, and sees a vagrant lurching toward him. In his fists, their nails like horns, are yet more soldiers. He is reaching into his pockets and casting them into the wind.

When he sees Kaspar, he stops. Carnikava is used to wayfarers. They tramp the roads of the coast, living off forage and the kindness of strangers. But this wayfarer is more brutish than most. His face is a lattice of scars, his nose misshapen, what teeth he has are rotted to pits – and all of that is hidden behind a beard so matted he might be part of the undergrowth itself.

Kaspar turns tail and flees – out of the trees, down the escarpments toward the coast, holding the little pinecone soldier all the way. Intermittently, he looks back. The vagrant is following after, but he has not changed the pace of his tread. He lumbers like a man who has come too far already, who would be happy to find a ditch and lie down until sleep takes him away.

Kaspar reaches home, that succession of wooden shacks, and scrambles inside to find his brother Emil leafing through the pages of a book – though neither Godman brother has ever learned to read.

'What is it?'

'There's a wild man, coming out of the woods.'

The door flies open, and there stands the very same vagrant. Emil leaps to his feet, cowers behind Kaspar (among all of the many things he is, Kaspar is first of all Emil's big brother and would do anything to defend him).

'Which one of you is Kaspar?'

This is not a man used to talking; his voice is of whispers and wind.

'I am,' Kaspar says, defiant.

'Where is your mama?'

'My mama is dead,' he declares, 'two winters gone.'

Only this gives the vagrant pause. Behind his mask of filth he is quivering, and the only sign of his tears are the patches of pink skin that emerge out of the dark. 'Then who looks after you boys?'

'We look after each other,' declares Kaspar, 'and we don't need nobody else.'

'Well,' says the vagrant, and his voice is different now, less bestial somehow, though equally deranged, 'you have me now. I'm your papa, and I need to sleep.'

Somehow, he knows where the old bedroom is, the one where Kaspar and Emil's mama had lain down to die. He crosses the shack and closes the door behind him, leaving only that coat of badly butchered hide behind. Seconds later, and for long hours to come, the sounds of his snoring reverberate in the house.

'What now?' whispers Emil.

'I think we sleep in the hen hut tonight, little brother.'

And that was exactly what they did, though there was precious little sleep to come. For that was the night that Kaspar and Emil waged the opening battle of the Long War. After dark, they stole back into the shack where this man who claimed to be their blood was sleeping, and found the interloper's overcoat pockets stuffed full with pinecone soldiers, ballerinas of bark, warhorses the size of thimbles. Kaspar took a handful, Emil took a handful, and out back, where the yard dog barked and the hens clucked anxiously at the suggestion of every fox, they played out the first skirmish in the campaign Cathy had just watched.

'It wasn't long after that that we left,' said Kaspar, taking care as he balanced one of the pinecone figurines upon Cathy's palm. 'Papa spent a few days scrubbing himself clean. He butchered every hen in our hen hut, ate every egg in the nests, quartered the piglets and smoked hard sausages on a pyre. We didn't know it then, we thought he was just an animal, but he was fattening himself up. Until then, he'd been skin and bone. It had taken him two years to walk home. He'd crossed all the Russias, but he wasn't stopping now. He wanted to carry on west, and he wanted us to come with him . . .'

'And you went, just like that?'

Kaspar nodded. 'It wasn't just because he told us to. And it wasn't just because of those soldiers he made! But, Miss Wray, he could have led all the village children away, if that was what he wanted. No, it was something in his eyes. Somebody needed to look after him. Emil and me, we decided that was us.'

'What about your dog, the one in the yard?'

'Left to go feral. It took us an age to forgive Papa for that, but he made it up to us, once we'd reached London. You've already seen Sirius, the first of all the Emporium patchwork dogs, tramping up and down on its cotton wad paws. It was a long voyage. I must have held Emil's hand halfway around the world. Then we were in London, and our papa showing us how to make toys. But that,' he smiled, 'is another story. I'll tell you it some time, but first ... isn't there something you want to tell me?'

Cathy realised she'd been staring at the soldier pirouetting in her palm for too long. Now, Kaspar's hand had closed over it, and she was forced to look up into his eyes. They were imploring her to tell, and every moment she remained with his hand touching hers, more and more of her wanted to say, 'Kaspar, it isn't so easy. Your story, it's full of adventure. Mine ...'

She might have said more (her tongue was threatening to), but before she could the bedroom door opened and Emil reappeared. He was comporting himself with more dignity than the moment he'd left, though his eyes were still swollen and raw. In his hands were more wooden soldiers. These ones were roughly hewn, still bearing the marks of his workshop lathe, but there was something magnificent in their minutely sculpted faces as well: once painted, this would be a unit of men of the same standing as the Imperial Kapitan. 'I declare an ambush,' Emil announced. Then, when Kaspar's eyes narrowed in an attempt to send him away, he spluttered, 'It's within the rules. Your troops have taken mine as prisoners. My reinforcements arrive late and ambush them on the way ...'

Those rules had been codified long before, and it took Kaspar too long to conjure up a reason why the battle had to wait. By then, Cathy had already taken her hand out of his and was hurrying away.

'Wait!' called Kaspar. In the doorway, pushing past Emil, she stalled. 'What are you doing on Christmas Day?'

'Christmas Day?' It would be a lie to say she had not thought about it. Christmases at home lingered long in the imagination: the pre-dawn stampede down the stairs, the stories of the night before, the incomparable delight of contemplating presents under the tree and remembering how it had felt when you were five, six, seven years old. Distance might have dulled the pain that she felt, but it only amplified the longing.

'There's the banquet,' Kaspar said. 'The Emporium Feast, for all of the shopkeeps who can't go home, all of the sweepers and joiners and tinkers. And ... all of us Godmans.'

Cathy faltered in what she meant to say, so instead she asked, 'Where?'

'On the shopfloor.'

Before she left, Cathy gave Kaspar a look that might have been either promise or regret. Five days would pass between this Midwinter's Eve and the Christmas Day when he would find out for certain. He would spend every one of them chasing down the meaning in her eyes, and every night he would lose another battle to Emil. And, in that way, the Long War would continue, while a new war was being waged in Kaspar Godman's mind.

On Christmas morning, Cathy woke ravenous with the dawn. Sally-Anne, she had discovered, had been secretly meeting with John Horwood, the Emporium caretaker, and he had taken her to a hotel for the evening; Ted Jacobs and Kesey and little Douglas Flood had ventured out into London as well, to go a-wassailing, see their families, or else lose themselves in some uproarious drinking den. The Emporium halls would be quiet without them. She rolled over with her hands to her belly, trying to assure herself that she was not truly alone. And yet – Christmas morning only intensified the feeling: without Sally-Anne to fill her head with gossip from the shopfloor, she felt the absence of her mother more keenly than ever. There were things she wanted to ask. Was it normal to wake up in the night and rush to the toilet bowl, barely to squeeze out a drop? Was it normal for her breasts to feel hard and tender, all at the same time? For the skin around her nipples to darken with tiny raised bumps? She asked the baby all of these things, but when even the answers she invented stopped coming, she knew there was only one option: sooner or later, she was going to have to leave the room.

Some time later she picked her way down the shifting Emporium stairs. And there, on the shopfloor, lay everything Kaspar had spoken of. In the night, the shelves had been rearranged, opening a huge plateau between the exhibits. Through the paper trees, now shimmering in streamers, a huge table was being laid. Mrs Hornung was directing the remaining shop hands like a general with his men. Somebody was bringing out steaming platters of potatoes and parsnips. Somebody else was carving a goose. Even up high, the smells reached out and wrapped around her, tempting her down.

When she came along the aisle and entered the plateau, one of the shop girls called out her name, and soon Cathy found herself laying out miniature wreaths of holly upon each plate. As soon as she had finished, a gong rang out. There must have been thirty shop hands left in the Emporium this Christmas Day, and now they all scrabbled for their seats. Only then did Cathy see that the Godmans were already among them. Papa Jack had a pre-ordained seat at the head of the table (somebody had hewn off its arms, so that he could sit overhanging each side), but Kaspar had found a seat a little further along, pressed up between one of the archivists, a girl with bottle-green eyes, and one of the boys who wrangled the puppets. Both seemed to be vying for his attention; when he looked up, he seemed to stare straight through her, preferring their flirtation instead. Later, Cathy would put it down to the steam billowing up from the food, but she felt herself flushing crimson as the blood rushed to her cheeks. Sirius the patchwork dog appeared, as if to beg for scraps from the table, and then wandered on; even he seemed to be drawn to Kaspar's company, curling up at his feet.

She was still staring at him when she realised that the figure levering into the chair beside her was Emil. Food materialised upon her plate, but in comparison to the mountain on Emil's, hers was only a foothill. Even so, the baby inside her began to cavort. She could barely restrain her hands as Papa Jack rose at the head of the table to wish good cheer on all of his guests.

'We haven't seen you,' Emil whispered as his father raised a glass to another Emporium Christmas, another dark winter shot through with Emporium lights. 'I thought, perhaps, my brother had ...'

'No,' said Cathy, 'nothing like that.'

'So you're ...'

'I'm well, Emil. I promise.'

She looked up, to see him nodding feverishly. 'I knew you were. My brother, sometimes he gets ... carried away. He thinks everyone ought to worship him. This time, it's those trees. I'd be sore as all hell if only they weren't so good. And they are good, Cathy. That's the problem. When I saw what he'd done with those trees, why, I ...' Cathy did not need him to finish the sentence. She had seen the look on Emil's face as his axe burst through the tree: there had been envy, that much was true, but eclipsing it was sheer delight. 'I've been trying seasons to work something quite as magical. And Papa, Papa must have noticed. If it wasn't for my soldiers, why, the game would already be up. Papa might as well have signed the Emporium to Kaspar and be ...' At the head of the table, Papa Jack was finishing his first toast. As the cheer went up, Emil lost track of his thoughts and, by the time the cheering died away, was rambling incoherent. 'You didn't want to go home?' he finally asked, by way of stemming the tide.

'No.'

'And your family, won't they miss you?'

She wondered what the house was like today, whether there had been presents and celebrations, or ...

'No,' she whispered, half trying to convince herself.

Somewhere in the conversation, as the first food touched her lips, she felt the baby twirling in unconstrained delight, and, by instinct, her hand dropped to the curve of her belly, to feel for it there. She was aware how tight her stomach felt, was marvelling at the way she filled even Sally-Anne's clothes, when suddenly something pushed back against her hand. She froze, but the sensation came again – and, when she lifted her hand, she could see it there, pushed up through fabric and flesh, a hand or a foot, the touch of her child.

She felt for it with the tip of her finger. Startled, the baby withdrew. Then, its courage returned. It kicked out again.

In the corner of her eye, she saw Emil tense. In an instant reality returned, the cheering from Papa Jack's toast reached a crescendo, and when she looked up, Emil was staring at the place where her fingers had been, his face livid as a bruise.

'Emil?'

'Why Cathy, surely you can't be—'

'Emil,' she said, and was surprised to hear how easily her own voice frayed, '*please . . .*'

But now his face was buried in his food; now he could not bear to look. And, inside her, oblivious to its discovery, the baby continued to turn.

STOWAWAY

PAPA JACK'S EMPORIUM, 1907

Consider Emil Godman: the youngest son of a youngest son, born to a toymaker who did not yet know that he was a toymaker, to a man who would one day find ways to invent whole worlds. On Christmas night, if you were the kind of creature to spy on him through a crack in the skirting boards, you would have found Emil in his workshop, tinkering with the toy held fast in the vice. He had been coming back to this toy for many long months, each time unable to make the adjustments that might have seen it taking pride of place on the shop floor. Something to transform the season, something to strike all mention of those Instant Trees from the Emporium record – something, *anything*, to stand alongside the magics with which his father, and now his brother, were imbuing their toys.

It was a mahogany case, lined in velvet, and when he opened it up it was to reveal a family of mice dressed as ballerinas. He wound them up, daring to believe when the mice unhitched themselves from the contraption and lined up in formation – but, when the music tinkled and the dancing began, everything was wrong. When the lead mouse turned a pirouette, she tumbled into the dancers behind her. When the second held an arabesque, she promptly fell over. When it came time for the climactic move, the whole troop turning their *tours en l'air*, the result was a chaos of arms and legs and tails, little grey legs windmilling madly in a heap on the tabletop.

Emil whipped them all up and set them back in the vice. He was about to take another turn, but something stopped him. At first, he thought it was his hands, treacherous as they were. He looked at them with fire – for why couldn't they be the ones plucking magic from thin air, taking the runners off a rocking horse and letting that horse go cantering around the store? Then he realised it wasn't his hands at all. It was his head. His head was too busy, too clouded with other things. How could he be expected to achieve real magic when his heart wasn't in toymaking at all? It was the girl. After what he had seen at the Christmas table, he couldn't stop thinking about the girl . . .

Christmas night came, and Emil breathed not a word. Boxing Day died, and still Papa Jack had not come knocking at Cathy's door, demanding to know why she had not told them she was conjuring a baby beneath their roof. Next morning, as the shop hands prepared the Emporium to open once more, there were no whispers in the Palace, no sordid looks from Sally-Anne and the rest. Doubting herself, Cathy ventured to the foot of the Godmans' stair, thinking she might catch him coming down, but Emil was already out, and soon the patchwork dog appeared to warn her away with its stuffed-pillow barks.

There was a deluge directly after Christmas Day, but the Emporium halls were never as busy again as they had been in December's earliest days. Cathy worked the register, or took children on rocking-horse rides up and down the aisles while the Emporium stable hands looked dutifully on, and by New Year she was courageous enough to return to the Palace each evening. By the end of that week she was beginning to feel that she was mistaken, that Emil hadn't really seen what he'd seen at all. In fact, as the second week in January arrived, and with it fresh flurries of London snow, she was finally starting to feel safe. Safety was a feeling that crept up on you. It was not like anxiety or fear. Safety did not descend in a rush, nor seize you in its hands; but here it was, all the same. A secret shared was a secret halved – and Cathy might even have convinced herself to confide in others, to take one of the more seasoned girls to one side and confess, if only Sally-Anne hadn't sashayed into the Palace one morning, stopped the breakfast revelries (Douglas Flood insisted on playing his fiddle even at breakfast) and demanded everyone's attention.

'Time to pack your cases ladies, gentlemen,' she declared, with a sad lilting tone.

At once, the shop hands understood. Cathy followed their gazes, to where Sally-Anne was now standing, up on the dais. In her hands was a single white flower, the hanging bell of a snowdrop plucked from the Emporium terrace. The thaw had come. This day at the Emporium would be the season's last.

The Emporium closed its doors on a frigid January morning, London encrusted in frost.

Mrs Hornung had prepared great cauldrons of stewed apples to see the shop hands on their way, but aside from this there was no ceremony. Papa Jack did not emerge from his workshop. Emil and Kaspar barely ghosted past. By the time Cathy was done packing what few possessions she had, most of the shop hands were already gone. She wound her way slowly to the shopfloor, already denuded of last season's toys, and stood at the open doors, feeling the bracing chill of the London air.

'You'll be back next year, dear?' said Mrs. Hornung.

'I will,' Cathy lied, and went out with both hearts beating wild.

At the end of Iron Duke Mews, Sally-Anne scurried past her, whispered 'Good luck!' and climbed into a taxicab her gentleman had sent to spirit her away. Then Cathy was alone, and London seemed suddenly so vast and unknown.

The Emporium had looked after her for a time. Emil had looked after her by saying nothing, ever since the feast on Christmas Day. Now there had to be another way. She supposed that the Emporium was looking after her still, for there was a secret place in her satchel where all of her winter pay had been stashed. If she was careful, it would see her until spring. But spring would bring with it new life in more ways than one, and it was a long time until this new year's first frost and the Emporium's reopening. How different life would be by then.

She set off, into the great unknown.

Decisions like this should not be made on an instant. And yet, that was what she was doing: deciding her child's future at every intersection of roads, mapping out its life story by gravitating toward one tram stop or the next. Without knowing it, she reached Regent Street, where horse-drawn trams and trolleybuses battled for control of the thoroughfare. North or south was the decision she had to make. The wind was coming from the north; so south it was.

It took her some time to find a bus bound for Lambeth and Camberwell beyond. Those places seemed as likely as any. Sally-Anne had spoken of grand houses along the Brixton road, carved up into tinier apartments for city clerks and railway workers. One of those might do, for ushering her baby into the world. The question of what happened next was one she was steadfastly putting to the back of her mind.

The bus was slow in wending its way south. Cathy took a seat on the lower deck, where the windows were fogged by the cold and London was a ghostly miasma through the glass. They had not yet reached the circus at Piccadilly when she felt somebody sitting down beside her. Though she kept her head down, she could sense that the stranger had turned in her direction. He was sitting uncomfortably close, his eyes roaming all over her face, her hair, her belly. Finally, she could bear it no longer. She looked up, determined to dress him down – she would rather be thought hysterical than stomach his scrutiny a moment longer – and there sat Kaspar Godman, looking half-affronted that she had not noticed him sooner.

'And where do you think you're going?'

'Kaspar, what are you—'

'You didn't think to say goodbye?'

'The Emporium's closed, Kaspar,' she said, quickly reordering her thoughts. 'Everybody left.'

'So where are you going?'

The bus had stopped while yet more passengers piled aboard. She searched for something to say, but each lie evaporated before she could give it voice. 'I don't know,' she finally admitted.

'Didn't you think about that before—'

Before he had finished, she cut in, 'What are *you* doing here, Kaspar?'

'Me?'

'It doesn't look right, you being out of the Emporium. It's like seeing a ... swallow in winter!'

Kaspar's face creased. 'Miss Wray,' he said, as his laughter subsided, 'why didn't you tell me?'

The words did not flay her as she had thought that they might.

'*Emil.*'

'Don't blame Emil. The way he's been moping around, I knew something was wrong. And when I found all those snowdrops hung up to dry in his workshop – well, it takes a lot for Emil to break the rules. He'd been plucking them, you see, every morning for the last week. Seems he didn't want the season to finish, that he didn't want someone to go. By God, I thought he'd fallen in love! There he was, mooning after one of the seamstresses or ... It was just rotten luck that Sally-Anne got to the terrace before him this morning. No doubt he'd have plucked every snowdrop until spring, tried to keep the Emporium open until the Royal Gardens are in full flower. So he had to tell me, you see? The idea I'd tell our father what he'd been up to ...' The bus was about to take off again, but Kaspar cried out for the horseman to stop, and extended a hand. 'Cathy Wray, don't make me be a gentleman in front of so many rabid onlookers. But you can't possibly think I'd let you – let you *both* – just wander off like that, can you?'

*

Back at the Emporium, the shop floor was in silence. The gloom that had settled was almost subterranean, and what wan light broke in from the skylights above could hardly penetrate the aisles. Kaspar brought Cathy in through one of the tradesman's doors, and now they stood in an alcove where pop-up books thronged the shelves. Each one of them held new delights, each page a cascade that could reach out and envelop its reader in lost worlds of dinosaurs and mammoths, of desert islands infested by cannibal hags, of fog-bound London streets and lonely Fenland locks. Mrs Hornung had already begun laying out the dust sheets, hiding the exhibits for another season. Kaspar made Cathy wait until he had scouted the aisle ahead, and only then did he usher her on.

Through the labyrinthine aisles they reached the paper forest and the Wendy House at its end. As Cathy passed under the branches, Kaspar lifted more Emporium Instant Trees from the shelving and cast them on to the floor. 'Just in case,' he grinned, barely flinching as they erupted out of the ground behind him. Now that the Wendy House was entirely encircled, it could barely be seen from the aisle beyond. He took her over the white picket fence and walked within.

Cathy stopped dead. 'You've been planning this for me ...'

Things had changed since the last time she was here. Beside the bed stood a cradle. Beside that, a Russian rocking horse had been draped in blankets and shawls. A miniature kitchen had been arranged, with a gas-fired hot plate, a kettle and a single casserole dish, burnt black around the edges. The rack above was filled with jars of preserves, flour and lard. 'Everything I could snatch from the kitchen without

Mrs Hornung beginning to suspect,' said Kaspar, turning a two-step across the carpeted expanse.

'I'm going to live here?'

'Why not?' It seemed so obvious to him. 'It has everything you could need. Not a soul on the shopfloor could see. And the walls, well, Papa made them so that a horde of children could play inside and barely a whisper would be heard without. There are three things a woman needs, Cathy. A roof over her head, food on her plate and ... delightful company. One, two, three.' At the last, he turned his index finger on himself.

'You haven't told Emil. Nor Papa Jack.'

'Strictly speaking, of course, it *is* against the rules. Emil can be a stickler, and my papa may not understand. Ever since that unfortunate business with that toymaker off the Portobello Road ... well, he's seen ghosts in every corner. I'm not suggesting he'll think you're a thief, but he may think you're in a thief's employ. What better ruse than a girl with child, come to prey on our sympathies?'

'You're making fun of me.'

'Cathy,' he said, more earnestly now, 'you can be safe here. You don't really want to have your baby alone in some Lambeth lodging, do you?'

She shook her head.

'Well, you don't have to. All you need is here. Let the Wendy House be a sanctuary for you. Let these walls hide you away. Why, all you'd have to do is lock that door and nobody would ever find you. My papa never made a toy that would stoop so low as to break in all of his life. These walls are a fortress. The Emporium might cave in and you'd still be snug and safe in here.' His next words were not so full of bravado. 'Let me do this,' he whispered, and then, full of bravado again, 'Why would you ever want anywhere else?'

Why indeed? After Kaspar was gone, Cathy walked the circumference of the Wendy House walls. Here was an entire life in miniature. She would have been lying if she had said she was not afraid, it would not have been true to say she did not wonder *why* – but above everything else was the relief she felt as she rushed to grill bread over the hot plate and slathered it with elderflower preserve. Kaspar's footsteps were fading on the other side of the paper trees, and Cathy Wray broke into the most mystified smile.

He came back to her that night, when the eerie hooting of stuffed owls on the shopfloor was keeping her awake. He had brought blackouts for the windows ('So you can light your lantern at night') and extra blankets for the bed; the snowdrops might have flowered, but winter was still bitter and deep. He had brought tea leaves as well, and soup from Mrs Hornung's pot. And, 'You're going to be bored,' he said, 'so you might tutor yourselves with these.' Onto the bedside he upended a hessian bag filled with pamphlets and old lithographs. 'Every catalogue and advertisement the Emporium's ever had. It's my own collection. One year we're going to have an exhibit devoted to it. "Kaspar Godman's Archive of the Emporium!" Here,' he went on, rifling through to find the oldest one. 'What do you make of that?'

The card depicted stuffed bears of dubious design. Above it were the words: COME TO PAPA'S EMPORIUM.

'That's my handiwork you're holding there. I'll wager you didn't know you were in the presence of an artiste *par excellence.*' When she did not challenge him, he added, 'I was eight years old. It was the same month that my papa made this ...'

Kaspar whistled, and into the Wendy House lolloped Sirius, the patchwork dog. On seeing Kaspar it butted affectionately against his leg, as energetic as a concoction made up of fabric and thread could be. Then Kaspar crouched and, in teasing its ear, directed its gaze at Cathy.

'Do you understand?'

In response, the dog lay down at Cathy's feet.

'He's to keep you company, for when I can't be here. Oh, I'll come as often as I can, but there's Emil to think of, and Papa too. They'll expect me to be up in the workshop, working out designs for next winter. If they don't see me slaving at it, they'll suspect.'

Cathy crouched so that the dog could nuzzle her hand. She still had no sense how such a thing might work, but the more time she spent with it, the less it seemed to matter. Such was the magic of an Emporium toy.

'Papa made him for us, to remind us of the dog we left behind. It was the winter we first came. We were living, all three of us to a single room, in one of those Whitechapel tenements a good girl like you won't know anything about. Papa didn't speak back then. He didn't really have the words. But he was making us those soldiers out of wood, and we were playing our Long War, and then, one night, Emil was crying, and I was there, holding him, asking what was wrong. That was what it was like back then. Emil would crawl over in the night and I'd have to hold him, tell him we were on the greatest adventure of our lives. And when he said he'd been thinking of our old dog, well, that got me sobbing too. I'd imagine you find that hard to believe. Me, *Kaspar Godman,* crying like that? Well, there was something about that night. Back then we barely knew a word in English. What we wouldn't have given to play with the boys on the floor below! But not one of them could understand a word we said. Papa was taking what work he could, tinkering around, and one night he came back with a pile of old trousers and capes. He must have spent three weeks hunkered down in the corner with those things – but then, one morning, there this dog was, all wound up and waiting to play. We named him Sirius, after the mutt we left behind ...' Kaspar clicked his forefinger and thumb, and Sirius rose on his haunches to beg. 'He was simpler back then. He couldn't do nearly as many tricks ...'

'I love him,' said Cathy, and meant it too.

'Cathy.' A note of seriousness had crept into Kaspar's voice. 'If you're going to keep him, there's something you have to promise me.'

'I know you, Kaspar,' she said, not knowing if that was true. 'You'd better tell me what it is first, or I'm liable to find myself in some sort of contract ...'

Kaspar took a deep breath before he proceeded. 'You have to keep him wound.' He saw the way she was looking at him, as if searching for a jest. Sometimes, Kaspar Godman found it hard to be taken seriously. It could be the most vexing thing. 'Ever since the day Papa gave him to us, he's never wound down. At first it was because Emil and I always wanted to play with him. But then ...' He hesitated. 'I don't know if I can explain it. You'll think it strange. Sirius has changed so much since then. Patches have been torn off and taken away. He's had new buttons for eyes.

Half of his tail burnt off once – I'll admit I was to blame for that – and we stitched him a new one. But he's never wound down. We wouldn't let it. And ... his contraption is old. I don't know what would happen if it stopped. What if he couldn't be wound up again? What if, once he ground to a halt, he was over, he was spent? Well,' he concluded, 'do you promise?'

Cathy said, 'I do,' and at that Kaspar turned, as if to hide his eyes. Soon he was hovering in the Wendy House door, ready to disappear into the forest.

'Kaspar, if he did wind down, if that contraption did break, couldn't you just make him a new one?'

'I don't think it's like that. It would be like somebody opening up your chest and giving you a new heart. How could anything – how could *anybody* – be the same after that?' He turned back to her, summoning up a smile at last. Things, he decided, had become far too maudlin; life was for levity, not despair. 'Do you think I'm awfully strange, Miss Wray?'

'Awfully sentimental, perhaps.'

'Aha!' declared Kaspar. 'Well, there you have it. For, if a toymaker cannot be sentimental, who on this fine earth can?'

Kaspar was correct; she quickly grew restless. The Wendy House was bigger than it had any right to be, but by the end of the second day it was already a prison cell. She spent long hours reading the old catalogues, charting the creations of Papa Jack and his sons across the years, but this could not sustain her for ever. By the fall of the third night she knew all about their first winter, when the Emporium was nothing more than the room where the Godman family lived and the boys from down the hall, who told the boys from down the road, who told the boys from further afield, that here was a family trading toys for winter fuel. She knew about the savings Jekabs Godman built up across that next summer and how, on the day of the winter's first frost, he made a deal with a fellow migrant, a man named Abram Hassan, to lease the derelict shopfront at the end of Iron Duke Mews. It was Hassan who convinced Jekabs that a stranger could rise up in London, that even a foreigner might prosper. Until then he had been working hard to lose his language, reasoning that English boys wanted English toys, but Hassan convinced him that, if this 'Emporium' of his was to succeed, a little exoticism went a long way. People could believe in magic from the frozen East, he said, so long as that East was further afield than Whitechapel or Bethnal Green. So that winter the rocking horses were painted with the red and green tassels of the Russian Steppes, and the bears were Arctic white with jet black eyes. Cathy held up the postcards with which Kaspar and Emil had capered around the West End, drumming up business while their papa slaved in his shop. It must have worked, because the next year's catalogue proudly declared the Emporium the toast of London town. Papa Jack's toys had garnered such a reputation that the freehold of the building was now his, and the first photographs of the shopfloor showed the aisles thronged with enchanted children, and equally enchanted mothers and fathers. That, Cathy supposed, was how the true fortune of the Emporium had been built: by making even grown-ups hanker after toys they might once have had.

Leafing through old photographs was distraction enough for the first few days. Yet the stretches between Kaspar's visits were achingly long, and when she spoke to Sirius her voice echoed in the cavernous Wendy House hall.

'I'll bring you more books,' said Kaspar one night. 'And games. Papa has chess boards that you can play against themselves, backgammon too. If you treat it right, the wood can *remember*. Beat those boards once and you won't beat them in the same way again.'

Time moved erratically in the Wendy House walls. Sometimes the tedium drove her back to bed in the middle of the afternoon. Often she only knew what hour it was by the fingers rapping on the glass that announced Kaspar's coming. Once, he arrived as she slept and she woke to find him urgently winding up Sirius, whose innards had started to slow down as she dreamt. 'Every night,' he was saying as the dog got back to its paws. 'Every night, with your prayers …' Cathy swore, then and there, that she would never forget again.

By the third week, she was spending too much time standing in the Wendy House door, gazing up into the paper branches. What a thrill it would have been to take just one step, and then one more! But Cathy was true to her word. She made a calendar to keep track of the days, and on it plotted the twists and turns of the baby in her belly. The kicks came with such frequency now. She could catch a heel or a hand and make it squirm inside her.

Somewhere along the way, she realised she had not thought of her mother or her father, nor even of Lizzy, in several weeks. Daniel himself was an outline in her mind; he might never have existed, were it not for the child turning inside her. Perhaps this was how lives changed: with new families always supplanting the last.

One night, when Kaspar arrived, she had rearranged the Wendy House floor. The bed she had shifted around, the curtains she had rehung; the nursery had been dismantled and rebuilt in a different corner.

'I know what this is,' announced Kaspar, depositing the evening's supplies on the bed. 'I've read about it in the Annals. This is what happens to polar explorers when they get trapped in their tents. It's a kind of hysteria. The white madness!'

'It is *not* hysteria. Or madness of any kind. It's ...'

'Next time I come, I'm likely to find you've built a little temple to one of your new gods.'

'It isn't that bad.'

'It isn't?' said Kaspar. 'Then, I'd hazard, you won't mind if I don't linger tonight. I'm in the thick of it in my workshop ...'

At first, eager that he not know how knotted she was feeling inside, Cathy shrugged – and, with a smile that was altogether too smug, Kaspar sauntered out of the door. He had only just breached the line of paper trees when he felt a ball of paper striking him on the back of the head. He paused, pretending it was merely a scrunched-up leaf, but when he strode on, Sirius hurtled to catch him. Only at the dog's insistence did he look back. Cathy was standing in the doorway, pointedly not taking the next step. What spirit she had to indulge in his game of brinkmanship was clearly fading away.

'Linger,' she said – so, with his air of victory barely concealed, Kaspar strode back through the Wendy House door.

'It's something. It's a start,' said Kaspar. 'And, truth be told, it was thinking of you that got me this far ...'

'Me?' Cathy asked, uncertain whether to be flattered or unnerved.

'Let me show you.'

On the ground between them was a small brown suitcase of perfectly utilitarian design. It was so unspectacular it didn't even have a handle. Kaspar knelt and opened it up, but it remained as humdrum as ever; all Cathy could see was the black felt of its lining. It was only as Kaspar stood, dangled one foot over the open case and plunged it inside that she realised the blackness had unaccounted depths – for Kaspar's foot seemed to have dropped below the bottom of the case, below even the lining of the floor. Then, after pausing to make sure of his balance, Kaspar lifted his second foot and planted it alongside the first.

Cathy studied him from every angle, while Sirius set up a pillowy hullabaloo. The case had swallowed Kaspar to the knots of his knees, but by rights it should not have reached his ankles.

'Am I going to get a smile?' asked Kaspar, ignoring the fact that he was wearing the biggest, most inane one himself.

'Explain,' declared Cathy, determined not to give him the satisfaction even as she battled to contain her surprise.

'Well, you already know how Papa can do the most extraordinary things with space. I've been trying to unpick it ever since I was small – but it wasn't until I started thinking about you in your hiding hole here that I started to see. And I was thinking: when you're here, inside the House, how could you ever hope to prove how big the House was outside these walls? When you're inside, why, it's as big as it feels – and that's all that matters. The perspective has shifted, don't you see? From the inside out, this is what's normal. And it's the same for that little ...' He flicked a finger airily at Cathy's stomach. '... creature in there. To that baby, your body's the whole world. The universe entire. So, with that in mind, I started tinkering ...'

Cathy waved her hand to order Kaspar out of the suitcase and took it upon herself to stand in his place. There was no unnatural feeling, no sensation that rippled in her ankles as she dropped in and found the bottom, some way below; it was the most ordinary thing in the world, and yet still she said, 'I have absolutely no idea what you're talking about.'

'It feels like I've done something real here, something just like my father, punched my way through whatever's been holding me back. Watch and learn, Miss Wray. Watch and *learn*. By the time this summer ends, I'll have more space inside my packages than you could hope to believe. The real question is – how to sell them? I've been picturing "Emporium Hiding Holes", for the perfect game of hide and seek. Or—'

'Toyboxes!' Cathy announced, at which Kaspar gave a wolfish grin. 'Toyboxes bigger on the inside, so a whole bedroom could be tidied away. Just open it up and cram everything in. Think about that, Kaspar. What mother wouldn't want a toybox like that?'

'You've a wicked mind, Miss Wray. It is mothers, of course, who hold the purses ...'

Cathy could virtually see the sales piling up in Kaspar's mind's eye. At once, he helped her clamber out of the box, snapped it shut, and darted away. 'I've much thinking to do. Too much thinking ...'

He stopped once before the doorway, to look back and make his goodbyes. As he did, a new look crossed his face; it seemed he was seeing her for the very first time. 'It's soon, isn't it?' he asked, considering her belly.

'Soon enough,' whispered Cathy, and only after he was gone did she realise quite how soon that was.

She had been given the gift of too much time. Too much time to think about it, too much time to wallow in ideas of what birth might be like. Time, she already knew, played tricks in the Emporium, but never as markedly as it did now: the days going by so slowly, but her body changing so fast. Kaspar came back across the next evenings, always bringing her some new version of his toy. Four nights had passed by the time he brought her a prototype toybox, plain pine inscribed with the tin soldier emblem of Papa Jack's Emporium. It was on the tip of her tongue to ask him to stay that night, but something held her back. Perhaps it was only pride, for Cathy had asked for so little in her life. She faced the emptiness of that night as she had all others – in thinking about the Emporium and its past, and trying desperately not to imagine the future.

The next night was the first that Kaspar did not appear. She gave up thinking of him (it was easier said than done; she realised, now, how eagerly she awaited his visits) and slept early, only to wake an hour, a half hour, a scant few minutes later – and, disoriented, stand in the Wendy House door. She spent the next day in solitude, but when Kaspar did not appear that night, nor the night after that, the feeling of imprisonment became too intense. There were only so many times she could prowl around the Wendy House walls, only so many times she could go back through the photographs of the old Emporium and search for some detail she had not yet noticed. She did not want to, but when she found herself back at the Wendy House door, it was the most natural thing in the world to set foot outside. And, when the world did not end, it was the most natural thing to keep going, over the white picket fence, under the first of the paper trees, up out of the alcove and into the first aisle.

Almost immediately the restlessness bled out of her. The knots inside her chest unwound. It was dark in the Emporium but she wandered along aisles lit by moonlight pouring in from the skylights above, and for the first time in many weeks she felt free.

It was intoxicating to be out. She spent an hour in the alcove where the pop-up books had been covered up, ferreting under the dust sheets and going through each book in turn. In the atrium the Russian rocking horses had been corralled behind a wooden fence, but she stole through and (mindful of her bump) climbed on to the closest she saw. Almost instantly, she could feel the wind in her hair, hear the pounding of hoof beats across some verdant plain. The sensations were so acute she quite forgot she was in the dusty old Emporium at all; the shop walls simply faded away, until what she could see in the edges of her vision was a wild, rugged vista of green, across which other rocking horses cantered in wild abandon.

After that she was tired, but it would not do to go back to the Wendy House, not when the night was still vast. Determined, she set off, ducking along an aisle where lace butterflies had once cavorted on invisible threads. In the insectarium at its end, the shelves were packed with boxes of grubs and larvae. On a whim, Cathy picked up the first, warmed the cocoon inside her palms and watched as a woollen house fly emerged. Only Kaspar, she thought, could have spent long hours concocting something so mundane as a toy fly. Papa Jack's were the golden dragonflies and grasshoppers, Emil's the bright furry bumblebees.

She left the insectarium by the back door and came, at last, to the carousel in the heart of the Emporium floor. The carousel itself had not turned since the night the Emporium closed its doors, and its painted horses, its unicorn and stag, now slept beneath blinkers and roughspun blankets. The depression in which they sat was surrounded by an avalanche of pillows, draped in the same dust sheets as everywhere else. Cathy remembered long winter nights when mothers and fathers had reclined on these hills and watched as their children were borne around by the carousel. Those slopes had always seemed so inviting; even now, hidden under thick sheets, they tempted her down.

She made her way over and lowered herself in. No sooner had the land given way underneath her, moulding to the shape of her body, Sirius reappeared and wormed his way up on to her lap. Sandwiched between the pillows and the patchwork, it wasn't long before Cathy's eyes grew heavy. Fleetingly, she closed them, content to float, for a time, on a mountain of pillows through the Emporium dark.

Noises woke her.

It was still dark on the shopfloor. The first thing she noticed was the cold, for Sirius was no longer on her lap. With the clumsiness of the half-asleep, she stumbled to the bottom of the slope and got her bearings.

She could see which way Sirius had gone for he had left marks in the dust now carpeting the Emporium floor, the tell-tale swishing of a hastily stitched tail. He had disappeared into the dark beyond the carousel, where the spiderweb of aisles had once housed all manner of delights. Panic gripped her. What if, somewhere down there, Sirius had lain down in the dust, his motors winding down? What, then, of the promise she had made to Kaspar?

Cathy took off. Past the carousel, the darkness in the aisles was absolute. She fumbled on one of the empty shelves, groping blind beneath the dust sheets – and came back triumphant with a glass jar in her hand, a relic left behind after the Emporium was closed. Fortune favoured her. She screwed the lid tight and the crocheted fireflies inside turned incandescent. They buzzed against the edges of the glass – and suddenly the aisle was lit up, serpents and soldiers cavorting in shadow on the shelves.

Cathy bore the light to the end of the aisle. She had not noticed this door before – but, then, there were so many doors in the Emporium, and the aisles constantly refracting or being rearranged. It was easy to get lost. And yet – there was something about this door that made her certain she would have remembered it. It was like the door to Papa Jack's workshop in miniature, oak with rivets of grey-black steel. Judging by the claw marks low down, the patchwork dog had scrabbled inside – and not for the first time.

She set down the lantern and opened it a crack.

'Sirius, you rotten hound, where are you?'

The door opened an inch, then an inch further. The first thing she saw was the dog. It was lying asleep, its feet twitching in whatever dreams creatures of cloth could have. Beyond where it lay, lit up by a string of firefly lanterns on a ledge beyond, Emil Godman sat hunched over a worktop.

At his feet were piles of felt, rolls of wire and a bail of cotton wadding. Toolboxes were stacked against one wall, sandwiched between crates of toy soldiers ready for sale.

Cathy had heard of Emil's workshop but until now had not caught a glimpse. Sally-Anne said the Godman brothers used to share a workshop, high up alongside their father's own – but here was Emil's, hidden in plain sight among the Emporium aisles.

She was whispering, trying to wake the patchwork dog, when Emil released a great cry of frustration and, whirling his arms like a toddler in the throes of some enormous tantrum, cast whatever he had been assembling from his worktop. A hail of wood and fabric arced over the workshop. What Cathy took for a pinewood hard-boiled egg landed square on Sirius's nose, waking him with a whimper.

'You wretched mutt, you're no help either. Why don't you go loping after Kaspar like you always do? Why do you have to bother me?'

Sirius beat his tail, whether in taunt or delight Cathy could not say.

Emil rushed at him, dropped to his knees and flipped him over. Cathy was about to leap out when she saw that Emil was only rough-housing with him, scratching the fabric of his underbelly and exposing the mechanism dangling there. 'Still ticking,' he grumbled, shaking his head in disbelief. 'And here am I, every night, just trying ...'

Emil rolled backwards, pulled one of the crates away from the wall and heaved out of it a bundle of rags and felt. At first Cathy took it for more spare parts, but when he set it down she realised it was a sheep, stitched together from old eiderdown and roughspun blankets. It was cruder than the patchwork cats and dogs that once populated the Emporium shelves, like a picture of a sheep a three-year-old child might have made. One of its black button eyes was lower than the other, its snout not nearly plump enough with stuffing.

Emil reached into its belly, wound it up and sat back, teasing Sirius's ears. In front of him, the sheep began to totter. It walked in a circle, emitted a pillowy bleat, bent to chew at some imaginary cud, and continued in that way until its motor had wound down.

'Useless,' Emil muttered. 'It's a toy, just a toy. There's no magic in it. It's just mechanics. Cam shafts and gears and four legs, up and down, up and down … What's the difference between *you* and *that*? What is it, you silly mutt? Why can't I …' Emil grabbed the patchwork sheep by the hind legs, tossed it back into the crate and slumped once more. 'At least I have my soldiers. Kaspar isn't interested in soldiers, so at least they're mine. And I've got something special, Sirius. Lined up and ready for next first frost …'

Emil marched into an alcove on the furthest side of the workshop, disappearing into shadow. Moments later, Cathy heard a chorus of rattles and clicks – and Emil emerged, his arms full of soldiery to line up on the opposite side. Standing proudly among them was his Imperial Kapitan.

Cathy watched as an army of wind-up soldiers marched out of the alcove, moving inexorably against an army on the opposite side. When they had crossed half the expanse, they stopped and lifted their rifles. Tiny pellets of wood exploded forth on strings, striking the advancing regiment just as they came within range. Under the hail of bullets the enemy fell; the only man who kept on marching was the Imperial Kapitan, impervious to the bullets.

'See!' Emil exclaimed. 'Kaspar won't know what's hit him. My riflemen will scythe his down, and nothing will topple the Kapitan. The next battle of the Long War, Sirius, it's going to be a massacre!'

At his outburst, the patchwork dog leapt to its paws. It turned to see Emil but, as it did, its black button eyes landed on Cathy – and though nothing in them changed (they were only black buttons), somehow Cathy saw the hint of acknowledgement in the way the fabric creased across its snout.

Its tail beat madly, and, as it did, Emil looked round.

Cathy recoiled back into the darkness of the aisle. She had taken only three strides when her feet, such treacherous things, caught one another mid-flight, sending her sprawling into the Emporium floor. The shock echoed in her body but, all the same, she picked herself up. She could hear footsteps behind her now – but it was only Sirius, coming to shepherd her home. More troubling was the voice that harried her along the aisle. 'Kaspar, you rotten spy, I know that's you! It's against the rules, Kaspar! Subterfuge and espionage, they're against the rules!'

Heart pounding, she found her way back to the paper trees and hurried through the Wendy House door. Only moments later she heard Sirius scrabbling to get in, and after that Emil's voice halloing through the trees. However intricate this toy was, nobody had fine-tuned its loyalty; it had led him straight to her.

She could hear the crunch of Emil's footsteps coming over the picket fence. First, he was cajoling Sirius to get out of the way. Then he was calling out his brother's name. Cathy looked around. In seconds, he was going to come through that door. And, no matter how vast this Wendy House was, it was still a finite space: four walls, no nooks and crannies, so very few places to hide.

That was when her eyes landed on the toybox, the dull thing of dovetailed wood that Kaspar had brought on his last visit.

The idea occurred in the very same moment that Emil's fingers landed on the door. Cathy threw herself across the Wendy House floor, heaved the toybox out and threw open its lid. Then, with one eye on the door, she stepped inside.

The floor was not beneath her, not where it should have been. She held on to the edges and pushed herself over the precipice – and then, at last, she felt it, somewhere below. When she stood, the toybox swallowed her up to her waist. The Wendy House door had started to rattle, but quickly she sank down, curling herself into a ball so that only the tip of her head could be seen. Then, as Emil shouldered his way in, she slammed shut the lid.

In the toybox there was only darkness. She could feel the walls closing in on her, the air growing warm and moist with her own breath. Yet, somehow it was holding her; somehow these four slats of wood had cocooned her in their heart: one pocket universe inside another, just like the child still kicking inside her.

'I know you're in here,' came Emil's voice, muted by the wood. 'Kaspar, don't be such a fool. There isn't any other way out.' For the first time, his voice faltered. 'Kaspar?'

She heard his footsteps prowling the edges of the room, heard him stop at the foot of the bed as if to check nobody was hiding underneath. By now he would have seen the nursery, the rocking horse and crib. By now he would have seen the collection of Emporium adverts lying strewn across the sheets.

The air in here was close; she felt it hardening in the back of her throat.

She was cramming her hand into her mouth, if only to keep herself from coughing, when she heard Emil's footsteps moving back in the direction of the door. She breathed out – but the relief was short-lived, for no sooner had Emil passed the toybox, than Sirius sent up a familiar howl. She contorted to look upwards, where a tiny sliver of light ran around the toybox lid. Now, it was marred by a patch of shadow: Sirius was looming above it, giving her away.

Emil's footsteps grew louder as he moved in her direction. Then his hands were on the toybox lid, drawing it up – and, from the incalculable depths below, Cathy peered up into his startled eyes.

'*You*,' he whispered, and fainted clean away.

It took some effort to heave herself out of the toybox. By the time she reached him, Sirius was lapping at his face with its darned-sock tongue, making the most dejected of noises with whatever motors lived in its throat. Cathy knelt beside him, peeled back his eyes. They were still flickering – and, no sooner had she closed them, than they opened again. As if startled for a second time, Emil scrabbled backwards. Cathy darted around to put herself between him and the door.

'Emil. *Please*. Listen. It isn't what you think …'

'What do I think?' he breathed, clambering to his feet.

'You think I'm one of those confidence girls, come to steal secrets. That I'm selling secrets to Hamley's, or that shop on the Portobello Road …'

'Well?'

'Well, look at me, Emil! Just look!'

She had almost shrieked it, for Emil's eyes were darting into every corner, searching out the secrets he was sure she had ferreted away.

'Emil, I have nowhere else. *We* have nowhere else ...'

His eyes landed on her belly. 'I'm sorry,' he said, berating himself by smashing bunched fists into his sides. 'I didn't think. I thought you'd go home. Why ever you ran away, I thought you'd go back and have your baby there and ... and then I'd forget about you and you wouldn't be back and—'

'I couldn't go home. I just couldn't.'

'So you hid here, on the day the snowdrops flowered. You've been hiding here ever since.'

It had been on the tip of her tongue to beg him not to blame Kaspar, to tell him none of this was Kaspar's fault, but somehow Emil seemed to be making the leaps of imagination for her, the story spinning of its own volition.

'I'm sorry,' she whispered.

'Oh no,' he said. 'No, no, no. Cathy, sit down. Please. Let me ... I should never have let you go. I almost didn't. I was going to tell Mrs Hornung but I knew there had to be a reason you'd kept it a secret and ... I'm sorry, Cathy. You believe it, don't you? Why, if I'd have had the idea, I'd have hidden you here myself ...'

He didn't know what to do, so instead he began pacing in circles, urging her to take the foot of the bed. When she did, he rushed to close the Wendy House door, lest anyone be spying from the paper trees. 'Mrs Hornung does her rounds. And Kaspar ... sometimes Kaspar creeps around here, concocting whatever he's concocting. You must be careful, Cathy. More careful than you've been tonight.' He stopped his pacing and Sirius, who had been mirroring him at his heel, promptly sat at his feet. 'How long will it be?'

'You mean my baby.'

He nodded.

'Soon,' she whispered.

'My mama was alone when I was born. Only her and Kaspar, but he was hardly a year old. Our house wasn't any bigger than this. Two rooms and a yard house and hens in the hut. And ... you did the right thing to stay here, Cathy. You mustn't do it alone. And I can—'

'You won't tell Papa Jack, will you?'

Emil puffed out his chest. 'I've never lied to my papa before, but I'll lie this time.'

'And ... Kaspar?'

On this, he seemed to ruminate for the longest time. 'Kaspar would know what to do. He always does. After our mama passed on, before our papa came back ... well, it was Kaspar who used to catch rabbits for our pot. Kaspar who taught me how to dig for mushrooms. It was Kaspar who told me we had a papa, and that one day he was coming home. Oh, he didn't believe it himself, but he still told me it, every night. And now ...' Emil came to sit beside her on the bed. Folding his hand over hers, he said, 'Mrs Hornung has some books. I've seen them on a shelf. And Papa has his taxonomies, the anatomies he uses for building his dolls. There must be something in there. And ... perhaps it's best, after all, if Kaspar doesn't know? Two can keep a secret, Cathy. But three ...'

It was on the tip of her tongue to say: you already told him I was pregnant. But then he would know, know that Kaspar had told her, know that it was Kaspar who brought her back here. That did not seem fair. All Emil wanted, all Emil had ever wanted, was something of his own, something he could stand alongside and say: look, this was mine, and I did as good a job as any. So, instead, Cathy squeezed his hand, rested her head on his shoulder and whispered her thanks – while, inwardly, she cursed her lack of courage. Why had her bravery abandoned her tonight? Even the baby, that half-formed thing inside her, was wiser than this.

Before he left that night, Emil gave her a pipe-cleaner bird – the closest he'd ever got, he confessed, to the magics of his father. It fluttered around the Wendy House rafters until all its energy was gone; then it dropped to the floor, where Sirius gnawed on it with relish. Afterwards, she picked up what was left and hid it underneath the mattress. Secrets and lies, she thought. She had thought she was skilled in both, but in truth she was a dilettante; she was going to have to do a lot better.

THE BROTHERS GODMAN

. . . .

PAPA JACK'S EMPORIUM, 1907

Consider Kaspar Godman. Tonight, if you were the kind of Emporium obsessive who collects a catalogue each year, whose home is infested with silver satin mice, who has saved and saved your pennies in the hope of one day taking a runnerless rocking horse of your own back home, you would have found him in his workshop, unwashed and unkempt as only a man in the throes of passion can be. Only, you would not have found Kaspar Godman locked up with an admirer; you would have found him in a storm of balsam and metal rivets, of paints and lacquers and varnish. Around him would be a half-dozen incomplete boxes, one upended inside another. One would be overfilled with patchwork animals, wound down and piled high. Another would have half a bedstead poking out. Yet another would be splayed open around Kaspar Godman's waist, as if trying to devour him whole.

The peripheries of the room were couched in the patchwork animals he had tried to make. A mermaid, meant for a good girl's bathtub, lay half-beached on a shore of wound-down patchwork bears. Kaspar had thought he would devote his summer to making patchwork so lifelike there was not a difference between his and his father's own, but there was a higher calling and he slaved for it now. He pressed his hands against the innards of the box in which he was standing, thinking he might shift its edges back just one more inch – but the wood began to buckle, the slats came apart, and instead of standing inside his own cavernous vault he stood in a disaster of splinters and jagged shards. Still, he did not abandon his calling, nor lament the world that was doing him wrong. He sat for a while, in the middle of the destruction, and gaped. Even in failure, what a life this was! He picked up one of his joists, slotted the broken shards back together and laughed. What a blissful way to spend your hours, your days and nights, making things up because nothing else mattered!

He was about to take another turn, but something stopped him. At first, he thought it was his hands. They were too tired. His whole body was spent. Then he realised it wasn't his hands at all. It was his head. What inspiration he had to achieve this, the thing that had first driven him to cobble the slats together and start teasing out the space inside ... it was the girl. Down there in the Wendy House, waiting for him to come back; the smile she had given when he stepped into his toybox, the way her face had crinkled, trying to resist her astonishment – and yet, and yet ...

What he wanted, most of all, above even beating Emil in the next round of the Long War, was to take a completed toybox down to Cathy and say, 'Look! Look at this thing I have done! You think it's only my papa who achieves the most vivid of Emporium magics – well, not any more ...'

It was the girl. He realised, now, that he was doing it because of the girl.

By the time he careened across the shopfloor, he was more convinced than ever. Cathy had never made a toy in her life, but she had opened something inside him, some untrammelled *desire*. Kaspar had never lacked inspiration (no toymaker could have made his paper trees without it) but this was different. He had never lacked shop girls to tell outrageous stories to, nor even to get lost with in one of the Emporium's many nooks, but this was different too. Being the best had always been important – but only to be the best. Being the best for somebody else, well, that was special . . .

He stopped as he hit the paper forest. His papa's Magic Mirror was hanging here, showing some corner of the Emporium storerooms where its sister mirror hung. He stood in front of it, his reflection imposed upon that shuttered room full of boxes, crates, the ranks of twitching skeletons waiting to be draped in patchwork, wound up and released into the Emporium playrooms. He was not, he had to admit, the most handsome sight. He made some attempt to style his hair with the tips of his fingers, straightened his shirtsleeves and the velveteen waistcoat he always wore (it did not do to wear common plaid, not when his work was so important) and proceeded, pausing to pick paper wallflowers on the way.

Before he went into the Wendy House, he peered through the window. And there she was: Cathy Wray, perched on the end of her bed. Her belly looked markedly bigger than it did even three nights ago, but it was not there that Kaspar was looking. He was looking at her eyes.

Cathy startled when the door moved, both hearts inside her leaping in fright. Her heart only half stilled when she saw that it was Kaspar, for wasn't there every chance Emil might come trotting behind? Kaspar looked more bedraggled than she'd seen him, yet still held himself with a peacock's pride. Cathy marched past, slammed shut the door and wheeled around. 'Where on earth were you?' she demanded.

'I beg your pardon?'

'You used to come every night. And now—'

'Am I to understand that you *miss* me, Miss Wray?'

It was a question Cathy was determined not to answer. And yet, 'I do,' she replied, angry with herself for admitting anything so foolish. The truth was hard to articulate: Emil was company enough, distraction from these Wendy House walls, but somehow it wasn't the same; Emil brought his worries – but Kaspar brought his wonders.

'It wouldn't have taken ten minutes to come to the shopfloor, just to—'

'I'm sorry. I've been selfish.'

'I'll say you have.'

'Have you been … very bored?'

Yes, she thought, boredom had been a part of it. But there had been Emil and, now that she pictured him, she did not want to be unduly cruel. There was sweetness to Emil and she hardly begrudged his visits, even when he came to her like a little boy does his neglectful mother, to pull on her apron strings and ask *have I been good*? She even enjoyed his company. He had brought her books: *The Compleat Confectioner*, being a collection of recipes for children by the 'Indomitable Mrs Eale'; *The Nursemaid's Oracle* – with advice on rearing and disciplining unruly youngsters – by one William Boulle; a sketchbook Papa Jack had made of the workings of the human body (this had more to say about joints and motion than it did the processes of giving birth – for which, Emil declared, there was a copy of *Gray's Anatomy* somewhere on a shelf, if only he could conquer his squeamishness enough to open the pages). Now that she thought about it, that was more than Kaspar had ever done. Kaspar was the one to bring her the reams of newspapers the Emporium collected for stuffing and packing, but leafing through them only reminded Cathy how close the walls of her Wendy House were – and what a world there was out there, if only she could reach it. London, which had once seemed so far away, sat denied on her doorstep. The front page of *The Times* showed the Royal procession moving along the Horse Guard's Parade – to think, she might have seen Prince George himself; Lizzy would have *died*! – while, inside, announcements were made for summer theatre in Regent's Park and an advertisement showed ladies in elegant tea gowns, walking through Kensington with the air of courtiers. There were only so many times she could read the list of debutantes being presented at court this season without screaming: *I don't care about coming out! All I want is to come outside …*

'I've been out of my mind.'

'I'll make it up to you.'

'How?'

'I'll think of something.'

'*How?*'

Kaspar brightened. 'You're not denying my ability to think, are you, Miss Wray?'

'Nothing of the sort,' she snapped, 'and do stop calling me Miss Wray. It's almost the worst thing about it.'

'The worst thing about what?'

'About *this*,' she said. 'Kaspar, don't you think ... isn't it possible I might have been better off if you'd just let me go and find a new home? Because if you're just going to leave me here ...'

At this, Sirius gave a solitary yap.

'You're upset,' said Kaspar.

'I am.'

'Perhaps you'd like me to leave?'

Cathy ripped one of the pillows from the bed and hurled it in his direction. He took it to the face and did not flinch, the perfect imitation of a man. 'I would not,' she begrudgingly declared.

'Cathy,' he said, more sincerely now, 'has something happened? Something untoward?'

'More untoward than *this*?' she said, as if to include the Wendy House, the patchwork dog, the Emporium itself. 'No ... not a thing.'

She had known, before Kaspar walked through the door, that she would not tell him about Emil. Either Emil would have confessed everything or he would have kept his silence – and she had always kept faith with the latter, because Emil had seemed so proud to have a secret of his own.

'Well, go on,' said Cathy, with something approaching a mild rebuke, 'tell me what you've been doing that's been so vitally important to the future of the Emporium that you couldn't spare me a single hour?'

Now that he was (mildly) forgiven, Kaspar marched into the heart of the room. 'It's my toyboxes. I've stretched the space inside one so that it's the size of a closet. I'm stretching it further, but something breaks inside, something breaks in *me*, and ...' He started gazing up, into the Wendy House rafters. Then his eyes dropped back to Cathy. 'I'm still unsure how my papa made all the space inside here, but it's near, I can feel that it's near ...' He did not say *every time I see you, it's getting nearer*, because how could she understand anything as ephemeral as that? The magic of toys was one thing; falling in love quite another. 'Imagine,' he said instead, 'a toybox the size of a train carriage, with a switchback stair leading to the bottom. And then – another toybox inside that, and another inside that. A boy could own an infinite number of worlds, all locked inside each other, if only I can ...' Kaspar stopped. 'You're looking at me in that way again.'

'I am?'

'The way that says, if I wasn't so charming, you'd have them drag me off to Bedlam.'

She gave him a pointed look and, in return, he roared in unadulterated delight.

Kaspar stayed until midnight, but Cathy had not yet fallen asleep when she heard a different tread approaching through the paper trees. Emil was more reticent than Kaspar; he knocked and waited to be invited within. Cathy rushed to the door and tried to bustle him through – but instead Emil stood, steadfast, on the step between the paper trees.

'No, Cathy. I've come to take you out.'

Cathy looked up. Mottled silver rained through the paper branches from the skylights high above.

'It's ... midnight.'

'Indeed!' Emil declared. 'A midnight ... feast.' And, on stepping aside, he revealed the picnic hamper he had been hiding. It sat squarely on the roots of a paper oak, opened up to reveal breads and preserves and all manner of other splendid concoctions.

Cathy needed no further temptation. She followed Emil through the trees and on to the shopfloor – but it was not until they came through the atrium at the Emporium's entrance, past the knights errant and the rocking-horse corral, that she realised they were not really going *out* at all. Now that she thought of it, the very idea was preposterous. Emil outside these Emporium doors was more of a nonsense than Kaspar. He simply did not belong. Far better that she follow him through the insectarium, along an aisle where a patchwork menagerie waited, gathering dust, for next winter – and on into a depression of land where the aisles pivoted apart.

'There used to be places like this all over the shopfloor,' Emil explained, 'but they get retired or they get moved around, and sometimes, if you don't keep up, you get to forgetting where they are. They get trapped behind aisles, or somebody builds a bridge over them, or the toys are placed in such a way the eye rather glances over the spaces in between. Me and Kaspar, we used to call them the Sometime Dens, because they're only ever there half of the time. But they're perfect, don't you see, for just not being seen ...'

There was a picnic blanket already lain out, in red and white chequered squares. Emil led Cathy down, guiding her as if past imaginary holes in the earth, and invited her to sit.

'May I?' Emil began.

Cathy nodded.

Emil opened up the hamper so that the moonlit picnic could begin. After the plates, knives and silver spoons, he produced a pair of chicken legs, roasted to perfection, a loaf of golden bread, a slab of butter that positively gleamed. There were bunches of grapes and quarters of cheese, an apple tart hidden beneath a lattice of shortcrust pastry. The sardines in the glass jar looked the most delectable of all, but it wasn't until Emil produced the jug of lemonade that Cathy realised none of it was real.

Her eyes caught Emil's. 'Please,' he said. 'Just *play* ...'

She picked up a bunch of painted grapes. They seemed almost good enough to eat. The adult part of her knew they were only orbs of wood, but another part could smell the crisp sweetness of the vineyard. The longer she held on to it, the more the feelings intensified. Just to test it further, she picked up a tiny teapot and pretended to pour a cup. The aisles that surrounded them fell away, she heard the tinkling of teaspoons, the drone of a dragonfly in the pristine parkland that now seemed to exist on the very edges of her vision. She could smell cake, buttery and rich with vanilla, though the only things beneath her fingers were paper and painted wood.

She put the grapes and teapot down and the parkland evaporated. Suddenly she was back on the dusty shopfloor. 'It's ... incredible, Emil. Did you make all of this?'

She looked up. While she had been engrossed, Emil had got to his feet. A few scant minutes ago his face had been open with pleasure; now he prowled the edge of the picnic blanket like a scalded dog.

If she had expected Emil to be heartened by her words, she was sorely disappointed. He simply picked up the cake, looked at it with disgust, and tossed it into the empty hamper.

'I'm sorry, Cathy. I so wanted to give you a good day out. But ... play a little longer, you'll find ants in the sandwiches. Storms in the sky.'

She ventured a grin, hoping it would dispel some of this madness. 'Then you've captured the experience of almost every English picnic there's ever been ...'

If Emil appreciated the joke, he did nothing to show it. He began to pack the hamper away, hands shaking in fury at the uselessness of a pinewood boiled egg. 'It isn't real. The feeling isn't right. Every cut I make, every little polish, it just slips further away. It starts out sunny and ends up with a storm. Why is that always the way?'

'You're too cruel to yourself, Emil. I could *taste* the cake.'

Emil lost himself in the mania of packing his creation away. 'I'm working so hard, Cathy. But Kaspar ...'

'What of him?'

'It's those toyboxes of his. Why couldn't I ... ? Why didn't I ... ? If he perfects it by winter, Papa will be so proud.'

Cathy sighed, trying hard not to let her exasperation show. 'Does it matter?'

'You don't understand. Papa, he's ... not a young man. Sometimes it seems like he never was. But he won't make toys for ever. And when he stops ... well, the Emporium, it has to *belong*, doesn't it? There has to be a Papa Jack. What if ...' Emil lost his words; perhaps this was a fear to which he had never given voice. 'What if he decided that, because Kaspar's toys ...'

'Emil, this is your home. He's your papa too.'

For a time, Emil remained silent. He toyed with a humble pork pie (balsawood, cork and pine) and seemed lost in his imaginings of it – and only when he reared up did

Cathy understand he'd been trembling all along, desperate to say something but uncertain if he dared say it. 'It wasn't always like this. When we were boys, those first years when Papa showed us how, I'd make *good* things, things every bit as good as Kaspar's – better even – and if you don't believe it, all you have to do is look at the pictures. Just ask my papa. When we were in our tenement, I made a sledge for the other boys to ride down Whitechapel Hill. It was so good those street boys stole it in the end. They said they could feel the snow around them, even in summer. And there was my kite. It burst into flight like a Chinese dragon, so light and strong it couldn't come down – and it just flew there, in the skies above Weavers Fields, until finally some men came up from the docks in St Katharine's and set light to its tether. And then it just flew away, burning as it climbed into the sun. Or there were the first years we were here, in the Emporium, and Papa gave us a workshop and said: do your best, boys ... And we did! All of my marching knights and pinwheels. My princesses in their towers! Oh, I wish I had one now, Cathy, and then you'd see – then you'd see it wasn't always Kaspar ...' He had to stop, but only for want of breath. 'Then there was that summer. You know how it happens. Kaspar grew six inches in a night. And his voice was different and he was growing his beard – and that was the summer, Cathy, that was the summer when ...'

'Emil, you don't have to say all this. Nobody's—'

'One morning, I woke up – and there he was, sitting at the end of my bed. I could tell he'd been up all night, because he had that bedraggled look about him. That elated look in his eyes. He had it every time he'd made a new toy he wanted me to try out. Well, I was still weary – but nothing woke me up, back then, like the idea of a new toy. So Kaspar put a pop-up book in my hands and, when I opened it, it just kept on opening – and suddenly, there I was, inside a jungle lair, with creepers and vines and monkeys swinging in the trees, and a little motor started spinning and a crackling voice came out. *"What do you think of this, Emil? What do you think of this?"* It was Kaspar's voice, and Kaspar's toy – and that, Cathy, *that* was when I knew. I spent the rest of that summer trying to make a book just like his, but I never could do it. And it's been the same ever since. No,' he went on, before she could console him any further, 'don't try and persuade me. A toybox like Kaspar's, it's worth as much as the whole of the Emporium. A hamper like mine, it might fill a few shelves, but will they talk about it on Speakers' Corner? Will children be jealous if their neighbour has one on Christmas morning?'

'Tell me something, Emil. Why don't you … why don't you do what *you're* good at? Not what Kaspar's good at, not what your papa's good at … what about *you*? What about your soldiers?'

'Yes,' Emil said, 'I'll always have my soldiers, won't I?'

'And you said it yourself – they come to the Emporium to see wonders, and maybe they even buy those wonders too, but not like they buy your soldiers. How many toyboxes can Kaspar possibly make? Ten? Twelve, if he doesn't sleep until first frost? Well, that's twelve customers at most. Twelve times the bell rings with a sale. Now, just imagine how many of your soldiers are going to fly out of the door this Christmas. I *saw* the things you've been working on, remember? Imagine how excited boys are going to be this

Christmas, to play battles with soldiers who can rally and shoot . . .'

The transformation in Emil was almost physical. He grew bigger, stood taller. 'Do you really think?'

'Treat yourself more kindly, Emil. That's an order.'

Emil nodded. Yes, Cathy thought, he likes being ordered around. And perhaps he would have marched away there and then, back to his workshop lathe and the hundreds more soldiers he might create before dawn, if only his eyes had not caught her hand hovering over her bump. 'I tried to talk to Mrs Hornung. But . . . she hasn't had babies of her own. And I . . . don't know where else to look. Mrs Hornung said the body takes care of its own. And I suppose there must be something in that, because . . .' He stopped, because he was blathering now. 'Are you afraid?'

'A little more each day.'

'It's no good me telling you not to be afraid. It isn't me who has to do it. I suppose you think I'm awfully selfish, coming to you with my toys, worrying about who'll own the Emporium when—'

'No, Emil.' She crossed the expanse and pressed her fingers to the back of his hand. 'I don't.'

It was the first time he had smiled all night. 'I'd like to help you, when it happens. You mustn't be alone.'

In her mind's eye, she saw Kaspar: Kaspar stroking the hair out of her eyes; Kaspar clutching her hand. The image was fleeting, but enough to make her snatch her own hand away. 'I won't be . . .'

Somewhere high above, a light exploded on one of the galleries circling the Emporium dome. Together they looked up. A figure had emerged. Even at this distance, there was no mistaking Papa Jack. He moved with the slowness of glaciers. He crossed from one gallery to the next and there he stopped, propped up on the balcony rail to look over the shopfloor.

'He can't sleep again,' said Emil. 'That means either he had an *idea* or . . .'

Papa Jack lifted himself to move again. Cathy was certain she was not mistaken; the old man was either crying or singing. Whichever it was, it had the quality of winter wind in the trees.

'. . . or what?'

'Or he's *remembering*.'

High above, Papa Jack disappeared through another door. The light seemed to move sluggishly after him, as if he wore it as a bridal train.

Emil must have realised he was standing too close to Cathy for he swiftly stepped aside.

'I'll come back soon, Cathy. I'll make soldiers so magnificent those toyboxes will sit around gathering dust. This winter, they won't even remember those paper trees.'

Cathy watched him race off into the darkness of the shopfloor. It was strange how easily Emil and Kaspar thought of the first frost, of October and November and Christmas beyond. Cathy laid a hand on her belly, where the baby was suddenly too big to cartwheel around. Before winter, there was autumn – and before autumn, summer. No wonder she could not envisage beyond, for what was life going to look like then?

The weeks flickered by.

Keeping Kaspar from Emil and Emil from Kaspar became a parlour game in which all three of them were embroiled (though only Cathy had any knowledge of the rules). When Kaspar was inside the Wendy House walls, the baby tumbled in panic – for what would happen were Emil to come sauntering through the paper trees right then? When Emil came by, to show her the Cossack cavalry he was devising, the miniature cannonade and musketeers fit for the Crimea, the baby tumbled again – for what if there were to come a knock at the door and Cathy were to open it, only to discover a perfectly composed toybox out of which Kaspar Godman unfolded himself?

There were tricks she learnt to employ. The gifts Emil brought could be hidden at the bottom of Kaspar's toybox. The signs of Kaspar's visits were easier to disguise, for he brought only his ideas – and the only sign he was there were the teacups he left behind, the impressions his body made on the bed when he lay back and told her how one day he would make her a Wendy House ten times the size, a paper garden for her baby, a whole world they need never leave.

And perhaps it was the way her eyes furrowed at this that prompted Kaspar's return at dawn the next morning. Evidently he had slept, for he looked less ragged than Cathy had seen him in weeks. He wore a woollen town coat and, over his shoulder, a satchel of waxed leather.

'You'll have to come quickly, if this is going to work.'

Still in her nightdress, Cathy felt suddenly naked. 'If what's going to work?'

'You've been a prisoner too long, Miss Wray. This Emporium of ours has its wonders, but sometimes you need a moment of normality to remember the magic. What do you say?'

'I'd say *something*, if only I knew what …'

'Outside, Miss Wray. London. But is has to be now – because once Emil starts pottering around the shopfloor, the moment is lost. Seize the day, Miss Wray!'

It was not the idea of seizing the day that propelled her to rush behind the screen and scramble into her day clothes. It was the thought of Emil wending his way down here, to share the fruits of his evening's endeavour, and catching her with Kaspar. For Emil, that would be a calamity too terrible to bear; she was, after all, *his* secret.

Hastily dressed, she stepped out from behind the screen and slipped her arm through Kaspar's. 'Do you know,' she said, 'it's somehow hard to think of there being an outside at all.'

'It can get you like that,' said Kaspar, and with a wolfish grin, he led her through the shadowed halls.

The coach was waiting at the end of Iron Duke Mews, with a horse already reined up. At first Cathy took it for patchwork, but it was only the enforced months of the Emporium tricking her eyes; this horse was very real. Kaspar helped Cathy on to the stage, where she sat among great felt sacks bulging with presents. She recognised sets of Emil's soldiery spilling out, boxes of paper trees, a floating cloud castle, weighted down so that it did not disappear, up above the London streets.

'What is all this?'

'There's a city to explore,' Kaspar began, 'but we have to earn it first. Come on, I'll show you.'

The sun was not fully risen as Kaspar drove the coach into the winding streets of Soho, but by the time they reached the Cambridge Circus it was lighting them in radiant array. Cathy had quite forgotten the temptations of sunshine. She felt brighter already. Outside the Palace Theatre, where a gaggle of stage hands called out to Kaspar as he passed – 'I used to come down here sometimes. The men in these theatres, they think they know magic. Don't tell Papa, but I leased them Sirius one season. They taught him stage tricks. They're the reason he can perform a tightrope walk' – they stopped to buy oranges, and with their fingers sticky with juice they wended their way south, down the Charing Cross Road and to the banks of the river.

There were places he wanted to take her. Somewhere, there was a poky little toyshop that specialised in miniatures – they were not without merits, Kaspar said, as long as you could overlook the fact that all they did was sit there, looking *small* – but better were the places he used to visit, secret places of his own. 'The Emporium might be the world, but summers there are long, Miss Wray. Sometimes you want … something else. I tried to bring Emil once. I had to put a halter on him just to get him out of the door. I forfeited two rounds in our Long War just to make sure he wouldn't tell Papa. But … Emil never did like escaping the Emporium. I don't think he's set foot outside in three whole years.'

Escaping from the Emporium seemed such a strange thing to hear Kaspar speaking about. She wondered how often he slipped through the tradesman's exits, what life he found out here, what people he knew.

It was on her mind to ask when the river hove into view and, hanging above it, the Houses of Parliament, the Abbey standing proudly behind. She had seen them in miniature on the Emporium shelves, but there they were, blotting out the skyline. How vast the world really was, when you started looking up! Kaspar drove the coach out over the river and for a time they lingered there, the boats turning underneath. She breathed in the ripe tang of the Thames and wondered that she was even alive.

Sir Josiah's sat beyond the railway arches and the Lambeth bridge. A tumbledown of brick buildings arrayed around a yard with wooden outhouses in between, it sat in shadow at the end of a row of buildings that looked bleaker still. The yard that sat in front was pitted with potholes where thistles and nettles burst up in inglorious rapture.

Kaspar brought the trap to a halt and, leaping down, extended a hand to guide down Cathy.

'What is this place?'

In reply, the doors opened and, across the narrow yard, out tumbled a horde of children. The elder ones stampeded the younger in their clamour to get past. Two of the grubbiest fought each other for the privilege of unlocking the iron gates but, once they had, nothing (not even the barking of the mistress who had appeared in the doorway behind them) could hold back the tide. Children of all shapes and sizes, not one of them wearing clothes that fit, lapped around the wagon. Kaspar slid blinkers over his horse's eyes, if only to stop his restless shifting.

'Think of it as the Summer Emporium,' Kaspar began – and, upon lifting the first of the felt sacks from the coach floor, submitted himself to a whirlwind of grasping hands as the children closed in.

After it was done, and the coach floor empty, Cathy watched the children tumble in orgies of delight around the yard, running wind-up armies against each other, squabbling for the affection of the litter of patchwork kittens they had awoken from their slumber, or clinging tight to the floating cloud castles for fear they might evaporate away. For some time, Kaspar was locked in conversation with Sir Josiah's schoolmistress (why this should have bothered Cathy, she had no idea, save for the fact that this particular mistress had a prim beauty about her); only when he had finished did he saunter back through the gates and join her at the wagon. Inside the yard, the battles went on. One of the patchwork kittens was already stuck, mewing for help from the top of a paper tree.

'Do you do this every year?'

'Once a summer. It stops one feeling … stifled.' He paused, reappraising himself. 'Don't look at me like that, Miss Wray! I'll admit – I enjoy the adoration.'

'I know you do.'

'Does it make me awfully selfish?'

Cathy was puzzled. 'To hand out toys at an abandoned children's home?'

'To bask in the glow of it.'

A thought cascaded over Cathy, one from which she could not escape. For mightn't her own child, the one squirming in her belly, have started its life in a place like this? Might it not be its face pressed against the window, waiting for a visit – from the Emporium, from a grieving family, from an old spinster desperate for a baby of her own?

'I think selfishness of that kind might be forgiven. Kaspar …' And here she hesitated, thinking she might take his hand. 'Can we …'

'Back to the Emporium?'

'Not that.' She tried to lift herself on to the coach again, but her body resisted; she felt the touch of Kaspar's hands as he helped her aboard. 'But not here.'

'I believe that's a thing we might do, Miss Wray.'

Some time later, having first explored the flower markets of Covent Garden, Kaspar accompanied Cathy through the Marble Arch and walked her, arm in arm, into the budding green of Hyde Park. It was unseasonably bright and the sunshine had already lured countless clerks out of their offices. Most were picnicking around the Apsley Gate, where handsome columns framed a frieze of charioteers riding out to war. Cathy could not ignore the furrowed looks as they noted the roundness of her belly, but it was not this that made her follow Kaspar on. She was, after all, used to a little scorn. Soon, they reached a stand of trees grown in such contortions that they seemed crowned in roots, growing down into the earth. Here patients from the hospital on the Hyde Park Corner formed a great horseshoe, fresh London air being deemed beneficial to their health, and even one of these (an elderly lady clinging to a velveteen rabbit from the Emporium stores) acknowledged Kaspar as he passed.

'They're looking at me, aren't they?' Cathy asked. Together they found the shade above the Serpentine and looked out across its glittering expanse.

'Let them look.'

'They'll think I'm the servant girl you've taken as your bride ...'

'Have they never seen a woman with child before?'

'You said it yourself, Kaspar. I'm sixteen if I'm a day.'

'You've never cared before.'

'I don't care now,' she answered – though perhaps it was no longer true. The Wendy House had spoiled her. It would have been like this every day, had she stayed at home.

There came the sound of a motorcar approaching along the Rotten Row, a trail of horse-drawn carriages trotting in its wake. Kaspar turned away from them with a sigh. 'I'd rather a runnerless rocking horse than a real horse almost any day.'

At least the stupidity of his sneer plucked her out of her own thoughts. 'Have you even ridden one?'

'I could make a patchwork horse twice as comfortable. Give it a little thought and I could make one twice as fast.' As if to prove a point, he darted for the roots behind him, came back with a fist full of twigs and lengths of dead grass, and set about meshing them in his lap. A few moments later, he set down a cavalry horse of sticks and made it canter toward her. Once it was in her lap, she held it aloft. It was only the sketch of a horse, and yet every muscle was demarked in dead grass; its halter was thistle, its mane made out of clover.

There was silence, punctured only by the riot of ducks on the water (the gentlemen from the motorcar had launched a punt and were helping their shrieking lady friends aboard). Cathy set the horse back down, tweaked its tail, and watched it canter to Kaspar. Moments later, he turned it back toward her. Each time it made the crossing, it frayed apart a little further; each time it lurched over a diminishing length of grass. And, as they passed it back and forth, Cathy's hands crept closer to Kaspar's own. At last, when the horse was spent, Kaspar's fingers touched hers.

He wants to kiss me now, thought Cathy. And, even as certain as he is (vain and cocksure as ever), I'd let him. But the baby had sensed something; it moved inside her, suddenly the only thing she could feel. The ripples across her insides. The ridge that moved across her belly.

She had waited too long. Masking his pain, Kaspar whipped his hand away, began tying knots in the grasses at his feet.

'Home?' he said.

Something inside her wanted to say more. There was so much with which that silence might have been filled. And yet, 'Home,' she finally replied.

By the time they returned to the Emporium, dusk was already settling. What clerks and daytrippers had swarmed Hyde Park were turning back to their townhouses and lodgings. At the end of Iron Duke Mews, the Emporium was a box of delights forgotten at Christmas and secreted away until the snow next fell. There was something forlorn about the idea that these aisles never saw summer.

Kaspar said so little as they made their way back to the aisles. He was hurt, that much she could tell. He had every right to be. He had told her so much, of the time before their papa, of the crossing they had made, of that wretched tenement where they had lived. All that he wanted was for her to say a little of her own life. Why, then, did it seem so hard?

He took her as far as the paper trees but would go no further. As she watched him go, something implored her to follow. And yet she remained, her feet stuck as fast as the roots of the trees that surrounded her.

Sirius did not rush out to join her. That would have been some consolation for whatever it was she was feeling – but, as she stepped through the Wendy House door, she realised why. The dog was curled up at the foot of the bed, and pinned to his breast was a simple letter.

I missed you.
Where are you?
Yours always
Emil

She clasped the letter to her breast, pitched down on to the bed and lay there as Sirius scrabbled up beside her. She was tired, yet thoughts of Kaspar kept cartwheeling through her mind, and the baby was pressed up against her, shifting in places that made her think the time was near. Where had this heaviness come from? It ought to have been a joyous day: she and Kaspar, out in the world. And yet …

She sat up. 'I've let him down, haven't I?' The paper tore where her fingers were straining at it. 'Come on, Sirius. You can lead the way.'

She stopped outside the door to Emil's workshop. Part of her hoped he wasn't there. But no, there he was, as besotted with his work as Kaspar before him. He had fallen asleep where he was sitting, slumped over his lathe with a unit of half-formed soldiers lined up in the vice.

Gone were the half-formed patchworks he had been trying to make; gone, his attempts at recreating Emporium Instant Trees; gone, the chaos of splintered parts that had put Cathy in mind of a child at tantrum. As hard as she looked, she could not even see the picnic hamper over which he had shed so many tears. Now, the workshop was an ordered production line. Units of soldiers occupied every surface and shelf. Some of them needed painting, some needed lacquer;

but all stood proud, defiant as any Emporium soldier had ever been.

She stole in, Sirius sloping after.

Cathy spent some time looking at the soldiers. Emil's original Kapitan was perched on his worktop, always at his left-hand side. There was something unbearably sad about that. Either sad or – why not? – the most magical thing ever. A little part of Emil was refusing to grow up. And that was how Cathy knew: no matter if he never learned to do the things Papa Jack could, Emil would always be a toymaker at heart.

She hated to think of him, waiting in the Wendy House for her today. Her hands danced across the thatch of his hair, until finally he woke.

'Cathy?' he whispered. 'I was worried for you. I was ...'

'I know you were, dear Emil.'

'But you came.'

She thought: *I almost didn't.*

'I did.'

She sat on one of the upturned boxes and watched as he kneaded the wakefulness back into his eyes. It was on the tip of his tongue to ask where she had been, and if he had asked it, she would have said; she did not have the strength of secrets in her tonight. All she wanted was to tell, to tell it all.

'Do you want to show me?' she asked.

'Show you?'

'You came to show me something, didn't you? And I wasn't there to see it.'

Emil came to his senses, leapt to his feet. In a flurry of movement, he had whipped away the dust sheet covering his work bench. On it sparkled a legion of soldiers, armed with their working rifles, flanked by proud dragoons and miniature cannonade.

Cathy had seen toy soldiers at battle before, but she had not seen them like this. They came at each other, stopped and let loose their fire. The barrels of the toy cannons jerked upwards and, out of their eyes, black orbs erupted to scatter the enemy like skittles. The devastation they wreaked was incredible to behold.

Gazing out across the ruin his creation had made, Emil trembled with pride. 'Oh, Cathy,' he whispered, 'what do you think?'

She only stared.

'When Kaspar sees this …' Emil began to place the soldiers back into their cases, handling his cannons with the delicate fingers a boy reserves for only his most special toys. When, at last, he was done, he gave Cathy a salute so long she felt quite ridiculous. 'No, I need to stop thinking of Kaspar. I didn't do this for Kaspar. Cathy, I hope you don't think it strange, but I must say it. Why, if I don't say it now, I never will, and then I'll perish. I … did it for you. I did it so you'd know I could do it, and that making my toys is done out of love. Love of sitting here in my workshop and making things happen. I don't do it for glory, I don't do it to win, I don't do it even because, one day, I want all of London's children to think of me, Emil Godman, like they think of my papa. I did it because you made me see. Papa and Kaspar have their magics, but I have my own magic, of a sort. You're my totem now, Cathy. I hope you don't think it foolish.'

Cathy dropped at his side, helped him put his new soldiers back in their boxes. It was safe here, with Emil. And perhaps she might even have told him: this is where I'm from, and this is why I ran, and this, this is what my mother and father wanted for me and my baby . . .

'Where did you go today, Cathy?'

The question cut through whatever she had been thinking. She could not tell him. Leaving the Emporium doors with Kaspar at her side, that moment in the park when she had almost – when she had wanted – to touch him with her lips. Those things would be like betrayal to poor Emil. So instead she told him how boys across London – across the world – would thrill this coming Christmas; and when, at last, she was back in the Wendy House walls, she wrapped her arms around Sirius, lay back, and wept.

It was true, what Kaspar had said in those first days after they met: you could never keep a secret in the Emporium aisles. Even if it took a week, a month, a year, the truth would finally out.

In the middle of the night, she woke to the strangest pain of her life.

It was dark in the Wendy House. The paraffin lantern had burned out, and as Cathy groped to relight it the pain reached a new horizon. Somebody had their hands deep inside her, holding on tight. She tried to sit up, upsetting the patchwork dog that had been lounging so happily across her legs, and when she did she felt the most insatiable urging in her bladder. There was a glass of water on the bedside table and she opened her mouth to throw it back. It steadied her, but everything seemed so far away; the walls, the door, the edges of everything, it was all in a haze.

She was hovering on the edge of the bed, trying to calm the patchwork dog that ran in anxious circles around her, when the pain ebbed away. For the first time, she regained her breath, got to her feet and struck a light inside the lantern. The room seemed more solid now. She sat and teased the dog's ears, and was whispering to it that she was all right, of course she was all right, when the pain returned. This time it was all in the small of her back. She could feel it swelling, taunting her with promises of more pain to come; then, when she finally thought she could bear it, the sensation exploded. She tried to take a breath but only half a breath would come; she tried to take another, if only to make up for the first, but again she could not fill her lungs. In that way she continued until, finally, the pain grew dull once more. She rolled back on the bed and felt the darned-sock tongue of the dog against her hand. It was this that brought her back to attention. She picked herself up, moved in awkward steps to the Wendy House door.

She had one foot within, one foot without, when the pain returned. This time, she held on to the doorjamb until it passed. Was it only an illusion, or had the pain come back more quickly this time? It felt like the tides that filled those old estuary sands, devouring the land a few inches deeper with every wave. As soon as she was lucid again, she set off through the paper trees – but stopped before she had reached the edge of the forest. If this was what it felt like, if what had started tonight was going to end with a squalling baby in her arms, she should be back there, back in the only place in the world she could truly call home. She looked over her shoulder, at the diminutive Wendy House with its diminutive door – but she had not taken two steps toward it when the pain soared up inside her.

She found herself sitting with her back against a paper tree, breathing quickly, breathing deeply, somehow finding a pattern that helped her steer a way through. When she looked up, the dog was standing forlornly in the Wendy House door. She beckoned to it and it loped over, its unmoving eyes somehow radiating concern.

'Fetch him,' she whispered, clasping the dog's jaw.

The dog seemed happy to have a command. Springing to attention, it took off through the trees.

She did not know how long she lay there. The tightening returned, coiling her body, and though she tried to be ready for it, somehow it was always a step ahead of her, always leading her on. The way to get through it was to roll over, not to resist. She breathed when she could breathe – and when she could not, she simply held on.

She was lying there still when she heard the voice on the other side of the forest. 'Miss Wray!' it cried, and she came to her senses – because Kaspar was coming to her now, and at least she would not have to do it alone. Then a second voice cried out. 'Cathy!' it hollered. And she froze; because the second voice was coming from the opposite side of the shopfloor, and the second voice was Emil.

The patchwork dog gave one of its muted yaps and shambled out of the forest gloom. In moments it was on her, pushing its snout into her belly. When it drew back, Cathy saw that its paws were dark and wet; she was sitting in a pool of her own water. She was trailing her fingers through it, daring to feel what was happening underneath, when the voices cried out again. 'Miss Wray!' Kaspar exclaimed, and then, 'Emil ... what are *you* doing here?'

And, in a frightened voice: 'Kaspar, how in God ... how in God do you know?'

'The dog came for me.'

'It came for me too ...'

Cathy looked into its black button eyes. It panted happily, proud to have done a good job. 'You brought them *both*? Why did you bring them ...'

'Stand aside, Emil!'

'Kaspar, you're only making things worse ...'

And then they were here. Abreast of each other they pushed through the hanging boughs, each one dropping at either side of her.

'Kaspar,' Emil began, 'you'll need to fetch some towels. Hot water too. Some of Papa's whisky, to dull the pain ...'

Cathy was riding the contraction, so she did not see the way Kaspar looked across her, as if disbelieving the evidence of his own ears. Was this really Emil, little brother Emil, brushing the hair out of Miss Wray's eyes, telling her she would be all right?

Emil's eyes widened. For a moment, he had the air of their papa, furious at being disobeyed. 'Please, Kaspar. We'll need to make her comfortable. There are drugs she could take, if only she were somewhere else. Morphine and scopolamine. Twilight Sleep. But she'll have to ...' He stopped. 'Don't look at me like that, Kaspar. I read every book I could. I sent Mrs Hornung out to track down the journals. I—'

Perhaps Emil meant to go on, but he had seen the incredulous look on his brother's face and, as he looked to Cathy to reassure her, he could not catch her eye – for she was looking up at Kaspar, her eyes locked with his. Her body was angled that way as well, moving there by imperceptible degrees. She was reaching out for him, thought Emil, reaching out for his brother.

He seized her other hand. 'I know what to do,' he whispered. Then, again, until it stopped being a statement and turned into a question. 'I know what to do. I do know, Kaspar. I know what to ...'

'Emil, you'd better raid Papa's cupboard. Brandy, rather than whisky. One of his liqueurs. And the pillows, the pillows from the Wendy House. I stashed a full set under the bed. We have to make her comfortable.'

How daring it had felt to be issuing orders, and yet how familiar to have them being issued at him. Emil was rising to the tips of his toes to do as he was told when a thought occurred to him. It opened up a great pit and swallowed him whole. 'You're the one who hid her here, aren't you, Kaspar?'

Kaspar's eyes darted at him. 'Well, what did you think had happened, little brother?' Then he was stroking Cathy's face again, drawing a finger gently along the line of his jaw. On the ground, Cathy's lips moved in imitation of his name. She knew she was close, but Kaspar seemed so far away. 'I want you to listen to me, Miss Wray. Listen to me and know: it isn't going to be easy, but it will be all right. Do you understand? Do you believe me, Miss Wray?'

Cathy opened her mouth to say yes, yes she did believe him (and damn you, Kaspar Godman, but I told you to *stop calling me that!*), but it was too late. Other hands had hold of her now. Kaspar held on to her left, Emil held on to her right, but those other fingers held the rest of her body in their vice-like grasp. She took a breath before they started to close in. Moments later they were squeezing the life out of her and there was nothing Cathy Wray could do but lie back and hope.

THE TRUE HISTORY OF TOYS

PAPA JACK'S EMPORIUM, MAY–SEPTEMBER 1907

Consider Jekabs Godman: older than you think him, though you already think him as old as mountains. Tonight, if you were the kind of person to have taken a post at Papa Jack's Emporium just to get close to the old wayfarer, to soak up his secrets as a tree soaks up the secrets of earth and rain, you would have found him asleep in his chair, for even toymakers of the highest renown grow tired, and, with the passing years, Papa Jack grows more weary than ever.

Watch him now, as he wakes ...

Perhaps it is a dream that stirs him. Perhaps you think Papa Jack dreams of yet more fantastical creations to populate his shelves, but he does not. Papa Jack's dreams are the dreams of wild places. They are the dreams of a young man who was once a carpenter, who might have been a carpenter still, if only his life had gone according to plan. These are not dreams any child wandering into the Emporium at winter should be permitted to see. If you were a caring parent you would shield your sons and daughters from memories like these. Better they remain where they belong, locked away behind those glacial eyes, while Papa Jack's hands do their everyday work, threading life into patchwork creatures, spiriting up space out of nowhere, unlocking the world as it appears to a child.

The first thing he saw, as he reared up from those dreams (lest they swallow him whole, as they had on so many nights), was Mrs Hornung. She had arranged his feet in front of the fire, draped the blankets over his lap as she did every night. The teapot at his side (bark, pine needle, nettle – for Papa Jack remained the wild man Jekabs Godman at heart) was still hot, so perhaps he had not slept for long. Mrs Hornung clucked to see him wake, in the same admonishing tone she once used to scold his sons.

'Is something wrong, Jekabs?'

Papa Jack picked himself up. At first Mrs Hornung thought he might topple, but as always he trudged slowly forward. In the fringes of the room, the patchwork creatures lifted their heads to follow him with their sightless eyes. A threadbare robin, loosely weaved, flapped its stubby wings and flew, in its own ungainly way, to his shoulder, where its motor promptly cut out.

Sometimes, the Emporium itself spoke its secrets to him, whispering through mortar and brick.

Papa Jack wound the little bird back up. As life returned to its motor, so it bounced upon his palm. Cupping it there, he left the Godmans' quarters and went out on to the gallery skirting the Emporium dome. Far below, the shopfloor was in darkness. The Emporium in summer was at once a sad and glorious thing, filled with anticipation, filled with promise, filled with *yearning*. Papa Jack brought the bird to his lips, whispered a word and cast it out, into the air.

Follow …

The robin swoops down, as gracefully as a robin made of felt and duck down can. Plummeting and flying are two very different things; this robin conflates them in a dance of its own. Down through the dark, over the tops of empty aisles it comes; then, at last, to the copse of paper trees where the Wendy House lies hidden. Here it crashes through corrugated boughs. In the emptiness beneath, the Wendy House appears. Now the bird can control itself no longer; its motor is tiny, and it must save what energy it can for the return journey. It pretends to peck at the ground, looking for fallen grubs – and, as it does, it looks through the Wendy House door.

Imagine what it sees.

The return flight is an epic. If patchwork creatures had patchwork poets, one would have spun for this robin a myth of classical proportion. As it is, we must content ourselves with the image of the robin's wings beating furiously as it fought gravity to return to the Godmans' quarters. There it found Papa Jack's palm once more. And there, before its motor wound down for a second time, it chirruped its last. Patchwork creatures have no language of their own; remember, they are only toys. But still, Papa Jack understood. Behind his beard, his face blanched as white as the Siberian snows. In seconds, he was in his robe, dark brown like the pelt of a bear; seconds later, he was holding his canes as he tramped through the door.

Papa Jack could not remember the last time he walked the shopfloor. The ways down to it were legion, but it had been so long that not even his feet remembered the way. He found himself in storerooms where patchwork mammoth lay; in the engine room where his flying locomotive still sat, awaiting the moment it might be needed again. He walked past the locked chamber where the Emporium Secret Doors had been barricaded (they opened in one place, but nobody knew where they went to; they had been locked away ever since), and only by sheer chance did he find the old night train and follow its tracks to the paper trees.

How furious he had been to hear of them rearing up, rupturing the boards of his shopfloor, and yet how majestic they now were! He would have stopped to marvel at them, but from deep within the copse there came a cry: somebody in pain, or terror, or both. Papa Jack had known pain before. He had known terror as well. It propelled him on – for there had never been such sounds in his Emporium, not this place he had created as a bulwark against the bitterness, the darkness, that was adult life.

He came out of the trees to find the Wendy House sitting there, crowned in paper vines. On a rock inside its white picket fence slumped Emil. The boy had his head hanging low so that, at first, he did not see Papa Jack arrive. But Papa Jack was a man whose presence could not go unnoticed. Emil felt a shadow cross him, and looked up to see his father.

What words Emil wanted to say withered on his tongue. But his eyes told a story. They directed his father to the Wendy House window. He had to crouch to peer in, for his great bulk towered above the Wendy House roof, his shoulders half as broad as the Wendy House itself. Inside, the space distorted with the quality of a kaleidoscope. And there, at the kaleidoscope's centre, was his son. Kaspar was on his knees at the edge of a bed, and in that bed lay one of the shop girls, the one who had arrived on first frost. Her legs were parted and her back was arched and she was clinging to Kaspar as if he was the only thing tethering her to the world.

Papa Jack turned his tundra eyes on Emil.

'Papa, listen ...'

'*No.*'

'Papa, please.'

'He's taken it too far, these flirtations of his.'

'No! It isn't ... Papa, it isn't *his.*'

Papa Jack looked, incredulous, at Emil. 'Then ...'

'Not me,' Emil whispered, with unexpected regret. 'It isn't mine. Papa, she had nowhere to go and—'

Papa Jack could listen to nothing more. He hunched over, meaning to push through the diminutive door – and perhaps he would have done so as well, but at that moment there came a different kind of cry, the air rent apart by the squalling of a newborn child.

Papa Jack hovered on the threshold, with Emil at his side. The fury he had been feeling faded away. Through the Wendy House door, Kaspar was cradling a blood-grey bundle to Cathy's breast. He was brushing the ragged hair from Cathy's eyes, leaving fingerprint marks where he touched her skin. He was bending down to kiss her brow, finding towels to dry her, a blanket to swaddle the child.

Papa Jack stepped backwards, over the picket fence and into the paper trees. He remembered a night much like this one, in that little hovel he once called home. Back then the trees that surrounded him were true black alder and Latvian pine. There were chickens in the yard and the weatherwoman, too late to attend the birth, arrived moments afterwards to find Jekabs Godman with his newborn son in his hands. 'We shall call him Kaspar,' Jekabs had said, and counted it the happiest moment of his life. A memory like that could obliterate every bad feeling in the world.

In the trees he looked back at the crestfallen Emil. 'When she's ready, tell her to come to my workshop. I shall want to be introduced.' Then he disappeared into the shopfloor dark.

The heart that once beat inside her was now beating up against her breast.

Cathy looked into her daughter's eyes. *Daughter.* She had thought it all along, but here she was, ten minutes old and already rooting for milk. On the other side of the Wendy House, Kaspar was brewing tea. Hot buttered toast was already piled on a plate. The exhaustion she felt was not the exhaustion of nights without sleep; her body was spent, and yet every nerve tingled with satisfaction. She floated on it, holding her baby near.

What had seemed so abstract only hours ago – *I am going to be a mother* – was suddenly so real: *I am a mother, now and from this moment on.* She propped herself up, allowed Kaspar to fix the pillows around her. She did not think twice as she pulled down her blouse to feed her daughter for the first time; Kaspar waltzed around her, doing what he must. By instinct she reached out and held his hand, still stained where he had lifted the baby to meet her for the first time.

'Do you realise,' she said, 'that yours are the first hands she ever felt? You, Kaspar Godman, tied to her for ever ...'

Cathy looked up, thinking she might even have made Kaspar blush, and there, in the doorway, stood Emil. She had not thought of him, not until now. He was holding a roll of crisp bedsheets from one of Mrs Hornung's cupboards, but he was carrying them like a penance, something he might offer up. He waited to be invited in, and that was the most saddening thing. 'Come and meet her, Emil. Meet ... Martha.'

Emil shuffled inside, reached the foot of the bed, and lay the bedsheets down – but he didn't know where to look. His eyes kept darting into the corners, unable to settle on Cathy, on Martha, on Kaspar – on anything at all.

Finally, he broke the silence: 'I was worried about you, Cathy.'

'You had no need to be, little brother.' Kaspar strode to his side, put an arm around his shoulder. 'She was in good hands.'

Kaspar had never felt Emil so rigid. Emil turned his shoulder but, when Kaspar's arm followed, he wheeled around, casting Kaspar bodily to the ground. Perhaps it was the night's exertions still taking their toll, for Kaspar was too weak and could not find his balance. He lay prone, dusting himself down.

'Papa was here.'

'Why, Emil,' Kaspar said, picking himself up, 'you little—'

'It wasn't me, Kaspar. You'll think what you like, but I kept the secret—' For the first time, his eyes found Cathy. 'I kept *our* secret all these months. Why would I ruin it now?' Emil knew the way Kaspar was looking at him: down his nose, imperious; it was the same look he used to wear on opening night, when the customers flocked to his creations and left Emil's to gather dust. He flailed around until he was back at the door. 'He says he wants to see you, as soon as you've the strength. I'm going there now. Cathy, I'll do what I can. But he's angry. He's angry and he's sad ...'

After Emil was gone, Kaspar marched to the door and slammed it shut. The noise reverberated in the Wendy House eaves, disrupting the paper leaves that had gathered in the gutters.

'Don't think of it,' he said, marching back to her side.

'How can I not think of it, Kaspar?' The tension tearing through her body must have been absorbed by the baby, for she threw her head back from Cathy's breast and started to cry. For the first time, the thought hit her: *I can't do this. Can I do this? I can't do this.*

'You're not going anywhere, Cathy. My father isn't a monster. If you knew ...'

'Knew what?'

'Knew the kind of man he is. So we'll go to him and we'll tell him it all and ...' His words faded away, his eyes drawn back to the baby in her arms. That girl was like a vortex, constantly pulling him down. 'Can I ... hold her?'

The baby had stopped its bleating. It turned its puckered eyes, as sightless as Sirius, on Kaspar – as if she might even have recognised his voice. And perhaps that was it: all those nights he had spent in these Wendy House walls, announcing the creation of his toyboxes; some of that, surely, had echoed in the womb.

Kaspar took Martha and held her up, as if to show her the world. Watching him stilled Cathy. Kaspar was right. He had to be right. A man like Papa Jack, a man who had devoted his life to the Emporium, could not possibly cast a mother and child into the outside world.

Exhaustion was coming over her, her body crying out for rest. She lay down, was aware of Kaspar laying Martha down beside her, buttressing her with pillows so that she would not tumble from the bed. And oh, that first night with the baby in the world, not knowing what to do, not knowing how to hold her or lay her down, nor even if she was breathing as she should! Emil might have gone, but Kaspar, she knew, would always remain. 'Sleep, Cathy. I'll wake you if she stirs.'

Perhaps she would have resisted – but, for the first time, he had not called her 'Miss Wray'. That, she decided, had to mean something, and as she lay her aching body down (was any other kind of pain as sweet as this?), the thought of Papa Jack's fury evaporated and she did not fear for anything at all. Kaspar was there, with her baby's fist closed around his finger, when she went to sleep, and he was there when she woke up, hours later, to her daughter crying and her chest wet and sticky with milk.

At dawn she fortified herself with toast and preserves, eggs Kaspar had lifted from Mrs Hornung's larder, and allowed herself to be led through the paper trees. In her arms, the baby gazed up. To her, paper trees were real; were she, one day, to walk in woodland beyond the Emporium doors she might take those real trees for false. *Perspectives*, Cathy remembered. Kaspar had said that the magic had to do with *perspectives* – and perhaps, one day, even she might understand.

Her legs did not feel her own, but Kaspar was there to catch her as they crossed the shopfloor and made the ascent to the Godmans' quarters above. Sirius followed, announcing their arrival with one of his cotton wadding yaps.

It was Mrs Hornung who answered. She gave Kaspar the same disconsolate shake of the head she had given him every time he was caught out as a child and, in return, Kaspar put his arms around her and held her tight. Then, Cathy followed him through. In the chamber, naked without the paper trees of Christmas, Emil was sitting cross-legged on the carpet, lining up soldiers as if to make war against himself. Perhaps he was making another war against himself too, for he barely looked at Cathy as she crossed the battlefield. Ahead of her, the heavy oaken door etched with Emporium insignia that led to Papa Jack's study was hanging open, a portal of blackness with dancing firelight beyond.

Kaspar bowed to Cathy (why did he have to pretend to be so ostentatious, even after last night?) and, leaving her behind, marched through.

'Papa,' Cathy heard him begin, 'you've every right to be ...'

And after that, Cathy heard nothing: only the miniature explosions of Emil's cannonade, the invective he muttered at his soldiers as they made battle, and the whimper of the baby asleep against her shoulder.

Soon, Kaspar reappeared. Resting a hand on each of her shoulders, he whispered four words – 'He's only my papa' – and stepped back to reveal the way through. She saw the embers of an old hearthfire, alcoves steeped in books. On a perch, a patchwork owl with snow white plumage was constantly revolving its head.

With Martha nuzzling into her neck, she entered the room.

Papa Jack was sitting in a rocker, needle and thread in his brutish hands. There was little room to approach, so instead she stood on the tiny square of exposed carpet, and felt an unnatural chill as the door creaked shut of its own volition. Of all the rooms in the Emporium, this was the smallest. Its walls seemed to taper in like the walls of a cavern, or the inside of a great kiln. Books hung precariously from the uppermost shelves, every one of them the clothbound tomes in which Papa Jack had inscribed his best designs. The only light came from the hearth's dying embers, the firefly jars pushed in between the books. And Papa Jack's face was illuminated like that: snowfall lit up by fire.

After a moment, the old man lay down his needle and thread.

'It's Cathy, isn't it?'

'Yes, sir.'

Papa Jack took her in, as if he was seeing her for the very first time. Was it Cathy's imagination, or was he looking through her, at some imaginary horizon?

'Tell me, have you named her?'

Cathy's blood beat black. 'She's named Martha,' she replied, shocked at her own steel. 'Sir, I understand you'll be angry. I know people have come here, before, to steal from you. That's not me.'

'I don't like liars,' he whispered. 'But I understand why you'd lie. Tell me – is there going to be trouble, Cathy? Trouble in my Emporium?'

In reply, she said, 'She's not yet a whole day old.'

'With your family, Cathy.'

'My family's right here, sleeping in my arms.'

'You're a runaway. I see that now.' His voice, like stones in snowfall. 'Had I seen it before, Cathy, you could still have spent winter in our Emporium. You might still have had your baby down there, in my Wendy House. So let there be no misunderstanding. The Emporium is yours for as long as you want it. There are rules, rules of hospitality I learned long ago, and I don't mean to work against them now. This child was born here, born in space I chipped out of the world with these two hands. That means a thing, to a man as old as me. But ... when people run, people chase. So tell me, is that how it's going to be?'

Cathy was still reeling, trying to listen to her own thoughts. The Emporium – hers for as long as she wanted? Her child, born into space Papa Jack chipped out of the world ...

'They don't want us,' she finally said. 'My family were sending me away. To a home ... And if it had been that way, there would have been a matron and she'd have been wresting Martha out of my arms, right here, right now, and then she'd have been with somebody else, with a different name, with a different ...' She paused. She would not tremble, not now. Strange how seeing Martha in the flesh had made her a mother; she had been a mother all of this time. 'I'm sixteen now. Girls younger than me have made it on their own. That's what I'll do if you ...' She thought she had the courage to say it, but when the moment came it was too much an ultimatum, and her tongue would not let her go on.

'Cathy, may I?'

Papa Jack opened his hands. For a moment, Cathy tightened herself – but it was only an instinct; she knew she was safe, here in the Emporium. She knelt and gently placed Martha on his lap, where his hands closed around her. How huge they were; she might have rested in his palm.

'This Emporium of ours, it has always been a place for runaways. I spent so long running, Cathy Wray, until I founded this Emporium. Mrs Hornung and our very first shop hands, all of them lost, with no place to go. It takes a special sort of person to make the Emporium their home. Now there's you ...'

Martha awoke, to see the gnarled face of Papa Jack looking down.

'A child born into my Emporium ought to know how my Emporium was born, don't you think?'

Cathy brought Martha back to her shoulder.

'If you're to stay, if you're Emporium through and through, it's important that you know. It isn't a story I'm fond of telling. It's important you know that as well.'

Papa Jack clapped his hands and, from beneath the shelfing, a toy chest picked itself up, shuffling across to him on a hundred pinewood legs. At his feet it lowered itself to the ground and opened its lid. Inside were rags, worn leather gloves, a nest of silver fur as of some eastern wolf. Sitting atop the nest, there lay a wooden contraption painted in dark forest green and sparkling white. Papa Jack lifted this up. Set down on his lap, it looked a simple toy: a diorama of dark pine forest and endless snow, a crank handle and simple figurines of men in brown coats, iron-capped boots, felt and fur hats.

'I made this long ago, so that I would always remember. So that my boys out there would know. If you're ready, Cathy, you might help me now ...'

She paused, suddenly aware of the door closed at her back. 'I don't understand.'

'Trust me, Cathy. Please.'

Cathy knelt again at the old man's feet and, at his behest, took hold of the crank handle on the end of the toy. Papa Jack's hand closed over hers. She was surprised to find his skin as soft as the baby she was holding.

'Don't be afraid,' he said, 'though I was more afraid than I could possibly be.'

Then, with his hand still over hers, the handle started to turn.

It began like this:

The crank handle turned and, with it, Cathy's hand.

Deep in the contraption, the cam shafts rose and fell, propelling the figures to begin their march. The toy kept them in place, rotating the diorama of icy tundra and black pine forest against which they walked, but this march was endless.

Cathy felt the first wave of cold as the numbing of her fingers. She tried to draw back her hand but Papa Jack's lay over it, holding her fast. 'Don't be afraid,' he whispered, and something in his voice gave Cathy the courage to continue, even as the cold reached up her arm, even as crystals of frost coated every hair hanging from her head.

She looked about. A whiteness, swirling and indistinct, was rising up the walls around her, obscuring the books on the shelves, the mortar and brick. Soon the walls fell away. The whiteness was absolute. It plucked her out of the Emporium and cast her down here, in this otherworld of Papa Jack's creation. A single snowflake landed on the tip of her nose and, when she looked down, she saw that she was wrapped in fur, that Martha was swaddled up tight beneath a fur-lined hat.

A voice sailed past her. 'You there! Stay in line!' She heard the tramping of boots, too many boots to hold in her imagination.

She had seen this once before. In the space between the aisles, Emil had spread out his picnic hamper, and the shelves had faded away to reveal a wildflower meadow, picnickers all around. Only hadn't that been the perfection of his toy, bringing to mind the thought of a summer's day so vividly that she created it for herself? Hadn't that been *imagination*? Whatever this was, it had to be something more – for these were not her memories, not her imaginings. These were coming from the toy and the man who hunched over it, still turning the handle with a perfect motion. Somehow she was inside his head, his imagination become manifest.

She was startled out of these thoughts by silhouettes on her shoulder. A column of figures opened up and marched around her, disappearing into the vortex of snow up ahead: men, countless men, in ragged felt coats and muskrat hats, some with packs slung over their shoulders, some dragging sleds in which other men were piled up.

'Where am I?' Cathy gasped. For the first time, trees appeared as stark silhouettes in the whiteness ahead. She felt herself being drawn to them, as if she too was marching in procession with the column. 'Who are they?'

'You see the man ahead, the man who stands apart from the rest?'

She did. He was walking with his head bowed low but, as she looked, he turned to her and held her gaze. Those eyes, they were glacial blue.

'Papa Jack, is that ... you?'

'Back then his name was Jekabs Godman. But yes, this is me. If you're to stay in our Emporium, you must go with him now.'

The figure had lifted a gloved hand. He was beckoning to her, but Cathy held fast. While she was here, one hand still on the crank handle, still feeling the touch of Papa Jack, it was possible to feel safe. Untethered, perhaps she would disappear, be swallowed whole by this toy and whatever magics it was performing.

'You'll have to hurry,' Papa Jack breathed. 'If he lingers too long, the gang masters will come for him. They are a brutal kind of man. They were once like Jekabs, prisoners every one, but they came back as guards. Please, Cathy. Jekabs is a ... decent man. He'll tell you it all.'

She tried to resist, but the wind flurried behind her, propelling her on. Her fingers slipped from beneath Papa Jack's, his eyes turned away from her, and soon she was whirling forward, borne by the snowfall itself.

Jekabs Godman was taller than the hunched mountain of a man he would become. He was, if it was possible to admit it, as handsome as his son Kaspar, with hair of jet black (now beaded in frost) and defiant features that over time would shift into peaks and ravines. He welcomed her with a smile. 'Walk with me,' he began, 'and beware of the rest. Don't speak to another soul.'

His voice was not the feathery voice it would one day become, but he still spoke far too gently for the ravaged landscape around. 'Where are we going?' Cathy asked.

'We are going into the east,' Jekabs Godman said, 'and leaving everything we knew. It will be six long years for me. They call this ... *katorga*. It is the most harrowing thing that can be visited on a man. Some of us will die on the way. Some of us will die there. But me? Well, you already know: I will survive. What you don't know is how. But come. We have walked but twenty-six of our miles. There are still six thousand to go.'

And then, as the column marched around them, Jekabs Godman told her his story.

Ten days ago, Jekabs Godman was a husband, a father, a carpenter of modest income but high renown. Now, he was nothing. Ten years ago, he was an apprentice, dreaming of the things he might one day make with his hands. Now, Jekabs Godman touched the burning indentations in his shoulder, the symbol that demarked his crime, still smelling of seared hair and flesh. The press of bodies against him forced him to look up. In front of them lay the east, frigid and featureless as the end of the world.

Ten days: all it took to destroy a world. Jekabs Godman was arrested on the first day. On the second he protested his innocence. On the fourth he confessed. On the fifth day he discovered the crimes of which he was accused, and on the sixth was found guilty. On the seventh day he was branded with hot iron and ink and, by the eighth, he had accepted his fate. Jekabs Godman: imperial saboteur and operator of an outlawed printing press. He had been using it, in the cellar of a well-acquainted friend for whom he had built cabinets, to run up leaflets for a stall he proposed to erect at Christmas, where he might sell some of the odds and ends he made to while away the hours between jobs: little wooden angels, delicate pine bears. On the front of the leaflets were Russian horses of the kind he dreamed he might one day build – and above hung the words: *'Are*

you a child at heart? Then ... Welcome to Papa Jekabs'
Emporium ...'

'Oh yes,' said Jekabs, and he put an arm around Cathy as
if to protect her from the imaginary winter wailing around,
'toys had always been my dream. I had a son, you see, and
another on the way. To play with my children with toys that
I made, that was almost the only dream I had. And until
that knock came at my door, in the dead of the night, that
was how life would have been. But they came for us all in
those days. If you weren't a killer or a criminal, you were a
sympathiser. As for me, and as for sympathy, well, I'd never
thought the world could have enough ...'

Night crystallised. On the plain the blackness was never
absolute, for the stars whose light was smeared across the
heavens were reflected in grain fields and hedgerows dusted
in snow. A fox, silver as the moon, darted across Jekabs' path
and in its eyes was the promise of something Jekabs would
never feel again: freedom.

They had walked through the vagaries of twilight,
prison outriders hemming them in just as assuredly as the
dark. Men on horseback thundered up and down the line,
keeping tallies in their heads but never breathing a word.
When the outriders sounded their horns to announce the
day's march had reached its end, they made camp in the
pastures of some farm whose service was rewarded by
the gratitude of the Tsar (eternal and enriching, but never
made manifest). The farmhouse sat at a fork between two
of the ancient cart roads that criss-crossed this corner of
the world, and in its reach were cattle barns and the ruins
of the farm that had sat here in centuries past. Here the
prisoners were corralled. Some were sent out to gather

firewood and forage. Others were set to butchering the pig dutifully trolled out by the farmer. Jekabs' duty was to wait and endure.

In the light of the farmhouse doorway there hung a little girl, watching her father deposit grain for the horses who drew the prison wagons. Kneeling, Jekabs picked up a length of twig. He sat on a stump and, first with his thumb and then with an edge of stone, scored lines and dug grooves. Another twig, a length of briar, a ringlet of leaves and pinecone for a head – and then, when he set it down, a stick soldier stood to attention. The way the wind caught it and whisked it along gave the figure the appearance of marching.

He was still gazing at the stick figure when a boot came down and ground it into the earth. Jekabs looked up to see a limping prisoner standing imperiously above.

'You don't sit with us, friend. Why do you never sit with us?'

Jekabs said not a word.

'What makes you think you're better than me, carpenter? Your kind have always thought yourselves better than everyone else ...'

Jekabs Godman had heard it said before, even though the place he had been born and raised was in the heart of the Russian Pale. The blood of Abraham, the blood of Isaac, was in his father's family and this did not, in itself, make him of the faith – but that had never stopped men like this forcing themselves into his face, telling him there was but one god, that his was false, that the ills of the world rested squarely on his shoulders.

If he focused hard, perhaps the man would go away. Jekabs reached down to pluck more woodland detritus from the pile. His hands moved of their own volition, lining up three more soldiers to stumble haphazardly with the wind.

The convict leant down and snatched them up. His face was pockmarked with the craters of old cankers, pointed and precise. 'You can be my friend, *toymaker*,' he said – only, now, one hand was cupped around his balls, the stubby protrusions tight against his trousers.

'Please,' said Jekabs Godman, and refused to wince when the torrent of phlegm caught him on the side of his jaw.

Downwind from the barn a cauldron of fire was burning. A cry went up – 'Chichikov!' – and the prisoner, torn between Jekabs and the fire, at last chose the flames.

'It was like that every night,' Jekabs continued, beckoning Cathy to sit with him. 'They'd come and they'd goad and, if ever one of us goaded back, that was it, we'd feel their fists, their boots – or worse. And I came to know: that was what was waiting for me in the east. More men like Chichikov. More nights like this. Two thousand of them between me and any chance of home. Those nights seemed enormous, yet tiny as a life. But later, when I dared look, that man, that Chichikov, he was sitting with others of his kind, and in the horseshoe of earth between them my three pinecone figurines gambolled backwards and forwards, colliding and spinning around each other while the bastards brayed. Tonight, those rapists and killers seemed like children, the same children I would have welcomed to my stall. I didn't know it then, but I had learned – no, *discovered* – something that night, something it would take me long months to understand.'

That night, somebody tried to run. He made it three miles but wasn't brought back. 'And let that be a lesson to you all,' said one of the outriders as he returned from the hunt, haloed in the orange and reds of the border fires. The lesson was: no more second chances. Look around you – this wild, white expanse, this tundra and taiga to which we're bound, *this* is your second chance.

'Three months can pass in the moment between one breath and the next. We continued east, beneath the glowering eyes of Cossack fortresses, lined up against the old Khanates of the south. Two days of marching, one day of forced rest: that was the pattern of my life, every step one step further from home. But at least I had something to cling to now – not memories, not hope, because what use were they? No, I had my pieces of pinecone, the long nights I spent whittling my soldiers and setting them to march in the snow. Every night they were taken from me. And every night, there they were, the killers, playing again. Some nights they were so engrossed they didn't steal anyone's ration, didn't force themselves on any of the weaker men when the outriders couldn't see. And I would remember it for ever: Chichikov, the lowest of all men, sleeping soundly, untroubled by dreams, one of my pine-bark ballerinas curled up snugly in his fist.'

Slowly, the old world faded. Memories of real life imploded, replaced only by the march. Jekabs watched the steppes, mountains and deep forests glide by, unable to absorb the vastness of the world. Every river forded was another river away from home, every barren plain another expanse in which his son, his wife, had ceased to exist. He could bear it all, all except those nights in the transit prisons when, shaven and deloused, he sweltered in the cells and had no curls of bark with which to make his soldiers. On those nights he sank into himself. He tried to hold his wife Sofiya, his son Kaspar in his mind, but all too easily their visages slipped away, replaced by Chichikov, Grigoryan, Grisha, all of the others who harried him and pressed up against him in the night.

Somewhere along the way, his wife gave birth. He marked the occasion by making a doll out of larch wood and leaving it on the trail for some peasant farmer to find. Perhaps they would make a gift of it to one of their children. Jekabs was a father for the second time, but whether he had another baby boy or been blessed by his first girl he might never know.

'It was December by the time we reached the timber camp we were to work, high above the Amur river. We came out of the forest and there it sat, our new home sitting on an escarpment shorn of all trees ...'

As Jekabs spoke, the winter exploded. The whiteness remained on the edges of Cathy's vision – but here, here in the centre, was the valley of blackened stumps of which Jekabs spoke, and in its basin a small township of timber shacks. Ahead of Cathy, the convoy began to wend down the hill.

'There'd been something reassuring about the march. I hadn't realised it until then, but that march had become life. But there, at the bottom of the escarpment, well that was the future, cold and unknown ...'

That night, on a stump by the barrack walls, one of the camp superiors put shackles around Jekabs' ankles and bound them with chain to the ones around his wrists. For the next six years they would stay that way, the chains relaxed only so that Jekabs could swing an axe or pull a hacksaw. Once the work was done, he was returned to the barrack house, where men made catcalls from the corners and crowed openly about which of the newcomers would be dead by morning, which in another man's bed, which would flee first.

'They came for me on the seventh night. Ursa Major and Ursa Minor, we called them, the *aides-de-camp*. They'd been prisoners too, but they were here for life – and lifers, well, they had privileges over the rest of us men. I wish I could tell you that they never beat me. I wish I could tell you that they didn't sell the timber I'd brought in to the other gangs and have me flogged for shirking. I wish I could tell you that the night I woke to find Ursa Major in bed beside me didn't happen, but this was the end of the earth and I am not here to lie. They came for us all. Any man they found wanting. Any man too soft for this world.'

The days were short this far north, but the work was long. The sun, when it came at all, barely roused the forest. Jekabs joined a work gang, where an old hand named Manilov showed him the rudiments of the hacksaw and axe. The first week was gruelling, the second an ordeal. By the third, Jekabs could feel his muscles hardening. Yet a vast hollow was opening inside him, and no amount of hard bread or thin soup could fill it. At least on the trail there had been forage. Here, his body was a chasm, and he himself was falling into it. On the cusp of the fourth week, he stopped on the sled trail, because the big black arc of the woodland was revolving. He could not tell the difference between the plain and the sky. It was only the threat of Ursa Minor's birch rod lash that drove him on. In the days that followed, as his body accustomed itself to dizziness and retching, he dreamt up good reasons to freeze to death.

Across the timber, he scratched out good reasons to stay alive. How craven he felt, for his children were not among them. Somewhere on the march he had passed through a veil; now he was working in some other world, where his children did not exist, except as figments of his imagination. Nothing as perfect as Kaspar, his firstborn, his son, could exist in a world which permitted this system of *katorga* to exist. Out here there was but one reason to stay alive: to spite that piece of you – that powerful piece whose influence grew day on day – which wanted nothing more than to lie down in the snow and wait for the end.

'Cathy, can you be brave?'

The world morphed around Cathy again, and the only thing that stopped her from panicking was looking back to see Papa Jack still there, turning the crank handle of the toy that had spirited all of this into being.

When the world reappeared, she was out in the woods, and around her the men in shackles were working in teams to drag timber into the thawed river and send them sailing downstream.

'I have to go now,' said Jekabs, his hand slipping out of hers.

'Go?'

'I'm sorry,' he said. 'But remember, all of this happened in the very long a—'

Jekabs did not finish the sentence, for at that moment two figures appeared from behind and, wresting him off his feet, dragged him into the trees. Cathy shrieked his name, hurried after. The world turned to mist around her, and then she was in the trees, Jekabs pinned on the earth with Ursa Major and Ursa Minor above him. She shrieked again, but her voice could not be heard, not in this world that was nothing but memory given form. 'We know what you are,' Ursa Major was bawling. 'We know what you do. Trading for supplies with those little stick soldiers of yours. Well, who made them *currency*? We're the only currency there is . . .'

They had torn Jekabs' coat off, made gashes in his shirt, when another cry came out of the trees – and there appeared Chichikov, his comrades Grigoryan and Grisha at his side. 'Hands off the toymaker,' Chichikov leered – and, when the Ursas only laughed, there was no second warning. Chichikov came forward, an axe in his hand, and the only thing that stopped blood being shed in the forest that day was the patrol who chanced across them, sending even the Ursas Major and Minor scattering into the trees.

That night, Jekabs Godman found himself lashed to a stump on the forest's edge, forced to face the night and all its howling demons. But he was not alone. For, his back still raw from the birch rod lash, there was Chichikov, staked to a stump beside him, and there was Grisha and there Grigoryan, all of them together.

The night was vast. Sleep came, but the cold always woke them.

'Why?' Jekabs breathed, when he could stand the silence no more. 'Why do that . . . for me?'

Beside him, Chichikov reached into his pocket and produced one of Jekabs' soldiers, plundered from him many nights before. 'Have you any idea?' he replied, his voice raw through the blisters. 'When I line up your soldiers, toymaker, I'm a boy again. I'm with my papa and he's lining up soldiers too. I'm in front of that fire, in Petersburg where we used to live, or I'm in the Gardens of Mars fighting with sticks. I'm ... not here, and ...'

Cathy imagined him about to say 'I'm not me', but the sentiment was too much for a man like Chichikov. He hawked up phlegm, spat it into the snow.

'No, toymaker, they won't touch you, not again, not while we still live ...'

'And that is how,' said Jekabs. 'How I survived, and how I knew what toys truly are. I'd found a kind of ... a magic, if you will. A way of reaching the soul of a man. Because even men like Chichikov, they would spend their nights parading my toy soldiers up and down. You won't believe it now, but a year into our *katorga*, Ursa Minor himself pulled a toy soldier from the floorboards in our shack and, that night, I saw him marching it up and down his palm as he stood guard. And I came to know – there's a shared heritage in toys. Take any man and show him a hobby horse, and a little piece of him will be a boy again, desperate to put it between his legs and take a ride. If you're going to make a toy, you have to hold one truth as inviolable above all others: that, once upon a time, all of us, no matter what we've grown up to do or who we've grown up to be, were little boys and girls, happy with nothing more than bouncing a ball against a wall. That's what I'd discovered in the East. I took something good from my *katorga* and it transformed my life.'

Jekabs reached out a hand and clasped Cathy.

'You must go now.'

'But ...'

'Back to the Emporium.' He looked sadly at his blistered, frost-bitten hands. 'I survive this, Cathy. I'll be seeing you soon.'

Behind Cathy, Papa Jack's hand froze on the crank handle and, as the toy stopped moving, so did the walls of the study reassert themselves. The wilderness of white faded, Papa Jack's ledgers returned to their shelves, and the cold that had worked in her body slowly ebbed away. The fur she had been wearing sloughed off her shoulders and vanished before it hit the ground. She heard the faint cries of Jekabs' fellow prisoners growing fainter yet – and then it was gone.

She turned around. Papa Jack sat slumped in his chair, his hand still on the crank handle though it moved no more. He looked spent, his face as white as the hair that fell around it. Cathy went to him and, kneeling down, took his hand. 'Jekabs,' she ventured. 'Papa Jack?'

He looked up.

'Didn't I tell you?' he whispered, smiling sadly. 'It's not a story I'm fond of telling. You see, now, why I wanted you to know? This is not only my Emporium. This is my life. I could no more throw out a mother and child than I could denounce a man like Ursa Minor. We all started in the same place, no matter where we end. That's how I've lived my life. That's how I'll die.'

'I'm sorry, Jekabs.'

'You mustn't be. The most terrible things can happen to a man, but he'll never lose himself if he remembers he was once a child.' Gently, he placed the toy back in its nest and the chest scuttled into its hiding beneath the shelving. 'You must be tired, Cathy. Go. Get some rest. I'll have Mrs Hornung bring you supplies. You might live in your Wendy House until the first frost of winter. By then, we'll find you a place. A place you might stay ...'

She was still too disoriented to do anything but whisper her thanks. In that way, she teetered back toward the door, certain that the books were opening and closing their pages to usher her on the way.

As she reached the door, a thought struck her. 'Your advert,' she said. 'The one that brought me here. It cried out to me. *Are you lost? Are you afraid?* I'm right, aren't I? It knew I needed help. That's why you sent it out, into the world – to find people like me. Mrs Hornung said that's what brought her here too. And when I looked at that advert – it was hovering, brighter than all the rest around it, and with that circle scribbled round it in ink. The advert that brought me here, it was one of your toys, wasn't it? One of your ... magics.'

Papa Jack had lifted his needle and thread, returned to the cross-stitched cadaver at his side, but his eyes came back to her now.

'The vacancy you came for, it was circled?'

Cathy nodded, uncertain what to feel. 'Your Emporium, a place to hide from the world out there, the world where bad things happen. A home for people who need it, people like you, people like me ... It found me, didn't it?'

He lay down his needle and thread. 'Cathy Wray, our advertisements are just advertisements. We need more shop hands every winter, even with those who come back year on year. There's nothing more to them than paper and ink.'

It couldn't be. She had felt so certain. 'But then ...'

'Whose newspaper was it, Cathy?'

'It belonged to my father.'

'And tell me, is your father the kind of man who reads that paper every night, looking at the situations vacant ... just in case?'

'He is.'

'And is he the kind of man who might know the right thing, even if he hasn't the words to say it?'

She thought, suddenly, of Jekabs Godman, of rapists and murderers, slavers and saboteurs: all of them, playing at toys; all of them, children in the once-upon-a-time.

'He is,' she whispered.

'Then, Cathy, that advert you saw, that ink sketched around it, perhaps that was the oldest kind of magic there is. The ordinary magic: a father who loves his daughter, telling her in the only way he knows how ...'

'Love?' Cathy said. 'Papa Jack, they tried to give *her* away.' She stressed the word, for that was what Martha was now: not the idea of a child, not some imagining of the future, but a person, flesh and blood with a heart separate from her own.

'Cathy, I brought you here to listen. But you have to hear it too.'

Papa Jack reached into his gown and opened his fist to reveal a pinecone figurine, one of the very same ones that Kaspar had shown her in the cabinet above. This was no soldier, but a girl's ballerina, crafted out of dead grass and bark. And yet – how lifelike its features were. How daintily it twirled *en pointe* on the tip of his finger.

'Whenever you feel that way about your mother, about your father, I want you to take this and remember: there was your own first frost, once. They'd have taken you to the step and showed it you, sparkling in the night. And there was a first set of clothes, a first birthday, a first present wrapped in ribbon that you couldn't quite unwrap yourself. Let it take you back there. You don't have to do anything, you never have to speak to them again if that's what you choose – just so long as you remember.'

Cathy took the ballerina, let it twirl around her palm and thought she knew what Papa Jack meant – for on the edges of her vision, she could see her old bedroom again, all of it reconstituted and only just out of reach. This was what had saved him, she remembered – this was the very same magic that had worked itself on Chichikov, Ursa Major, Ursa Minor, all of the rest. She looked at him now and tried to picture how his life had been, in those places at the ends of the earth, bartering for his life with enchanted creations of dead grass and bark. What was it Kaspar had said? *A toy cannot save a life, but it can save a soul.* How many souls had Jekabs Godman saved, shackled in those frozen prison camps? Could it be real that the man sitting in front of her, the man she trusted entirely to cradle Martha in his hands, had spent so many years out there, among murderers and rapists and thieves, and turned them all into friends with the toys in his hands? She had seen so many magical things in the Emporium, but surely this was a magic too far. And yet, every time she fingered the pinecone ballerina, she felt the same as those prisoners had done. Tiny flashes of halcyon days forked across her eyes: walking along the tow paths with her mother and father ('hold Mummy's hand!' she had shrieked, delighted, 'hold Daddy's hand!'), or watching from the kitchen table as her father stole another slice of cake and rewarded her with a corner for not giving him away. Birthdays and Christmases; a ride on a steam train;

the smell of her father covered in talc or her mother's cheap perfume. These little things, and more, exploded in those pockets of recollection hidden behind the eyes; and all her bitterness faded away.

She tried to picture how it might have been: her father, pacing the day away as she and her mother travelled up to Dovercourt and back, prowling along the estuary sands with one hand clasping the other; the way his head had been buried as she came home that evening – might that have been fear, not fury? In her mind's eye she saw his fingers trembling to clasp his inkpen. *London*, he might have thought. *Yes, you could disappear in a place like that. People go missing in London all of the time.*

Ordinary magic. All of the Emporium's wonders around her, all of the things Papa Jack's creations could do, but how much more powerful was this?

'Papa Jack,' she said, 'thank you.'

Outside, Kaspar was waiting.

'Kaspar,' she said, 'there's something I have to do. Will you help me?'

'Anything, Cathy. I'm your servant.'

Emil was still staring as they disappeared out to the gallery together, Sirius following obediently behind. Then, alone, he returned to his soldiers, began to lay each of them down in its red velvet case. Last of all came his Imperial Kapitan, the original and most precious of the thousands he had made. Emil held him close, a much smaller boy trapped in a young man's body, until finally he felt foolish and tidied him away.

In the end, it was weeks before she was strong enough to venture out.

Kaspar stayed with her in the nights that came, his toyboxes sitting half-finished on his workshop floor. When Martha woke in the night, so did Kaspar; when Cathy needed somebody there, to bring her tea or toast – or only to tell her that it was good to be tired, that being tired meant she was doing everything that she must – there was Kaspar, beating back his own exhaustion to sit at the foot of her bed. Those nights were long and empty and, when she was not nursing Martha or rocking her basket to try and get her to sleep, she asked Kaspar about his father and those things she had seen. And, 'Papa's life is very different to our own,' he said. 'Sometimes I wonder if that's the reason, if that's why those things he can do seem so natural to him, but so strained to me and Emil. Mightn't it be, Cathy, that, until you've seen the dark, you don't really know the light?'

'I hope you never see that dark, Kaspar, not for all the magic in the world.'

They made plans to leave at the start of Martha's twelfth week. By then, the thought of returning to the world beyond the shopfloor was not tantalising, but disconcerting. 'I feel as if she's never really left the womb,' Cathy said as, with Kaspar and Sirius, she crossed the shopfloor and carried Martha out on to Iron Duke Mews.

Summer was giving way to autumn, the sun growing too weak to properly dispel the London chill. At the bottom of Iron Duke Mews, the motorcar Kaspar had hired was a boxy thing, gleaming black and with wheels half as high as Cathy herself. Sirius was first aboard, sniffing at the leather seats with his cross-stich nose. Only when he was satisfied did he scurry back to allow Cathy aboard. She lifted Martha in carefully, settled her basket on the seat and steeled herself.

To run away by train and return in her personal carriage; what they would think of her when she appeared!

Kaspar fancied himself a driver of estimable talent, but driving the carts he and Emil had created up and down the empty Emporium aisles each summer had taught him only recklessness and haste. Cathy had to bark at him more than once, or grapple out with her arm to wrest him from the wheel, as he joined the flow of traffic heading east, along the river and out of the city.

Beyond London the roads lay empty and still. It was a revelation to see greenery again, that trees might sprout leaves in summer that were not curls of paper and corrugated card. Yet nothing was more revelatory than the smell that hit her as they came close to the sea. That smell, only salt, seaweed, perhaps even the barest hint of sewage, was intoxicating. She lifted Martha to breathe it in. Smells, she decided, were like the pine-bark ballerina hidden safely in her pocket. They could make you feel five, six, seven years old again.

Leigh had not changed in the months she had been away. The streets were the same, the shopfronts, the boats basking across the mudflats like beached wrecks. She directed Kaspar quietly, until at last they arrived at the street she had once lived. She had been gone mere months, had travelled only thirty miles, and yet a whole world existed between then and now.

'Are you certain of this, Cathy?'

She lifted Martha, wrapped her up in a shawl. She had not cried once, in spite of Kaspar's driving, but as Cathy stepped from the car she strained against her shoulder, putting up a protest.

Before Cathy could approach the first house, Kaspar called out: 'Miss Wray, wait ...'

Before he went after her, he reached into the back of the carriage and produced a lady's leather purse, with ornamental clasps depicting butterflies in flight. In the middle of the road, beneath the brilliant reds of twilight, he presented it to Cathy.

'It's for you. I've seen mothers staggering up and down our Emporium aisles with such bulging bags, but not you, not with this ...'

It was difficult to tear herself away from his eyes, but when she unclasped the purse and looked inside all she saw was blackness, rich and deep. She reached in but her fingers could not find the bottom.

There were all sorts of things that she wanted to say. She wanted to tell him thank you – for this purse, for bringing her so far away from his Emporium, for the way he had knelt at her side and told her she was strong, that she could do it all, as Martha came into the world – but, instead, she turned to face the old house and said, 'You've never asked me who my baby's father is.'

The statement seemed to catch Kaspar off guard. 'It isn't that I haven't wanted to ask. But ... you came to our Emporium with your secrets. They're yours alone.'

'No,' she whispered. The façade of the house seemed to glare down at her. 'Not any more.' She found the courage to face him again. 'Kaspar, I owe you the truth. I've been a coward. But the truth is, I haven't thought of Martha's father in so long, it already seems another life. He was a friend to me, for a little while. Nothing more.'

Kaspar's eyes twitched. 'A *little* more, Miss Wray.'

'I thought you'd stopped calling me that.'

'Where is he now?'

Cathy barely knew. 'Gone, off to some other family, some other future. He didn't come looking, Kaspar. But I've already told you – it wasn't as if it was ... love.'

'Not love,' said Kaspar, 'but there are ... responsibilities.'

Cathy turned the word over. In the end, she supposed, Daniel's responsibilities to his father had outweighed any responsibilities he had to a child who was barely an *idea*. But then there was Kaspar: a boy to whom ideas were everything.

She turned and walked some distance, crossing the street to reach her house in three loping strides. When she looked back, Kaspar was still staring after her.

'Kaspar, about that day we were in London, when you took me to the park. I ... wanted to. I want you to know that. And I might have, if only ...' How to say it without – not hurting his feelings, because sometimes Kaspar Godman behaved as if he had no feelings to be hurt. Perhaps it was only – without seeming foolish. In her heart, she had wanted to. But it was her body; her body had wanted different things. Things like rest, like food and water; like being able to sleep on a night without waking every second hour. People talked about the heart and the head being at war – but, when you were pregnant, the body was separate, and the body ruled all.

She lifted Martha to her shoulder, tightening the shawl around her. I'm not pregnant now, she thought – so what is it, what's stopping me? Propriety? Could that really have been it? Because she had never once cared about being proper. She had spent the year, hadn't she, in Papa Jack's Emporium, instead of *there*, as her parents had planned ...

She strode back toward him. It was captivating how silent he was. He did not flinch, even as she lifted a hand to stroke the hair out of his eyes, even as she rose on to her tiptoes (the baby sandwiched between them) and planted a kiss on the thin stubble that lined his cheek.

'I knew you'd understand, Kaspar. If anyone could, it would be you.'

Then, cooing at Martha, she walked into her house.

It was cold out on the estuary. Kaspar took the motorcar down to the sand and watched the tide glittering as the stars revealed themselves, one by one. For a time, he walked along the shale, listening to the waves. A pair of old lovers sat out on the rocks, holding each other as they gazed into the gas lamps on the other side of the water. Kaspar sat higher yet, the darkness solidifying all around. Without knowing he was doing it, he twisted a length of sun-baked seaweed into the skeleton of a sailing boat and, giving that sailing boat wings, let it fly out into the blackness over the water. Those two old lovers, perhaps they had come here every night since they were children. Perhaps they would come here every night until, finally, one of them did not. And, as he watched, he got to thinking: what if they had been born two streets distant? What if they had not been sent to the same schools, or if their parents had not met in the same beer hall, or walked the same routes through the same parks? What if ... she had not run away to his father's Emporium, and he had not found her there? What if those boys had not crashed into his paper trees and she had not taken shelter, with him, in the Wendy House at the bottom of the aisle? What, then, of life?

An image, perfectly simple, seared on to the back of Kaspar Godman's eyes: he and Cathy, as old as these two wrapped up together on the estuary's edge, wandering the aisles of their Emporium, a threadbare Sirius still lolloping behind.

What if she had never fallen pregnant by some other man and been driven into his world? The baby he had helped birth might never be his, but he could love her all the same – for that, and everything else.

Kaspar took the motorcar back to the streets and stood outside Cathy's house. The silhouette show against the curtains was like one of his father's puppet theatres. He watched Cathy twirl. Figures stood and then sat down. He thought he heard laughter, and that was a beautiful thing – until he remembered that only happiness might make her stay, here where she surely did not belong. After that, fear was like a seed sprouting shoots in his belly. He went to the door, but checked himself; went to the door again and started at the voices within. A man his age hurried down the street, and the thought of him knocking at the door – for was this Cathy's estuary boy, come back to be a father? – made all the jealousy he had not known that he had flower.

The door opened and, framed by the light, there stood Cathy.

Behind her hung figures Kaspar thought he would never see: her mother, her father, a sister taller than Cathy with striking blond hair. It was the sister who was holding Martha. Kaspar froze, allowing himself to breathe again only when Cathy took her daughter back into her arms. One by one, she embraced the family around her. They had not come to claim her back, he saw; they had come to see her off. Her mother was stiff as Cathy held her, but her father gave in. His fingers teased the fluff of Martha's hair.

Cathy joined him at the motorcar and, in silence, allowed Kaspar to help her inside.

Some way along the estuary, with the lights of Leigh fading behind, he dared break the silence.

'Are we going to be all right, Cathy?'

When he said *we* he might have meant Cathy and Martha, or he might have meant all three of them. She nodded but said not a word, for there were tears in her eyes and she did not know what they were for: what she had lost, or what she had gained.

'You look like your daughter when you cry.'

'Kaspar!' she snorted, and dried her eyes on the hem of her skirt.

'Well, it's true.'

'My father said that too. He said seeing her was like seeing me.'

'You might have stayed.'

Cathy nodded, trying to make sense of it all. 'After all of this, they would even have had me. A few lies here, a compromise there, we might have made it work ...'

Into the silence that followed, Kaspar said, 'There was a piece of me, a tiny corner, that thought you would. That your life might be here ... where it started. And, while you were in there, that thought, it just kept on growing. I couldn't stop it. I think that must be what ... *doubt* feels like. Cathy, I hadn't thought it until now, but the thought of you not there, in the Emporium, it ...'

'Hush, Kaspar,' she said. 'Take me *home*.'

The car drove on, back through the late summer night.

The Emporium was silent when they returned. Emil and Mrs Hornung had been busy replenishing some of the aisles, anticipating the first frost yet to come. Emil's soldiers looked resplendent on the shelves.

In the Wendy House, Kaspar slid Martha into her crib, the only sound the suckling of her own thumb. Together, they watched her squirm against her blankets, undisturbed by the world.

'Will you go back?' Kaspar asked. He had crossed the room to hover in the Wendy House door, as if uncertain whether he should be in or out. It was such a nonsense to see him uncertain; it did not suit Kaspar Godman well, and the idea infuriated her.

'Or they'll come here. My sister Lizzy, she may even apply for one of your situations vacant ...'

'She would be in good company. But ...'

Cathy rolled her eyes. She marched to meet him. 'Kaspar, you fool. You keep asking yourself why I didn't leave. What you might be asking is why I stayed. Who I stayed for.'

Kaspar was still. Then he raised his hands to hold her.

'You're saying ...'

'I'm saying I'm an Emporium girl, through and through.'

Then he was kissing her, and his hands were in her hair, and hers were in his – while, in the paper branches, a pipe-cleaner owl fluttered its wings and the thin rustle of confetti snow began to fall down.

MANY YEARS
LATER . . .

THE HOME FIRES BURNING

PAPA JACK'S EMPORIUM, AUGUST–NOVEMBER 1914

The sun had never touched the aisles of Papa Jack's Emporium, but this summer it was bleaching the London streets. The yard at Sir Josiah's was white as chalk, the sky a vista of cerulean blue. Even the grief-stricken waters of the river Thames seemed to sparkle, reflecting back the purity of that sky; and if ever there was a reason to think this summer a dream, there it was – for Cathy had never known the river anything but turgid and grey.

The children had flocked out to watch the Emporium wagons on their way. Ruddy faces watched from the rails, holding to last Christmas's treasures: backwards bears, Martian rockets, more wind-up soldiery than a boy could ever find uses for. In the street beyond, a motorcar drew around. Kaspar Godman, black hair rippling behind, rose to the tips of his toes, threw the boys a flurry of salutes, and drove on.

Trips out of the Emporium were few and far between, but Cathy relished each one. Winters had always passed in the same controlled chaos she had known since she arrived at the Emporium, but summers could be stultifying. Too much time in the shadowed aisles was not good for the soul, no matter what Emil said; a turn through the summer sun was the restorative Cathy needed, and a trip to Sir Josiah's always renewed her faith in what the Emporium was for.

Kaspar was about to steer into the controlled pandemonium of Regent Street when Cathy clasped his arm, directing his gaze at the girl sitting beside her. Eight years old and the mirror image of her mother, small and dark with darting green eyes, Martha was peering over the side of the motorcar, gawking at the great billboards of the Piccadilly Circus as if it was these things, not the wonders of Papa Jack's Emporium, that defied all reason. She wore the same look every time they emerged from the Emporium, constantly finding adventure in the ordinary.

'Do we have to go back quite yet?'

'What was I thinking?' Kaspar gasped, in mock surprise. Martha beamed up at him. 'A change of heart never hurt a soul,' he declared and, bellowing at a horse and trap about to cross their way, he arced the motorcar around and sped off along the broad way.

The afternoon was growing old, Hyde Park in full blossom. He drove them up and down the Rotten Row, turned dramatic circles around the Apsley Gate, and finally – when it was growing dark – plunged headlong into the grand parades of Belgravia, where men in tall frock coats (didn't these people know it was summer, and a twentieth-century summer at that?) looked aghast at these deplorables come to ruin the afternoon. One man barked at them to show some respect, and this was a thing that delighted Kaspar and Cathy both. They turned to blow kisses – and would have followed through with dainty little waves if only the air had not been suddenly filled with invective, the hollering of a brawl and, next moment, the sound of shattering glass.

Belgrave Square, an explosion of green among the grand terraces, was drawing people to it like ants to spilled sugar. As it met the crowd, the motorcar had to slow to a crawl. Two tradesmen crossed their path with impunity, barely flinching when Kaspar ordered them out of his way. One of the men clasped a rock in his fist. Brazenly, he tossed it from one hand to another, then brought his arm back and let it fly. Over heads and the crowns of treetops it flew. It fell short of the house behind the black railings, but the second and third were better thrown. Glass shattered. Somebody sounded an alarm.

'Head down, Martha.'

'But Mother—'

'Head down, *please*.'

From Martha's lap, a patchwork face picked itself up. Sirius had grown a little more ragged with the years. His black button eyes had been ripped off by over-eager hands, stitched on and restitched again; his patches were thicker where they had been replaced, and what mechanisms still drove him purred a little more incessantly every time he moved his limbs. Martha held on to him, her face screwed up in a scowl. This was the problem with living in the Emporium, thought Cathy. You did not develop an instinct for the real world when all you knew was toys. Martha had no reason to fear for she had never seen anything like this – but then, so Cathy supposed, neither had she. Two men were scrambling into the boughs of one of the trees, the better to observe the carnage.

'It isn't safe,' she whispered. 'Kaspar, what do you think it is?'

'It's ... the embassy.'

Sirius was up on his haunches, hackles raised as if to protect Martha. A man crashed alongside the car, brought his arm back and let fly with another rock. More glass shattered in the face of the building above, the volley followed by a dozen and more.

By now the motorcar had ground to a halt, an island in the sea of men. Kaspar tried to hallo one of them, but to no avail. Instead, he reached down and grabbed him by the scruff of the neck.

'What's happening here?'

'See for yourself, mister,' a voice barked back, and soon Kaspar found an afternoon edition pressed into his hands.

Kaspar unfurled the rag while another stream of men, bank clerks and bricklayers, buffeted the wagon to join the crowds on the other side. With a flick of his wrist it rolled down his arm. Three striking words leapt out of the print:

HIS MAJESTY DEFIED!

Kaspar dropped the newspaper into Cathy's lap, where she read on: war begun without formal declaration, a dreadnought sunk by German privateers in the northern sea, heroes recalled from summer holidays in far-flung climes. And there, underneath it all: YOUR COUNTRY UNDER ATTACK.

'Can I read, Mama?'

In silence, Cathy folded the newspaper and placed it underneath her seat.

'Perhaps we should return home, Mrs Godman?'

Mrs Godman. Even now it was a novelty to hear it, in the same taunting tone he used to say *Miss Wray*.

Home, she thought, and into her head came an explosion of atriums and aisles, the quarters above and workshops deep below; the pack of patchwork dogs over which Sirius ruled; the phoenix that sat, at all times, in the rafters wherever Papa Jack roamed; and that little Wendy House, hidden now in the paper trees, where it sometimes seemed her very life had begun. 'Yes,' she answered, '*home*,' and put an arm around her daughter as the cacophony faded behind.

Come back to the Emporium now. It has changed much since we have been away. Eight years have seen the aisles transformed, but so too the sky above them. The cloud castle that floats, forever churning out the steam on which it survives, in the Emporium dome, belongs to Emil; the patchwork pegasi that gambol around it, those were built by Papa Jack. The paper trees that you must remember have long since put down roots, rucking up the floorboards for aisles around. The Secret Doors have been unleashed, their entrances and exits finally tethered together, so that now a customer might enter on the shopfloor and exit on to a gallery high above. The *Midnight Express*, Emil's endeavour of two summers past, is a miniature locomotive that will ferry customers from the atrium into the new showrooms, bigger on the inside than the out, that Papa Jack has chipped out of the world. There are too many new delights to mention (though let me mention Kaspar's Masques – put one of these on and you might find yourself becoming the animal whose likeness you have taken), but some things will never change in this Emporium of ours: Kaspar still cavorts recklessly around, Emil still lines up the soldiers he has diligently made, and Cathy still makes certain their

Long War does not rise up out of the battlefield into the Emporium aisles. Yes, come back to the Emporium with me now. You have been away too long ...

The letters arrived before the end of the month. Emil, who was up every morning at dawn to turn his workshop lathe, brought them to Papa Jack's breakfast table where the whole family gathered. Mrs Hornung had served up devilled eggs but, this morning, there was not an appetite in the entire Emporium. Sirius begged for scraps but, every time Martha sneaked one into his cotton wadding jaws, he turned up his nose, uncertain what to do with things as alien as toast and griddled fish.

'Douglas Flood,' Emil began, reading the first letter aloud. 'Kesey and Dunmore. They're saying they'll be back by Christmas, that we needn't worry. This thing will be over by first frost, that's what they're being told. But what if it's not?'

Kaspar, embroiled in one of his breakfast battles with Martha, would not be drawn on the subject. Cathy saw him pointedly keeping his eyes down.

'Let's send some more notices into the wild,' Papa Jack began. His voice was more feathery than it had been; Emil's rattled like Vickers gun fire, but Papa Jack's remained a whisper. 'There are always shop hands.'

'Not good ones. Not like Douglas and Dunmore. Even Robert Kesey! How could we teach a new team to wrangle the rocking horses, or to make more soldiers ... or even where everything is? Can you imagine a first-year shop hand teaching one of your unicorns how to walk, let alone the pegasus foals to fly? By the time we were done the snowdrops would be up and ...' There came a knock at the door and Mrs Hornung reappeared, a telegram in her hands. When Emil tore it open, his face blanched. 'John Arthur,' he swore. 'John Arthur signed up too. Well?'

But the faces around the breakfast table bore the news without the panic that had turned Emil's features to a parody.

Kaspar flourished his finger in one direction, drawing Martha's gaze. While she was looking the other way, he snatched an egg from her plate, made it reappear in her pocket – and, when she cracked it open, it revealed not gleaming white and vibrant yolk, but a patchwork chick who squawked, waiting to be fed. 'Emil, is there a time in life when you might *not* think it's the end? Do you know ...'

Papa Jack lifted a granite hand. 'Your brother is right to be afraid.'

'I didn't say I was *afraid*, Papa ...'

'If this is truly what they're saying it is—' and here Papa Jack brandished the newspaper '—then we would do well to watch ourselves. Godman is a name that might pass, not like Schneider or Schmidt, but there can be scarcely a boy in the city who doesn't know us for what we are. That we're not like *them*. Bring them into our Emporium, sit them down with our toys, and they would see that we were all children, once – but, passing in the street, or looking up at the shuttered-up shopfront with a rock in their hand and a belly full of beer? No, not then.'

Emil twisted. 'The Russias are ranged up against the Kaiser, father, just the same as us ...'

'A little thing like that oughtn't matter to the man on the street. Given the excuse, a certain sort of man would put a stone through your window if you so much as had a different colour eye. No, I've seen this before. London loves its toymakers from the frozen East ... until it doesn't. Love and hate, they are such very similar things.'

Cathy had heard quite enough. However much Kaspar was trying to distract her (he was using his pencil to draw figures on the tablecloth, and now those figures were dancing, pulling faces, battling each other back), Martha's eyes kept darting to Papa Jack. When Papa Jack spoke, the world stopped turning on its axis so that it might listen.

'Martha, perhaps it's time you cleared the plates away.'

Martha's face turned to a rictus. *'Mother.'*

'Now, Martha.'

Kaspar could see where this was going; the only time Cathy ever turned brittle was when Martha glared like this. But she had Cathy's pluck, the same pluck that had brought Cathy to the Emporium doors, and that was something that couldn't be quashed. Better that it be diverted instead. Even the wildest rivers could be diverted.

'Mademoiselle, shall we?' In moments Kaspar was bustling Martha through to the parlour where, together, they would tempt Sirius to lick the crockery clean.

After they had gone, Cathy looked between Emil and Papa Jack. 'If you must talk of this thing, there are enough locked doors in the Emporium.' She stood so that she might look down on them, as if it was they who were her children. 'Whatever this is, she's eight years old.'

Emil spent the morning in his workshop, scything more soldiers out of wood while his Imperial Kapitan watched from on high. It was meant to be cathartic work, but today his hands were separate from his body. They kept slipping, so that he planed a soldier's arm down to a stump, or opened up his belly to reveal the cavity where the wind-up workings were to slot inside. Finally, he gave up. The Imperial Kapitan was still watching, his painted features as proud of Emil's trembling hands as they were when he spirited perfect soldiers out of scraps left on his workshop floor. It was time, Emil decided, to stop. Down on his knees, he ranged up a troop of wind-up soldiery and set them to battle each other.

Ordinarily watching his soldiers lifted him out of himself, but today the feeling was not the same. The battle being fought behind his eyes was too strong. The calendar on the wall, which Emil had inscribed himself, read 5 August. There were still two months until he would dare stay up each night, searching for signs of first frost – and yet he was thinking about it every day, and had been since the moment the snowdrops flowered on the Emporium terrace and last season's magic came to an end. That sweet anticipation, even the anticipation of the anticipation, was enough to sustain him through the long, lonely (yes, he used the word at last) summer. He did not mind the endless days with only him and the Imperial Kapitan, did not mind listening to the sounds of Kaspar and Martha playing in the aisles, nor even of Kaspar and Cathy playing through the bedroom walls at night, not when he knew there would come a day when Douglas Flood and Robert Kesey, Dunmore, John Horwood and all the rest would stream back through the Emporium doors and light the aisles up, play battles in the Palace and stay up late with him, concocting all sorts of stories, playing all sorts of games. Emil had long ago observed that he himself was like one of the Emporium's backwards bears: in hibernation through the summer, only truly alive when winter was at its most fierce. A whole year's life could be lived in the space of an Emporium Christmas. And yet ... the thought of a winter without them, his boys so far away while Emil remained alone in the Emporium, well, that was what was clouding his thoughts. That was the reason today's soldiers lay dismembered on the bench, their faces as crude as the ones on sale in all the lesser toyshops of London town.

'What do you think, little thing?' he said, eyeing the Imperial Kapitan. 'I'm going to have to talk to you. If I don't talk to somebody, I'm bound to go mad, and you're the only one there is ...'

The Imperial Kapitan eyed him with its unflinching face.

'If only you could talk. Why, then we'd see ...'

Clasping the Kapitan, Emil ventured on to the shopfloor. There would be the customers. His days would be filled with showing boys battles, or restacking shelves, or taking the most brave shoppers on tours of the jungles his father was planting, where all manner of patchwork creatures would frolic in the vines. It wasn't as if there would be no joy. The world would stop turning before there was an Emporium winter without any joy.

A noise from above drew his eye. Kaspar was dangling from one of the galleries where the frame of Emil's cloud castle was tethered, its towers and portcullis borne up by a reef of churning steam. Moments later, Martha perched on the balcony beside him and, goaded on by Kaspar, dropped over the edge. Together they released their fingers – and would have plummeted down, if only Kaspar's longships with their dragon head prows had not appeared underneath.

Kaspar dropped into the first, Martha into the second – and the dragons, opening their jaws in the way Kaspar had designed, took off, as if swimming in the cloud castle's moat.

Laughter fell around Emil like a deluge of rain. The longships swooped and turned at the command of their mechanical oarsmen, but what was keeping them afloat Emil dared not guess. Impressive as his cloud castle was, any engineer with half an interest in atmospherics might have achieved the same thing. But those longships? Those longships had sailed straight out of Kaspar's dreams and into the Emporium air.

Another voice joined the laughter above. And there was Cathy, at the same balcony rail with Sirius yapping at her side. She had been admonishing them (she always admonished their escapades), but as Kaspar's dragonboat completed its circle and drew near, something changed. Emil saw her head drop to one side (how beautiful she looked when she disapproved and yet approved at the very same time!); then, timing her leap perfectly, she propelled herself over the side.

The dragonboat tilted as she hit it. Moments later she and Kaspar were off, hunting Martha in the mist, the dragon heads showering sparks as the laughter continued to pour down.

Yes, the Emporium was a place of joy, but without the shop hands this winter the joy could never be Emil's. 'What would you have me do?' he whispered, but the Imperial Kapitan offered no reply.

That evening, Martha would not listen to her stories. She asked: 'What does it mean, Mama? Is there to be a real war, like the ones Papa and Uncle Emil play? With cavalry charges and a noisy cannonade?'

Cathy stroked the hair out of her eyes. 'Why do you say that, my treasure?'

'None of the shop hands are coming, are they? They're to fight their real wars. But why do people fight wars, Mama? Why, when there are toy soldiers to do it for them?'

What an Emporium thing to say! Only a girl raised in these aisles could think such a thing. And yet, she thought, why not?

'Whatever happens, whatever things they do out there in the world, it won't touch us, not here, not in our Emporium. What you saw at the embassy, that isn't coming here. You're safe here, my treasure, safe with your mama.'

When she reached their own chamber, Kaspar was already in bed. Cathy ordered Sirius away, off to guard Martha through the long night, and would have sat down herself, if only her feet hadn't kept on walking.

'I've seen you like this before. You're prowling, prowling like a caged tiger.'

'I'm frightened, Kaspar.'

This was new. The Cathy Kaspar had fallen in love with had never admitted such a thing. He lifted himself from the covers. 'Whatever happens, whatever things they do out there in the world—'

'That's precisely what I just told Martha. You can't pull the old lines on me, Kaspar. We wrote those lines together, remember?'

Kaspar said, 'There's no need to be afraid.'

'But Dunmore and Kesey and little Douglas Flood ... off to carry bayonets like it's just another game. If they've gone, how many others?'

'Thousands, I shouldn't wonder. Thousands and thousands and thousands.' Kaspar had said it dreamily, but now he came to his senses. 'Whatever happens out there, it won't be like the Long War. What sort of madness might that be? To wind up a battalion of living things and march them at one another, as if *that* might win a war?'

Kaspar took her by the hand, drew her down to the bedsheets. If the Emporium's magics would not make her forget the outside world tonight, well, there were other ways. He rolled over her, staring at her dewy-eyed until she could no longer contain her laughter. He looked pointedly absurd when he glared at her like that, and he knew it.

'You're a fool. War declared, our shop hands gone, panic in the aisles and blood on the streets – and you, all you can think about is this ...'

All the same, it was Cathy who kissed him first.

That night, in bed, she had dreamt about blood on the streets; three mornings later, there it was, in lurid smears up and down the Emporium doors, a dried-up pool of viscera spreading out into Iron Duke Mews.

Mrs Hornung was already on her hands and knees, the pail of water at her side frothing with scarlet soap, when Cathy arrived. Cathy had come in search of a letter, for Lizzy wrote often and her stories were better than anything in the *Reader's Digest* magazines, but no postman had dared a delivery this morning. A pig's head sat in the middle of the filth, warning strangers away.

'Mrs Hornung ...'

'Don't you mind me, girl. I was here to see it happen, opening up to flush out the cobwebs when they bouldered up the mews. *Foreign dogs*, they shouted. *Foreign dogs*, as if their mamas and papas hadn't brought them to these same doors every Christmas and spoiled them with Mr Godman's toys. I tried to reason with them, but those butcher's boys had their bucket and ...'

For the first time she stopped scrubbing and turned to face Cathy. The pig's blood had made a merry mess of her apron; it ran in the creases of her neck, giving the impression that somebody had come for her with a knife.

'Let's get you upstairs, Mrs Hornung.'

'Not a chance, girl, not until this is done. I won't have those blackguards winning. It's like Mr Godman says. We was all babes once. English and German and even Spaniards, I should say.'

Cathy rolled up her sleeves. 'Two backs are better than one, Mrs Hornung. You move on up, those flagstones are going to need some working ...'

She had not yet broken a sweat (though the work was hard, the blood needed scouring from each stone) when she heard more footsteps thundering up Iron Duke Mews. Instinct told her this was another villain come to daub their Emporium walls – just as they had daubed the fronts of every emigrant bookseller, locksmith and chocolatier since the day war was declared – but, when she looked up, an altogether more bewildering sight was coming their way. Emil was hurrying back into the Emporium in great, loping strides. His chest was heaving, his fists were bunched, and though he hopped ungainly through the sea of dried blood, he kept his head steadfastly up, refusing to acknowledge Cathy and

Mrs Hornung on their knees at his feet. 'Emil?' Cathy cried out, but in response he contorted past them and was lost to the darkness of the summer aisles.

Cathy stared for a long time after he had gone. 'When was the last time Emil left the Emporium, Mrs Hornung?'

'More than out here, to sign for a tradesman? I should think it's been half that boy's life.'

Mrs Hornung had not broken her rhythm. She was still scouring the flagstones into submission. But, after that, and though she kept on scrubbing, Cathy's mind was not on the task at hand, nor even on the pig's head that stared at her with such derision. She could still picture Emil's face, seen as if from below. She was not mistaken: Emil had been crying.

Emil did not appear when the gong sounded for dinner that night. Martha (whose tutor Mr Atlee had just departed, leaving her with a composition on the works of Charles Perrault) was the last to the table. After that, Papa Jack recited some words of thanks in that language Cathy still could not understand, and then Mrs Hornung served up her rich chicken broth. When Emil had still not appeared by the time she wheeled out her suet pudding and plum sauce, Cathy teased Sirius's ears and sent him down to the workshop on the shopfloor. Who knew how Emil understood the patchwork dog, but before the plates were clean, there he was, forearms raw with scratches from the workshop lathe. He made a muted hello, took his place at his father's right hand, and set about devouring what was left.

'This thing isn't going away,' Papa Jack began. Ordinarily newspapers were good for only one thing in the Emporium – every gazette that came through the door was shredded up for papier mâché, or used to line the workshop floors – but he had a collection at his feet and, brushing aside one of the patchwork cats who had escaped from its packing, he lifted up the first. Liège had been broken, Alsace and Lorraine were overrun, but so too were islands in the South Pacific rearing up. French and British soldiers had marched into Togo and taken it from its German governors, and into the fray marched legions from that vastness Jekabs Godman had once called home. The Russians were in East Prussia and marching west. 'I think we have to accept that. Two hundred thousand English boys already in France. That changes everything. Cathy?'

Cathy had wanted to usher Martha out of the room, but the girl would only listen with an ear at the wall. Standing up, she held forth a leaf of paper. The letter had arrived with the day's second post. She had known it was Lizzy by the florid script on the front (her father sometimes sent cards, but his was a simple, workmanlike hand), but she had not known what its contents would be. 'She's going too. They're taking nurses out of Homerton and sending them out, with the British Red Cross. My little sister, going to war.'

It seemed scarcely credible, even as Cathy gave it voice. Lizzy Wray, destined to marry rich and live a spoilt life, was off to save lives while the world frayed apart all around her. Something had changed in Lizzy the year Cathy ran away. Cathy had thought she might come to the Emporium, spend seasons with her and Martha in the aisles, but instead Lizzy had landed in Homerton to train as a nurse. Cathy had often wondered: was she looking for her own Emporium? Well, now she had found it, in the makeshift barracks and tents of some French field.

Cathy trembled as she read out the letter. It was so inordinately foolish, so incredibly brave. Lizzy Wray, who wouldn't get dirt beneath her nails without causing a fuss ...

'Well,' said Mrs Hornung, because somebody had to fill the silence, 'we must all do our part.'

By the head of the table, Emil sat bolt upright, spraying suet pudding. 'Just what do you mean by that?'

All eyes turned on him. His face was purpling with rage. When nobody answered him, he was on his feet. When they kept staring, his fists were up. Beneath the table, Sirius yapped.

'I'm the one who *tried*, aren't I? I'm the one who went out and *tried* to do my part, while you all sat here just talking about it. And now you dare to stare at me like this, like I'm some ... some *coward*? Is that it? Well, I'm sick and tired of being the odd one out in this Emporium! I'm sick and tired of being overlooked. I tried and—'

His anger had carried him so far but now his words were failing him. Another tortuous silence threatened, until Cathy – who had never liked seeing Emil squirm – ventured, 'Oh, Emil. You tried to sign up.'

So that was why he had come storming back into the Emporium this morning, unable to look her in the eye.

'I did,' Emil breathed – and, now that his valiant feat was acknowledged, he sank back into his seat. 'But what would you know? They wouldn't have me. Asthma, they told me. A weak heart. They've said I should find a physician. Well, I've more heart than any of you. I *tried*, didn't I?'

Sadly, he spooned in the last of his pudding.

ROBERT DINSDALE

'This morning, pig's blood sprayed all up the shopfront.
You might have thought they'd brought that pig, kicking
and squealing, and cut its throat there and then.' Rage
was infectious; now Mrs Hornung seemed to be purpling
herself. Cathy touched her forearm, as if to soak up some
of the anger, but instead she started to feel it too. 'It's a
shame you didn't make it, young Emil. Somebody ought to
give those *bastards* – there, I said it! – filled with their fear
and hate something to think about. Show them all foreign
born aren't to be reviled. Why, they'll come here and play
with your toys one winter, then come to vandalise the next.
Well, we ought to be showing them, we'll stand up to be
counted – and not because we're English, because we've no
need to be. Because we're people.'

Emil had finished his suet pudding but continued to
scratch at the bowl.

'Mealtimes are not for fighting,' Papa Jack began. 'There
is enough warring outside these walls to make war among
ourselves. Emil, you are my son and I love you. Today you
surrendered a part of yourself. That they sent you back here
does not diminish the trying.' He paused, clasping Emil
with one of his mammoth hands. 'But you are right, dear
Mrs Hornung. I have longed to make the Emporium apart
from the world – but we are, and will always be, a part *of* the
world. This morning proves we are not forgotten. And they
will come again.'

'We need to do our part,' said Mrs Hornung, repeating
it like a petition.

'We must,' said Papa Jack.

There was silence. For a time, nobody could look at
Emil. They kept their faces buried in their bowls. Then,

when it was not enough to ignore his anguish any longer, their eyes seemed repelled, moving as one along the length of the table, past Papa Jack, past Cathy, past Mrs Hornung, to its other end. There sat Kaspar, engaged in a suppertime skirmish with Martha (his salt cellar was advancing on her fortress of interlocked knives and spoons). Until now he had pointedly been ignoring his brother's disgrace, for a look from Kaspar could have turned Emil's rage incandescent. Now he looked up, to see his family staring back at him. His face opened wide, in dumb realisation.

Cathy curled up, Kaspar around her. Small as she was, she fit perfectly inside the arc of his body.

'How are we going to tell her?'

'We'll tell her her father is a brave, brave man.'

'She'll miss you.' Cathy paused. '*I'll* miss you.'

'Don't think I haven't thought the same. I've spent almost every day with you since I shuttered you up in my Wendy House, Cathy. It isn't the Emporium that's my universe. It's you. Of course, they may not take me yet. They may find a weak heart ...'

'Oh,' Cathy sighed, '*please.*' Then, more seriously now, 'You don't have to do this.'

But I do, thought Kaspar – and, as soon as he thought it, the idea solidified around him. Kesey and Dunmore, Douglas Flood and John Horwood, they were already part of a battalion, the Artisans Rifles, and they were in training, or they were over the water, out in the world. Those last words, *out in the world*, transformed the way he was thinking. 'Do you know,' he whispered into Cathy's ear, touching it with his lips, 'I always wanted an adventure. It used to be that sneaking out of the Emporium in summer was enough. But I think back on that journey we made with our papa, over the oceans with a man we barely knew, and – for all the wonders in the Emporium aisles, was anything as adventurous as this? I'll be gone mere months. I wouldn't even miss first frost. I could be out there, with those Emporium boys, and back by opening night. Perhaps – perhaps this is the adventure for *now*?'

Cathy turned in his arms, to face his naked chest. 'You'll write.'

'I'll write. The most florid, extravagant letters a wife ever received.'

She held his hand, searched for the simple wedding band there.

'And keep it on you always, no matter where you are or whatever you do.'

'Until I die,' he whispered.

Sirius was at the foot of the bed. He let out a disenchanted moan.

Daybreak found Emil in his workshop. If he had cared to look in the mirror this morning (he did not, for fear of the man who would be glowering back), he would have seen his eyes bloodshot and red. If Papa Jack, Cathy or any of the rest had pressed him on it, he would have told them it was exhaustion, and the evidence of that would have been piled up around him – for last night toy soldiers had sprung out of his lathe like a plague, and the red on his fingertips was the residue of the paint he had used to dress them in their finery. But he would have been lying. For last night, Emil had ventured into the Emporium attics, those great antechambers where whole childhoods are stored away, and unearthed the first games he and Kaspar used to play. Crude toy soldiers and their three-legged mules; maps they had painted across which they fought the first battles of the Long War; a spinning top that Kaspar had given to Emil that first Christmas they were English boys, its edges grooved so perfectly it hummed a lullaby as it spun. It was spinning now, up on the shelf above his worktop, spinning beside the Imperial Kapitan. It had been spinning all night and, though there was no magic in it, not like the toys Kaspar now made, still Emil kept seeing memories manifesting themselves in the edges of his vision: he and Kaspar gambolling through the empty Emporium, the first morning their papa took the lease on the place; he and Kaspar, kindling a fire together, that night they got lost in the shifting aisles and couldn't find their way back.

The spinning top stopped, skittering up against the Imperial Kapitan.

Emil was about to set it spinning again when he realised he was no longer alone. In his workshop door, Mrs Hornung was waiting. 'Emil, it's time.'

'I'll be out presently.'

'Young man, your brother is leaving *now*.'

Emil ground his teeth. Why was it Mrs Hornung always made him feel like this? He was a little boy again, clinging on to her apron tail. He remembered, starkly, the time he had mistakenly called her *mother* and the look of consternation that had flickered across her face. That night, Papa Jack had come to smooth his bedsheets around him, while Mrs Hornung took a day's leave. Some boys, all they wanted was a mama.

'I can't.'

'You must.'

He spun around. 'But I mustn't, don't you see? He's going off and it ... it should have been me. I should be the one. If it weren't for my heart, I would be. And now it will be ...' He stopped. Seemingly he had changed what he was going to say, because when he spoke again it was with a new, forced lightness. 'Kaspar has a daughter.' *She should have been mine too* was the terrible thought that entered his mind. 'He has a wife.' *And Cathy, Cathy should have been ...* 'He shouldn't have to leave them, and all on my account.'

'This isn't on your account, Emil. There are thousands of men like Kaspar crossing over the water.' She touched him like a mother might touch him, and that only made Emil hate himself more. 'You'll regret it if you don't.'

Kaspar was in the half-moon hall when Mrs Hornung and Emil made their way up the aisle. He was crouching down, his arms wrapped around Martha and, when he stood up, the girl would not let go; she was dangling from his neck. It took Cathy to prise her away, and then she herself needed prising. Papa Jack clasped Kaspar by the hand, drawing him into a mountainous embrace. And Emil, Emil lingered on the edges of it all.

'Back by first frost,' Kaspar declared. He took each of them in until, finally, his eyes landed on his brother. 'You'll look after them for me, of course.'

Emil tumbled forwards, betrayed by his own feet. He wrapped himself in his brother's arms, fumbling a fist into the pocket of his greatcoat. Then, he unfurled his fingers.

There were words being whispered into Emil's ear. 'Look after our Emporium well, little brother.' And, 'I love you, Emil.'

Emil did not say it in return – but, as Kaspar reached the end of Iron Duke Mews, he knew it all the same. A little spinning top had been tucked into his pocket and, as he walked, it was humming a tune he had never forgotten.

The Emporium was empty that day, more empty than the most barren of summer days. Cathy busied herself fixing the braids of Papa Jack's ragdolls. Martha's tutor, Mr Atlee – whose own sons had already gone where Kaspar had followed – arrived to teach her the simple precepts of trigonometry (and to bore her senseless to boot). Mrs Hornung lost herself in a maelstrom of cookery, filling the kitchens with the scents of Kaspar's favourite foods, of kasha and dumplings, as if that might keep a little part of him here, where he belonged. And Emil waited nervously outside his papa's workshop door, watching through the crack as his father stitched more flaming feathers into his phoenix's hide.

'Papa,' he said, finally pushing through. How many times had he come to this workshop as a boy, sat cross-legged on the floor and watched as his father brought some new fantasia to life? 'Papa, are you well?'

It was not often that this man as old as mountains looked bereft, but he looked bereft now.

'Don't be sad, Papa.'

'There are times when it is good and right to feel sad,' Papa Jack whispered.

It was only now that Emil noticed that the wind-up mechanism from the trunk beneath the shelves, the one with the little figurines and a barren snowscape, had been set on the mantel. Papa Jack had been playing with it, then, visiting that place in the tundra where he had first learned the magic in toys. In that moment, Emil understood the weight of his father's sadness – for wasn't Kaspar going where Papa Jack had gone before, marched off into the world with a pack on his shoulder and no certainty he was ever coming home? A new, terrible feeling rose into Emil's gorge: I want it to be me, he thought; I want it to be me, so that I can be close to my papa.

'Kaspar will be home soon.'

'We can hope, at least.'

For a time there was silence. Emil found a felt sack, filled with tiny leather balls, and sank into it; a chair sprang up around him, moulding to the shape of his body. 'It's going to be strange without my brother, but we can do it, can't we, Papa? The Emporium is still going to open. There's still going to be first frost. And ... the people will still come. Kaspar or not, Iron Duke Mews will be filled with them – and, and ... they'll be expecting miracles. They'll *want* them, this year more than any. Opening night can still be a spectacle. I know I have my' – he had to rush the word, because he barely wanted to say it at all – 'limitations, Papa, but I can do it. I ... promise I can.'

Papa Jack threw himself to his feet, the phoenix tumbling to the floor (where it picked itself up and looked disdainfully on). In two great strides he had crossed the workshop and smothered Emil in his arms. It had been an aeon since Emil felt his father up close, smelt the powder gathered in his beard, the heady scent of wood chippings, axle grease and glue.

'I don't want to hear you say those things again, Emil. You're my son, just as Kaspar is. Your toys belong in these aisles just as much as mine, just as much as your brother's. We have a ship to sail, boy. Let's do it together.'

Out on the balcony, Emil stared into the shell of the half-finished cloud castle and listened to his father's words reverberating in his skull. One of his papa's patchwork pegasi had wound down by the castle portcullis. Kaspar had planted instant trees along the moat, so that the unfinished walls were hidden in tumbling foliage and paper vines. Emil could build neither of those things. He could not replace the magic that had marched off to war with his brother. And yet ... a new idea was forming. Not an idea for a toy, nor an idea about opening night – but an idea about himself. His father's words had opened up something inside him. There were, he decided with something approaching confidence, a dozen different ways to be *spectacular*. Magic might have been one of them, but there were others. And, if Kaspar was not here this year, if opening night was not to be his, well, perhaps there was something he, Emil, could do. Perhaps this was his moment to stand up, to be noticed, to get the recognition he and his toy soldiers had always deserved.

As he stood on the balcony, he imagined the aisles below thronged with customers. He imagined boys pouring into the dells he had made between the stands, where epic battles were being fought, the air alive with cries of exhilaration and delight. *His* winter, he thought. *His* Emporium.

This would be the winter of the Long War. With that in mind, he made haste for his workshop. There was much work to do, and mere months to go.

Kaspar wrote every day, as he promised he would. Days passed without letters, then arrived in a flurry: four, five, six of them landing on the mat, or ferried up to the quarters between Sirius's soft, felt jaws. Each night Cathy sat at the end of Martha's bed, Sirius lounging between them (asking either for his tummy to be tickled or for his gears to be wound tighter, that he might beat his tail with even more loyalty for his missing master), and read them aloud. After that, she retired to the empty bed and savoured each sentence alone.

> *At night the skies are open and Douglas Flood makes merry with his violin. In our billets we eat snail and French sausage and talk of the Emporium this Christmas. I am well my Cathy, my Martha. The French air is bracing and as we march (we march for the sea) I imagine an Emporium in Paris, or one in Liège (one in New York, when I forget where I am, one in St Petersburg, all the grand places of the world) and what we might do together, one day. For the world is more vast than you can tell, and I am living in it now. (PS Here is a design for a Constant Burrow, that boys and girls might have underworld dens in their gardens. We are digging in ourselves now and it is exhilarating work. Perhaps Emil might construct one?)*

Sometimes there were notes, hidden in the letters. The capitals might spell out *Remember Our Wendy House*, or in minute script (illegible except to a magnifying glass, sentences looped inside tiny o's or crammed up inside a question mark) *You would love Paris, Cathy, and I will bring you here when the war is finished. Summer in Paris is divine. Winter would be perfect.* Mr Atlee had Martha compiling a scrapbook, all the places her father had seen, all the foods he had eaten and the people he met. Cathy kept a scrapbook of her own and, in it, she counted the days.

August became September. October arrived more swiftly than it ought. Paris was saved from what had seemed a certain fate. An armada of taxicabs came together to deliver soldiers to the city's defence. Odessa was ravaged by shells from the sea, the Turks drew lots and entered battle in the East; but inside the Emporium, the world did not change. The aisles were replenished in anticipation of first frost: toy soldiers and princesses, patchwork dogs and all the toil of Papa Jack's summer. The cloud castle anchored in the Emporium dome grew a drawbridge and walls. In the workshops, patchwork reindeer were taught how to walk, then, finally, how to fly. The movements of autumn, heralding the movements of Christmas, were the same as in every other year – and yet sometimes Cathy woke in the night to find her bed empty (or, worse still, that Martha, haunted by some phantom image of her father, was occupying the place where Kaspar once lay), and this was her constant reminder: this year was not like every other, not at all.

Then came the night when Cathy walked through the paper trees, telling Martha the story of how her life had started here, in the little Wendy House beneath the boughs, and looked up to see the glass at the height of the Emporium dome was incandescent with tiny droplets of ice.

'Look, Martha.' Her daughter's eyes were agog as Cathy lifted her up, the better to see the way the crystals caught and trapped the moonlight above. 'The first frost of winter ...'

A magical moment, one for which every devotee of the Emporium hungered, and yet this year it was tinged with sadness, for Kaspar hadn't made it home after all.

Daylight had not yet fallen upon the grand arcades of Regent Street when the shop hands lined up at the Emporium door. Those who had chanced to see the first frost forming had rapidly packed their bags and made their pilgrimage to Iron Duke Mews. Among them were the flatterers, confidence men and tricksters who thought to try their luck and sneak within – but Emil stood diligently by the door, turning away any ne'er-do-wells who gathered in the alley. When he was done, he hurried back across the shopfloor – and there he met Cathy, standing in the aisle. He looked white as the frost itself.

'It's down to you now, dear Cathy. I can't recall an opening night with so many new hands, not since our very first!'

There were familiar faces this season, but in the half-moon hall the new shop hands gathered, nervously awaiting their introduction to the aisles. Cathy, who had sifted through the letters of entreaty that piled up on Papa Jack's mat, knew already that most would be girls, but in her mind she had imagined them as images of herself, the runaway coming to the Emporium with little more than the clothes she stood up in. Instead, she found mothers and grandmothers, elder sisters and aunts – the rags of families left behind this Christmas, eager for change.

At least Sally-Anne was here. That calmed Cathy. 'Just us this year, girl. We're to sail this ship, are we?'

'We still have Emil,' Cathy replied.

'Oh,' she said, rolling her eyes, 'we'll *always* have Emil ...'

It seemed a spiteful thing to say – but then, Sally-Anne had not seen the way he grew purple with shame that day he tried to sign up. In the weeks approaching first frost, Cathy had seen how feverishly he worked. It meant the world to Emil that this season should not suffer, because Kaspar was not here to sprinkle his magic up and down the aisles.

Cathy stepped forward, facing the crowd. 'I remember the first day I stood in this hall,' she began – and she vividly did: the cold at her back, the emptiness gnawing in her belly, the exhilaration of escape. 'Savour it, because, though this could be the first of many Emporium seasons, you will never have a first time again. Tonight the spectacular will happen. Christmas begins. And I know how much you all need Christmas ...' She paused, thinking of Kaspar behind the lines in some derelict barracks. 'But there is work to do before those doors open, and so few hours to do it. I hope you're ready ...' At this point a mechanical reindeer, all of its patchwork sloughing off, came cantering down the aisle, Sirius chasing wildly behind. Cathy closed her eyes. This was going to be more arduous than she thought. 'You'll need to show some of them how to wrangle them,' she whispered to Sally-Anne. 'Papa Jack has so much in store.'

'Let's take them on a tour. Show them what they're letting themselves in for.'

Cathy nodded. 'But don't go losing one of the grandmothers in the storerooms. We haven't time to organise search parties.'

Sally-Anne grinned, 'Not this year ...'

Sally-Anne relished playing mother hen and led them into the aisles. A diminutive grandmother with tight white curls, a middle-aged couple who clasped each other's hands as they filed past, a young man dragging behind him a lame leg and somebody's spinster aunt; the Emporium would have a motley crew this Christmas, but motley did not have to mean miserable.

Cathy was about to follow the procession when a girl caught her eye. She might have been no more than fifteen, sixteen years old, with hair as red as anger, and somehow this struck Cathy as familiar. Her eyes were grey and marked by freckles, her teeth just crooked enough to be noticed. She had been fixing Cathy with a look, trying to pluck up the courage to talk.

Being a mother made you think impossible things. There must have been only six or seven years between them, and yet by instinct Cathy put a comforting arm around her shoulder. 'You mustn't be nervous. This winter you'll see such magical things.'

'You're Cathy Godman, aren't you?'

'I am.'

'My name's Frances,' she ventured. 'Frances Kesey. My brother, Robert ...'

Cathy beamed, 'You're Robert's sister.'

She nodded, finding her nerve. 'He spoke so much about this place. That's why I'm here, you see. To see all the things my brother talked about ...' She spoke in the same broad Cornish that Robert Kesey had spoken, even more his sister in voice than she was in the flesh. 'Oh, we didn't believe it, Mrs Godman, that first Christmas he came here. We thought he had a girl, or was just trying to be contrary, because that was his way. That maybe he'd been gone from home so long just to spite our parents. Robert liked to tell a tale, and when he talked about patchwork dogs and trees bursting out of tiny wooden shells and ... why, Wendy Houses bigger on the inside! Well, we could be forgiven for thinking he was having us on. It wasn't until the next year, when I woke at New Year and there were paper trees all over our garden, a whole forest of them sprouted overnight, that I knew it was real. After that, he'd bring gifts every year. I have a ballerina, a mouse, who turns pirouettes up the walls, across the ceiling. I have a dress that shows me how to dance.' She stopped. Cathy thought: how strange for the girl to be overcome with such emotion ... 'He was going to bring me here one day. We would ride on runnerless rocking horses together, or we'd sneak into the storerooms and see the patchwork giants Papa Jack makes in secret. Woolly mammoths and cave bears and – are there truly spiders, the size of a horse, sleeping in the cellars? So you see, I had to come and see it for myself. I want to feel the things he felt. Eat dinners in the Palace each night, and make merry with the other shop hands and maybe, just maybe, open up my own patchwork dog and be the first thing its black button eyes see when I wind it up ...'

The girl's words exploded. Now they were formless, ugly things as she tried to contain her tears.

'I'm sorry, Mrs Godman,' she said, straightening herself up. 'You must think me frightful. And I have been, ever since that telegram arrived. My mother and father, they don't know I'm here, you see. But I had to come. To honour Robert. To remember.'

By now Sally-Anne and the rest had reached the heart of the shopfloor. Over the aisles, Cathy could hear her dividing them into parties, assigning roles, assigning tasks.

But Frances Kesey's words had given Cathy a chill for which she was not prepared.

'You'd better run along, before they get ahead of us.'

Composing herself, Frances Kesey took off up the aisle.

'We'll look after you here,' Cathy called. Frances Kesey looked back and allowed herself a wan, half smile. Perhaps Cathy's words had brought her comfort (perhaps this winter was everything the girl needed, for all she would have to do was touch one of Papa Jack's toys and be spirited back to the childhood games she and Robert once shared), but her own words had opened up a chasm in Cathy. Robert Kesey dead. Dozens of letters from Kaspar and he hadn't said a thing.

Martha had hardly slept the night before, dreaming of the magics of opening night. In their quarters, where Mr Atlee diligently tried to instruct her in the basic structures of Latin, or the secret meanings hidden inside her mother's old edition of *Gulliver's Travels*, her excitement could barely be contained, manifesting itself (as it often did) in lack of interest, contrary questions and downright insolence. Mr Atlee – who would, if you had badgered him, have admitted to a tingle of excitement himself – was ready to accept defeat and would have done so right then, if only he hadn't heard Martha's mother marching past the study door.

Bracing herself, Cathy strode into the bedroom. Kaspar's letters were kept in a bundle in the bedside dresser. She lifted them out and spread them on the eiderdown.

My own Cathy, read the first letter. *My only Cathy,* read the second. She read about his basic training and his journey across the water. She read about the barracks in which the Artisans Rifles spent their nights, the scent of wildflowers in a Flanders meadow. She read about the card games they played after dark and the wagers they made. It was only when she went looking for it that she noticed: a month ago, all remarks about Robert Kesey had evaporated from Kaspar's letters. He still spoke fondly of Andrew Dunmore, of John Horwood and Douglas Flood, but Robert Kesey was dead and it hadn't merited a mention.

A lie of omission was still a lie. She sat for long hours, reading the letters over and over and only now did she see: these letters were about nothing at all. They were bedtime stories, things he had contrived from the banal moments of his days, letters designed to protect her and nothing else. To protect her from *knowing*. To protect her from the truth.

She was trembling (this was fury like she had never felt) when there came a tentative tapping at the door. By the time she turned around, Emil was already nosing his way in. Cathy thought: *Get out! Get out now!* But Emil was wearing that same anxious look he had on the eve of every opening night, and something in it made the anger bleed out of her.

'Cathy, it's time.'

Her eyes shot to the window. The afternoon darkness was hardening to night. Her entire afternoon, wasted in these letters, while a fresh band of shop hands were tasked with preparing the Emporium for its biggest night of the year. She felt the shame of it, hot and urgent.

Martha appeared beside Emil, Mr Atlee hovering behind.

'Mama,' she grinned, 'come on! We mustn't miss it!'

Cathy gathered the letters together, not caring when they crumpled in her hands. As she crossed the room, she caught sight of herself in the mirror, still in her day dress with the dust of forgotten aisles up and down her arms. Her hair was a mess, her fury had deepened the creases in her cheeks, but this would have to do. A gong was sounding on the shopfloor. The seconds were counting down.

As they reached the shopfloor, Cathy's shame turned to relief. What magics they had worked while her head was buried in those letters! Around her, every aisle was garlanded with lights. High above, the Emporium dome was swirling with pinpoints of white, like a constantly falling snow. The arches that opened each aisle were wreathed in holly leaves of crêpe paper and card; plump red berries of papier mâché hung from every leaf. Pipe-cleaner owls stood in the boughs of the paper trees, the carousel turned and sang, and the vaults above the aisles were a circus show of dragon longships, patchwork pegasi, and a white lace wyvern whose body was wrapped around the turrets of Emil's cloud castle.

The shop hands were all flocking in the same direction. The aisles had separated and moved while Cathy had been up above, and now they all led into a single great boulevard, charting the length of the Emporium floor. Where there had once been polished floorboards, now there were the cobbles of an open-air market, and it was here that the confetti fountain constantly burst forth, painting the air with images of horses mid-canter, great dragons and knights. She and Martha joined the procession and stopped where the crowd was gathered in the half-moon hall. Here, through frosted glass, she could see Iron Duke Mews thronged with mothers and their excited broods.

The bells stopped pealing. All was silent on the Emporium floor. From the forested alcoves to the cloud castle halls, not a creature was stirring, not even a mouse. Then, without being touched, the doors opened. Winter rushed in with its perfect icy breath, and on it came a tide of shoppers.

In the half-moon hall, the first customers froze. Before they could fan out, their eyes were drawn upward. Cathy looked the same way. Above them, the cloud castle drawbridge was lowering, and out of the vault inside a red carpet rolled. Instead of dropping from the precipice, it slowly unfurled, charting a crimson pathway over the tops of the aisles – until it landed here, at the feet of the first family. From up above, the sound of sleigh bells could be heard. The swirling lights of the castle interior revolved, and through curtains of rippling white the heads of two cloth creatures emerged. Black button eyes and embroidered noses were followed by antlers of crocheted bone. Soon, two patchwork reindeer stood regally at the top of the crimson road; then, each with a nod to the other, they began to canter down.

Behind them they trailed a simple wooden sled, its rear piled high with presents wrapped with silver paper and bows. No passengers descended with the sled, no driver flicked the reins to drive the reindeer on. They cantered, without hoof beats, to the half-moon hall, and there they came to a stop in front of the first family to have breached the doors. The first reindeer nuzzled the hands of the mother, the second reindeer nuzzled the hands of the children, and in that way they directed the family aboard. Then the sled drew around, parted the gathered shop hands, and took off along the cobbled aisle.

Somewhere, gramophones began to play. The carousel burst back into life. The shop hands came together in one last burst of applause – and then it was done. Opening night had begun.

'Danger! Adventure! Glory! Have you got what it takes? Step up, be courageous! Fight the brave fight, beat the unbeatable foe, win the unwinnable war!'

Emil stood atop one of the monstrous bears, which had been armoured and saddled like some monster plucked out of Nordic myth. The glade between the aisles was one of several waiting to be discovered on the shopfloor. In front of him, two dozen expectant faces looked up. More were being drawn from the neighbouring aisles, boys straining on their mothers' hands.

Beneath him – Emil, the god of the battlefield – lay a medieval village in miniature, a rustic landscape where a hand-crafted windmill turned the waters of a stream, where paper trees the size of a boot made forests against the banks, and the hilltops rose in gradients of felt, cloth and papier mâché. The houses were tumbledown creations crouched around a market square, where wind-up pigs and cows troughed in the fountain.

Soldiers were descending from all sides, the village the scene of the battle.

'Take cover!' Emil cried, and one of the boys shuffled his soldiers into a barn. 'Enter the fray!' he exclaimed, waving at another boy about to deposit his soldiers to the battle. 'Keep tabs on your sergeants, on your captains and mercenaries! You there—' he waved at a nervous boy, who was opening a package his mother had purchased and finding a rag-tag set of soldiery within '—those soldiers were peasant farmers just two days gone, but they'll need to see battle. Then—' Emil whipped out another package, which he gave to the boy. Inside were tiny pantaloons, leather jerkins, private's tunics and redcoats. '—dress them as you see fit, as they rise up through your ranks! This is the *Long War*, boys, and it is only just beginning!'

Emil threw his arms out. Battle was being joined all around him. Boys had dragged their mothers to the counters, rushed back with their new toys and set them loose at once. Above him, the great banners of THE LONG WAR! were held aloft by patchwork robins. The walls of the glade were built from boxes that boys might buy. They said Kaspar had enough imagination for an entire Emporium, but they had never seen this. In one box a troop of medieval knights were waiting to be wound up, ready to joust. In another were horse dragoons and musketeers; in another, Roman legionnaires. The boxes of the new Long War game came with a set of soldiers ready for battle, but boys could get together with their friends and make armies as big as the imagination allowed. This was *how*, Emil knew as he let himself be borne up by the excitement around him. There might not have been true magic in the glades, the children here might not have been witnessing the impossible – but this was magic, all the same. Not the showmanship of Kaspar and his ostentatious toys, but the simple showmanship of business. The ordinary magic. *This* was how he might be remembered.

Emil was so engrossed that he did not notice, at first, the women who had entered the glade and looked disapprovingly down on the battle. There were five of them, four matrons and one woman much younger, dressed in grey finery with huge white collars. The younger woman had a most severe look, elegant and cold, with hair that was turning from blond to a brilliant white and eyes almost as pale. It was she who set foot in the battlefield, to the consternation of the boys whose soldiers were about to meet. The cries of foul play went up around them, boys scrambled to right their soldiers – and Emil, who was already referring to the *Rules of Engagement* inside each Long War box, did not notice that it was to him that the woman was purposefully striding.

'Sir?' she began.

'One moment, madam, this is an emergency ...'

'There is one more emergency at hand, good sir.'

Emil looked up from his notes and was perplexed to see the woman standing imperiously above, like she was the goddess and he the lowly soldier sent out to do battle. Pinched between her fingers stood a single white feather. It trembled in the warm Emporium air.

All of his world zoned in on that single feather. The rest of the Emporium faded. When it returned, Emil saw that some of the boys had stopped making battle to stare at him. He came to his senses with a resounding crash.

'We are representatives,' the woman began, as if reading from a hymn sheet, 'of the Order of the White Feather. We are the champions of fairness and courage. We who are forbidden from defending our King and Country must do our part nonetheless. And it is with this ambition that I present this feather to you, as a mark of your cowardice, your lack of brotherhood, your childishness, that you are not with our fathers and brothers, defending the realm.'

The feather was in Emil's fingers before he could reply, the woman turning on her heel to join her elders, who had been looking admiringly on.

That feather, that *white* feather – and it hadn't even belonged to a swan! It had been torn from the wing of some scrubbed-out seagull, its quill still marked with the poor bird's blood.

He felt the eyes of every boy playing his Long War on him. That *they* should think him a coward was the most injurious of all. Letting the feather slip through his fingers (it floated dreamily over the battlefield; the toy soldiers must have thought it some angel from above), he took off at a run.

The women were already marching back along the aisle. They had handed a white feather to one of the Emporium customers as well, a boy barely out of short trousers who had (to his playmate's horror) been gazing up at the dancing ballerina bears when the Order descended.

They were leafletting too. Handing *leaflets* out in his Emporium! Emil tore one from the hand of a stunned mother as he cartwheeled past.

*

TO THE YOUNG WOMEN OF LONDON!
Is your best boy wearing khaki? If not, don't <u>YOU THINK</u>
he should be?
If he does not think that you and your country are worth
fighting for – do you think he is <u>WORTHY</u> *of you?*
If your young man neglects his duty to King and Country,
the time may come when he will <u>NEGLECT YOU</u>
JOIN THE ARMY TO-DAY!
*

Emil tore it into a thousand shreds, cast it all around him to join the confetti snow. Then he ploughed after the woman, up into the half-moon hall.

'I don't have to explain myself to you. This is my Emporium, *mine*, and you're here at my consent or not at all. But, since you've flaunted your way in here to make your accusations, I'll have you know this: I was the first to sign up. I was at the recruiting office when summer was still high. I'd be in France now, doing my part for my King and my Country, if they would have had me. Coward? Walk into my Emporium and call me a coward? I'm no coward, madam. My name is Emil Godman and, what's more, I am no one's *young man*. I am nobody's, do you hear? I'm not in danger of neglecting a soul, because I don't have a soul I could neglect! Do you understand!?'

The woman had stopped in the doorway, while her elders streamed out into Iron Duke Mews. She turned. Now that she was alone, without those harridans on her shoulder, she did not look as imperious, nor as severe. Her pale eyes were even beautiful, Emil thought, and that was such a terrible thing to have noticed.

'Nobody?' she asked, and Emil stood there dumbly, wondering what on earth she could have meant.

By special dispensation, and in accordance with the benefits of its Royal Warrant, Papa Jack's Emporium opened long into the night. The sounds of games being played, the roar of a winter dragon, all of this carried out into Iron Duke Mews and the quiet cityscape beyond. Joy was infectious and London deserved its joy, in this of all winters.

When the shopfloor was finally silent – and Sally-Anne leading the shop girls in their nightly parade of the aisles, rooting out any adventurers hoping to hide out overnight – Cathy slipped through the refracting snowflaks and up the servants' stair. As was his habit, Papa Jack had not been there to watch over opening night (though perhaps he watched through his phoenix's eyes, entangled with the spyglass hanging over his workshop hearth). The toymaker remained in his workshop, spiriting new creations into being – and that was where Cathy found him, with his hands deep in the innards of some patchwork beast.

'A spider,' he said as Cathy stepped through. 'A giant, to hide in the cellars and scare boys adventurous enough to venture down. Perhaps, a legend to last the winters to come …'

Cathy strode across the workshop and, before Papa Jack lifted himself from the beast, she cast the bundle of Kaspar's letters on to the trunk at his side. There they splayed open, Kaspar's florid hand across each: *Mrs K. Godman, Papa Jack's Emporium, Iron Duke Mews.*

'He's lying to me. He's been lying all along. Robert Kesey is dead. Who knows how many more?' She did not tremble, for she had done her trembling now. 'None of them made it home by first frost, so it isn't as if they're the only ones who lied. The whole world is living a lie, one that nobody cares to acknowledge. It will be fast, they told us. It's barely even a war. Who would dare stand up to our brave British boys …' She paused. 'I'm afraid for him, Jekabs – but, if all these letters are lies, if he daren't tell the truth, well, then he doesn't care for me at all.'

Papa Jack stood, the gears in the spider's chest winding down. 'Hush now, Cathy, he's your Kaspar. Don't call them lies. Instead, call them … fancies. Hasn't Martha slept more easily at night, knowing her papa's safe and sound? Haven't you?'

Cathy was about to reply when something stalled her. 'You ... knew?'

Sighing, he sank into his chair. The arms rose up to give him comfort.

'My boy has been writing to me as well.'

Secrets, thought Cathy with a curse. Her life in the Emporium had been secrets before – but only secrets shared, never secrets between them.

'You must understand the position he's in. Do you think they would let him write with such news? No, you'd receive letters scoured out, big lines of black. It is an act of love, Cathy, truly it is. What good would knowing—'

'He told you, didn't he?'

'I am his father.'

'I am his *wife*. He'd have me thinking he's out there, basking in a rose garden, tasting borage and mint, until the day his letters don't come and, instead, there's a telegram at the door, some secretary writing for some general, and that's it, the end of Kaspar's life, the end of my family. Just like it happened for Robert Kesey.'

She marched back to the door.

'Cathy, don't you—' Papa Jack opened his hands, taking in the letters she had left behind.

'Keep them,' she said. 'What use are they to me?'

She was already in the hallway, among hanging jack-in-a-boxes and dismembered clowns, when Papa Jack begged her to stay. Cathy had never liked the sound of Jekabs Godman uncertain of himself, and it was this that compelled her to turn around. Back in the workshop, he was lifting something from the trunk where he kept his winter toy. He grasped a little leather journal in his hands, the stub of a pencil dangling from it on a ribbon.

'I made them for my sons, the year the Emporium opened. Oh, they were secretive little boys, and me barely a father, so long had I been missing from their lives. All they truly had was each other. They had their own language, a feral little tongue I could no more understand than the English around me. This journal, this one you're holding, this was Emil's. The other Kaspar took with him. I entangled the two together, you see. Go now, open it up. See for yourself ...'

On the first page were the words, DOES IT WORK? and, below that, in Kaspar's very particular scrawl, IT REALLY DOES! PAPA IS A GENIUS! The pages after had been torn out, perhaps in some childhood pique. The next were all filled with Kaspar's hand – and yet the date he had scratched out at the top read 31 August 1914, the very night he had left.

'How can that be?'

Papa Jack rolled his fingers, urging her to turn the pages.

Here was more of Kaspar's writing, more and yet more: 2nd September. 19th. 1st October. 2nd, 3rd, 4th. Pages and pages were filled with his missives. She saw Robert Kesey's name leap out. Robert Kesey is dead.

'He writes to you in it,' said Cathy, 'he sends you letters through his journal ...'

'One more of the old toys you know about, now. One more secret. I built these so that my sons could whisper secrets to each other from one end of the Emporium to the other, or tell stories in the dead of night. Mostly they used it to taunt each other in that Long War of theirs – but boys, as the English say, will be boys. They forgot about them, in the end. Well, there were so many other new toys in those days. Every season some new fascination for them to explore ...'

Papa Jack returned to the floor, where he delved again into the belly of the giant beast.

'Jekabs ...'

'Take it,' he said. 'He hasn't hidden a thing from me. I can assure you of that. It's all in there, if you want to see it, all of Kaspar Godman's war.'

THE TOYMAKER'S WAR

PAPA JACK'S EMPORIUM, NOVEMBER 1914–AUGUST 1917

Sirius was waiting for her when she returned to her bedroom. Perhaps he recognised the journal from Kaspar's boyhood days, for he nosed at it with his cross-stitched snout. 'Off with you now,' said Cathy, first making certain his motors were wound. If she was going to do this, she was going to do it alone.

The Emporium at night could be an eerie place, in winter most of all. You could hear the skittering of toys left wound up, and the shop hands – those not making merry hell in the Palace – still roamed the aisles, readying for the morning rush. But Cathy locked the door, remained in her own private world – and, when she found the courage, opened the journal. Kaspar's handwriting was so like him, elegant and wild, full of bold flourishes and curls.

My papa, I had not known you kept our old journals, but when you pressed this into my hands the morning I left our beloved Emporium, I felt a rush of such nostalgia I cannot set it down in words. But perhaps you know it. I treasured this collection of paper and thread once, and I will treasure it now, as I head into the unknown. My papa at my side! Promise me that you will keep what news you can from Cathy and Martha. To them I send missives of love. To you, who have seen so much more than me, the truth unvarnished.

We have completed our training and embark for Belgium before dawn. Tonight Douglas Flood and I play cards against Robert Kesey and Andrew Dunmore, but I have been forbidden from dealing the pack (they consider me a conjuror). It has been strange to be away from our Emporium for more than a night, and for myself I find it stranger still to remember there was a time when the Emporium was not home. For the boys I travel with, tomorrow will be their first taste of foreign air. They ask me about the world as if I know anything of it, when the truth is that, to me, those years before the Emporium are a dream.

Stranger still is being without Emil. We dedicate meals to him (the food is not near Mrs Hornung's delectable standard, but Emil would like it all the same), and think of him often. No doubt you find it some comfort that he remains to look over the shopfloor and cultivate marvels this summer, and I admit I find it some comfort that he will be there for Cathy and Martha as well, but I remember the look in Emil's eyes when the physicians declared him exempt. Of course, they say we shall be home by Christmas, and – adventuring aside – it is that which I hope for. I should like to see Martha marvelling at opening night, and wake with Cathy to give her our gifts come Christmas morning.

There was more. Kaspar described his training in details meant to delight his father, lampooning the other recruits and singing the praises of every Emporium shop hand – who, or so Kaspar professed, showed dexterity beyond the requirements of mortal man, and thus had proven themselves particularly adept at fixing a bayonet, patching a sand-bag, and shoeing a malcontent horse.

> *Shoeing a stallion is quite different from appending a runner to a rocking horse, but in the end it is not nearly as difficult. Do you remember the Arabians we built for the Christmas of '99? I recall them as more dastardly than any warhorse I am likely to meet. And this reminds me, Papa: Douglas Flood has been assigned as an ostler's assistant. It means he must shovel manure all day. Not a duty with which he ever had to contend in the Emporium corrals ...*

The next time Kaspar wrote he was in Belgium, where the 7th Division had arrived too late to prevent the fall of Antwerp and had turned, instead, toward the Flemish town of Ypres, already overrun. Cathy knew the town only from the stamps on the bails of linen delivered to the Emporium doors, but the image she had of it proved to be remarkably similar to Kaspar's own: a tumbledown town of stone walls and turrets, more weathered and steeped in history than any model village or foldaway fortress the Emporium had ever made. It was here, Kaspar declared, that the Division would halt the enemy's advance. And,

> *Tell me about Cathy. She has written to me that all is well, that Martha remains proud of her Papa and*

makes pictures of me each night. But – what is the truth,
Papa? Are they well?

Cathy almost shut the journal then. The temptation to cast
it across the room was almost insurmountable. 'You'd have
known, if only you'd asked,' she whispered, and her vitriol
showed itself in spittle showered across the page. Wherever
Kaspar was now, perhaps the ink in his own journal was
smearing just as the ink in this.

On the next page Papa Jack had written, for the first
time, back to his son.

My Kaspar, how good it feels to see your words. The
Emporium continues as you can imagine, with
long days and nights, empty of everything but the
invention. I will keep my promise, my boy, and say
nothing of our communications to Cathy and Martha
– yet perhaps you do them little credit, for they are
thinking of you and know you too well to believe in
the fairy tales you send.

Your patchwork dog whimpers at your bedside at night,
but Martha and Cathy are keeping it warm.

Sometimes the missives came in a flurry. Other times, there
were weeks between each and Papa Jack filled the silences
with quiet reports of interludes at the Emporium. As Papa
Jack wrote of the patchwork spider he was planning, Kaspar
found himself marching the flat lowlands of the Belgian
border, those farms and coppices of ancient Flanders. '*It is a*
challenge to reach the sea,' he declared, with the glee of one

boy defying another to beat him in a race, '*and by this many battles will be saved.*'

Cathy's breathing stilled as she read the next pages. For Kaspar had not reached Ypres, not without seeing his very first battle. Those same farms and coverts that he described so gaily, that was where he had first fired a gun. And, '*It was not nearly as I had thought, Papa,*' was all that he wrote. '*Yet now we have reached Ypres. Through the darkness we can hear them in the fields, but the town is ours ... and it is here I shall spend my opening night.*'

The next letter described the Division at rest as winter approached. Ypres was a welcome distraction from the camps and barns they had barracked in on the march. There were beds and soft linen and (Cathy winced) French girls in the beer halls at night. There was food, as well, better food than the tins and dried army rations on which they had marched. Not Mrs Hornung's Emporium fare, that much was true, but delectable all the same.

> *Papa!* (read the following page) *First frost across Ypres. What magics on opening night?*

And, beneath that, in Papa Jack's own hand:

> *Alas, no frost across the Emporium roofs! You are not so very far away, my son, but winter keeps its own pace. Be safe and be warm.*

She had startled at the thought of Kaspar seeing battle, but it was the idea that, for the very first time, Kaspar had known a different first frost to the Emporium that made Cathy soften toward him. She looked at the date Kaspar had scrawled at the top of this missive. Two weeks had passed since that date – and she pictured him, standing on the ramparts (did they have ramparts in Ypres?) and gazing out over Flanders fields, bejewelled in white. How homesick he must have felt, even with the shop hands around him.

All the same, the next pages revealed Kaspar content with his lot. He professed his fears for Cathy and Martha often – but, of Ypres and the villages behind the front where the Division made its barracks, he spoke in glowing terms.

> *I am making us toy soldiers, Papa. Little trinkets to sit in our barracks or carry with us on patrols. Nightly we must walk them and a man can feel awfully alone, marching in file through farms and forest he does not know. A toy soldier in a pocket can be great comfort. It tells us we are part of a tribe. I wonder, Papa, about the years you spent in the frozen East, and what your toy soldiers meant to you ...*

He spoke, too, of the days spent digging the line, reshaping the land. Robert Kesey had struck up a romance with a local girl. They had no language in common, but Kesey delighted her with a patchwork mouse he had secreted in his packs.

Two days after the first frost in Flanders came a declaration from Papa Jack.

> *This year we have a new friend to work the shopfloor. Perhaps you will not remember Wolfram Siskind, who until this summer worked his chocolatiers' in a little Bond Street mews – but I can assure you, your ten-year-old self*

thought his shop an extravaganza to set our Emporium to shame. You will recall the scenes outside the German embassy, how they threw rocks and lay the little red door to siege? I am afraid Wolfram suffered a similar fate and, since the summer, his shop has been lain to waste too many times. So, for this winter only, he will sell his concoctions of chocolate and honey and spun sugar from a grotto here on our own shopfloor. The truth is, Wolfram has struggled in his work for some time. He is an artiste in his chosen form, but across time his spun sugar mice, his chocolate hawks, his bears sculpted from toffee and nuts have grown so that they feel too real – and not even the most merciless child could bring themselves to eat them. Instead, they take them home and make them beds from cotton wool, or keep them in their doll's houses as toys. For Wolfram it is a triumph, but one suspects his creditors take a different approach. Whatever we can do to help him, we will. You would find him a man after your own heart.

Your loving Papa.

The next page was filled with a scrawl so fierce that Cathy was taken aback. There was violence in that hand. Beneath it there had once been words, but Kaspar had scoured them out so deeply not even their impressions remained, only a spiralling chaos of black ink.

On the next page, the words could be read, but the hand still unsteady:

On patrol this night Robert Kesey dropped dead by my side. His body will be laid to rest come the dawn. We returned fire into the pitch of night and, Papa, I have killed my first men. Do not tell me a German could ever be after my own heart.

To which Papa Jack had simply replied:

Never forget – once upon a time, those men played with toys too.

And it put Kaspar Godman to such shame that he had not written since, not even when his father begged and begged and begged.

It was late when Cathy closed the journal. The clock on the wall, with its manifold faces, told her it was after three. Frost had grown in fractures across the window glass, winter starting to harden. It would, at least, bring custom to the shopfloor.

She ventured out, and into the rest of the Godmans' quarters. In the workshop the fire had burnt down to embers, and Papa Jack was asleep in his chair. It was so rare that he retired to his bed, not in these long months of winter. She was about to replace the journal on his lap, when his inkpot and pen caught her eye. And, damn it, why *shouldn't* she? She was his *wife*. She picked up the quill and pressed it to the page.

Kaspar, she wrote, I <u>know</u>.

Beneath it she signed her name. Then, because her anger had faded with the night, she forced in the words 'my love', cramped up so that he might still think it an afterthought.

In her dreams that night were patchwork dogs and razor wire. Kaspar Godman had a contraption in his back and Robert Kesey had to wind it up so that Kaspar could march. She woke in a cold sweat, and another Emporium day began.

The gall of the white feather was nothing compared to the gall Emil felt on seeing its giver again – and yet, the next day, as he stood god-like over more battles of the Long War, there she was, watching him from an alcove between the aisles. It was most distracting. It had taken only a day for the rumours of the new Long War game to spread across the schoolyards of London town. Boys had dragged their mothers to the Emporium directly after their school days finished. Others, Emil knew, would be planning trips from Gloucester and Cirencester, Edinburgh and the Yorkshire Wolds. Pilgrimages from far and wide, all to see his soldiers, and there *she* was, like a ghost at his feast.

One boy had tugged on his hand and told him how he wanted a troop of soldiers *just like my daddy*, and this had given Emil the biggest thrill of his life.

When Emil could stand it no more, he stepped from his pedestal, called the boys battling away to a parley, and told them he would be back soon.

For a time it was enough not to be in her line of sight. He worked at the register, wrapping presents, and in the work found his composure – except, when he looked up, there she was again, lined up in the queue with all the other shoppers. By the time she got to the front the blood was roiling in his veins.

'Hello,' she ventured. 'Sir?'

There was only so long Emil could keep his head down.

'You haven't asked me my name.'

Emil snapped, 'I'm aware of it. I hadn't planned to. I'd planned to order you out of my Emporium, but we don't turn a soul away. It's one of our dictums.'

'Dictums,' she said, with a smile. 'Emil Godman, you have the quaintest turn of phrase.'

This only infuriated him more. He had so few words.

'As a matter of fact, I've come to tender an apology. I have a cousin on the Board. I verified your record. You're no coward, Emil Godman.'

This caught Emil almost wholly off-guard. He fumbled with wrapping paper, tied his hands to a box of the Long War with ribbon.

'My name is Nina Dean. I'm afraid I was … too eager. I would like to make restitution.'

Restitution, thought Emil. *You have such a* formal *turn of phrase.*

'What kind of restitution?'

'I was thinking of a home-cooked dinner, from one supporter of King and Country to another.'

'If you hadn't guessed, this is my busiest time of year. A home-cooked dinner indeed!'

Emil snorted, imitating disgust, yet even now he was thinking of roast potatoes on a plate, gravy thick with dripping, bread and butter and …

'Then I might cook for you here.'

'I think Mrs Hornung may have a *moment* at the thought of a stranger rifling in her larder.'

Miss Nina Dean returned Emil's snort, turned on her heel, and marched away. Still flushing red, Emil returned to his wrapping. Only now did he realise how his heart was pounding. He was glad she was gone, he was sorry he was gone, and the two were curdling into the most unholy grumble in his stomach. A shadow fell across him. 'Yes?' he snapped – and, on looking up, saw that it was none other than Miss Nina Dean, her arms laden down with dozens of boxes of soldiers.

She deposited them on the counter with a crash.

'I shall take them all, these and a hundred more. My aunts and I shall deliver them to the boys' homes, for they're bound to swell this year when fathers stop coming home. And I shall want a dozen boxes of ballerinas as well. Dainty ones, who can spin *en pointe* and hold perfect *arabesques*. And *then* – then, after you're done with your wrapping, done with your *harrumphing* and general discontent, *then* you can accept my apology, consent for me to cook for you, and *look me in the eye.*'

Emil's gaze shot up. His whole body was quaking.

'Does that sound like a thing you might do for me?'

And Emil said, 'Yes. Yes, I suppose it does.'

My papa is a scoundrel, wrote Kaspar. *I had sworn him to secrecy and took it as a pledge. But there you are, dear Cathy, dancing across the page. As fortune had it, I was awake and staring at the page as the words appeared. I followed you with every etch of the pen. And I know you were angry, Cathy. It was there, in the rush of ink. So, first of all, let me say now how sorry I am. I wanted to spin you a yarn, a tale of adventure, but that is not what life is, and I should have known that from the first. So, now that you are here, every unvarnished thing ...*

She could not remain bitter, not for long. Bitterness was a kind of privilege afforded to those in better times – and how could she be bitter, when at least he was still alive, and Robert Kesey cold in the ground.

I have missed you Kaspar. That is all. And I want nothing but the truth. I want to know you.
The truth.
And nothing but the truth.

The truth, Mrs Godman. But my truth is dull these past days. We are sent down and behind the line, leaving others in the 7th to their patrols. To be a soldier, it appears, one must stomach long bouts of nothings and short bursts of every thing in the world. Tell me news of the Emporium, Cathy. Tell me something I can tell the boys. We have already missed opening night ...

So much to tell, thought Cathy, but where to begin? She watched as Kaspar's words materialised and thought: he needs some levity, he needs some hope. And what better hope than this?

Emil, she wrote, and hesitated on the word, *is falling in love.*

It was the dawn of December, two weeks since she invaded the Emporium kitchens to make good her apology to Emil, and Cathy thought she had seen Miss Nina Dean every day since. If she was not there when the doors first opened to wish Emil a good day, she was there in the afternoon, on her hands and knees in the Long War glade, first learning the rules of the game and then directing others. On the second of the month, when London hunkered under its first real snowfall of the season, Cathy gazed out from one of the galleries and saw her leading one army, a gaggle of boys around her, while Emil led the opposing force. Emil's cries of celebration at routing one of her units flurried up into the Emporium dome.

'I haven't seen him as elated, not even when he used to play with Kaspar.'

Mrs Hornung was at her side, her face screwed up in concentration. 'Do you trust her?'

The question gave Cathy pause.

At first I was uncertain, she wrote to Kaspar that night.

To waltz in here as she did and call Emil a coward, right there in front of his customers — well, that is a slight from which it must be hard to recover. And yet recover from it he has! It helps that she is forthright, it helps that she brooks no nonsense, it helps that she is more sure of herself than almost any other lady I have met. In truth, she can seem more like mother to Emil than she does admirer. Her affiliation with the Order of the White Feather, Emil explains, was at the insistence of her aunts, that coven who marched in here on opening night and witnessed Emil's humiliation. When quizzed upon it, Emil insists that it took more courage to return to the Emporium and make amends than it did to come in with an accusing finger — and on that he is correct. And *yet Mrs Hornung's words have stayed with me today and they linger still. Miss Nina Dean has a cold exterior, but sometimes the light shines through. Certainly, had she no genuine affection for Emil, she would not have spent today on her hands and knees battling with toy soldiers. It cannot be her interest, so she must do it solely for him. And when I catch myself asking why, I must stop and scold myself. For why shouldn't a woman look at Emil and feel the same things I first felt that summer you helped me stowaway in the Wendy House walls? Do I think so little of Emil to deny him even that? What kind of a friend, of a <u>sister</u>, would that make me? So, yes, I do trust Miss Nina Dean. I choose to trust her because Emil chooses to trust her. That should be enough.*

In the morning, when she checked the journal again, Kaspar had made just three marks. '!!!' he had scribbled – and, in his next missive, told her of the moment he broke the news to the Emporium boys.

First they roared with surprise, and then they roared with delight. Please convey our best wishes to my brother and tell him: if there is no band on her finger, nor new children to roam our Emporium halls, by the time the Peace has arrived, he must forfeit his birthright and cede me every last aisle!

They wrote more sporadically as Christmas approached. Perhaps Kaspar's days were too exhausting, for Cathy's certainly were. The new shop hands, inexperienced as they were, ran her ragged, and when she sank into bed at the end of each night, it was all she could do to write the words '*I love you*' in the journal, then fall asleep with its pages pressed up against her face.

The snowdrops came late on the Emporium terrace that year, January already gone by the time the shoots opened up into perfect white jewels. Emil, who held them in the palm of his hand, stepped back through the plate glass doors, crossed the Godmans' quarters and went out on to the gallery beyond. Every season ended with this same plummeting feeling in the pit of Emil's stomach, but this year it was more terrible than most – for there, in the glade of the Long War, Miss Nina Dean was laying out soldiers for a battle of epic proportions and boys (and girls; Miss Nina Dean was drawing more and more girls into the glade) were choosing sides.

He lifted the Imperial Kapitan out of his pocket and set him to marching on the balcony rail.

'I'll have to talk to you,' he said. 'There isn't anyone else.'

The Imperial Kapitan lifted his arm, as if in salute.

'If she goes away now, she might not come back next winter. It'll be off to Society and those harridan aunts of hers and … next year, who's to say she'll even think of our Emporium at all?'

So what are you waiting for? he thought, unable to voice it even to the Imperial Kapitan. Down below, Miss Nina Dean had started up the battle. She shrieked with glee that soared up and reached Emil, even standing so high above. He could, he supposed, march down there right now and say: I should like it, if you were to stay. We need help this

year more than any, and you have already proven yourself
so adept ...

His eyes revolved to find the Wendy House, where it still
sat between the paper trees. He could see its steepled roof
between the branches. Only Kaspar knew how the branches
sprouted fresh leaves each summer – but in winter they were
skeletal as trees in the wild, revealing the Wendy House
beneath. Kaspar had never got much further in learning how
their father stretched out the space inside (that summer his
toyboxes were abandoned, because he had a baby to care for,
and babies eclipsed everything else, even toys ...), but the
Wendy House remained the most magical of all places on the
shopfloor. Not just, Emil thought, for the way it staggered
and amazed when you stooped through its door. There was a
different sort of magic attached to the Wendy House now, one
from which no one could escape. What a perfect story: Kaspar
and Cathy and the Wendy House where they used to live.

Sometimes thinking of her just spirited her into being –
and, as if by magic, Cathy appeared far below. On seeing
her, Emil had to tighten his hold on the balcony rail. He
tried to force himself to look back into the glade, but his
eyes (such treacherous things!) kept drifting back to Cathy.
He remembered visiting her in that Wendy House as well.
The books he had read, when he thought *he* might be the
only one holding her hand as she—

His knuckles whitened. He thought he heard the
Imperial Kapitan cry out – *Stop being a fool, Emil!* – but
it was only the sound of his own conscience, drumming
against his skull, trying to get out.

Because – what do you really think is going to happen,
Emil? That this winter, this winter you rule the Emporium

floor, she'll see what she didn't back then? That she'll come knocking late at night and tell you she was wrong, that it should have been you, you to help her push Martha out into the world, you to curl around her in bed at night, you to take her hand and marry her, down there in the paper trees? Or (and he hated himself, even as he thought it), are you really thinking … what if he didn't come home? What if Kaspar stays out there, just like Robert Kesey, and she needs you – needs *somebody*, but it just happens to be you – to fill the place where he used to lie, a faux-Kaspar, a shadow, something to cling on to, something to fill the void … *Is that really what you think?*

She wouldn't even have to change her name.

It was an effort, but he stared at Nina until he was certain Cathy had passed from sight. And he realised, then, what he had never realised before. This jealousy had started out for Cathy, but the feeling had blossomed and changed. He was jealous of it all now, of Kaspar being a father, of the games he played with Martha, of … I never had a mama, thought Emil, but I've always wanted to be a father. Even as a boy I would think of one day having boys of my own, and playing with them on the carpets as my papa played with me.

So, yes, he thought, perhaps there is a different way of looking at life … and, in the same moment he thought that, Miss Nina Dean looked up from the shopfloor. She had the look of a sculpture and she had caught his eye.

The Emporium (Cathy wrote) *is closed for another winter, but there remains great excitement. Emil is to be married.*

ROBERT DINSDALE

*Perhaps you are not surprised, given all the stories I have
brought to you, but to us in the Emporium it remains
a great shock. On the day the snowdrops flowered,
Emil cornered me in the storerooms and – can you
believe this? – asked my permission. I believe it was only
his nerves manifesting. Dear, sweet Emil will never
conquer those nerves! He needed my emboldening to give
him courage and, duly bolstered, he arrested Miss Dean
before she left by the Emporium doors, and led her to the
gallery above the Emporium dome. Then, at his signal,
Mrs Hornung – who was in place in the aisles below –
pulled a cord that wound up a hundred soldiers at once.
High above, Nina saw them march out – and there,
according to Emil's design (what geometries it must
have taken to make it happen!), they wound to a halt
in such a way to spell out his proposal, Will You Marry
Me?, in letters across the Emporium floor. I am pleased
to say that Nina wept openly, there and then. Through
her tears, she agreed to be Emil's wife.*

*There is secret history to this. Nina's brother, Emil tells
us, perished at the defence of Muscat. Their grandfather
has interests in Arabia and had been tutoring his
grandson there when hostilities were declared. He
served bravely as an officer, at only twenty-one years of
age, and lost his life in that service. The tragedy has
hardened Nina to what she wants from life. This, she
knows now, is our brother Emil. She has spent the last
weeks in cleverly disguised misery that the end of the
season might be the end of their relations. Now she will*

stay with us all summer long and be welcomed to our Emporium famille.

Cathy sent the dispatch expecting a reply as soon as Kaspar opened the journal, but by fall of night none had come. She lost herself, that morning, in joining Martha for her lessons; then, in the afternoon, they threw themselves into the brave task of accounting for the winter's takings before the man from Lloyd's arrived for his annual account. When no reply had come by fall of next night, the fear she had been holding at bay finally broke through. Now she stood on the threshold of Papa Jack's workshop, wondering whether she dared venture in, if what she was about to say might tear apart his world.

At last she found her courage, marched into the workshop – and there Papa Jack slept, his phoenix on his shoulder, Sirius curled up at his feet. He looked so like Kaspar when he slept and something in the image soothed her. She slunk back to her quarters alone, looked in on Martha as she too slept, and lay back in the marital bed.

In the morning, letters reeled across the journal page:

Cathy, please forgive my silence. I am delighted for my brother and wish to fill these pages only with good tidings and salutations for Emil's future wife. I know I will find my home much changed when I return to you. But I can keep the truth from you no longer. I am writing to you from the base hospital at Arras, behind the line. But Cathy – I am alive.

It was the way Kaspar's hand had trembled upon writing that final line, causing the letters to tumble uncontrolled across the page, that stopped Cathy's heart. She sat upright, raced to read on.

By the time the snowdrops had flowered on the Emporium terrace, Private Kaspar Godman had become Lance Corporal, with the Emporium shop hands and a group of other men under his command. Spring had brought with it the thaw that closed the Emporium doors, and it was this same thaw that returned Flanders to open war.

Cathy, they came for us. We had long thought it was coming and waited, each night, for the horns to sound. But when it finally happened, they did not send men. They sent great reefs of gas, ghosts to do their bidding. When men set their minds to it, they accomplish the most terrible things.

Kaspar had not been on the line on the day the gas first came, but he had watched from behind as the French soldiers staggered through. Some had run, cascading out of the little hamlets they had taken oaths to defend. Others, too trusting or too defiant to understand, had stood their ground. But battle could not be fought against an enemy invisible to the eye, and hundreds had perished there, amid the budding leaves of spring, before any had understood what was happening. Kaspar had watched the ambulance wagons flowing, like a line of ants, into the west.

And I wondered, Cathy, how many men made it to their beds, or how many were left in the dirt along the way.

Across the next days there were gaps in the line, which men raced to defend, but always that same dirty yellow on the horizon, or the reef breaking through a line of blasted trees. Sometimes, you could see them coming through the smoke, the shapes of those German boys in black. They were stripping what they could from our fallen boys. And I tried to hold on to what my papa said. My men and I were sent to hold a copse of willow at the Salient's deepest point and I was telling myself: they played with toys too. Yet, when the gas came and I saw their shadows loom, it mattered not at all that they had rode on rocking horses or thrilled at tumbling skittles, not when I saw what their gas had done to Andrew Dunmore's lungs. I fired and fired and fired.

I was at the clearing station before I started coughing up blood. And now here I am. Arras is not so far from the line, and yet the streets still stand. Ypres is a ruin, but the ruin is ours. And yet, can it be that my body itself has been conquered? The physician tells me I have my heart, I still have my stronghold, but the salient around me is withered. It is a strange feeling to be weak. But I am alive, Cathy. Isn't that a thing?

Cathy lifted her pen to reply, but her fingers had no grip, and her blood was beating so fiercely that she thought she would better run to France and hold him in her arms than write a single word. She was composing herself when she heard Martha's voice at the door and the girl scrambled in, meaning to lose herself in the hugs and kisses with which every morning began. Cathy embraced her, slipped the journal beneath the bedsheets, and thought: *he's alive, he's alive, he's alive … but for how long?*

Across the next months, the missives flew back and forth between the sleeping Emporium and the base hospital at Arras. Kaspar's recovery was slow. Cathy charted it in how often he wrote, the steadiness of his hand. Summer had already come, and plans for Emil's wedding were in full swing, by the time she saw a change in him. His letters grew long, he was writing in the thick of night, and the passion with which he wrote was evident in the way his pen pressed against the page. Kaspar was energised as she had seen him only once before, that summer when he was first learning to make caverns inside his toyboxes – for, stranded in Arras, co-opted by nurses and orderlies to help ferry around patients more critically wounded than himself, Cathy's husband had returned to his old vocation.

> *I am making toys, Cathy. Toys for the ones who go to sleep at night and will not wake in the morning. Toys for those men I hear crying for their mamas. And might I confess? Cathy, they are the most beautiful toys I have ever built.*

Daily the wounded men came through, and daily they were sent away – back to the line in boots or far from it in boxes.

> *The man beside me died last night. I was holding his hand as he faded – and I think I know, now, what I did not know before. A secret has been revealed, and finally I understand the true meaning of toys, something my*

papa learnt long before me. When you are young, what you want out of toys is to feel grown-up. You play with toys and cast yourself an adult, and imagine life the way it's going to be. Yet, when you are grown, that changes; now, what you want out of toys is to feel young again. You want to be back there, in a place that did not harm nor hurt you, in a pocket of time built out of memory and love. You want things in miniature, where they can better be understood: battles, and houses, picnic baskets and sailing boats too. Boyhood and adulthood – any toymaker worth his craft has to find a place to sit, somewhere between the two. It's only in those borderlands that the very best toys are made. So let me tell you, Cathy, about a new toy I have made ...

There is a moment, before the end, when a man knows he cannot be saved. I have watched some go to it in a state of quiet awe, but that is not the story of most. Most men feel the encroaching dark and rage against it – but a man can no more fight that battle than light can battle shade. In these hospital beds they hold themselves until they can hold themselves no longer; after that, they are men no more. They are like boys with a fever, wanting only to curl up beside Mama, with old blankets on their laps, and be sung to and told stories. What better way for a man to go out than the way he came in? With the milk of mother's love.

It was my papa who taught me how a toy must speak to a grown man, how it must fill him with the simplicity, again, of being a child. Children come to the Emporium for adventure, but adults to be reminded that adventure was once possible, that once the world was as filled with magic as the imagination will allow. Emporium toys have always taken us back in time. And, as I have lain here in Arras, watching my fellows die around me, I have wondered: could a toy comfort a man in his final hours? What if he was not here, rotting in a bed in which another man will rot tomorrow – but twenty years ago instead, curled happily in the crook of his mama's arm, knowing that all is good and right in the world? What kind of a toy could be so perfect as to take him back there, the magic so adept that, for brief snatches of time, he might even forget the reality of his life? What if, in his final moments, those memories were manifest around him? Wouldn't that be the Perfect Toy?

She was not sure why the letter made her uneasy, perhaps only for the idea that Kaspar and Death made such common bedfellows – and were it not for the fact that his next missive was so joyous (for first frost had come early to Arras, and Kaspar's senses were enlivened by the thought of an Emporium in full swing), she might have known it sooner. As Christmas grew close, Kaspar's letters showed him, if not his old self – gleeful and fizzling and bursting with ideas – then at least renewed. After he returned to the line, and found Douglas Flood, John Horwood and the rest, his humours returned; he wrote no more about his Perfect Toy, turning instead to questions of Cathy and Martha and professions of how he missed the shopfloor. It was, it seemed, a restorative to be among Emporium friends once again. But Cathy noticed, in the way his letters still quivered across the page, in the way the words disintegrated as each sentence moved on, until sometimes they were illegible even after many hours of trying, that all was not right with her husband. The lies had started again: the lies of omission, the lies of *keep your head up and soldier on*, forgivable only because, this time, Kaspar was lying to himself as much as he was his wife.

Kaspar's body had survived the gas, but something else, some other part of him, lay bedraggled and maimed, gasping for air.

And still Cathy kept writing, for it was the only thing she could do.

Emil Godman and Nina Dean were married on the morning after the snowdrops flowered, bringing the next Emporium winter to its end. Such a sight it was, to see Emil in his morning suit and Nina in her bridal gown. They spoke their words and made it formal before a city registrar, but Papa Jack raised a chapel on the shopfloor, and into it streamed every shop hand who still survived (along with the ghosts of those who had perished on the way). Emil spoke his vows with a tremble in his voice, Nina with the sharp authority that was her everyday tone. Martha scattered paper flowers in their wake while satin butterflies, released from the insectarium, cavorted overhead.

Emil had no best man (Cathy wrote), *for it would have been you, Kaspar, to stand at his side and settle his stomach in those few hours before the service, when he knew not how to button a shirt, nor how to fasten a tie, nor even how to put one foot in front of another. You would have laughed to have seen him, but you would have put an arm around him too. Instead it was me who dusted his morning suit down (he had spent the morning in his workshop, dressed in all his finery, whittling more soldiers for the sweet release it brings him), me who told him not to put cufflinks into sleeves that were not French cut. Me who told him you would have been proud.*

She told him it all, about how Nina's family had gaped to see the patchwork pegasi soaring in the Emporium dome; about how the toast Papa Jack made harked back to his own wedding day and the wife who was lost while he slaved in the frozen East; how Nina (cold, hard Nina) had shed a tear as Emil told the congregation how he had never envisaged a future as perfect as the future he envisaged now. She did not tell him about the fleeting glance Emil gave her when his speech reached its zenith, for it spoke of indecision, of an instant's hesitation, of an actor at odds with his part; it spoke, she thought, of a stowaway summer long ago, and things that were better left unsaid. She filled pages instead with details of the many-tiered cake Mrs Hornung had prepared, the trinkets Martha had already made in anticipation of the cousins to come. She told him all of these things, and sat up through the night waiting for the letter she was certain would come in response – but that was the first time in all of their writing that Kaspar never wrote back at all.

＊ ＊

DOLLIS HILL TO PAPA JACK'S EMPORIUM, SEPTEMBER 1917

After all this time, Cathy could not get used to riding in a hansom carriage. In her heart, she supposed, she would always be a tram girl – but life, like almost everything else, rolled constantly on. This morning, when she stepped out of the carriage, she felt so ostentatious she could not keep her cheeks from turning crimson. It was not right to come to a place like this dressed in finery, nor to have arrived in so cavalier a fashion.

Dollis Hill House had been built to a grand specification and had lost little of that glamour in the century since. A resplendent farmhouse with whitewashed walls, it looked out across the manicured wild of Gladstone Park. This far out of London the approach was flanked by willows in russet leaf. Some of the convalescents were tending to the estate's empty flower beds and, as Cathy began the long approach, they turned to watch her. Makeshift wooden huts, like the barracks she imagined Kaspar had once called home, had been erected in a horseshoe along the farmhouse's eastern flank.

The sister was there to meet her. Her name was Philomena and she was the daughter of a local teacher, one of those who had been instrumental in initiating the hospital fund back when the war began. That had been three years ago, though the hospital only opened its doors in 1916. 'We only had twenty-three beds at the start,' Philomena explained as she took Cathy into a dimly lit reception area, once the farmhouse porch. 'Now we have seventy-three, and every one of them taken.'

And every one of them needed, thought Cathy. 'My sister is a nurse. She's in Dieppe. It's only through her that we knew. It's hard to put in words but, after a little time, my husband stopped writing at all ...'

It had been a slow process. It happened in stages. One week between missives, then two, then three and four. Once his letters had been long and florid; then they were short, perfunctory things. It got so that he said almost nothing of his days – and that was when Cathy knew for certain that he was in some kind of hell, trapped there, alone, all of the Emporium hands gone from this world and Kaspar left as officer of a group of young boys, some so young they must still have thrilled at trips to the Emporium each Christmas. She had told him, once, that he must never lie to her again, so instead he drew within himself, wrote letters with silly, nonsensical verses for Martha, or wrote not at all. Three summer months had passed without a word when the letter arrived on the Emporium doorstep. It was Martha who had brought it to her, sobbing even before the envelope opened; Cathy had wanted to sob too, for a letter from Arras certainly meant her husband's death. Instead she had found a hand she had almost forgotten: the delicately practised hand of her sister:

Cathy, forgive the brusqueness of this note, but I write on a matter most unexpected and no less urgent. As you know I have been stationed in Dieppe these past months. Two months ago I made an exchange with a nurse close to the line, whose nerves demanded she be relieved from the front. In this capacity I have been nursing in the base hospital in Arras. The work is relentless, the hours long, and perhaps if it was not this way I would have known sooner. But there is a face here you would know well. He awoke from his injuries one week past. I believe he even recognises who I am.

Cathy, you must prepare yourself. He has suffered. But ...

Sister Philomena was disappearing into the twilight of the hospital interior. Coming out of herself, Cathy hurried after.

'Tell me, have you come far?'

'London.'

The Sister paused, as if the information did not tally with what she had been told.

'Please forgive me,' Cathy explained. 'We only discovered my husband was here three days ago. My sister wrote that he would be repatriated to England, but that was all. One of the other convalescents penned us a letter when he arrived here, but it took some time to find us.' The envelope had said EMPORIUM and nothing more, the manic scrawl of a soldier come back from Reims, where – or so he professed – his body had been made an offering to the fire.

'I see,' Sister Philomena said, and Cathy was grateful when they drew to a halt outside the door of what had once been the farmhouse study. 'The doctor will see you now.'

Through the doors sat a physician who Philomena introduced as Norrell. He was a small man, and when Cathy stepped into the study he was buried in reams of papers. After studiously finishing the final leaf, he looked up and said, 'Take a seat, Mrs Godman.'

'I should like to see my husband, if it pleases.'

'And I shall take you to him soon. Lieutenant Godman isn't going far, but first there are things we ought to discuss. Please, Mrs Godman. If the lieutenant is to return home with you this day, and he's professed no resistance to the idea, it's important that you understand.'

What was there to understand? Kaspar was coming back to the place he belonged. Papa Jack's Emporium had been waiting for him for three long years.

The look on Norrell's face compelled her to sit.

'When did you last see Lieutenant Godman, Mrs Godman?'

How she wished they would stop calling him that. Lieutenant Godman, as if he was anything other than the wild-haired boy who had secreted her in the Wendy House all summer long. Anything other than the man who had spent Midwinter's Eve of five years past painfully recreating a lost bear in spider silk and fur, so that Martha would not miss it on her pillow when she awoke.

'I know about his injuries,' she said, suddenly strident. 'But I'm his wife. You'll think it ought to matter, but you don't know me, and you don't know my husband.'

Doctor Norrell gave a simpering look that seemed to say: *they all think that, in the beginning.* But then he said, 'Lieutenant Godman's injuries were not insignificant, yet his body has borne them well. He'll walk again, I'm certain of that. No, Mrs Godman, what I want to talk about are the injuries we do not see.' For a moment he was silent. 'This is a convalescent hospital, Mrs Godman. It is not a hospice.

It is my duty to repair our men and return them to the front, where they are needed most. I'm taught to watch for malingerers, for confidence men, for men of ill honour. But not every wound is one you can stitch together or cut away, and not every man who isn't fit to return is a malingerer. I'm speaking, as you must know, about maladies of the heart. And of the head.'

'My husband isn't mad, Doctor Norrell.'

'Madness is relative. Do you know, in Ypres, they called your husband the God Man? *The* God Man – on account of the things he did that put him in harm's way. His record demonstrates him a ruthlessly efficient leader. He's been promoted and decorated. The boys in his platoon look up to him enormously, and the same cannot be said for many of the NCOs whose paths have crossed mine. And yet ... Mrs Godman, your husband has not breathed a word since the day he arrived. There has been no crack through which I can shine a light, to better understand what goes on behind his eyes. Mrs Godman, you may not want to hear what I have to say next, but it's important that you do. Your husband was dragged from the mire by two of his men. By the time they reached the field station, it had been eighteen hours since the explosion that felled him. He had spent every one of those hours with his head buried in the cavity of his second lieutenant's chest. When the field ambulance reached him, they believed him to be dead. The God Man, they said, dead and gone. And yet he awoke, in the hospital behind the front line. By some miracle, his wounds were not infected. He is still there behind his eyes, Mrs Godman, but there has been no way in. Most of my colleagues would tell you that silence settles the mind, that the lieutenant is doing everything he can to return to himself. But there is another school of thought – and it is my sincere belief – that, for maladies like your husband's, the only cure is in the talking.' Again, he stopped. 'Do you understand my meaning, Mrs Godman? Your husband cannot be cured if he remains hidden inside his own head.'

'What you're saying,' said Cathy, 'is that my husband is here – and yet he's not.'

The doctor laid down his papers. 'Perhaps it is time that you saw the lieutenant for yourself.'

Kaspar was classified as a cot case and, as such, was in the ground-floor ward, among the other bedridden and fresh amputees. Sister Philomena was emerging from the room as they arrived. Inside, makeshift curtain rails divided the beds – and there, propped up in bed with his head hanging down, was the man Cathy had loved for so many years. Lieutenant Godman. The God Man. Her Kaspar.

He was old. That was the thing that struck her. She could see the bones of his cheeks; they gave him the look of a sculpture, though without any of a sculpture's classical poise. Upon his lap sat a wooden box, carved with the fractures of a thousand snowflakes, and on its top a varnished plate spun at the same pace as the crank handle Kaspar's hand was turning. On the plate danced two circus acrobats, mahogany mice in braces and long pantaloons. The melody from the contraption inside was lilting and sad, a nursery rhyme as played by a harpist of great renown. It slowed and sped up, according to the whim of Kaspar's hand.

'Did he make that thing?' Cathy whispered.

'Sister?' called Doctor Norrell – and, at his command, Sister Philomena returned to the room. 'The music box, did the lieutenant …'

'It was in pieces, and part of his packs,' she explained. 'The first days he was here, he rebuilt it out of every last splinter. Sometimes, he lends it to the other men. They're besotted with it. And it's the queerest thing – whenever Lieutenant Godman's without it, he comes out of himself. He gets out of bed, he starts pacing, he *prowls*. I do believe he has an attachment.'

Cathy took three great strides into the ward. Some of the other soldiers revolved to face her, but Kaspar – her poor, beautiful Kaspar – did not flinch; his eyes saw only the twirling mice, his ears heard only that sweet, sad refrain.

'Bring me a cane,' she said. 'I've a carriage waiting outside. Doctor Norrell, my husband is coming home.'

The spyglass was one of Martha's most treasured possessions. Her papa (not her blood papa, who she understood – in the storybook kind of way she understood these things – to have perished in the Aegean) had made it for her. It had an ivory handle in a pearlescent design and, if you pressed one eye to the glass, you could watch everything that was happening through its sister piece, hidden out on Iron Duke Mews. That was how she knew of her mother's return even before the Emporium doors opened. As soon as the spyglass revealed the hansom carriage approaching, she scrambled for the dirigible tethered between the paper trees. She was in the stern, preparing to toss ballast over the side, when Sirius lolloped out of the trees and set up his thin, cotton whimpers.

'Oh, come on then,' she said with a dramatic roll of her eyes – and Sirius, so elated to be included, turned top over tail as she hauled him aboard. Now that they were ready, she threw the last of the sandbags to the Emporium floor, heaved up the tether, and clung on as the dirigible rocketed skywards.

Up they went, up and further up, up past the Wendy House roof, up past the paper branches – and, finally, through the canopy, into the Emporium dome. Martha had flown this route before, but now came the most perilous part. Timing was key. Above her, the cloud castle was hoving into view. When it was almost upon them, she reached out for the rope dangling from its drawbridge. By using her body as an anchor, she slowed the dirigible's rise and heaved it to a mooring by the drawbridge winch. Then, with burning arms and pride in a job well done, she helped Sirius clamber over the side.

Down below, where the empty aisles were draped in dust sheets, the Emporium doors were opening up. The first figure who came through she knew to be her mother, both because of the ostentatiousness of her hat (Martha rolled her eyes) and the day bag hanging over her shoulder. That bag, she knew, had been a gift from her papa – the girl had hidden inside it once, just to see how deep down it could go. The figure who came next was hunched over, dwarfed by the grey greatcoat he wore. In one of his hands he held a cane, which he seemed to be using as a third leg, and he moved with mortifying slowness.

'What do you think?' Martha whispered. 'Is it him?'

Sirius's tail had exploded in delight.

'It is!' she exclaimed. 'Papa! Papa, up here!'

It was her mother's face that looked up. Her papa seemed not to have heard. Surely he couldn't have forgotten the days and nights they'd camped up here, the stories he'd told her, the games they'd played across the cloud castle floor? It was here he'd told her about the birth of Sirius (or at least the first time he'd been wound up), the day he met her mother, the time he'd grown a labyrinth out of his paper trees and got trapped inside it for six days and seven nights, eating only papier mâché fruit to survive. She had doubted the veracity of that last story, but she'd loved it all the same.

From this distance, it was difficult to tell – but it seemed that her mother was glaring. Possibly she was instructing her to stay away, but since she couldn't be sure, she felt no great desire to obey. With one hand still restraining Sirius, she skirted around the castle walls to return to the dirigible. A few more sandbags heaved aboard would send her crashing back through the paper trees. Down, down, down they came. So filled by thoughts of reaching her papa was she, and so distracted by the delirious twirling of the patchwork dog, that she misjudged the landing. The dirigible came down hard, struck the roots of a paper oak, and listed wildly. By the time Martha had picked herself up and checked Sirius for tears to his fabric, the shopfloor was empty again.

Too late, her mother had taken her papa into the quarters above. Martha hesitated before following. All of her excitement had evaporated, and in its wake were only nerves. She stamped her foot. It was not fair. Nerves were what happened to other people.

'Let's make him a present!' she declared. 'Something to welcome him home. Something he can't possibly ignore ...'

ROBERT DINSDALE

Turning on her heel, she marched back into the aisles. 'Well, are you coming?'

Behind her, Sirius looked suddenly downcast. Denied his master's return, he hung his head and sloped after her, grovelling as he came. Human beings, he had decided, were the most inscrutable things.

'Here we are,' said Cathy. 'Might I take your boots?'

Kaspar stopped in the bedroom doorway, tilting his ragged face up to take in the room. Cathy hoped it was stirring something in him, for what he saw was a snapshot of the day he had left the Emporium behind. In the three years since, she had not touched a thing, dusting carefully around each ornament, making certain every toy soldier would be standing to attention just as on the day he had left. If only to have something to say, she bade him sit at the end of the bed.

Levering off his boots was easy. He winced as the shock waves worked through his body, but his legs were weak and they slipped right off. So many parts of his body were unfamiliar. His left foot had only three toes and on the right the ends of each were worn down to stumps. Yet there was a silver lining in every black cloud; Kaspar was so detached that he did not see her recoil, nor how her left hand grappled her right to stop it from lifting to her mouth.

Did he need rest? Did he need air? Did he need company? She had no way of knowing – and so, falling back on the lessons they had learned together as they watched Martha grow, she promised to return with milk for his bedside and a hot water bottle for his bed.

By the time she came back, Kaspar was propped up in bed, an angular form beneath the blankets. In his lap the music box played its lament while the mice danced erratically on top. His head was hanging down, lost in the twirling of the mice, but all around him were splinters and shards of broken wood. Every toy soldier who had stood so proudly on the shelves, waiting for their general to return, was destroyed. All that was left were pieces of painted faces, peering expressionless out of the ruin.

That night, she crawled into bed beside her husband, not knowing if it was the right thing to do. The heat from his body had warmed the sheets and that was the most alien thing. His back was turned to her. She tried to hold him but it felt all wrong. She turned against him and that felt wrong as well. So instead she lay awake. Some time in the night, Kaspar must have woken too (or perhaps he never slept at all?), for she heard the lilting melody of the music box. Soon after that, he returned to his slumber, more peaceful than before. The melody did nothing for Cathy. In the morning she woke and went about her business, but Kaspar remained.

Sometimes he could be seen in the workshop. He took out tools he had not touched in years and tinkered with the music box, then retreated with it to his room, or some unseen cranny of the Emporium floor. The shopfloor itself had changed since he had been gone; Cathy was afraid he'd get lost, but Sirius took to following him at a distance, always ready to lead him back. In the evenings, Mrs Hornung brought him food. At first the plates came back untouched, but soon she understood that he had reverted to the dishes of his boyhood, that he found comfort in those old textures and tastes. After that she made only his *vareniki* and kasha broths. Sometimes Papa Jack sat with him as he ate. Other times Emil came. He was desperate to introduce Kaspar to his wife, to fill Kaspar's head with the stories of the seasons he had missed, but Cathy pleaded with him not to. Kaspar took it all in but said nothing, returning each time to the music box in his hands. Whether it was day or dead of night, his fingers were never more than a whisper away from it. Even when Martha stole through to sit at the end of his bed, he would not acknowledge her. He wound and rewound the music box and lay back, stupefied.

'He doesn't want to be back, does he, Mama?' Martha sobbed as Cathy put her to bed at night.

'Your papa is very unwell, Martha. But one day ...'

'It's the music box. Why does he always listen to the music box?'

Cathy did not know, but she resolved to find out. That night, when he slept, she teased it out of his hands. Without its touch, his sleeping grew fitful. She took care not to wake him and sat at his bedside, her fingers trembling over the crank. Why she hesitated, she did not know, and yet it took some courage before she began to play it. The contraption turned at her command, the mice began to dance, and the music drifted up to bewitch her.

It was a sensation like so many other Emporium toys. The sounds were so perfect, the dance so particular, that she no longer felt like Catherine Godman, twenty-seven-year-old mother and stalwart of Papa Jack's Emporium; the toy had touched her, somewhere deep inside, and now she was Cathy Wray, five or six or seven years old. The edges of the bedroom she shared with Kaspar seemed to evaporate, and out of the haze appeared the furniture and fittings of that little room she and Lizzy used to share, in an age that seemed so long ago. The longer the music played, the more real things seemed, the richer the colours, the deeper the textures. On the bedside sat the copy of *Gulliver's Travels*; on the shelf, the wooden rabbit. She had felt this way once before, that moment many years ago when Papa Jack gave her one of his pinecone ballerinas, and soon the only reason she knew it was not real was because, when she looked down, it was the hand of an adult still turning the handle of the music box.

The music soared and, suddenly, she could perceive the Emporium no longer. Whatever spell the toy was weaving, her childhood had grown solid, undeniable around her. There was movement in the corner of her eye and, when she looked up, the door opened to reveal Lizzy, five years old. By instinct, Cathy opened one arm to receive her. It was then that she saw: she no longer had the arm of an adult. It was a child's arm that reached out to Lizzy. She was wearing the white pinafore dress that her mother kept for Sunday best. Lizzy nestled into her shoulder and Cathy gave in, returning the embrace. 'Let's play, dear Cathy!' Lizzy cried (and the voice, so familiar, echoed in her body). 'Do you remember Polly?' Cathy did; it was the name of a game of skipping they used to play, up and down the estuary sands. She found herself saying, 'But I can't, dear Lizzy.' And, 'Why ever not?' asked her sister. 'Don't you see?' said Cathy. 'I'm not really here. I have to keep winding. If I don't keep winding, none of this exists …'

Her sister looked at her quizzically. 'Winding what, dear Cathy?'

Cathy looked down. By some miracle, both her hands were free. The music still played, but it was distant now, a solemn song at the back of her head – and of the music box, she could see no sign.

'Where is it?' Cathy cried. She leapt to her feet. In her panic she did not see that her arm was adult again. Something in her frenzy had brought it back. She whirled around, spied the music box sitting on the bed and snatched it up. The crank handle had been turning of its own accord. She seized it, stopped it from moving. The mice resisted, determined to dance on, but she held it fast and watched, with relief, as the old bedroom fragmented around her. The last thing she saw was Lizzy's plaintive face, calling out. 'Come back, Cathy. Cathy, come back. Don't you want to play?'

The music stopped. Cathy cast the music box down and, when she looked up, she was in the gloom of the Emporium again. Kaspar whimpered in his sleep, words without form – though their meaning was clear. In his dreams he was three hundred miles away, trapped in a foxhole in the French earth.

She slid back into bed beside him. Now, at least, she knew where Kaspar was whenever he went away. He was twenty years away, in a world without Cathy and Martha, a world without death, a world in which the only wars were waged across the Emporium carpets – back when he and Emil were brothers-in-arms, and if he wanted to stay there, thought Cathy, and live those moments again–well, who was she to say otherwise?

As she lay down, Kaspar called out. He cried for his mama, and somehow his sleeping fingers found the music box where it had landed. Cathy heard that haunting melody again and wished him well on his way.

Stay away from him, Martha, her mother had said. Give him his peace. Lord knows, he's earned it. Well, what about *her*? What had she earned across all those years? Three Christmases without a father. Three birthdays. One thousand nights of going to bed and folding her hands and saying her prayers. Sometimes she had dreamed about him. She'd written little notes, tied them to the leg of a pipe-cleaner bird and hoped it might somehow flutter all the way to France. All that had to count for something, or what was everything *for*?

Martha strained with the bamboo cane in her hand; she strained too hard, and it snapped. No matter – she would just start again. She had resolved that she was going to finish his gift today, and nothing was going to stop her. Accordingly, the Wendy House floor – for it was this that she had designated her workshop – was itself a battlefield, littered with the carcasses of her past attempts. This morning her frustration was mounting. She did not want to give up.

The principle was simple, but only as far as every Emporium toy seemed simple on the surface. A steam train, built from a frame of bamboo, would hurtle along until it crashed headlong into a wall. The resultant explosion would crumple the bamboo in such a particular fashion that, when it sprang back into being, it would now be a locomotive headed in the other direction. In that way, the train could bounce back and forth between two workshop walls all day long. Imagine the games that could be played! Martha thought – but then, upon seeing the wreckage spilled around her, her heart sank. Ambition, Papa Jack had said, was only the first step to producing a perfect toy. After that, you had to have art.

It was, she reluctantly decided, time to get help.

Her mother would not be any use. Papa Jack would be sleeping, so Uncle Emil it would have to be. She found him in his own workshop, whittling yet more toy soldiers out of a great trunk one of the Emporium's foresters had delivered at summer's end. His favourite toy, the Imperial Kapitan, was watching over him as always it did.

'It doesn't work,' she said, depositing the tangle of canes and cotton twine at his feet. 'I know what it's meant to do, so why won't it … do it?'

Emil, who had been too engrossed in his own work, looked up. This was a sentiment he had known all of his life. He set down his lathe, moved aside the paints and pots of varnish, and considered the concoction Martha had brought.

'Let me see,' he began, and sat cross-legged beside her. He lifted the mess, rearranged the canes and joists until it took the form of a locomotive again. She had planned a miraculous design, but it was little wonder she had not made it work. A thing like this took a lifetime's nuance – yet he found himself inordinately proud that she had envisaged it. She was, without doubt, an Emporium girl.

'It's for my papa,' said Martha as Emil continued to fiddle.

'I see.'

'To make him better.'

Emil remained silent, working out a particularly knotty joint.

'What do you think is wrong with my papa, Uncle Emil?'

Emil whispered, 'I don't think I could ever understand.'

'I thought a toy would help. It's what Papa Jack says. A toy can't save a life, but it can save a soul. Well, my papa's alive, but ...'

'*There,*' Emil said, thankful to be bringing the conversation to an end. He set the toy down and now, when Martha looked, it seemed sleeker and more crisply defined than ever. The key in its back would set it running. Martha turned it and watched it fly. Soon, it was hurtling toward the naked wall, its whistle (Martha had not thought of a whistle; it must have been Emil's addition) trilling all the way. She rose to the tips of her toes in anticipation. The train bore down on the wall, there came an almighty crash – and the next thing she knew, the canes had concertinaed, parts fanning out and twisting around. An instant later, the threads binding it all together grew taut, contained the explosion, and the flying parts collapsed back into place. Now, just as she had hoped, the locomotive had reassembled itself, facing in the other direction. It came screaming towards her. She threw her arms around Emil and gushed out her thanks.

As Emil watched her leave, he felt that strange longing again, the one that had been plaguing him ever since Cathy brought Kaspar home. How he hungered to go up there and hold his brother's hand! How he hungered to show him the Long War, to settle down with Kaspar and make mindless battle across carpets, floors and aisles. And yet – something always stopped him, something always held him back. Whatever it was, it would not permit him to sit at Kaspar's side, so he sank back to his workbench, picked up his lathe, and continued his work. Sometimes, it was the only thing that could bring him peace of mind.

With the locomotive cradled in her arms, Martha burst through the bedroom door.

Inside, it smelt of the bedpan and sour milk. Her papa was upright in bed, buttressed by pillows on every side. In his lap, a papery hand, ridged with veins, was turning the handle of the music box; occasionally, as the mice danced, his lips twitched with a smile. Sirius was lying across his feet, guarding his shrunken legs. He eyed her warily, judging if he ought to let her near.

She had decided that she would be strident. And so, ignoring the smell, ignoring the growling of the dog, she strode to the edge of the bed and held up the train. 'Papa, it's for you!'

Kaspar remained as he was, mindlessly turning the crank, but Martha would not be deterred. She set the train down and watched with mounting glee as it exploded against one wall, reassembled itself, and then exploded against another. She watched the volleys three times, cheering with every collision, before she turned back to her father. And still Kaspar remained, lost in the melody and whatever cherished landscapes the box was creating.

He wasn't even in the room, Martha realised. Wherever he was, it was not here.

She leapt on to the bed. Before she knew it, she was straddling him, her two hands grasping the music box and trying to tear it from his lap. She did not realise, until much later, that Sirius had closed his muslin jaws around her leg. He was wrestling with her just the same as she was wrestling with her papa. Despite the way he slumped, there was strength in her father's fingers. Those brittle things would not release the music box, no matter how hard she tried. Even as she fought, he was continuing to wind it. The music billowed up around her.

'Papa!' she screamed and, realising at last that Sirius was mauling her, she kicked out and sent him flying from the bed. 'It's ... for ... you!'

Something cracked inside the music box. At last, she ripped it from his hands. His fingers were left clasping the crank handle, but the box was hers; she flung the wretched thing aside, down past Sirius, down into the path of the unstoppable locomotive. Had she tried, she would still have been too slow to stop it. The steam train whistled in fury and barrelled straight into the stranded box. Canes exploded, strings drew taut, and though the locomotive reassembled to hurtle raggedly in the other direction, the box was no more. Parts of it arced in every direction.

The music was dead, but the silence was oppressive. Martha rocked back, Kaspar still unmoving underneath her.

'Papa,' she repeated, 'it's for you ...'

Still he said nothing. He looked straight through her, and that was when Martha gave up. She clambered off her father, not caring for his cadaverous body underneath the sheets, and tramped back across the room.

She did not take the toy train with her. It had been for her father and, whether he wanted it or not, that was where it would stay. That was what presents were for. Disconsolate, she dropped back to the Emporium floor. She had almost reached the sanctuary of the Wendy House when her mother caught her. Her mother had a sixth sense that told her when she had been crying. She clawed angrily at her eyes, as if that might mask the tears.

'Darling, has something happened?'

Martha could not hold it in, no matter how hard she tried. 'It's my papa. He won't ...'

Her sentence faltered, for another sound was filling her ears. It was the clanking of bamboo pistons, the shrill call of a whistle – and, from along the aisle, the miniature locomotive burst into sight. It passed between Martha and her mother, disappeared into the paper trees and returned, slightly worse for its explosion against the Wendy House wall. Martha tracked it with her eyes – back along the aisle, back through the open boxes where Emil's Long War boxes were waiting to be displayed, and between the knock-kneed legs that had loomed into view.

She gazed up. There stood her papa, a wraith in a dressing robe, black hair entangled with black beard. His whiskers were crusted in the white run-off of his drool.

'Kaspar?' her mother breathed – but she was the second to reach him. Martha was already there, with her arms wrapped around his legs.

THE RISING

....

PAPA JACK'S EMPORIUM, WINTER 1917–1918

October turned into November, but still there was no frost. News came that John Horwood, the Emporium caretaker who had been presumed dead on the Somme, was alive and well (though none would recognise him if he ever returned, for his jaw had been left in the Flanders earth and now he wore a new one made of ivory and India rubber). Every day the Emporium shelves grew deeper, new displays appearing in the alcoves and other expanses. It was the time of year that Cathy liked best: those evenings of anticipation, wondering if tonight was when the first crystals of white might appear. And this year, more than any other, she had reason to cheer – for there was her Kaspar, back in his workshop, working on his toys.

Here he was now. Cathy peeped through the gap in the workshop door, and watched as he turned the concoction of felt and fabric in his hands, adjusting its insides with the miniature tools from his bench. He held his body (that body he would never let her hold) differently now, but in his eyes something of the old Kaspar remained. Around him, the workshop counters were littered with fragments of the music boxes that, in his weaker moments, he had been trying to recreate; that he had given up on each new version was the thing that made Cathy know he was still as proud and stubborn as the day they had met.

Her heart gave a flutter when she saw him set down his new creation and smile. Never had one of those smiles – once so irrepressible, so infectious – meant more to her than it did now.

The patchwork rabbit was a dainty thing. It had a key in its side that was slowly winding down and it hopped along, as rabbits do, until it found a few scraps of fabric left on the workshop floor. At these it bent down and started to eat. Kaspar sprinkled more felt and the rabbit hopped after its forage and gobbled it up. Next, Kaspar scattered bits of bent iron, a few screws, a length of copper wire. The rabbit devoured it all. Then, at the last, it stopped hopping altogether. It hunched against the cold furnace wall, furrowed its embroidered eyes – and, out of a knot in the fabric of its posterior, there popped another rabbit, this one even daintier than the last. As the adult rabbit's motor wound down, the baby's came alive. Eagerly, it hopped back toward Kaspar, searching out any scraps of food its mother had missed.

Sensing movement behind her, Cathy turned to see Martha approaching along the shadowed hall. Putting a finger to her lips, she whispered, 'Come and see …' and, with a footfall soft as Emporium snow, Martha scurried to her mama's side. She was about to peep through the door, where another patchwork rabbit was birthing a kit, when a sound echoed up the hall. Three short blasts – the sound of a bugle, the sound of *the* bugle that announced first frost. Martha looked up at her mother, her face opening in delight. 'Oh, Mama!'

Cathy pushed open the door. The room was silent. Where Kaspar once sat, there was only an empty chair. Around its legs the patchwork rabbits gave their last little hops as their motors wound down. With no felt left to feast on, or transform in whatever intricate motors Kaspar had devised, they huddled together as they grew still.

'Where is he, Mama?'

'Go to the shopfloor,' Cathy whispered, forcing a smile. 'They're going to need all the help they can get.'

Cathy took off, through the cluttered workshop and up the servants' stair to the quarters above. She had hoped to find Kaspar in the bedroom – but he was nowhere to be found. She checked every cranny before she returned to the workshop below. She was hurrying through when she recalled the forest green toybox from the summer Martha was born. There it sat, crammed between two crates of cast-offs and a bale of satin lace. The lid was askew, hinting at the darkness within.

Cathy heaved it aside. Being one of the earliest Kaspar had made, it had always been the smallest of the toyboxes. From the lip, she could see Kaspar lying six feet below, seeming to cringe from the light.

'Kaspar. My love. It was only the bugle. It's to be opening night.'

Kaspar rolled; for a moment Cathy thought that he was fitting, but it was laughter that rattled his body. 'Mrs Godman, you must think me awfully strange.'

Cathy remembered a conversation of so long ago. 'Awfully sentimental, perhaps.'

'Aha!' sighed Kaspar. 'Well, there you have it. For, if a toymaker cannot be sentimental, who on this blasted earth can?'

Tonight, the heavens inside the Emporium were laid bare for all to see. As the doors opened and the first families flocked in, constellations exploded above them. Stars were born, died and re-formed. Angels of light galloped through the blackness, a heavenly host was picked out in cascades of paper, and, as the swirling mass settled, the outlines of toys could be seen, gazing back down. Here was the constellation of the Patchwork Dog; here, the Imperial Kapitan and his loyal wind-up soldiers. It was snowing across the Emporium and cheering erupted in every alcove and aisle.

In one of those alcoves, grasping Martha by one hand and Cathy by the other (and with Sirius, loyal as ever, sitting at his side), stood Kaspar. His eyes pointed upward but his body was quaking. As the snowfall broke, his trembling slowed down.

'Is it good, Papa?'

A night of falling stars, of explosions in the heavens. More magical than any other opening night – and yet, these things, they were not so out of the ordinary for Kaspar.

He was still trembling as he said, 'They put on a good show. I couldn't have done it better myself.' But then he broke free of both their hands and stepped into the aisle, where the first customers were hurrying through. It had been all women last year; women and their children. Now there were others: a cripple on his crutches, a gentleman who wheezed with every breath. No wonder they were drawn back, thought Cathy. After everything that had happened, who wouldn't long for the time before?

'I should like to see some toys,' said Kaspar. 'There's so much I've missed.' And Cathy, thinking that a good thing, let him drift on.

*

Cathy had much to attend to, for most of the shop hands, three seasons old, still needed her to cluck around them like a mother hen. Martha, meanwhile, was determined to keep watch. She followed him at a distance, pretending to peruse shelves whose contents she knew by heart.

Kaspar headed first for the carousel, and next for the corrals where the children were riding rocking horses with wild abandon. Kaspar recognised some of these horses, but many others had been crafted since he left. Martha watched him clamber on to the one she called Black Star, the king of all rocking horses the Emporium had ever made. He rode for some time, eyes screwed against an imaginary wind, before he clambered out of the saddle and wandered on.

Sometimes he got lost. Aisles had been torn down, reassembled and torn down again – and he took to asking Sirius for directions, following wherever its nose led. And that was how, some time later, Kaspar strode into the glade where boys were playing at war.

A dozen skirmishes were being played out across the carpets. Gangs of boys crouched around what toy soldiers they had scavenged from the open boxes, wound them up and let them go. Tiny bugles sounded, wooden bullets flew, and all at once images raked across Kaspar's eyes: the first time he went up and over the top, the time he battled Emil in the bedroom while the new shop girl, mysterious Cathy Wray, watched on. How energised he had been then! How in awe! Now, he was compelled to look the other way. The battle cries were too insistent, too loud. He cringed and found himself looking, instead, at a tower of cardboard boxes, decorated by an expert hand. The stencils across the sides were surrounded with a weave of

Emporium soldiers in interlocking design. The words read: THE LONG WAR.

He had made an industry of it, then. While Kaspar discovered real war, Emil brought their game to the world.

ADVENTURE! the box declared. GLORY!

YOUR COUNTRY NEEDS YOU!

Kaspar turned away. There was a cabinet of other toys behind the tower and, hoping to distract himself, he picked one up. It was another of Emil's creations; he could feel it in the weight and heft of the piece. Touching its crank handle, he felt the axle meshing with the mechanism inside.

Against a diorama of crosshatch hills and skeleton trees, tin soldiers were presented on spikes, as if peeping out of their foxholes. When he turned the handle, the soldiers rose, swivelling as if to bring their rifles to bear. Then, because a toy could only ever capture a moment in time, the soldiers retreated again, back into the safety of their dugouts, bound to repeat the same manoeuvre over and over: never seeing real battle, but never going back home. As Kaspar turned the handle for the third time, he heard, as if in the distance, the horns of war begin to sound, a single trumpeter turning into a chorus. A fourth time, and the edges of the aisles filled with sporadic bursts of tiny artillery fire, the miniature thunder of cavalry stampeding past, the alarm call of whistles and officers bellowing at their rank and file. Kaspar did not look up from the toy but, as he turned the handle again and again, the borders of the shopfloor fell away, the shelves dissolved into a blasted battlescape of trenches and barbed wire. It was then that the terror hit him. The rational part of him knew that he was safe, that it was only a game, the toy working on his imagination as toys are meant to do, but it was not the rational part of him in charge of his fingers. They kept turning the crank, solidifying all that he could see. And then he was back there. Back where his fingers were grimed in scarlet and black. Back in his uniform, with pieces of his second lieutenant's brain smeared across his face. His ears were full of the sounds, his nose was full of the smells. He screamed and screamed and screamed.

It was a sound that had never been heard in the Emporium. Cathy was wrestling to wrap up a herd of toy sheep when she heard her husband's cry. Abandoning her post, she hurried into the aisles.

She found Kaspar where he had fallen, his hands over his face. Sirius was trying to nuzzle him but he didn't seem to know the dog. Martha was standing over him, asking 'Papa? Papa, are you there?' as if she had not been asking the same thing every hour of every day since he returned. 'What happened?' Cathy asked. Customers were being drawn into the glade. They craned to take a look over the tops of the aisles.

Martha looked at her, face contorted as if that was answer enough.

'Help me get him out of here,' Cathy said, and, avoiding the thrashing of his limbs, tried to get her arms under his. 'Martha?'

'I'll fetch Uncle Emil ...'

She was already darting off when Cathy shouted, 'No, don't tell Emil!' She did not know why, but somehow that seemed important. 'Just ... stop them all staring.'

With strength she did not know she had, Cathy lifted Kaspar to his feet and laboured him out of the depression.

Though his arms had stopped thrashing, now he was a dead weight, slumped against her shoulder.

By the time she reached the aisle where model tigers prowled the uppermost shelves, Martha had done her job. The cloud castle drawbridge had opened above them and yet more lights were fountaining out, painting extravagant snowflakes in the air. This was distraction enough. Eyes no longer followed her as she dragged him along – and, in that faltering way, she brought him through the paper trees.

In the Wendy House, she laid him down. Sirius had followed. He whimpered miserably in the corner.

'Kaspar?'

On the bed, he rolled, drawing his knees up to his chin. What a thin, angular body his was. At least he was in the room with her now. His eyes recognised her, but still those guttural noises came from the back of his throat.

Cathy made room at the bedside. No matter what he wanted, she would touch him now. She went to grip him by the shoulders but her fingers resisted. She had to battle herself to do it.

'Kaspar. My love. What happened?'

He choked with laughter again. 'It's supposed to be a toy. How could a toy ...' But then the laughter was silence, and into the silence came his sobbing.

She tried to hold him closer, drawing him on to her knee, but there was strength in him yet. He rolled away, fists bunching up the bedclothes.

'My love, you have to tell me. Tell me what I can do.'

This time, he looked at her. He opened his hands and said, 'There is nothing.'

'You did it for me. You held me here, on this same bed, and told me I could do it, told me I was strong. So tell me, why can't I do it for you?'

'My Cathy, you can't—'

Her body was at odds with itself, just like his. Part of her wanted to throw herself down and lie beside him, but other parts could not bear to be there, her body repelling his just as his repelled her. Her disgust disgusted her, but that way lay madness; that way lay hate. Finally, she screamed, 'Then you have to do it! I don't care what it is. I don't care how. But if you won't let me, then there's only you left. Do you understand? You didn't die out there, Kaspar. You came back to us. Was it for a reason? Was it just plain luck? I don't know. But if you didn't die, you have to live … because there isn't anything else.'

Kaspar's breathing slowed. His eyes, which had darted into so many corners as she spoke, settled on hers.

'She missed you, Kaspar. I …' Her voice cracked. She was as bad as him. Since when had she lost the ability to say what she meant? 'We waited for you all this time and you came back and …'

'Then tell me. *Tell me.* How am I to—'

'I don't know,' Cathy said, 'but you do. I've watched you build boxes with caverns inside them. I took shelter in here with you, while paper trees rained down from the sky. You transform things out here, Kaspar. So why can't you transform things … in there?' After that, they stared at each other for the longest time. Soon, Cathy heard footsteps beyond the Wendy House walls. 'She's coming back. Kaspar, promise me. You're alive, aren't you? You are alive.'

*

That night, Emil took his time to disrobe. First, he picked every splinter of wood from his arms, where they had matted in the bristles of hair that grew thicker each year. Then he hung his work clothes carefully in the wardrobe, ready for another day's labour. Only after dousing himself liberally in the little tin sink did he step behind the screen and don the nightclothes Mrs Hornung had left out for him. In the bedroom, Nina was already upright in bed, reading one of her novelettes.

Emil had taken his notebook to bed, as had been his practice ever since he was a boy, but the marks he made tonight were scrappy and inconsequential. He drew the face of a soldier, supposed to be as regal as the Imperial Kapitan, but instead the image looked bedraggled, worn, like a body whose soul had been spent. *Like Kaspar*, Emil caught himself thinking – and promptly scoured the image clean away. He had not yet told their father about the scene Kaspar had made in the glades of the Long War this evening; he wondered if he ever should.

'Emil?' Nina had been watching him all along. 'Do you want to tell me what's wrong?'

Emil lay with his hands folded beneath his face, the imitation of a sleeping angel. He rolled to face Nina. 'I don't know what to do with him, Nina. I see Cathy trying to cradle him, and he won't be cradled. I want to go to him myself but ...'

'But what?'

'But how can I? I'll say the wrong thing. I'll make out like I understand. But I don't. How could I?'

Nina ran a finger along the thick thatch of his eyebrows. 'This is your home, Emil. You shouldn't have to creep around it like you don't belong. Don't you belong here? Don't I? What your brother sacrificed, that shouldn't have to ...'

'You don't understand. He's *Kaspar*. He's the one who made the paper forests. He's the one who built the toyboxes, with all those caverns inside. We've been waiting for him to—'

'Do you know what I see when I see your brother, Emil? I see a man. That's all. A lonely man. A broken man. But still just a man. Look at what you did these winters, Emil. Look at the ledgerbooks. A paper tree, that lives and dies. But a game like the Long War? That goes on and on and on ... children devote themselves to it. You don't think that's a marvel, just as good as all of the rest?'

Everything she was saying was true, and yet, 'I miss my brother,' he whispered. 'It isn't right to say it, and who knows if he missed me, but ... I miss him, Nina. I want him home.'

'He is home.'

Emil shook his head, as fierce as a toddler just discovering the motion.

For a while Nina said nothing. She lay with her own hands folded beneath her face. Then she reached out, took Emil's, and guided it down. Emil tried to resist (this was not the moment, how could she feel romantic when ...), but gave in when he found his hand had been cupped around her belly.

'I know you miss him, Emil. I think it might be the sweetest thing about you, how much you love your brother. But your family's bigger now ... and it's growing bigger still.' She paused, waiting for the gears in Emil's mind to start turning. 'I saw my aunt's physician. It's certain. He believes ... there may even be twins.'

Emil's eyes widened with every utterance.

'Imagine it, Emil. Twin boys, gambolling up and down the Emporium halls. *Your* boys, *our* boys, making their futures here. I'm sorry for your brother, I'm sorry the Emporium isn't going back to how it was. But – and this is important, so listen to me, my love – these last years, *that's* what the Emporium is to me. That's all the Emporium I've ever known. I don't want it to go back. I want it to go forward. I want you to be fit and fighting strong, and for the Long War to make your fortune ... because your children –' she smiled, the simplest and most meaningful smile, and saw it mirrored in Emil's opening face, '– are going to need it.'

On the first day of December, with ragged snow streaming through the Marble Arch, Cathy wrapped herself against the winter and took the trolleybus west. Hyde Park was not blanketed in snow, but its pastures were dusted in a whiteness at the same time dirtier and more pure than the confetti snow with which she usually spent her winters. The banks of the Serpentine, where she had dozed with Kaspar in that summer so long ago, were alternately crisp with frost or deluged in dirt – but it had not stopped the families turning out to see the new memorial, nor the patients from St George's venturing out to fill their lungs with the crisp, frigid air.

St George's loomed on the corner, half-hidden behind colonnades. As Cathy approached, a horse-drawn ambulance had stopped and orderlies were striding out to help its occupant through the doors. Cathy followed after, to the whirlwind smells of iodine and carbolic soap. At a counter a nurse was filling in papers.

'I'm looking for a Lizzy Wray,' she began. 'My sister. She's . . .' And here she brandished the letter she had received, its postmark already two months old: Lizzy, back from the base hospital and using her service leave to volunteer. It all seemed so unlikely.

'I don't know a Lizzy,' the sister replied. 'But there's a Beth Wray working on second ward. Might that be . . .'

Second Ward was not difficult to find. A convalescent floor, its patients reclined in the sax blue suits and scarlet ties that marked them out as soldiers at rest. Some of them were cajoling each other from the spaces between their beds, but more still were asleep, or gathered on a terrace looking out at the snow. Only one nurse drifted between them, fixing sheets and piling bedpans on a trolley.

When she finally looked up, Cathy realised how long it had been since she had seen her sister. Lizzy was older now, her eyes greyer, but above all else (in spite of the uniform, the places she had been, the grime beneath her fingernails so alien to the girl she used to know), she was still the same beautiful Lizzy Wray.

'Cathy!'

'Beth?' Cathy ventured, with just a hint of admonition.

Her sister rolled her eyes. 'It was time for a change,' she said. 'Oh Cathy, I wasn't sure if you'd got my letters. Now I see that you have, I . . . I would have come to the Emporium. You know that, don't you? Only . . .'

Cathy understood; what could first frost matter when set against everything happening inside these hospital walls?

'The truth is, I'm only here another week. After that I'm putting in a favour for a girl at Endell Street. It's women only there, did you know? Women nurses and women doctors, the whole thing. But by Christmas I'll be gone. Cathy,' she whispered, 'I've met somebody. He's back in Dieppe. Convalescent to start with, but back home he was a medical doctor, so now he's working the rounds.'

For a little while they talked of other things. Their mother was well, their father resigned from the cockle sheds to keep books for the munitions works on the other side of the estuary. If nothing else, and unless he did anything foolish, it would keep him from France. After that, there were only the small utterances and stilted conversations of people with too much time in between them. But Cathy had not come here to be reminded of what she had left behind. In the silences she kept circling herself, searching for the courage to say what was on her mind.

'Kaspar's home,' she finally said. It felt better to get it out and, after she had said it, the words came more freely. 'You saw him, Lizzy. What it did to him. Well, his body's healed, and yet . . .'

Lizzy rushed forward, smothering her in her arms.

'He's *alive*,' she said.

'I keep telling him the same thing. But he's changed as well. I thought he would come home and we'd pick up our lives, that we might even have all those children we'd talked about, brothers and sisters for Martha to play with in the Emporium halls. But how? How if he'll never touch me? How if I don't want to . . .'

Lizzy shepherded her to a corner of the ward, where the beds sat empty, awaiting the next convoy. 'It changes them in different ways. I've known men lose whole days. Some stop talking. Some talk about nothing else.'

'It used to be I could tell what he was thinking just by the creases of his eyes. Don't they say eyes are the windows to the soul? Well, with Kaspar, they're like the Emporium's secret doors: you look into them, but you don't see what's behind. I want to talk to him, but he doesn't want to talk. I want to hold him, but he won't be held. With other men, it would be the drinking. But with Kaspar ...'

That morning she had stood in the doors of his workshop. Felt rabbits had birthed more felt rabbits until there were no more left to birth. A woollen sheep was baaing incessantly, searching for the rest of its flock, oblivious to the fact that Kaspar had yet to craft them and probably never would. The silk suit that hung on the back of the door was grappling out with empty sleeves, wanting only to be hugged – and finding nothing to hold. Such things had been pouring out of him in the last days.

Sometimes she woke in the night and he was not there. Sometimes she woke and he had been lying there all along. And as the weeks went by, it was increasingly difficult to tell one night from the next.

'I don't know if I love him.'

It burst out of her, dripping with the shame she had been drowning in for days.

'Oh, Cathy ...'

'I mean – I don't know *how* to love him. Can that be real? Can it wither like that? It's like a rot.'

Lizzy didn't say a thing. She reached out and held Cathy's hand.

*

On Christmas Day, as every year, the tables were laid out on the shopfloor and the shop hands who remained brought up platters of food from the kitchens underneath. Mrs Hornung, who was already a part of Emporium legend on account of her figgy pudding, had surpassed herself with the goose. It was stuffed with a partridge which was, itself, stuffed with a songbird; the pastries were stuffed with pheasant, brought into the store as payment by a gamekeeper whose wallet was empty, but whose children deserved so much more.

Cathy and Martha busied themselves until, at last, the table was a mountain range with crags of roast gammon, foothills of potatoes roasted and mashed. A wilderness of parsnips reached up one of the escarpments and made a crown at its summit. The shop hands were already filling their plates when Emil and Nina appeared along the aisle, helping Papa Jack between them. As he settled, Cathy saw that he was balancing a pinecone soldier between his thumb and forefinger, constantly twirling it around.

The toasts were short and sweet. 'To the Emporium,' said Emil. 'To our families and our friends, at home and abroad. To moments like these. To my wife, and my sons yet to come, and my papa who started it all. And to my brother's return ...'

At this he lifted his glass. His eyes followed it but did not look down again. Cathy looked the same way – and there was Kaspar, balanced on one of the galleries above.

She started. Martha had started too. Cathy had to rein her back into her seat and, by the time she had dealt with her muttered protestations, Kaspar was gone.

'I'll fetch him,' she whispered in Martha's ear.

'We didn't even invite him …' she was saying. 'Why didn't we invite him to our Christmas?'

Cathy was barely out of her seat when he appeared along one of the aisles. From here he was slow in coming, resting on one of his canes. Twice, he caught her eye and gave a mute nod, as if to promise he was fine.

As he grew near, some of the shop hands didn't know where to look. 'Eat!' insisted Papa Jack. Sally-Anne took the order to heart and continued to pile her plate high. Others moved reticently – but not one of them looked in his direction.

Emil reached Kaspar in the same moment that Cathy came to his side. 'I can still walk, little brother,' Kaspar said, barely concealing his frustration. Then he was at the table. No place had been left for him, so suddenly Nina was on her feet. 'There's really no need,' Kaspar said. 'It's customary to stand to make a toast.'

Kaspar held out a hand. Martha passed him a glass. 'My friends, my family, my daughter, my wife.' He was looking at them all so fiercely, but on his lips was that same infectious smile of old. 'It has been a considerable thing to come home. To find you all here again, where you surely belong. With my hand on my heart, I can say that, through every night I spent out there, I kept the image of you all in my mind. My papa and my brother. My Cathy and my Martha. Kesey and Dunmore and little Douglas Flood.' His brittle hand had fallen to dance through Martha's hair. She squealed at his touch, looking up with little thrills of delight – and Cathy had to fight the compulsion to draw her away. It was only Kaspar, she told herself. The only father she'd ever known. 'The Emporium is my home,' he went on, and something in his voice began to show the frailty he'd been working so hard to keep at bay. 'This place is my beating heart. Its storerooms and aisles. The dens where I used to play. And I know, now, that that is the only reason I came back to you, while so many of our friends perished. Because how could a man ever die, when he doesn't carry his heart with him? When he's locked it away here, at the bottom of his toybox, with everything else he holds dear? The world outside those doors knows more sorrow than I dare remember – but in here? In here, there is snowfall of paper and rocking horses running wild. There are forest glades and butterflies of satin, trains that loop impossible loops and patchwork dogs that never grow old and die – and there is the memory,' he whispered, 'of when we were two little boys, who knew nothing other than our games.'

Emil had started to clap, but perhaps it was premature; not one of the other shop hands joined in.

'The Emporium has changed since I embarked,' Kaspar went on. 'But I'm home now and, I'm sorry, Emil, but the Emporium must change again ...' He stopped to survey the room, taking in every face that was staring at his. 'From the moment the doors open tomorrow, and for ever after, the Emporium will sell no more toy soldiers.'

There was silence, less stunned than perplexed, around the table.

'Let us put that in our past, like everything else.'

'Kaspar,' Emil ventured, 'what do you mean, no more—'

'It is a simple matter, my brother. There are so many magical confections in these halls. Why must we sully ourselves with soldiers any longer?'

'Now, Kaspar,' Emil said, sterner now. 'Listen here, the Long War—'

'—is still going on,' said Kaspar. 'I know it is.' He leant down to plant a kiss on Martha's brow. Then, pitching into his cane, he returned along the aisle from which he had come, ignoring the cries that harried him on his way.

'Eat!' Emil exclaimed, and the shop hands, who until now had maintained a reverential hush, began their mutterings as the tinkling of plates and forks dispelled the silence. 'Well, it's preposterous!' Cathy heard Emil go on. 'To think he can waltz in here and make a judgement like that, a judgement on us all. It's ugly, that's what it is. Isn't it, Papa? Well ...'

But Papa Jack said nothing. The old man sat slumped in his chair, his pinecone figurine still clasped between forefinger and thumb.

Trade began slowly next morning, as it always did once the festivities had died down, but by the small of afternoon a steady trickle of customers were filling the aisles, the rich children of Knightsbridge coming out to indulge their Christmas allowances. Emil, who spent the morning prowling the shopfloor (if only to make certain that the boxes of the Long War still took pride of place on the carousels) put on his usual ebullient show whenever a boy asked him the way into his cloud castle, or the secret tune that could make the dancing bears perform a fandango. Yet in his quiet moments his eyes kept searching, lingering on the galleries above in case his brother dared to be seen.

The day was almost done, the shopfloor emptying as customers gave up the dallying in which they had spent their days, when he heard the commotion. Balancing on one of the units, trying to draw down a dirigible, he pirouetted around. By the counters at the front of the store, a rotund man was remonstrating with Cathy, his face (behind whiskers waxed as if to look incensed) turning scarlet with rage. A small crowd of onlookers had already formed.

Through bobbing heads and arms flung skyward, Emil watched as the man set up two small units of soldiers on the counter, wound them up and let them go. It was a battle like any other, just the same as the thousands that had already been played with Emporium toys. In perfect formation, the soldiers marched at one another. These were infantrymen, armed with only bayonets; they would do and they would die, and whichever was left standing would be the victor.

It took only seconds for the soldiers to meet. Yet, as they came together, it was not battle that Emil saw. No infantryman sent another cartwheeling over the edge, or snarled itself in its enemy's arms. As one, the soldiers stopped. Each lifted a hand and grasped the hand of the soldier it had, only moments ago, been sworn to kill.

'Well?' the rotund man was demanding. 'What is the meaning of it?'

Emil was already grappling the tow rope of the dirigible that had been floating above. Holding it firmly, he took a step off the shelving and heaved down, to land clumsily at the bottom of the aisle. By the time he had picked himself up, the man at the counter was demanding the return of his money (and a payment in recompense for the distress his sons had shown on Christmas morning). Emil lumbered in that direction, his chest heaving.

The first rule of storekeeping was not 'the customer is king'. The real first rule was 'don't assault the clientele'. It was a rule Emil ignored as he forced his way through the crowd. By the time he reached the counter, Cathy was patiently counting coins back into the customer's outstretched hand.

'Has something happened?' Emil asked, still straining for breath.

'You're the toymaker, are you?'

'I am.'

'Then it's you to blame, is it, for toys that won't play? Shame on you, sir. They were only boys. They wanted nothing more than a game. And all this, while our boys are still fighting out there ...'

The man would brook no further questions. The crowd parted to allow him through, unwittingly closing ranks as Emil sought to follow. By the time they fanned out back into the aisles, the customer was gone. Emil stared after him, searching for footprints in the confetti snow.

He turned to see Cathy packing the soldiers away. 'Let me see them.'

Cathy stood in silence as he wound the soldiers up, deployed them, and watched them broker their peace.

'It's *him*,' said Emil, unable to speak his brother's name.

Cathy touched him on the arm. 'You don't know that.'

'Oh, but I do. He waltzed in and made his declaration and now he's done this ... He's done it to spite me. And all because I ...' Emil hesitated before saying the words, but Cathy heard them all the same: *because I wasn't there.* 'It's sabotage. That's what it is. Well, we've had saboteurs before. We'll see about—'

He was on the verge of striding through the counter and into the warren of stores and antechambers above, when Cathy said, 'Emil, let me go to him.'

Emil was about to say no when a trio of boys tumbled out of the aisles, with boxes of the Long War in their arms.

'Sir,' announced the first. 'It's these ones too.'

'We were playing in the glade, but these wouldn't work. We'd thought they were broken, until that man ...'

Emil fell to one knee and took the new soldiers in his hands. 'What use is a soldier if he won't do battle?'

He opened the mechanism of the first soldier, as if he might find the answer inside – and, while he was ferreting within, Cathy slipped into the shadows behind the counter. Moments later, past the register and up the spiralling stair, she was standing in front of Kaspar, the patchwork rabbits having proliferated around his feet. Martha crouched among them, feeding scraps of fabric to one of the tiny kits.

'Martha, might I speak to your father?'

'Oh yes, Mama.'

'*Alone.*'

Martha scooped a selection of rabbits into her arms and, with a vengeful glare, tramped out of the room.

'Kaspar, tell me it truthfully. Have you ... tinkered' – she could find no better word for it – 'with the soldiers on the shopfloor?'

Kaspar's lips parted in a smile.

'Kaspar?'

'It's you who told me, Cathy. That I had to do it, that it had to come from me. Well, my love, this is how. You understand, don't you? Why it has to be this way? Because ... they weren't going to listen. They all look at me like I'm an intruder. Well, this is *my* home. And Cathy, all I want is to come back ...'

'Kaspar, here you are. *Here.*'

'Emil was never going to listen. He's wanted to win the Long War ever since we were boys. Well, now there'll be no winner. Now it can end – and this Emporium, this place we have, it can *live* again ...'

At that moment, the workshop door flew open. Patchwork rabbits scattered for the shelter of shelves and upturned crates.

Emil stood in the doorway, his cheeks bunched and red. 'What did you do?' he breathed. 'Tell me what you did!'

Kaspar lifted a consolatory hand. 'Let me show you, little brother.'

A toy soldier was lying inert on the floor by Kaspar's feet. The cavity in its back was still open, so Kaspar tinkered within. What adjustments he was making, Emil did not know. Yet, when he set the soldier down, suddenly it wouldn't march. Emil wound it up, but instead of sallying forth, it folded its legs and took a seat. Then, with sinking inevitability, the key stopped turning.

'It's supposed to march. They form a unit, so boys can play battles against each other.'

'Oh yes,' sighed Kaspar, 'and win a few square feet of carpet for every ten soldiers lost.' His eyes darkened. 'I told you, little brother. The Emporium isn't to sell toy soldiers any more. We are, none of us, butchers. So why must we raise our children that way?'

Emil snatched the recalcitrant soldier in his fist. Three years his brother had been gone. And if, in those years, Kaspar had seen and done things of which Emil might never know, well, that did not make Emil's own years worthless. He had Nina. The Long War was a triumph. He was to be a father, a real father ... And the Emporium did not belong

ROBERT DINSDALE

to Kaspar. It belonged to them all, to their families, and, 'Damn it, Kaspar! What do you want from me?'

To Kaspar the answer was so banal there was no point in asking the question.

'I want you to grow up.'

'I deserve more than that, Kaspar. Well, Cathy, don't I? You fought your war, but I ... I kept our Emporium afloat, didn't I? I did it in the only way I knew how. And my soldiers, they're ... everything.' He had started out softly, but now his voice reached new heights. 'The Long War is our best-selling toy. That's what boys want. Soldiers to put on their shelves and think of their fathers. Little tin tanks that can roll up and down on their tracks. Cavalry and artillery wagons. Boys come here for them. Girls too. They take them home and collect them and make battles and come back for more. The Emporium might have sunk without you, Kaspar. Papa slowing down and you gone for so long and ... give me one reason, just *one*, why you've any right to waltz back here and end it all!'

Kaspar levered himself to his feet, refusing the offer of Cathy's hand. When he spoke, white spittle flew from his lips. 'Haven't you ever thought how it might *feel*? Two battalions of these things, all wound up and marching at each other – and then they fall down, and get picked back up, and have to do the whole thing all over again, dancing to somebody else's tune. These soldiers don't get a choice. It doesn't end for them, Emil. They don't even get the sanctity of death.'

'Kaspar,' Emil said, more softly now, trying to cross the expanse between his brother and him in awkward, stuttering steps, 'you're home now. They're only toys. They can't *feel*.'

The look on Kaspar's face was incredulous. Emil might as well have told him there were no stars in the night sky, that their mama still lived and walked among them. 'Didn't Papa teach you anything?' he asked – and there they stood, each one staring into the other, while on the shopfloor beneath a hundred disappointed voices began to make themselves heard.

IMAGINARIUM

. . . .

PAPA JACK'S EMPORIUM, 1918

Dawn, and the aisles of Papa Jack's Emporium lay in wild disarray. Had you been there that night, had you crouched on one of the galleries and peered through the rails as Martha Godman did, you might have thought that the crooked servants of London's ordinary toyshops had come to lay the Emporium to waste. But had you looked more closely, you would have seen two familiar figures toiling in the gloom: Emil and his wife Nina, whirling together in the Long War glade as they tore open every box, shredded every soldier's wrapping and set them to march. Now, in every corner of the glade, toy soldiers shook hands and agreed an armistice, rather than raise their rifles or even march on. As the dawn's first light spilled over the cloud castle turrets, waking the patchwork pegasi from their roosts, Emil sank to his haunches and laughed, laughed in wild despair.

'Pack them all up. Wake Frances Kesey and all of the rest. If one of these soldiers leaves the Emporium today, the shop hand who sells it is finished.'

Nina went to console him, and for a moment Emil let himself be smothered in her arms. Then he took off, into the darkness of the untended aisles.

Follow . . .

Up, up and up; Emil Godman might have run ungainly, but he could run when he needed to. Into the shadows of mammoths, through the log piles where paper trees had been felled; patchwork dogs and cats watched him from their enclosures; the runnerless rocking horses stopped grazing in their corrals and wondered at his flight. After a long night's labour, Emil was too tired for the endless stairs, so he clambered into a dirigible balloon, heaved its tethers out of the earth, and soared up, up, up into the dome above the shop floor. From the gallery rail, Martha watched him hurtle past, then lost him in the reef of mist on which the cloud castle sat.

By the time he reached the Emporium terrace, he was quite out of breath. Great billows of white curled through his nostrils as he burst on to the rooftop where his papa's garden spilled out of chimneypots and terracotta, rising up through dislodged tiles. From here you could see the world. A single snowflake pirouetted down to land in the hair of Emil's naked arm.

Snowflakes, snowflakes all around – but, of snowdrops, there was no sign.

Chest burning, he crouched down, pressed his fingers to the earth. He was searching for colour, for a speck of green, anything that might convince. The bulbs were down there, down where they hid all summer long. And if there truly was magic in the Emporium, if this thing they called *magic* existed at all, then surely it would call itself forth now. Surely a snowdrop would rise from the earth and open itself to reveal a perfect bell of white.

But no magic came for Emil. No magic had ever come for him at all.

ROBERT DINSDALE

He pressed his fingers through the frost-hardened earth, delved down until the dirt grew thick in his fingernails, riming the creases of his hands. It was, he realised with a sense of revelation, delicious to be doing something so ... untoward. He risked a look over his shoulder, but in the Godmans' quarters all was still. Then, back to his task, his fingers found what they were looking for. He pulled his hand back, trailing a snowdrop bulb and all of its roots. It had already started to shoot, struggling for the surface.

Now that the crime was done and all his adrenaline spent, Emil hurried to hide the misdeed. He flattened the earth beneath his boot, scraped the soil from his hand and hurried inside. Perhaps Mrs Hornung would notice the boot prints he left behind him, but she would not say.

The Imperial Kapitan was watching him from its place on the mantle, where he had left it after dinner the previous night. On seeing it, Emil felt a rush of such shame. How many seasons had he gone to the terrace, willing the snowdrops to stay beneath the earth? Now he dragged them up with his hands, desperate for winter to end.

The necessary tools were in his workshop. With a scalpel blade he opened the flower's head, spread back its unripe layers. A little paper, a little felt; his fingers had painted such delicate things on the faces of his soldiers that surely they were up to this task. He worked quickly, he worked with purpose, he locked the magnifier to his eye and hunched over – and then, then when he heard footsteps behind him, then when he was holding himself so tight he felt ready to burst, then he was finished. He turned around to find Nina waiting. Her belly was rounded, his two sons grown firm.

'They're ready for you.'

Emil strode across the workshop, squeezing her hand as he brushed past. Out on the shopfloor, the shop hands were nervously milling. Cathy lingered, unseen in the darkness, watching him keenly.

Emil shook as he lifted his fist, opening it to reveal the snowball bulb with its flower standing tall and firm. 'It's over,' he said. 'Finished. We'll see you all next year.'

A month had passed by the time real snowdrops filled the Emporium terrace. Cathy wove them into Martha's hair, Papa Jack retired for his long summer sleep, Kaspar continued his tinkering – and down below, locked in his workshop day and night, Emil opened up the soldiers that had once been his, removed their mechanisms and took them apart piece by piece. Scalpels he had at his side, screwdrivers and tweezers and wrenches small enough to shift the most tiny of cogs. He lifted out springs and stretched them, looking for faults in the coiling. He put his magnifying glass to the teeth of the wheels that drove the pistons that drove the soldiers' arms and legs. He dismantled and rebuilt and dismantled again, and still he couldn't discern by which simple trick of engineering Kaspar had corrupted his Long War.

'What am I missing?' he said, to the Imperial Kapitan sitting static up on the shelf. 'What did he do?'

Spring was here, the days already growing longer. They would, Emil decided with a sinking finality, all have to be destroyed. All of those hours spent at his workshop lathe, all of those unsuspecting toy soldiers put to the torch, so that he could begin again.

He was scratching out figures on a slate, trying to quantify the amount of timber he would need, the number of shop hands he would have to hire to replenish the shelves by the time Christmas came, when fists hammered at the workshop door. Behind him, Cathy hung in the frame, gasping for breath.

'Emil, you must come.'

'I'm nearly there, Cathy. Whatever he's done, I'm certain—'

'No, Emil. *Now*. It's now.'

Emil was slow to understand. He began to protest – this was *his* time, all he needed to do was think, the answer was here, if only the world would let him find it – but then Cathy's silence revealed all. He dropped his pencil to the worktop, watched it roll down to the feet of the Imperial Kapitan. Then he was up on his feet, finding neither his words nor his balance.

'Now? But Cathy, there's a month, two months to go ...'

'It's twins, Emil. The midwife said, they come sooner if they're twins ...'

Emil stuttered out on to the shopfloor, stumbling over himself as he twirled to look at the galleries above. Perhaps it was only imagination, but he thought he could hear Nina, even all that distance away.

Cathy took him by the hand. 'Now,' she said, more firmly.

They reached the Godmans' quarters by the back stair, the one that couldn't possibly have climbed so high into the rafters as it did. Martha hung by the terrace door, standing on the tips of her toes. Papa Jack clasped his hand as he came. Mrs Hornung, or so Cathy said, was already by the tradesman's entrance, awaiting the arrival of the midwife; and Kaspar, well, Kaspar was behind one of those doors, his head in a manual, oblivious to the nephews about to make their entrance to the world.

Nina waited alone in their bedroom. When Cathy left she had been prowling back and forth; now she sat on the edge of the bed, trying to ride the early contractions.

In the passage outside, Emil stopped dead.

'Cathy, I don't know if I can.'

How his heart must have been pounding. Cathy stood as close to him as a wife ever could and whispered, 'You've been waiting eleven years. You were ready to help me then, and you're ready to help her now. Don't you remember? All of the books you collected, all of the questions you asked? Emil, not once, then or now, did I doubt you could do it. Just go in there, hold her hand until the midwife comes. Tell her you love her. She's going to need it.'

Emil whispered, 'Thank you, Cathy,' and then he was gone through the doors.

Seven hours later there was cheering in the Emporium halls. Cathy – who had waited so anxiously while Emil paced the quarters, panicking each time the midwife emerged to collect more towels, more water, toast and butter to give his wife strength – heard the squawking of a newborn through the wall and breathed out. Until that moment she had not known she was holding so much tension within.

At her side, Emil was suddenly on his feet.

'Shall I . . . Should I go, Cathy?'

There were two voices crying now; she was certain of it. The midwife would already be swaddling them. Nina would already be . . .

Mrs Hornung appeared in the doorway, her sleeves still rolled up as if she herself had been there at the bedside. 'They're asking for you, Emil. It's time.'

But he was rooted to the spot – and until Cathy put her arms around him, and whispered that his work was about to begin, he did not dare take a step.

After he was gone, Martha clung on to Cathy's hand. 'Can *we* go, Mama? Can we see them?'

Cathy made her wait. She remembered the exhaustion that came afterwards, the feeling of plunging back to earth from that otherworld where all that existed was the breathing, the body put to its only real purpose. It was not until darkness had fallen, and the shopfloor lit by the haloes of Papa Jack's falling stars, that she caught a glimpse of her nephews for the first time. Emil had carried them – tiny as twins often are – out on to the gallery, where they might sneak their first look at the shopfloor. He was whispering to them as Cathy approached: 'We'll set it right, the three of us, and there'll be stars falling every opening night, just like there are now, stars for the two of you ... There's the cloud castle where we'll camp, and there's the paper forest where we'll go hunting patchwork deer – and there, there's the glade where we'll play our Long War, all three of us together. They'll come at Christmas and try to take us on, but nobody will ever win a battle, not against us Godman boys ...' Cathy was almost at Emil's side, and now he looked around.

'Cathy,' he beamed, 'they're boys. Come over! Come and meet my boys ...'

On the first day of summer, Cathy watched from a gallery high above the shop floor as Emil opened the Emporium doors and a gaggle of shop hands she had not seen before tumbled within. Demanding their silence, Emil produced a flurry of papers, took signatures from each and marched them into the aisles. In the last weeks he had given up tinkering with the toy soldiers and devoted himself, instead, to reordering the shopfloor, erecting barricades along the apexes of aisles, planting Secret Doors that would entrap all but the most ardent cartographer in an infinite loop. The next season's creations had been left to Papa Jack (who slept, most nights, in his workshop, enduring this family feud with the same stoicism that had once helped him survive a frozen prison camp), and all the while Emil *conspired*. Cathy watched as he marched the new shop hands into the copse of paper trees – and, once in their heart, to the Wendy House door.

Cathy had seen Mrs Hornung provisioning it. It had bunk beds stacked seven high, sacks of potatoes and crates of canned beef, tea leaves enough to quench the thirst of an army and mint cake enough to sustain an Antarctic expedition. Only now did she understand what it was for. Alone, she saw Emil march the new shop hands inside – and later that day, as she and Martha worked the shopfloor, she saw the boards that nailed the door shut, the blood red sign screaming KEEP OUT!!! and the crude patchwork wolves that had been set to prowl the perimeter as guards. Unsophisticated things, all they knew to do was march and bark.

Later that night, she stood at the workshop door as Martha sat at Kaspar's feet, learning the intricacies of patchwork design. 'And he's locked all the soldiers up in there,' Martha was saying, darning an eagle's feathers. 'And his new shop hands, they'll undo everything you did, Papa. And how will we ever get in, because Uncle Emil's turned it into his fortress ...'

Kaspar's face creased with some memory half-forgotten. 'Let me tell you something, little Martha. When Emil and I were boys, he simply couldn't bear to lose. He'd build fortresses back then as well, but there was always a way in.'

'There really isn't, Papa. Mama and I marched all around, even when those wolves had wound down. He's put boards across every window. Those shop hands aren't coming out until opening night, and by then it will already be too late.'

It was strange to see how buoyed the bad news made Kaspar. In a moment he was up on his feet, dancing an ungainly two-step as he dislodged a wooden crate from one of the counters. This he set down by Martha.

'See ...'

Inside the box were toy soldiers and parts of toy soldiers. He set one down and, closing the cavity in its back, instructed Martha to wind it. A second he began to tinker with. 'I've been holding it in my mind for so long. Sometimes all it needs is time and a puzzle works itself through. But I perfected it last night. It doesn't matter a jot what Emil does in those Wendy House walls, not when ...'

With a final exhalation, Kaspar snapped shut the mechanism in the second soldier and wound it up. For some time, nothing miraculous happened. Then, as Cathy watched, the first soldier – which had been marching in ever-decreasing circles – began to wind down. As it neared its end, the second soldier – still with life left in its mechanism – approached the first, took its key in its wooden hands, and began to turn. Energised again, the first soldier sprang back to life and continued its dance.

Martha clapped her hands in delight, just as the second soldier's mechanism began to slow. This time, the first came to its rescue, winding it back up. When, minutes later, its own mechanism slowed once more, its comrade sprang to its defence. The soldiers marched on and on and on. As long as they were with each other, they would never stop.

'Emil never learned how to think. He's good at what he does, that much is true, but he can never think beyond it. He doesn't understand. Perhaps he never will. But these soldiers don't have to do his bidding any more, not if they can wind each other up. They don't have to fight in any Long Wars. Why, they don't have to be soldiers at all. They can take control, be whatever they want to be. My Martha, the world is bored of armies. It can't bear another boy to die. It doesn't need killing. It needs farmers and tinkers. Shepherds and railwaymen and grocers. It's time we set the soldiers free.'

'Oh yes, Papa! Oh yes!'

Martha dove into the box and plucked up another soldier to set it marching with the rest. This one's mechanism had not yet been doctored and it knew nothing of winding up its comrades – and yet, when it wound down, the others sprang to its defence, keeping it running long after it ought to have stopped.

'You see?' grinned Kaspar. 'That isn't soldiers, killing each other just because they ought to. That's *people*, helping each other just because they can. Isn't it a beautiful thing?'

*

A Report On a MOST Miraculous THING
by Martha Godman (aged 11 ¾)

The Topic I am to write about this week is What I Wish To Be. Do I wish to be a school teacher or do I wish to be a mother? Do I wish to be secretary to a rich Financier, or do I wish to be a LADY EXPLORER. The question set is interesting in and of itself but (Martha licked the tip of her pencil here, certain that Mr Atlee would disapprove) a more interesting question presents. How to get what One Wants, with reference to toy soldiers of Emporium Design.

What if One was trapped in a Circumstance of which one disapproves? What if One was made to be a way One did not wish to Be? How might One take charge of One's own JOURNEY THROUGH LIFE. Destiny, we have been taught, is resolute. But what if One wishes to change one's God-given Destiny?

Step the First
It is the directions, assumptions and Privileges of Others which keep us in place.

Point 1st: A toy soldier must be wound at all times, or else perish.

Point 2nd: If a toy soldier can be shown to Wind Himself, he need never rely on the Privileges of Others.

Step the Second
Helping Oneself is nothing if One does not help Others. A movement can only succeed when what is Revolutionary becomes that which is Ordinary and Accepted.

Point 3rd: If a toy soldier can be shown how to help others Wind Up, they too can be RELEASED FROM SHACKLES.

Point 4th: Soldiers released from SHACKLES can release others from SHACKLES. As we are taught disease spreads from hand to hand so too does Knowledge and Freedom.

Step the Third
A journey is begun. Who knows where it might lead? The first step is to learn GOVERNANCE OF THE SELF.

Soldiers do not want to be soldiers and if you give them the CHANCE to DECIDE, the most Miraculous Things will MANIFEST.

(Composition by Martha Godman, August 1918)

Cathy put down the paper and felt Mr Atlee's eyes considering her above the bronze of his pince-nez. It didn't matter how old you were; a schoolteacher's gaze would always be withering.

'Am I to imagine she is making some veiled analysis of Women's Suffrage? We have covered as much in lessons, and your daughter has never been less than forthright ... But all of this? Understanding what one wants, casting off shackles, rewriting one's own destiny? Your daughter is, dare I say, a little young for radical politics. And this business with toy soldiers? Some risqué comment, I imagine, on conscientious objection? Her, with a father who sacrificed so much to keep this country free?'

Cathy hung her head.

'Quite apart from anything else, this egregious use of Capital Letters is alarming. I am certain she does this just to spite me.'

Of this Cathy was quite certain: she had caught the girl practising the most ostentatious capital letters by torchlight in bed.

'I'll speak with her.'

'See that you do,' Mr Atlee declared, gathering his papers. 'It is for her own good. Mrs Godman, goodness knows, I admire this place, I'm grateful for my years of service – but have you ever thought that, perhaps, just perhaps, Martha might benefit from some exposure to the *real* world?'

Cathy waited some time after Mr Atlee had taken his leave before she set out to find Martha. Mr Atlee had set her arithmetic problems to work through before his next attendance, but as ever she was not to be found with her books. Cathy found her in the Godmans' quarters instead, fussing with one of the twins while Nina tried in vain to spoon stewed apple into the other. At six months old they were developing the same ursine look as their papa, the same paunchiness too.

'Martha, a word.'

'No, Mama, he doesn't have *words*. It's only babbling. He just makes sounds.'

Cathy thought: it's as if Kaspar truly is her father; the knowing look, the deftness of tongue, she gets it all from him.

A simple glare compelled her to set the youngest Godman down and come to her mother's side. Retreating to the corner, Cathy unfurled the report over which Mr Atlee had remonstrated and asked her, 'What does it mean?'

'It's all true, Mama. I wouldn't tell *lies*.'

Cathy thought: she wouldn't; the truth delights her too much. 'But what *is* it?' she asked.

'It's the soldiers. Papa will show you. Come on ...'

Martha took her hand and led her up the back stair. At the top, the door to Kaspar's workshop sat for ever ajar.

Kaspar was sitting in the rocking chair that once belonged to Papa Jack, while dozens of self-winding men were lined up in battalions before him. Somebody had been making tallies on a board with chalk. The workshop floor was a parade ground where units turned and fell over, picked themselves up and formed rank and file again. Across the parade ground, whenever a soldier began to slow, one of his compatriots would twirl around, fit his hands into the grooves chipped into the key at his back, and wind him back to full strength. It was, Cathy thought, like watching the dancing of honeybees. The wind-up army moved as a swarm, or not at all.

Kaspar was keeping metronomic rhythm with his foot, but when Martha started tugging on his sleeve he looked up. 'Cathy,' he said, 'look! They're drilling. We've been trying to persuade them to drill differently – why should they stand in battalions if they're not to be soldiers any more? – but it's bred into them. Something in the way that they're made. So – look!' Kaspar's hands revealed a mountain of miniature overcoats, woollen jumpers and shirts. Tiny Wellington boots in forest green and navy blue. 'Dress as a soldier and perhaps you're a soldier. But dress as …'

'It hasn't worked,' Martha chipped in. 'They don't let you put them on.'

'And then we thought – why should they? They've been being told what to do for far too long. Who am I to tell them how to dress? Oh, Cathy, they do the most remarkable things. Cathy, they can *learn* …'

Cathy crouched down. At the sudden intrusion the toy soldiers formed ranks and routed, re-forming on the other side of the workshop floor.

'They need a leader,' said Martha. 'Sometimes they just whirl and twirl and collide with one another or end up shaking hands. If they had a leader, they might smarten up a little. That's what we think.'

'It's like nothing else in the Emporium. They perform the same action a hundred times, and for every hundred times, one will go wrong. Perhaps it upsets them, so they simply try over again. But when it offers them an advantage …' Kaspar's eyes sparkled like frost. 'All year they've been discovering new things.'

Kaspar opened up a box by his side, one emblazoned with the insignias of the Long War, and set down a static soldier. Moments later, the battalion marched forward to where it lay. From here on, their drill was deftly orchestrated. The soldiers worked in two groups – one to open up the cavity in the soldier's back, and another to make sure the first group never wound down. The soldiers tasked with attending the static soldier moved with nuance that had not been possible one winter ago. They reached in and upset gears, lifted out a cog to replace it with three of smaller design, shortened the cam shaft and inserted more guide wires into the soldier's arms. When they were done, they wound their new brother up for the very first time.

Soon, he had taken his place in the battalion – and, to Cathy's mounting surprise, was winding up the fellows around him with newfound aplomb.

'You built them to build each other?'

'It's better than that,' beamed Martha. 'Papa didn't build them this way at all. They built *themselves*.'

Emil was diligent in releasing the new shop hands at the end of each summer night. First locking the Wendy House door behind him, he lined the workers up among the paper trees and ran his hands over each, searching for what blueprints or implements they might be stealing away, then marched them in file to the half-moon hall. If any minded the way he emptied their pockets, they did not say it; men returned from war with only half a leg, or mothers raising their children alone, needed what work they could find. And, as Emil released them into Iron Duke Mews each night, he reminded himself: they are not your friends, they are not your friends. They were his workers, that was all, and this seemed the most important lesson of his life.

Tonight he locked the door, made one last circuit of the boarded-up Wendy House, and walked back through the paper trees. There, waiting for him where the forest met

ROBERT DINSDALE

the shopfloor, was Nina. Their sons squirmed in their pram, angling for a look at their father, and Emil dropped down to rub his bristly face in theirs.

'How is it?' Nina asked.

'The finishes aren't right, but there's time for that yet. Still two months until first frost might come. We've boxed up enough to fill the shelves, but they need paint and lacquer. Only I can do that.' Another night he might have seemed defeated, but on this night he was filled with hope. 'We'll be ready. If there's an armistice this winter, it will be out there, in the world. Not here in my Emporium.' Emil squeezed Nina's hand, her fingers threaded through his. '*Our* Emporium.'

They walked together through aisles that would soon live again, past the Long War glade that would soon ring with the sounds of battle – and, as they went, they were so caught up in talking about the way things would be, the first opening night their sons would ever see, that they did not realise there were already toy soldiers walking across the shopfloor, watching their every move. They did not see the wind-up army that marched in the cavities along the bottom of the shelves, did not see them stopping to wind each other up as they came. If only they had looked behind them, they might have seen the army as it marched into the paper trees, turning circles around the Wendy House where more of their kind were being chipped out of branches and trunks.

Emil did not see the soldiers as they fanned back into the aisles, looking for others of their kind. He was already carrying his children up the stairs to bed by the time they discovered the aisle with his old workshop waiting at its end – so he did not see them venture in, and he did not see them venture back out, carrying one more inert soldier between them. If he had, perhaps things would have turned out differently for Papa Jack's Emporium – for there, on the shopfloor, the toy soldiers lay down the Imperial Kapitan, so regal and strong, so perfect, the leader for which (or so Martha believed) they cried out. They gathered about him (they could not have been *admiring*, because their minds were only useless blocks of wood) and worked in pairs to turn him over. And there, as in Kaspar's workshop above, they opened his insides, lost themselves in industry, and finally wound him up.

The Imperial Kapitan picked himself up. There was something different about the way he lifted his arm in the salute for which it had first been made, something different in the way that, when one of the soldiers beside him began to wind down, he stepped forward and wound him back up.

The Imperial Kapitan stood where he belonged, at the head of the army. The wind-up host marched on – and not a soul in the Emporium saw it, so not a soul in the Emporium believed.

Cathy always knocked before she entered Papa Jack's workshop. It was a habit she meant never to shake. It had been a long time since crossing that line made her remember the frightened girl she had been when she first came here, but something of that feeling returned tonight. She did not wait for an answer, but stepped directly through.

Papa Jack was in his chair, where he always was. She had thought to find him stitching more feathers into the hide of his phoenix (the feathers so often failed to survive the bird's conflagrations, though the mechanism lived on), but instead he was asleep, his fingers twitching in whatever dreams of wilderness and winter still plagued him.

He opened his eyes before Cathy came to his side. That was a habit from those wilderness days as well.

'How has it been?'

The spectaculars of opening night had diminished in the year Kaspar left for France. It had seemed, to Cathy, an echo of the loss she had been feeling – for how could the Emporium ever be as filled with enchantment as when Kaspar walked its aisles? – but, in truth, it had been because of shipments not reaching London's wharves, and merchants biding their time while prices rose and fell. In the winters since, Emil and Papa Jack had spent long nights lost in each other's counsel, seeking a way to dazzle and delight even in these austere times. What did it matter what commodities were at hand? Papa Jack had insisted. Once, he had been a toymaker with only leaves and lengths of twig – and weren't those toys every bit as fantastic as the things that brought people to the Emporium twenty years later? Tonight had been testament to this, the most muted Opening Night in the Emporium's history – but the joy in the aisles had been of a different pitch than ever before. First frost had come on the night of the tenth of November, and rumour had it there was an armistice in France, that, this time, all of their boys truly would be home by Christmas night.

'It was a special kind of chaos, just as it always is. But ...'

She did not tell him how the Long War was already off sale, how Emil had filled the shopfloor with his recast soldiers, only to discover hours later that the glade had been pillaged, every box opened and emptied, the toy soldiers he had slaved over all summer gone. She left out the moment Emil tore into Kaspar's workshop and demanded to know what he had done (even though Mrs Hornung insisted he had not left the workshop all morning and, indeed, had been asleep for almost all of opening night). Perhaps Papa Jack needed no protection, not even in his old age, but those things did not seem right, somehow, to mention.

'Papa Jack, listen. There's something I have to ask. It is going to sound foolish. I hope you don't take me for a fool.'

'Sit, Cathy. We've talked about so much, you and I.'

Cathy sat at his side.

'Now that I come to it, it seems a question Martha ought to be asking, not a grown woman like me. But, Papa Jack, is it possible ... I mean to say, *might* it be possible ... that a toy might ...' Now she knew it truly was foolish; she had never been as foolish as this, not even as a child. '... come to life? Oh, we read about it in books. There are always puppets growing into real live boys.. And of course they come alive in the imagination and that, that's where a toy truly *lives*. But I don't mean that. I mean *life*. I look at Sirius and I wonder ...'

Papa Jack had taken Cathy by the hand. She flushed to look at him, so foolish did she feel. 'I've wondered too, my girl. Of all the patchwork dogs and cats and wolves and bears we've sent out into the world, what sets Sirius apart? He was made the same way, made with these same hands.' And he lifted them up, like a magician might do to show: no tricks. 'Sometimes you see understanding in those black button eyes, and no cogs and gears could ever account for that.'

'So what, then? What might it be?'

'My boys, and now you, have kept Sirius wound since the moment I made him. Wind down has never come to that poor patchwork dog. He just keeps going and going. They show him new tricks, and soon his gears strain to mimic them. They take him new places, and his paws record the way. They poured their teaching into him without even knowing that was what they were doing. And with every new trick he learned, every new habit, well, knowledge grows. The braille cards in his motors that tell him when to walk or when to run, when to sit up or when to wag his tail, they get imprinted with more and more knowledge. And then ... why, then, mightn't that knowledge rub up against itself? Mightn't one piece of knowledge touch or complement or clash with another? Suddenly it isn't just a list of tricks. It's a way of comparing one trick to all the rest. And maybe, just maybe, things begin to mesh. Maybe that meshing is a kind of ... intellect. These things are more mysterious than a mere toymaker could hope to account for. But sometimes, when I look into those black button eyes ...' Papa Jack paused. 'It would feel like murder to let him wind down, would it not?'

Cathy nodded.

'You cannot murder what never lived, so isn't *that* life?'

As if knowing he was being spoken of, Sirius sidled into the room, snouted at Cathy's hand, and curled up, right there, on her lap.

'The shop hands have been complaining, complaining about ... scuttling in the walls. They think we've got mice, or rats – and of course we do, because this is London and ...' Cathy lost her train of thought. 'What you say about Sirius, is it possible it might happen to other toys?

More quickly than you've said ...' She took a deep breath. To give voice to it was to make it manifest. 'Emil's soldiers. Kaspar changed them so that they can wind themselves. He did it out of spite, because Emil wouldn't listen any more, not when Kaspar tried to tell him what it was like, to be a soldier and have no control over what you do, where you go, who you are ... But since then, they're ... changed, and changed again. Martha showed me them drilling. They took an ordinary soldier and turned it into one of their own.' And now, she thought: the glades of the Long War brought to ruin, all of the hundreds Emil crafted all summer long, all of the thousands ... Toy soldiers, proliferating up and down the Emporium aisles. Emil had ordered the shop hands to lay barricades across the seventh aisle, to shut the snowflake stair. And she couldn't escape that feeling: the scuttling in the walls, it was nothing to do with mice ...

Papa Jack was staring. She thought he would speak of the soldiers but instead he said, 'How is my son?'

'I want to talk to him about it. We used to talk. The physicians say he has to, but he won't. This thing with the soldiers, at first I thought it might help. But now ...' She steadied herself, tracing the blue veins on Papa Jack's palm. 'I'm going to speak out of turn, Papa Jack, but you're the one who showed it to me, so perhaps you won't mind. All that time ago, when they dragged you into the East, when they chained you up with men like Chichikov and Ursa Major and all of the rest. It did something to you. It could have killed you, here, *inside*' – she lifted her hand from his to touch him on the breastbone – 'but you came home from it. You survived.'

Papa Jack whispered, 'But not the *same*. Never the *same*. It all does something to you. The little things as well as the big. You might go to sleep one person and wake so slightly different, and all because of a dream you had. You can't hope to go back. Men lose themselves trying it.'

And Cathy thought: those music boxes, the ones Kaspar tinkers with, even now. Even Cathy had felt the pull of the past, wanting to drag her down, wanting to immerse her.

'Might you speak with him, Papa Jack? You're his father. Perhaps he'd listen.'

Papa Jack said, 'I'll try.'

When Cathy got to her feet, Sirius followed. By the time she was halfway across the workshop, Papa Jack had closed his eyes. The worry was sloughing off her with every step. That was what Kaspar needed, she thought: only to talk.

As she stepped into the hall, Papa Jack stirred. 'Cathy,' he called out. She turned around to face him. 'I haven't forgotten how you stood here in front of me that day you first arrived. Even then you understood our Emporium, though you didn't know it. But can a toy come to life? My dear,' he breathed, 'it isn't foolish at all. All of the magic, all of the love we pour into them. I should think the only foolish thing is to wonder why it doesn't happen all of the time.'

Sleep came more easily when Cathy returned to her bed. Even so, she awoke in the pitch black, to the sound of scurrying in the walls and her heart beating wild. Instinctively she reached out for Kaspar – but he slept on and, in his sleep, cringed from her hand. She trembled as she lit the candle at her bedside, illuminating every corner in dancing orange light. The only thing that moved in the room was Sirius, the bellows of his lungs lifting his fabric hide up and down. And still that infernal scuttling in the walls.

Perhaps it was her imagination, but the scuttling seemed to move up and down the walls, as if the mice in the cavities were constantly surging one way and then the next. She followed it out on to the landing and pressed her ear against the wall. Sometimes it was strong and sometimes it was soft, but always it was there. Not mice. There was no point in keeping up the pretence. She took a deep breath and prepared to retreat to her bed – and it was then that she noticed the candlelight flickering under the opposite door. Martha's room. Evidently the girl had fallen asleep with her head in a book, and her candles still guttered on the ledge. Inwardly, Cathy sighed. This was how the Emporium would end: in a dancing inferno, patchwork beasts darting hither and thither, paper trees turned to columns of raging ash, and all because of a little girl who loved to read too much.

Quietly, she pushed through the door. Martha ought to have been there, wrapped up in sheets with the old copy of *Gulliver's Travels* splayed open on her lap, but instead the bed was empty, the covers drawn back and left in a heap at the end.

Cathy rushed to the window. The girl had left it open and the chill air clawing in made the candle stubs dance a wild fandango on the ledge. For a moment, there was terror – for the window opened on to a steepled roof, and all that separated the roof from the drop into Iron Duke Mews below was a length of iron gutter shot through with rust. She thought to call out, but the November air robbed her of all breath and, when she turned against it, she saw, for the first time, that the closet door was hanging ajar, and more candlelight coming from within.

Cathy stole forward and opened the door.

Here were Martha's dresses and here were Martha's coats; here were the costumes Kaspar himself had stitched, that might whisk Martha away to the court of some Imperial Tsar or the pleasure gardens of a Parisian palace. The candlelight, weak as it was, came from somewhere beyond.

She parted the coats and crept through – and there, in the back of the closet, sat Martha, gaping upwards with the candle at her side.

'Martha Godman, what on earth …'

Martha lifted a finger to her lips. Then, 'Look!' she whispered.

So Cathy looked.

The wall above Martha was a woodcut panorama from head to toe. The candlelight picked out grooves that had been scored into the wood, shapes and swirls of some primeval design. There were spirals and boxes, amorphous shapes that gradually took on the details of faces. Cathy followed them as they grew: the first, just a blob; the second, an orb with barely defined eyes, a mouth open wide as if in a scream. There, at the end of the row, the face of a toy soldier was recognisable at last.

She knelt down, bringing her candle close to the wood. The artist, whoever it was, had grown confident in the telling. At her foot an etching showed ranks of toy soldiers lined up against one another. The next showed two soldiers, crude stick men with tall charred hats, reaching out to shake each other's hands. In the next frame, what she could only take for a God (for he was vaster than any toy soldier) towered above the regiment. A second God was drawn leaner, more handsome, where the second was corpulent with eyes of deep engraved black.

In the final frame the soldiers lined up in procession. Cathy doubted herself at first but now she was certain: the soldiers were winding each other up while, from above, the good God looked benevolently down.

'It's Papa, isn't it?' Martha began. 'And the other ...' She pointed to the corpulent god, the one whose mouth was a wide black vortex, 'that's uncle Emil.'

She dropped the candle.

'Did you do this, Martha?'

Martha barely had time to shake her head when Cathy, with a rising panic she did not fully understand, snapped, 'Martha, this isn't a joke. If this was—'

'It wasn't!' Martha protested. 'Come and see.'

Outside the closet, Martha got to her knees and prised back a piece of skirting board from the wall. 'They scuttle through here, Mama. I hear them every night. So one night I got a chisel from Papa's workshop – I'm sorry, Mama, I'll put it back, I swear – and opened it up. I thought I might catch them, whatever they're up to in there. That's when I found this ...'

The etchings inside the skirting board were not nearly as nuanced as the ones across the closet walls. If the closet wall was a Bayeux tapestry of details and delights, the skirting board was the first foray of some Neanderthal cave dweller, scratching out bison and mammoth on his cavern wall.

Cathy took Martha's candle and pushed it into the gap. The sounds within were unmistakable. The toy soldiers might have been no more than inches from her hand. She imagined them gathered together, watching her in the dark.

'They're everywhere, Mama. Up and down every Emporium wall. It's an ... infestation.'

Cathy revolved to look at Martha. The words she wanted to say seemed absurd, but the evidence was there in etchings across the skirting board, up and down the closet walls.

'It's more than infestation. Is it possible ...' She paused, hesitating even now. 'Martha, have they learned how to *think*?'

THE FOREVER WAR

PAPA JACK'S EMPORIUM, 1919–1924

Emil opened the Emporium door, oblivious to the smells of the London spring. The snowdrops had flowered late along the Emporium terrace this winter, and a month later the circles that darkened around his eyes had still not disappeared. Sleep had been coming to him only in snatches; the memories of the season kept turning in his mind: the obliterated Long War, the barricaded aisle, the disappointed faces of the children who had flocked to their door, only to leave it empty-handed.

The man standing in the doorway had the look (like they all did) of somebody only just demobbed. Emil invited him inside and, taking care not to stare at the bright red birthmark that discoloured his right cheek, tramped with him into the aisles.

'I can hear them already,' said the man. He had a broom handle in one hand and a leather satchel into which had been stitched the words ANDERSENS' EXTERMINATORS. 'There must be a nest. It's the time of year for a nest. O' course, every time of year's the year for a nest these days. It's on account of the End Times. Plagues and wars and infestations. Well, we've already had two, so the third's on its way. You'll see.'

Emil did not intend to talk theology with a ratcatcher's apprentice and had already marched on when he looked back to discover the exterminator on his hands and knees, listening to the floor. 'Good Lord, there's a fair few. Have you got a sewer running under this shop?'

'I'm sure there's nothing of the sort.' Impatience came too easily these days. Emil pressed his face into the palm of his hand, hoping to cram whatever insult had been forming back into his throat.

'Well, there's *something*. I can hear hollows. There they are again!' And the exterminator, still squatting, scuttled to one of the walls. 'Do you mind?' he asked – and, before Emil could answer, he was back on his knees, a crowbar in hand. Soon, he had popped a length of skirting out, revealing a long black cavity beyond. 'It's the most vexing thing. Ordinarily, you'd jimmy up something like this and see spoor. Spoor here and spoor there. You see?'

Emil bristled.

'But – nothing!' Now he had a torch in his hand and was extending it into the hollow. 'You get to know the signs of rats in this profession. London has some big ones, o' course, but none as big as them we had in France. Nasty black fellows, big as cats. You remember things like that, don't you? It's silly the things you don't forget. I forget the sounds, but I don't forget the rats ...'

'I wasn't in France,' Emil uttered.

'Flanders, was it?'

'I wasn't there.'

'Ah, well,' the ratcatcher said with a modicum of impatience, 'you won't know rats then ...'

At last, Emil could take no more. He exploded: 'Whoever said they were rats?'

'You did call for a ratcatcher, sir. Now, I'm not one for riddles, but what do you call a ratcatcher for if you don't want to catch rats?'

'They're toy soldiers, you fool!'

Emil marched over and, kicking the neighbouring stretch of skirting aside, revealed a trio of soldiers standing stock still in the blackness. Poor fools, but their keys had wound down – and here they waited until some of their brethren happened across them on their patrols.

The ratcatcher laid down his torch and looked up. 'This some sort of trick, sir? Trying to catch me out, are you?'

'I just want them gone,' Emil breathed, but the ratcatcher was already on his feet.

'It might not seem much to you, sir, not with your flying galleons and castles in the air, but ratcatching's a noble profession. I've caught rats in palaces and sewers. Ain't no difference between them both.'

The exterminator marched back towards the doors.

'Please!' Emil cried after him. 'They're up and down the walls. They scurry all night. I haven't slept properly since Christmas.' His words were having no effect. 'I have two sons. Surely you can do *something*. Lay down traps. Put down poison. Don't you have ferrets you send in for this sort of thing?'

At the door, the exterminator turned on his heel. 'I could've been smothering fleas in Buckingham Palace,' he declared – and, on that dubious note, he was gone.

Screams sundered the Emporium night.

Cathy and Kaspar were in the Godmans' quarters, around the table with Mrs Hornung and Papa Jack, when the screaming began. The doors to the terrace were open, but there was no mistaking this for a scream coming from some Regent Street reveller, or drunkard on his way home. Cathy was on her feet in a second, pulling Martha near. The plates in front of them, piled high with *vareniki* and chipped potatoes (since she was a babe, Martha would not sanction a meal without chipped potatoes), sent up curls of steam.

'That's the boys,' said Cathy. 'Where's Nina?'

'Dinner in his lordship's workshop,' Mrs Hornung muttered darkly – for it had been months, years even, since Emil would sit around a dining table with his brother, and Mrs Hornung was compelled each night to deliver service to the shopfloor.

'Go for them, Martha. I'll be in the nursery ...'

Cathy hoisted her skirts and was already off, through the door.

The nursery was on Emil's side of the Godmans' quarters. As a bachelor, Emil had needed so little, sleeping wherever he fell, but when Nina arrived at the Emporium the old living rooms and larder had been partitioned and new bedrooms built where old storerooms used to lie. Cathy had often wondered if the rooms they all lived in were of a kin with the Wendy House sitting shuttered up on the shopfloor; she seemed to walk down halls too narrow, into rooms that threatened to be the size of a wardrobe but opened up into grand, palatial suites.

The nursery door was closed and the screams still coming from the other side. Cathy lunged for the handle and the door toppled inwards.

The boys were in their beds, old cots shorn of their sides, but they were not alone. The window was wide open, net curtains rippling in the breeze, but no crook nor kidnapper had shimmied up the drainpipe to carry away the Godman boys.

All around, toy soldiers swarmed.

They had come out of the skirting. Cathy could see, in the corners of her eyes, places where little portals had been chipped away, doors opened into the wall beyond. Now they stood along the rails at the foot of the boys' beds, marching where they could across the undulating battlefields of the bedspreads themselves. Little siege towers and scaling ladders, cobbled together out of salvaged wood (and, Cathy saw to her surprise, pieces of shelving harvested from the shopfloor), had been pushed into place against the beds, and up these the soldiers were scrambling. A scouting party had reached the giddy heights of the window ledge using crampons and cotton rope, while others worked with miniature axe heads (Cathy took them for skittled pennies) to carve notches in the bed legs, like foresters hard at work.

The boys must have been sleeping, safe in their dream worlds, when the toy soldiers arrived, for Cathy saw now that they were lashed down with crimson ribbon. There were bales of the stuff in the storerooms, and perhaps that meant that the Emporium basements had already been breached. The soldiers were plundering wherever, whenever and whatever they could.

Bound so tightly they could barely lift their heads, the boys strained to look at Cathy. She thought she had never seen such fear.

The soldiers had not yet noticed Cathy hanging in the door. She watched with horror as one, more surefooted than the rest, advanced across the bedspread of the closest boy, marched up his breast and lifted his rifle. Before Cathy took another step the soldier fired; a little wooden bullet exploded forth, falling short of the boy's face, and was promptly wound up again, back into the barrel of the soldier's gun. Soon, the boy's screaming had turned into a succession of quiet, breathy sobs.

'Off them!' Cathy cried out, and was about to throw herself into the room when somebody pounded up the hall behind her, barrelling Kaspar and Papa Jack out of the way, and thrust her bodily aside.

Emil came into the room in a thunder of footsteps and launched himself at the first bed.

The soldiers turned as one. The mountaineers on the window ledge tumbled in surprise, grappling out for their ropes as they plummeted to the flatlands of the floorboards underneath. A trio emerged from the foot of the bed, lifted their faces at the giant tearing at his son's ribbon shackles, and scrambled back. Some valiant soldiers lifted rifles and let wooden volleys fly; others turned to escape into the skirting. The siege tower, several of the scaling ladders, were already turned to a ruin under Emil's boots. He had lifted his first son out of the bed and, cradling him to his shoulder, caught Cathy and Kaspar frozen in the doorway, as he turned to rescue his second.

'Don't stand there gawping! Do something! Cathy, you of all people ...'

Cathy knelt to loosen the ribbons that bound the second boy. Until now he had been silent, but at the moment of rescue he started shrieking. There was a toy soldier tangled in his hair and, when Cathy lifted him, it dropped to the bedspread.

Emil flailed out with his foot, sending the second siege tower skittering across the room. The soldier on the bedspread marched from one end to the other, finding no way down to the floorboards below. His painted features gave no hint at what he was thinking (if these things, Cathy had to remind herself, really could think), but the way he turned gave the impression of panic.

Emil's boy was sobbing into her shoulder. She cooed for him to be quiet, told him that he was safe. Now that the worst was over she stepped forward, as if Emil might take him – but his eyes were on the bed, the soldier who marched in circles searching for a way down. It was only now that Cathy noticed its uniform of crimson red, the valiant features with which its face had been etched. The Imperial Kapitan. The soldier who had stood, for so long, on the ledge of Emil's workshop, looking over everything that he did. Now, he was one of the things building their doll's house world up and down the Emporium walls.

The venom was gone from Emil. Crestfallen, he stuttered backwards – and, seizing its chance, the Imperial Kapitan cast itself off the edge of the bed. Then, picking itself up (and perhaps amazed that the fall had not corrupted its workings), it joined the last soldiers flooding back into the skirting. On the threshold it turned, threw Emil a defiant salute, and vanished into the dark.

In the hallway outside Nina had arrived. Forcing herself between Kaspar and Papa Jack, she demanded the boy from Cathy's arms. Before she took him, she drew back a hand and whipped it directly across Kaspar's cheek. Kaspar turned, only fractionally. Not a word passed his lips.

'Emil?' Nina began, as if reminding him of some private discourse.

Emil's eyes had been on the skirting, but he came to his senses now. 'It's gone too far, Kaspar. *Too far*. You're to call them off. Summon them up or issue some proclamation, or whatever it is you do, and tell them what's what.'

Kaspar stammered, 'Emil, you can't possibly think *I*—'

'I do,' Emil declared. 'I saw it. That was *my* Kapitan. Why else would you take him and fit him out like all the rest, if not for spite? Well, you've done it now, Kaspar. They've crossed a line. They're only boys. They're your nephews, for what that's worth. Call them off. Call them off or I'll …'

'We'll burn them out,' Nina said, as poised as Emil was fevered. 'They come for my sons, well, we'll come for them. So what's it to be?'

'Emil,' Kaspar began, 'are you going to let her speak to me like this? This isn't *my* doing. I haven't told them to do a thing. That's the very point. What they do, that's up to them. It's you who *tells* them. You who …'

Nina opened her other arm, took her second son away from Emil. For a moment, Emil resisted; then he let the boy go to his mama. In the doorway, Nina hesitated, both boys dangling from her neck. 'Are you coming?'

Emil shouldered his way out into the hall. 'I'm sorry, Papa,' he said, 'but this is just intolerable. They're only little boys. What did they do to deserve this? To be victimised in their own home? And if he won't even—'

Kaspar reached out, but Emil only shook him away.

'Hands off me, Kaspar.' He had gone three steps before he spoke again. 'Do you know, we were doing fine. I thought it was going to be impossible without you here.

I thought it was going to be hell. I thought there'd be customers turning away, and all because you weren't here with your fanciful designs. Well, it wasn't like that. Do you know what the biggest shock was in those years? It wasn't that the customers didn't miss you, for I'm certain that they did. It was that ... I could do it too. I could make things they'd talk about. Oh, they mightn't have been the same as yours, but they didn't have to be, because they were mine. I could bring them in and I could show them how, and, and ... and I could have a wife and I could have a family too. The Emporium is *ours*, Kaspar, and you just couldn't stand it, so you had to ...'

Cathy had been listening from the bedroom, but at last she joined them in the hall. 'Emil, it's better if you go. Be there for your boys. Nina will thank you for it. *You'll* thank me for it, in the morning.'

'Thank you? Thank *you*, Cathy? Do you know, *you* were better in his absence as well. There isn't a thing your wife can't do, Kaspar, and you haven't deserved her, not for one second since you've been back.'

Emil disappeared down the hall, into the room he and Nina shared. The reverberations of their argument moved in the walls, just as surely as the tramping of toy soldiers, but Cathy tried to put it from her mind as they returned to their own side of the quarters.

As soon as the outer door was closed, she heard the crying. She had thought to plead with Kaspar, for there must have been something he could do, but instead she was drawn to Martha's bedroom door. At the foot of her bed, Martha sat in a ball, her knees tucked into her chin, Sirius trying to inveigle himself inside to give her what comfort he could. Cathy rushed to her side, falling to the floor so that she could wrap her in her arms.

'It's all my fault,' Martha said, between breathy gulps.

'What is?'

'The boys. I saw them through the door. I didn't mean to, Mama, but ...'

Kaspar was hovering in the doorway and, with one arm wrapped around Martha, Cathy gestured for him to come in. When he remained outside, her face set hard and her gesture became a demand. She hated to concede it, but Emil had been right about one thing: those years when Kaspar had been away, those endless summers and testing winters, somehow they had been easier than this.

'Martha, my treasure, how could any of it have been down to you?'

Martha got to her feet and brought Cathy the book that had been half-hidden beneath her pillow. Cathy remembered the book well, though now it was falling apart. The stitches in its seams had long come undone. Martha dropped it into her hands and it fell open at the colour plates in its middle.

Gulliver's Travels. In the illustration, the giant Gulliver lay on his back among hills of rolling green, and crawling all over him were the tiny Lilliputians, men no bigger than the little finger of Gulliver's clenched fist. In his sleep Gulliver had been lashed down with ropes. Scaffolds of wood and wire had been built across both of his shins, his midriff buried beneath the beginnings of a rudimentary fort.

'I hear them, every night, in the wardrobe and the walls ... and I thought that maybe they wanted to listen. Maybe, if I read to them, they might come out and line up and ... they did, Mama. They did.' The tears were threatening to come again, but Martha had learnt stubbornness from her father (perhaps Cathy had something to do with it too) and fought to contain them with a single, sticky snort. 'I wasn't sure if they understood. Not at first. But something must have got through, because the second night more came, and the third night even more. After that they just kept pouring out of the wardrobe. It was like they were telling each other, in the walls: come and listen, come and listen to the story ...'

The first nights they sat in perfect stillness, the only sound the steady rattle of their motors winding down, and *listened*. It was weeks before they started reacting. Martha would tell them how Gulliver was enslaved by the Lilliputians and the soldiers would be on their feet, twirling around in what she could only define as sheer, unadulterated joy. When she reached the moment in the story when Gulliver, found guilty of treason, was sentenced to be blinded in both eyes, the righteousness among the soldiers turned into a riot. 'The Imperial Kapitan had to order them to stand down. He was marching through them and putting them in place and ... I think he still cares for Emil, Mama. Maybe he remembers everything that happened before he ... woke up. How they were friends, back then.'

In the doorway, Kaspar still lingered. 'I don't believe so. Back then the Kapitan was only sandalwood and teak, a little varnish, a little paint.'

Cathy had heard quite enough. Besides, what story Martha was telling was quickly lost in the resurgent scuttling in the walls. On her feet, she stepped through the closet door, parted the hanging dresses and coats, and gazed at the mural carved into the wood. A new etching had appeared among the rest, one with all the florid detail of the best Renaissance painters. Surrounded by soldiers bearing guns, two little boys were lashed to their beds. The giant that was Emil stood horrified behind them. There was something in the way his face had been rendered that gave the impression of despair, of terror, of submission. The way they depicted it, the soldiers had cowed the monster.

Cathy lifted her hand to her mouth.

Back outside the closet, Kaspar had come into the room to sit beside Martha. 'What if they could learn more, Papa. They might ...'

'They planned it,' Cathy cut in. 'They'll have other plans as well. Surely you could talk to them? They know you, Kaspar. They trust you. They think ... they think you're gods. You the light and Emil the dark, and all because of that stupid Long War of yours.' What she was saying ought to have seemed a fantasy, but she had been too long in Papa Jack's Emporium to believe anything else. It meant the soldiers had minds, it meant those minds were growing – but she knew that already, from the way their etchings grew more sophisticated, the way they grew more organised and bold. Her eyes dropped to the copy of *Gulliver's Travels*, and she thought of how Papa Jack had described Sirius: his mind a collection of tricks, things performed by rote, until suddenly came ideas and knowledge, intellect and invention. *Personality.* What else had the soldiers drawn from the story? Stories were like entire lives lived in a few dozen pages. How more swiftly might a mind grow if it could read, if it devoured one story after another?

'I couldn't speak with them,' Kaspar replied, 'not even if I wanted to. I could only speak *at* them, and that would never do. I won't tell them how to live. That would make me as bad as Emil. Worse, because I'd be doing it against my conscience. Something of which my brother is in dire need.'

'And if they come again?' Cathy pictured Martha lashed to the bed, but then thought: *no, they would never come, not for us, not their saviours* . . . 'Whatever you think of him now, he is still your brother. And if you won't tell them what to do, then . . . we could explain. Come to a parley.'

Kaspar dragged himself back to the door. 'It's for them to decide,' he said, as if betrayed. 'They're to choose their own lives.'

After he was gone, Martha went to her mother. 'I'm sorry, Mama.'

'Don't be. Your papa will come round.' He has to, Cathy thought, or else everything is lost. 'Martha,' she ventured, 'what your papa said is true. He could talk at them, but not with them. But . . . when you read to them, when they understand, have they ever . . .'

'Tried to talk back? Mama, they whirl their arms and march on the spot and throw the wildest salutes. It has to mean something.'

Cathy bent down and kissed her on the brow. 'If you hear a whisper from the wardrobe, you fetch me that instant. Do you understand? And, for heaven's sake, leave something out for them. A page from the book, a little coloured stone, one of your dolls. Anything so that, if they come out of the walls while you sleep, they know we're friends, that we're not angry for what happened tonight . . .'

The idea thrilled Martha. It was the way medieval villagers might leave out a butchered calf (or some humdrum village girl) to curry favour with the dragon from the mountaintop, or the demons who rose up every All Hallows' Eve. She chose one of her ballerinas, thinking that those poor soldiers deserved at least one girl in their lives, and climbed back into bed. Her tears were dry at last. She picked up her *Gulliver's Travels* and then, thinking better of it, turned to Jules Verne. These toy soldiers were certainly a thing of which Mr Verne would have approved.

She was halfway into her chapter when a thought occurred, a memory resurfacing as memories sometimes will. Martha had been up in the boughs of one of the paper trees (a place she was forbidden to go) on the day Emil proposed marriage to Nina. Martha had known, even then, that she did not entirely approve of the idea of Nina living among them, not while her father was so far away. But the way Emil had made his proposal had stirred even her to a fit of admiration. The way those toy soldiers (then just simple, wind-up things, without even a mind between them) had been set to march so that they would spell out the words had been an ingenious thing.

The way ideas formed in the mind of a toy soldier was not so different from how they formed in the mind of a girl. One idea gave rise to another, that idea gave rise to an idea greater still. Shapes came together to create bigger, more convincing shapes ...

To speak with the soldiers? To teach them how to spell and march out words – not like Emil had done, through timing and expert design, but by thought, by their own volition? Yes, she thought, that would be an accomplishment of which even that stinker Mr Atlee might have been proud. She returned to her Jules Verne with newfound aplomb and (thinking nothing of her mama's instructions) began to recite out loud.

That night, down on his knees, Emil piped putty into every hole or crack in the skirting. He tossed handfuls of nails into the cavities beyond, smiled as he pictured clots of soldiers entombed in the dark, nothing to do for eternity but endlessly wind each other up. What minds they had were simple, primitive things. It would take so little to drive a mind like that mad ...

Nina lay in their bed with her arms around the boys. It had taken some time for them to sleep. Now they rested fitfully, feet kicking out with every dark turn of their dreams. 'If it isn't safe to be here,' she said, 'we cannot be here.'

Emil continued his work.

'If our boys can't sleep soundly in their own home, well, what kind of home is this? What kind of a father are you?'

Emil tensed, contained himself, then returned to his work.

'Are you listening to me, Emil?'

Emil stood.

'I'm going to make it safe.'

At that moment, there came a burst of scuttling in the walls. In their sleep, the boys grasped their mother more tightly still.

'I'll be back,' Emil said.

In the boys' bedroom, he heaved the beds away from the walls. Here was where the soldiers had streamed out. Evidently, they had returned while he was gone, for the wreckage of their siege engines had been dragged back into the skirting. On his knees, Emil began his own fortifications.

More nails, more putty, more wooden boards. If only half the Emporium had not been wood, he would happily have put them to the torch.

Emil planned to sit up that night, and for all the nights to come, watching over his boys. He would sit with his fishing net and a bucket of rotating blades and, if ever a toy soldier appeared, he would scoop it up and scythe it back into splinters. But after that night, the boys never did return to their own room. Their mother would not allow it. And because there was no room in the marital bed for Emil to join them, that night (and for all the nights to come) Emil sat up alone, or slept where he fell. In his son's bed he listened to the scuttling in the walls, smiled at the panic he sensed when the soldiers ran into one of his traps of shattered glass, and tried not to think of the Imperial Kapitan, his sparkling creation, standing unyieldingly on his son's breast with his wooden rifle raised.

If nobody else would help him, he would have to do it himself.

That winter had been punishing, but they had made it through. What a sorry feeling it was, to be actively waiting for the first snowdrops to flower, to long for the big, empty days when the Emporium was closed so that, at least, it was done for another year. This Christmas the customers had still come, but how many came back when they were told to find their toy soldiers elsewhere? How many told their friends? How many remarked upon the ramshackle aisles, the places where the skirting boards had been levered up to reveal great holes in the walls, the constant sounds of chittering in unseen corners? And what of the boy who had come to the shop with his own toy soldiers in his pocket, only to discover them gone when the time came to leave? Where were they now, Emil wondered, if not patrolling the walls with the rest?

Well, Kaspar was not the only talented toymaker among them.

Emil shook his boys until they awoke and, rubbing blearily at their eyes, they clambered out of the bed where their mother still slept. 'What are we doing, Papa?' one of them asked. 'It's a midnight adventure!' the other announced. But, 'A midnight raid,' Emil replied, 'and I wouldn't let you miss it for the world. We're going to end this thing once and for all. Your papa has a plan ...'

Nina would surely not approve, but Nina was still asleep, so Nina would never have to know. With his boys marching behind him, Emil made his way to the shopfloor. There, in the half-moon hall, a crate fastened with steel rivets was waiting where he had left it. Emil made his boys stand aside as he jimmied it open. Inside, wrapped in crêpe paper, were a hundred soldiers of his own design. 'An elite guard,' he announced. 'Worthy to be generals, every one. Your uncle might have realised the wildest ideas, boys, but he never surpassed me with my soldiers – not when we were little, and not now ...'

'Is it going to be a battle, Papa?' At four years old, the idea of a battle ought to have been the most thrilling thing of all, but since that night when the soldiers attacked all talk of battle had been banned by their mother.

'My boys, it's going to be a massacre. Your uncle has to learn that this Emporium isn't his to do with as he pleases.

It's ours, it's *yours*, and these soldiers of his have to be told. Wind them up, boys. I'll prepare the way.'

The boys scurried to their task as Emil crowbarred a piece of skirting away from the wall. Then, at his command, the boys released the soldiers and stood back as they marched into the brickwork, dividing into two columns as they went. If Emil had calculated correctly, they would fan out into the cavities he had mapped – and somewhere, in the unseen crevices around them, battle would be joined.

'It's happening, Papa! Listen!'

In the walls around them, a thousand tiny footsteps could be heard. There came no battle cries, only the thud and crunch of wood against wood, the hollow pops of mahogany bullets letting fly. Emil whirled around, dancing on the spot. First, there was battle on his right; then, battle on his left; then, finally, pitched battle beneath the soles of his feet.

Eventually, all around him was silence. For some time, not a toy soldier moved. It was a joyous sound; Emil had not heard silence like it in many long months. Some of his own soldiers would have wound down by now – but that had always been their fate, to fulfil the decimation for which they had been made, and slowly grind to a halt, down there in the dark. They were warriors, and would have been proud. No matter what Kaspar would say, to die for one's country was a sweet and glorious thing.

Emil counted slowly under his breath: one, two, three, four. Then, as he had planned, the footsteps started again.

'Stand back, boys, it's nearly time!'

The boys reeled as toy soldiers burst out of the wall. Emil's elite guard, those who had survived, streamed on to the shopfloor – and there, pursuing them, came the self-winding host.

The trap was sprung. Emil reached out, pulled a cord at his side – and from a second silver crate sprang a patchwork wolf. The wolf was coiled so tightly it hurtled forward, skittling elite guard and self-winding soldier alike – but it had only one command. In the middle of the battlefield, the wolf wrapped its jaws around a soldier in glistening red and, when it came to deposit it in Emil's hands, the jaws opened to reveal the Imperial Kapitan, his legs milling in wild panic.

Emil took the Kapitan in his fist, held him up so that the fleeing soldiers might see. Some of them stopped on their way back into the skirting. How did they perceive him then, through their wooden eyes, their general dangling up above? 'He's ours now. Come on, boys. I'll show you how we're to sleep safely in our own homes.'

The boys followed their father across the ravaged shopfloor, down the tapering aisle to the workshop at its end. Such a magical thing for the boys to come into their papa's workshop. They held hands and gaped at the stars plastered across the ceiling, the nightjars on the shelf.

At the workshop's end, a brass birdcage stood on its stand. The boys recognised it from last Christmas, for this was the roost Papa Jack's phoenix kept on the nights he soared over the shopfloor. Its wires were tightly meshed; a padlock dangled from a door where there was no real need.

The Imperial Kapitan hung limp in Emil's hand. Now, he wound him up and cast him inside. As he fumbled to lock the door, the Kapitan picked himself up. Perhaps Emil was only imagining the rush of feeling as life spread back through the Kapitan's heart, along every piece of wire and catgut in his body. The toy soldier flexed his finger joints, threw a salute (was this mockery, or just confusion as his mind – if mind it truly was – came back into being?), and marched on the spot.

'See, boys?' Emil whispered, drawing them near. 'He's here now, and he's here at our mercy. Without us, he'll wind down. Without us, he'll cease to exist. And if those other soldiers know what's good for them ...' He took a broom handle and beat out a rhythm on the skirting, up and down the walls. 'They'll do as I tell them.' He opened his mouth to roar out. 'Go back to your walls! Live your doll's-house lives! But stay away from the shopfloor or ...' He rounded on the birdcage again, and the Imperial Kapitan who had once been his friend. 'Wind Down. Wind Down for you all!'

How to explain what was happening in the walls? Days passed. Weeks and months. Sometimes the soldiers were quelled, but sometimes they grew confident, determined to win back their Kapitan – and that was when the workshop walls came alive with the tramping of a thousand wooden feet. Emil ran sorties when he discovered a build-up behind his workshop door. He built patchwork ferrets and sent them into the skirting to hunt; when they came back at all, it was with their backs pierced by wooden lances, their stuffing ripped out. So long did he spend conniving ways to stop the soldiers proliferating, blocking up holes in the skirting and cementing up the burrows his boys kept discovering, that for long months he made no new toys for the winter to come. All the while, Papa Jack worked long into the nights, so that the aisles might be full again by the time first frost came. And because he was locked away, with only his toys to confide in, nobody noticed the new cough that was wracking his chest, nor the way his fingers were finally – after decades of intricate work – beginning to seize up. They did not notice the first time his memory failed him, because he recovered of his own accord and continued to make stitches in the hides of his seaside serpents. They only went about their business, and he about his, and the only ones who truly knew were the soldiers standing dumbly in the walls.

In Martha's quarters that summer, when Mr Atlee came to give her lessons, the wind-up host gathered to listen. She took to opening the skirting board so that they could hear her teacher drone on about arithmetic and parables, kings and countries and the Proverbs of the Bible. Sometimes, she came back to her bedroom at night to find that they had scaled to the top of her reading desk and were marching up and down her thesaurus, as if trying to understand the mysteries written within. At night, she read to them from Gibbon's *Decline and Fall of the Roman Empire* – but of armies and soldiers, no matter what the sort, they didn't want to hear. Instead, she read them Perrault and the Brothers Grimm, stories from the *Arabian Nights*. She read them Jules Verne and HG Wells. And when Cathy came to wish her goodnight, she was shocked (but not surprised) to see the soldiers perched on every shelf around the bedstead, the sounds of their constant motors turning all around.

Stories, Martha thought. It was stories that could help them think …

The first frost came late in that year of 1923 – so that, by the time the Emporium opened its doors, the ledgerbooks looked barer than ever, and when Mr Moilliet, the man from Lloyd's, came to consider the annual accounts, he departed with a sombre look and promises in his ear that surely could not be kept. There was no grand spectacle that night. When the first families flocked through the doors, they were not met with flying reindeer or cartwheeling stars, but only by a shopfloor half the size of the year before, its outer reaches boarded up to avoid the sense of empty shelves. There would have been more magic, the customers whispered, in a night at the Palladium, and this was a thing that had never been said before.

If you had returned to the Emporium that Christmas (as so many men did, seeking reminders of earlier, more innocent times), you would not have recognised it as the Emporium of your youth. You would have turned into dead-end aisles, would have seen hollows where toys had been bought and never replenished; the Wendy House you used to marvel at would have seemed a grotty woodland hovel, its windows still boarded up; and, above all else, you would have floundered over the looping railway lines that had erupted all over the Emporium floor – for there had been an industrial revolution in the walls that winter, the toy soldiers seeking better ways to cross the vast distances between them and unearth stores of more inert soldiers they could fit with self-winding designs. Emil and what shop hands he could afford had spent days prising up the new railway lines, but as fast as they worked, the wind-up army worked faster. By the time the first frost came, Emil had already ceded the mezzanine, the carousel, half of the windward aisles to the soldiers, in the hope they might be satisfied – yet, at night, the hooting of train whistles filled the shopfloor, and each morning, the aisles were a little more ragged, another paper tree felled or another tow-rope severed, upending the cloud castle above. And if you had been like any of the other shoppers come to the Emporium that winter, you would have taken one look at the ruin and thought: is this it? Is this the place I used to dream about coming every year? Have I changed, or is the Emporium really gone?

It had been a quarter of a century since Papa Jack last saw an opening night, but tonight he emerged from his workshop tomb and gazed out across the shopfloor. He watched his patchwork pegasi, threadbare after so many years, cartwheeling through the towers of the listing cloud castle and, closing his eyes, shuffled on his way.

The Godmans' quarters stood silent, Cathy, Martha, Emil and the rest attending to the shopfloor below, but here lay Kaspar, curled up in bed where Papa Jack had known he would be. When he slept there was still a way of believing he was thirty years younger – only now the demons that danced in his dreams were built out of memory, not childish fancy or imagination. Papa Jack lowered himself to the seat at his bedside.

'Kaspar,' he whispered. 'Kaspar, my boy?'

At Papa Jack's touch, Kaspar turned toward him, as a child might reach out for their papa in the night.

'Opening night used to be so special to you, Kaspar. I want it to be special again. Cathy asked me to talk to you. I promised I would, but until now I could never find the words. Because – how do you solve a life, my Kaspar? How do you solve a life like yours ... and mine. A life is not such a very easy thing. So the weeks started passing, and then the months passed and the years, but ... Kaspar, here I am, where I've always been, ever since I came back and found my boys. *Here. I. Am.*'

In his sleep, Kaspar had reached out and threaded his fingers into his papa's. Papa Jack's hand dwarfed his. He held it fast.

'I've dreamt of what I might say. I've longed to find it. I've thought for so long I don't have any more time to think, so here it is, everything I have ...' He took a deep breath because this thing he had come here to say, it did not want saying. 'You cannot go back.' He paused. 'When I left my *katorga*, I wasn't the same man they snatched away when you were so small. I thought I could be, but I was wrong. And all that year, as I wended my way back into the west, as I stopped to make toys in the villages and bought favours and rides and a roof over my head with toy soldiers and ballerinas and bears, I understood it more deeply than ever. I wasn't really walking back the way I had come, because this man that I was, he wasn't the same man who'd made the trek east. With every footstep I was somebody new.

'You're new too, Kaspar. A man can't go out and see the things you've seen, do the things you've done, and come back to his old place in the world. This Emporium of ours, it crystallises childhood. It makes us long for those days when all the world was a toy and all of life was the adventure you had when you closed your eyes and made it happen. But Kaspar, if you go on like this, there isn't a happy ending. There's just more of ... this. I had to find a new way to be. I found my boys and I took them into new lands and I made something for us there. I made this Emporium. I got away from the wilderness by finding something else. And Kaspar,' he whispered, and brought his head down to his son's face, and planted a kiss on him there, 'perhaps you must too.'

A single tear rolled from Papa Jack's eye to land intact upon Kaspar's cheek.

Papa Jack took the back way to his workshop, unwilling to look out over the shopfloor one last time. Once inside, he shut the door. Somehow Sirius had found his way within. The patchwork dog rested its muzzle in his hands. Then it lifted itself, lapped him once with its darned sock tongue, and whimpered as it left.

Alone now, he studied his workshop.

Eyes were watching him. This was another of those things he had carried with him all of his life; he could always tell when he was being watched. He made himself tea from the pine needles and samovar Mrs Hornung always left out and, as he was stirring through syrup, he saw the flickerings of movement in the edges of his vision. 'I see you,' he whispered, with a smile. 'Yes, I see you now. You may come out, if that is what you wish. Your secrets are safe with me.'

Without looking down, he retreated to his seat. The arms rose up to hold him and he realised, with a starkness he had not felt before, how good it was to be held. It had been so long since he felt the warmth of human arms. Desire did not die, not even after all this time.

As he breathed in the scent of pine forest floating up on the steam, the scuttling arose at his feet. He felt them before he could see them. Then he was down on his knees among them, the wind-up soldiery milling around.

There were ten of them. More gathered at the skirting where a loose board released them from the walls. Papa Jack lowered himself until they were of a level, staring into their delicately painted faces with his own of flesh and blood. 'How handsome you are,' he ventured, and extended a palm as if to invite one aboard.

The soldiers milled frantically, uncertain of what they were being asked.

'You may go back to your skirtings, should you like,' Papa Jack began, 'but I should be grateful of some company tonight.'

As if emboldened (or was it in empathy?) the soldier closest to Papa Jack marched forward and set his little wooden jackboots upon his palm. Gently, so as not to topple him, Papa Jack lifted himself back into his seat. The sight of their brother at ease in the giant's hand drew yet more soldiers from the skirtings. They lined up in battalions at Papa Jack's feet.

'My sons made such magic here. They made it together, if only they could see. I can see my Emil's hand in your finish. I can see my Kaspar in how you … live. Yes, I believe I shall use the word, tonight. And at least I am not to be alone.'

The soldier in his hand was winding down. It turned frantically, seeking out its brothers on the workshop floor – until Papa Jack whispered, 'May I?', and the soldier, nodding in spite of his panic, stiffened as Papa Jack twisted the key in his back.

The soldier was renewed. The only soldier since the Rising to have been wound up by a man. 'The honour,' Papa Jack began, 'is mine alone,' and, setting the soldier back down, he reached into the trunk at his side. When he brought his hands out he was clutching twists of pinecone and grass, bundles of twig and dried bark.

'It was with these that I bartered my life,' he said, and lay them down. 'The first toy soldiers a Godman ever made, but you should take them now. It is your ancestry, after all.'

The soldiers gathered, and perhaps they saw themselves in the dried husks, in the same way a man might see himself in the skeletons of prehistoric apes strung together for a museum dais.

The edges of the room were growing indistinct. Papa Jack closed and then opened his eyes. Look around you, he thought. There is nothing in the history of the world, no aspect of life nor of death, that is not being charted here, in this workshop, tonight. Half of Papa Jack's life had been lived alone; what might life have been like if he had had somebody at his side, somebody to wind him up when his heart began to slow?

In the air around him, memory and waking life merged. He was in his workshop and yet at the same time he was suckling at his mama's breast. There was a bear he used to have, little more than a stitched-up fur, and he had carried it about the village where he grew up until it clean rotted away. He thought he would like to hold it now, to cuddle it or to play – but there was no need; toys didn't need playing with any longer, for they were playing with themselves. And, 'I would have liked to have seen what becomes of you,' he said to the waiting host. 'We have all come so very far.'

Every man was a child in the moment that he died. Jekabs Godman closed his eyes and, with a hundred wooden faces watching, he slipped slowly from this world.

THE LITTLE ACT OF A LONG GOODBYE

. . . .

PAPA JACK'S EMPORIUM AND HIGHGATE CEMETERY, 1924

Consider the Imperial Kapitan: born on a workshop lathe, given form by chisel and file; one Emporium soldier brought into this world to rule over them all. Tonight, if you had been wandering the deserted shopfloor, breathing in the dust and musk of the Emporium in summer, you would not have heard its screams, nor it pleading for mercy. Leave aside for a moment the fact that it has no voice. It is, after all, only a toy. (Or at least, keep telling yourself that, if you – like poor Emil Godman – still refuse to believe.) The Imperial Kapitan neither screams nor begs because it is not the way he was made. His pride is there in every groove etched into his face. Even if the mechanism that is his beating heart were designed to give him words, he would not scream, not for you and not for anyone else.

Imagine for a moment what the Kapitan thinks and feels (*believe*, now, that toys can think and feel) as he watches the workshop door open from behind the bars of his birdcage prison. His motor is almost winding down and, with it, comes a slowing of the world. He knows his death is near, but this is not the first time he has been wound down and it will not be the last. There is still a chance he can rise again. So he watches this figure, this behemoth, hove into view – and the last thing he sees, before the blackness of Wind Down comes (as it must come, in the end, for all of his People) is a vision of Creation: the daemon-god who chipped him from dead timber is stomping in his giant's stride across this crucible, this Work Shop, where all life began, opening the birdcage door and taking him in his fist.

The last thing he feels are fingers, vast as the trunks of trees. The Imperial Kapitan thinks: *how like us he is, and yet how different we are. The gods made us in their own image …* But the thought is stamped out, for Wind Down is here and all things must end.

Life returns, with a feeling like his insides being wrenched. It is the bite that comes with Wind Up, so gentle at the hands of his brothers, so violent in the fist of a god. The world solidifies slowly. He would struggle if he thought it would do any good, but the god is holding him aloft, whirling him across the workshop, to where great Fires burn in the Hearthland.

The god sits back in a chair. He sobs, the great fat tears of a god.

'You were mine,' he says (and the Imperial Kapitan thinks: no, I am *mine*). 'I made you here, right here …' (And the Kapitan thinks: no, I was made with my first idea, my first thought; or I was made when the tree from which I was hewn sprouted; but not here, never *here*). 'He thinks it's a miracle, *his* miracle, and this the final insult. Everything that was mine, turned to his. He couldn't let me have one moment, one moment to make my papa proud, one toy that might last so my children could look back and say: there, that was my father, how great he was. And now … Now

Papa's gone, and he thinks this place is *his, his* to do with as he wishes ... And what he wishes is to cede it to *YOU*.'

The daemon-god grapples the Kapitan forward, until the heat of Fire starts to taint the colour of his wood. Paint and varnish run, the Kapitan's lifeblood dripping on the god's fat fingers.

'Well, it isn't going to be that way. Do you hear me? You're toys. You're not real. The Emporium is going to survive, and my sons are going to play here, safely, where they belong. And ...' He voices a fear; the Imperial Kapitan knows it for what it is by the tenor of his voice. '... my wife is going to stay. She won't take my boys from me, not when you're gone ...'

Fire again. The Imperial Kapitan has been turned so that he must face it. And in the flames he believes he sees an image of the daemon rendered in red and orange. *Daemon Lord who sent us out to fight the Long War. Daemon Lord who set us against each other, who forced us to kill our fellows. Daemon Lord who revelled in war, war without end ... Wind Up and Fight, Wind Up and Fight again ...*

The feeling of wood turning to charcoal is not like Wind Down at all. This is the Always End of which their prophets sometimes speak. The Imperial Kapitan prepares himself but, at the last moment, the daemon stays its hand.

'Did you think it would be that easy? One terrible moment, and then gone? No, you're not to be destroyed. You're to be *paraded*. Paraded so that the rest of them know. Paraded so that they know who I am and what they are. I'm the *Toymaker*. This is my Emporium.' Then his voice breaks and, with a lilting sadness he says, 'It didn't have to be this way. You were mine, once. We used to play together.'

The Imperial Kapitan finds himself cast back into his birdcage prison. There he picks himself up and, as he watches the behemoth retreat into the Outer Dark, thinks: *but where is the other of which the daemon speaks, the Angel who saved us? The god-of-light who put the Long War to an end. Who saw the slaughter and thought: NO MORE! Why is he not here to take me in his hand and deliver me back to Skirting Board and Ward Robe?*

It is only as he starts to feel the dull ache of Wind Down once more that the Imperial Kapitan remembers: the one they call Kaspar, the brother god of the daemon, he did not set us free by his own hand. He gave us, instead, the power to wind ourselves and, in so doing, make decisions for ourselves. These decisions, they are the magic we call Life. He did not speak commandments, nor ordain from on high. It is the daemon who seeks to direct us with *Rules of Engagement* and forbids us from laying down our weapons. The Kaspar God helped us only until we could help ourselves.

He did not say *THOU WILL!* He said *THOU MAY* ...

The spark of revelation is bright inside the Imperial Kapitan's wooden mind. Had you been inside there, trapped in the swirling grain of sandalwood and teak, you might have seen connections springing together, the wood fusing in strange new patterns. This is the magic as thoughts coalesce.

He has to save himself.

But there isn't much time. Wind Down grows closer each second and, here in his prison, only the daemon lord could help. So the Imperial Kapitan waits for his moment, reaches for the birdcage bars, and begins to strain. He has already seen a knot in the floorboards, and perhaps this is a way back home.

The morning of Papa Jack's funeral dawned crisp and white. Cathy gazed into the open skies above Iron Duke Mews and wondered: how white were the skies, in that faraway world where Jekabs Godman had become Papa Jack? Last night, she had crept into his workshop and lifted his toy from the trunk with a thousand legs – but when she wound it up, and though the cams drove the prisoners onwards with their march, the walls of the room did not dissolve away, winter did not come howling in, and no phantom Jekabs Godman was waiting to accompany her on the ride. Papa Jack's story was finished, and the Emporium behind her suddenly seemed a shade more drab, a shade more grey.

She had been up before dawn to help Mrs Hornung in the kitchens, but now she waited in the frigid morning air. Seven dawns had passed since the morning they found him sitting in his workshop chair, and she had spent so long wondering what Kaspar thought, what form his grief was taking behind those sad, vacant eyes, that only now did she ask what she herself was feeling. It had been Papa Jack who welcomed her to his world. She remembered the way he had intoned those questions, so weighted with understanding: *are you lost? Are you afraid?* And she thought, suddenly, that she would write to her father soon, or visit them out on the estuary sands.

At the end of Iron Duke Mews the first carriage, bearing the coffin, was already manoeuvring to leave. Martha was helping Kaspar up into the second carriage, Nina corralling her boys with stern words and promises of sweet treats to come. Cathy was preparing to join them when the tradesman's door flew open behind her and out barrelled Emil, his head tucked down like a scalded child. She could see he had been in his workshop by the soot and flecks of woodchip that still coloured his hands. He had been painting too, for his fingernails were rimed a deep and dirty red, the colour of the Imperial Kapitan.

'For your papa,' said Cathy.

'For my children,' said Emil and, ignoring her further, took his place aboard the carriage.

How strange it was to venture out of the Emporium together. The procession took them north from Iron Duke Mews. Rounding the rails at King's Cross, they followed the York Road, past the empty granaries and canalside wharves, through the tumbledown redbricks where soot-stained faces ogled them from the terrace – until, finally, they rolled through the green fields of Highgate. Here the cemetery yawned open.

As the funeral procession ground to a halt, Cathy saw the well-wishers already lining the spaces between the graves.

'Who are they all, Mama?'

Cathy stared. In spite of Kaspar's whispered protestations, Emil had taken out an announcement in *The Times* and, accordingly, the grounds were filled with customers past and present. Shop hands from seasons past had come to show their respects. The wives and daughters of those who had been lost along the way had come to catch a glimpse, again, of the gilded world their husbands and fathers once left behind. Beneath hanging hawthorn, Frances Kesey was dressed in funereal grey; Sally-Anne (who later declared that Papa Jack's was a life of colour and he did not deserve to see only sadness on this, his final day) had come in vaudeville black with lurid sapphire and emerald brocade.

'Are you ready?'

Wordlessly, Kaspar nodded.

Together, they emerged on to the cold hard ground between the graves. Martha, dressed in one of Nina's black gowns, cringed from the wind. Cathy took her hand, thinking her still a little girl, but Martha did not resist. In turn, she took Kaspar's – and, to Cathy's astonishment, he did not resist either. Cathy looked up. Sally-Anne was right. There ought to have been patchwork horses drawing chariots of fire. The pegasi ought to have been set loose to cavort in the open skies, and to hell with the damage they caused when their motors stopped whirring and they came crashing back down. Ballerinas ought to have twirled *en pointe* while every tree in Highgate Cemetery was smothered in the tendrils of spreading paper vines. The trees, the sky, the world seemed so ordinary today.

Behind them, Emil and Nina were emerging from the hearse, their boys dressed in miniature black suits. Emil, whose own suit seemed suddenly too small, waited while the pall-bearers lifted the coffin out of the carriage.

'Are you certain you can do it?' Cathy asked.

Kaspar's eyes had not left the coffin for a second. 'Do you want honesty?'

'Always, Kaspar.'

'Then I'm far from certain. But I'm certain that, if I don't, I would never forgive myself. So I'll stand at Emil's side, if only for today.'

Cathy led Martha along the frost-hardened trail, as an honour guard grew up along the wild, untended banks. At its end, the earth was open and the gravediggers standing by. Cathy stood at its head, staring into the ground that would soon swallow Jekabs Godman whole. She had been telling herself: it's only his husk, only what he left behind, and he left behind so much more, back in our Emporium. But seeing the earth made thoughts like those seem so facile. Jekabs Godman was gone.

'Mama, there's something changed in Papa today. Did you see? He held my hand in the carriage.'

There were so few excuses she could make. The years had been a long litany of explaining her husband away, and Martha was not a girl any longer; she could not be persuaded to believe what her heart held as untrue.

'Today is a strange day.'

They were coming along the trail now: lean, angular Kaspar, still walking with a limp; ragged, rotund Emil, who looked as if he hadn't slept in nights. Behind them two hired hands bore the second half of the coffin.

'I remember being scared of him, up in that workshop. Can you believe that? Warm fuzzy Uncle Emil and Papa, just being Papa ... and then there was Papa Jack, big as both of them, and with those eyes, and those hands, and that ... would you call it hair, Mama?'

'Tangled and matted, like he hadn't had a wife in a century or more. But, yes, Martha, I'd call it hair.'

Martha grinned.

'I was scared of him too. The day I turned up, they took me up to his workshop, and he fixed me with those eyes and asked me those questions and ... somewhere along the way,

ROBERT DINSDALE

it clean melted away. He stitched you a bear out of spider silk. You lay in his hands, that day you were born, and, do you know, by then I wasn't afraid at all. I would have let him carry you away.' Cathy paused. 'Here they come ...'

The funeral procession had arrived. In a succession of stutters and false starts, Kaspar and Emil guided the coffin to the ground at the graveside. Moments later, the cowled undertakers stepped in and began to attach cords.

The graveside was growing crowded at last. There were faces here that Cathy knew, but so many more to which she could put no name. She reached out for Kaspar, guided him to the grave beside her.

'Are you ...'

Kaspar gave her a knowing look. 'My papa was the heaviest of men.'

The crowd had gathered. The undertakers were in place. The coffin hung, suspended, over the grave – and then, inch by inch, Papa Jack vanished into the ground.

At the head of the grave Emil waited nervously for his moment. The silence around him was absolute – and, with his boys at his side, he began.

'My papa was a simple man. My papa was a great man. My papa was my world. The Emporium he created occupies such a place in all of our hearts that we would not be the people we are without it – and that is why we have joined here today, to commit my papa to the earth, to give our thanks that he was a part of this world at all.

'Papa Jack is gone, but the Emporium lives on in all of us, in our hearts, and in the memories that exist out there – of everyone who ever shopped in the Emporium halls, the boys and girls and the games that they played.' Cathy saw his eyes roaming the crowd until they found his brother, whose head was still bowed over the grave. 'Our papa's work lives on as long as the Emporium does. As long as we're making toys. As long as we're …' His voice threatened to break, but he conquered it again. '… keeping magic in the world, never forgetting we used to be small – making the world better, one toy at a time.'

From the clouds above, thin snowflakes started to fall. They sifted through the cemetery trees, dusting the graves – but they were not paper, so it was not right. Emil helped his boys throw handfuls of dirt on to the coffin; the gravediggers were waiting to do their task, but soon all of those gathered were tossing in more handfuls. In that way, Papa Jack's coffin disappeared from view.

At Cathy's side, Martha threw a handful of earth. Cathy did the same, removing her glove to feel the frozen dirt on her fingers. She turned to deposit some into Kaspar's hand – but there was another figure between them now, somebody sidled up from behind to make his offering.

He was old as Papa Jack had been, with the look of a weasel and the only hair he had left hanging in a curtain of grey around the back of a scalp mottled with age. The suit he was wearing was freshly bought, and the raw red of his skin gave Cathy the impression that he had spent long days scouring away the filth in which he ordinarily lived. He smelt of cheap talc and peppermint lotion and, when he looked up, she saw that one of his eyes was made entirely of glass.

'Are you the son?'

His voice had the same inflection as Papa Jack's, of a language learned long into life and peppered with old, harsher sounds never forgotten. It took Kaspar a moment to realise it was him to whom the stranger had spoken. 'My name is Kaspar,' he said. 'Tell me, did you know my father?'

'A long time ago and half a world away. But, yes, I am proud to say that I did. You might say that I was his apprentice, though perhaps he would not himself have used such a word. I am sorry for your loss, boy. Men have lived worse lives and lived on and on.'

The stranger touched Kaspar's hand with the ruin of his own, then drew back into the crowd. In the gap he left behind, Cathy caught Kaspar's questing eye. She tracked the man as he left.

'My papa?' Kaspar said. 'An apprentice?'

Cathy had no strength to stop him; Kaspar disappeared after the man, angling his way through the mourners. By the time he breached the last of them, the man was already shambling into the hawthorn, disappearing around the looping trail. He had drawn up his collar, lost himself beneath a tall Homburg hat, and Kaspar had to strain to catch up. Finally, he grappled for the man's elbow.

'My papa never took an apprentice,' he gasped. 'My brother and I, we—'

'Calm yourself, boy. I didn't mean to alarm. Of course, I use the word loosely. I only ever set foot in your Emporium once, and by then I pray he did not recognise me. In the days I knew your papa, he was a different man. All of this – all of this was for the future. The Jekabs Godman I knew was a carpenter, but he turned sticks into soldiers, just for something to do with his hands, and he …' The man stopped. 'Your family, they are waiting for you, are they not?'

Kaspar looked over his shoulder. Cathy was watching him from the graveside.

'They have been waiting for me longer than I can say. They can wait a little longer.'

'It has been a lifetime since I saw your father, but when I saw the notice of his death ... I had to come and say my farewell. I believe ...' The man's face seemed to crumple for an instant, lending him a haggard, almost leering air. '... I would not be alive were it not for him. Certainly, I would not be the man I am today. You might say that Jekabs Godman saved my soul. He didn't know that he did it, and he never knew what I did with it – he never knew that the little soldiers he showed me how to make went with me back home, never knew all the places I travelled to share them, places where the children don't have any toys, places where they deserve to be reminded. Toys made me ... good again. Perhaps you can understand? I had never thought of myself as a good man, not until I met your father.'

At the graveside, as the crowd fanned out, each to their private griefs, Cathy watched her husband embrace the stranger, then let him go, off into the trees. Martha was already gone, helping Nina corral her boys, by the time Kaspar returned. His strides, as he returned along the trail, had new purpose.

'We should retire. Back to the Emporium.'

Cathy was still staring after the man, long after he had vanished.

'Who was he?' she asked.

Kaspar put his arm through hers and, together, they followed the path.

'A stranger. Papa knew him long ago. Long before he knew either me or Emil ...'

Halfway along the trail, when the carriages were already in sight, a thought hit Cathy and she dug her heels into the frozen earth, straining on Kaspar's arm until he too came to a halt.

'That man,' Cathy said, 'did he say what his name was?'

'Chichikov,' Kaspar answered. Then he drew his collar up, against the cold and wind. 'The man said his name was Chichikov.'

Seven days is an aeon in the lives of toy soldiers. For simple wooden minds, a day might be a lifetime; a week, time beyond measure. And though they were there on the night Papa Jack passed away, their best and bravest seeking communion with him as he slipped from this world, up and down the skirting board he has already passed into legend. All they know, now, is that the Old One is gone, that a season has passed with not a heart beating anywhere in the Emporium halls; and that, now, the two younger gods and their families have returned. The toy soldiers lurk in the skirting boards now, silent but for the ticking of their motors, spying through thin cracks in the wood. And what they see is this: on one side of the room, the daemon lord is playing with his children. On the other, the Kaspar god is seated with his wife and their daughter, the one who tells the soldiers Truths out of Books. Between them sits a table, heaped high with the foods of Banquet – and not a roast potato, not a glazed carrot, not a *vareniki* or bowl of hot broth is being touched. Instead, the gods remain famished on the borders of the room, casting each other glances whenever the other one is unaware.

And the toy soldiers think: to whom does the world belong, now that the Old One is gone? Which one is it? The Lord of Light, or the Lord of Death? Are we to live in peace, or be sent back to wage the Long War, from this day on and for evermore?

Cathy was late to bed that night, for in the kitchens Mrs Hornung quaked over the wasted food, the mountains of crockery, the pots and pans that needed to be scoured and stacked away. For hours they worked in companionable silence, and only once did either one speak. Her arms deep in soap suds, Mrs Hornung uttered, 'He was a good man,' and after that returned to her work with newfound fire.

Some time later, when the Emporium clocks were tolling and Cathy was ready to leave, she spoke again. 'Those two boys have been squabbling since they were young. But there was love in it back then. Tell me, Cathy, is there love in it now? Because all I see is hate ...'

'There's love,' said Cathy. 'No understanding, but there's still love.'

'Well, that's boys for you. All the love in the world doesn't match a little scrap of understanding.'

Cathy dwelt on it as she went back above. By now Emil and Nina had retired to their separate beds, Martha reading Perrault to the toy soldiers in the walls. For a moment, Cathy stopped in the doorway to listen. The story was Bluebeard, and the terrible chamber to which his young wife was forbidden to go. She wondered if the soldiers understood, yet, the horror they were hearing. Then she drifted on.

Kaspar would be asleep by now, his back turned against her as it always was. She opened the door …

… and there he sat, in a whirlwind of paper dolls. They danced like sprites as he scissored them from the rolls at his side, taking off and floating like some heavenly host.

He looked at her through the angelic storm. 'For you,' he said. They hung in the air: paper centaurs, paper nymphs.

'Kaspar, you're awake.'

'I was waiting for you.'

'Waiting for me?'

'I didn't want to sleep, Mrs Godman. Not without you near.'

Words were such slippery things. She wanted to hear what she thought she was hearing, but there was so much distance between the two of them; languages grew and changed, and perhaps the words had a different meaning when they left Kaspar's mouth to the moment they touched her ear. She snuffed out the light, slid under the covers. As always, the no-man's-land stretched between them. 'Tomorrow's a new day,' she ventured. 'Remember that. We'll always have new days.'

Something had changed in his breathing. Then – she had to check herself, for this too had the quality of dream – she felt movement at her side. Kaspar's hand had stretched out into the no-man's-land. It was reaching for hers and she allowed it to be taken.

'Cathy, there's something I have to do. You might think it frightfully absurd.'

This last he said with a grin, and Cathy felt certain it was not her imagination. She felt more certain still when his other hand found her, lying on her belly before gliding north. It was such a strange sensation, so unexpected, that she could not drive the tension out of her body. She flinched, recoiled, then laughed, as if she had never been touched before.

'Kaspar, are you …'

'You ask me if I'm well by the hour, every hour. You won't need to ask me again.'

He had rolled toward her, drawing her into the no-man's-land – but then this, she supposed, was where everyone ought to meet.

'Do you think we might … try?'

It was no good holding herself so rigidly. She was a part of this too. She had to force her hand up to touch Kaspar's face but, once she had forced it, her fingers remembered the line of his cheeks, the knots in his skin, the peculiar savageness above his left eye. The body had a memory, just like the mind. To hell with those music boxes he used to make; this, right now, was like stepping backwards in time.

In the night she woke knowing he was near and, when she rolled toward him, his arms folded around her and she felt the beating of his heart. Later, when she woke, they had come apart, each dreaming their separate dreams – but that was good, that was as it should be, and when she stretched her body he stretched his, as if reflecting her in a mirror. For a time, the images that played across the backs of her eyes were not true dreams, but recollections, fragments of lives yet to be lived. She and Kaspar had a tiny emporium in Paris, where they sold patchwork frogs and the toy soldiers lived in peace. She heard the deep bass of his snoring, then she heard silence – and until she woke up, with dawn's first light, to feel the emptiness beside her, the cold air playing at her back, she had no idea that he was not there with her and had not been for hours.

Kaspar was gone. His slippers, his robe, the canes with which he walked; all of those things, gone as well.

It was not so unusual for Cathy to wake up alone – and if, after last night, she had imagined them lying together until the day was old, that was only because, on the edges of sleep, it was possible to believe she was still the sixteen-year-old runaway who had first fallen into his arms, to forget the fact that she was a mother, a wife, part of the gears that kept Papa Jack's Emporium alive. Perhaps it was not such a shameful thing to admit that, if only for tiny pockets in time, it was a joy to be nothing other than herself.

The idea struck her that he would be in his workshop, for after last night anything seemed possible. She went there now, expecting to find him lost in some miraculous new design, but the workshop was empty – and, it occurred to her now, she could hear no scuttling in the walls, none of the regimented march of toy soldiers that had coloured their days for so long. Sometimes it was more reverential in Kaspar's workshop, but as she returned to the quarters she crouched at the skirting, pressed her ear to the wall. In the cavities there was only silence, dull and absolute.

'What are you doing down there, Mama?'

She turned. Martha had been reclining on one of the armchairs all along, one of her novels in hand.

'You slept there all night, little one?'

Martha shrugged. 'Not on *purpose* … Is something wrong, Mama?'

What could she say? *Silence*, Martha. *Peace.*

Cathy lifted her robe and hurried back through the quarters, up the stair to the place where her bed lay bare. She could see the indentation Kaspar's body made in the sheets, but his absence was like a vortex in the room. It pulled her down.

The window was ajar, the frost of morning whispering through, but though she peered out, she did not see him hanging from a ledge, nor reclined up on the roof tiles, taking in the morning air.

Through the walls she heard the chatter of Emil's children. Nina was already barracking them for some imagined mischief.

As she stepped back from the window, her eyes fell on Kaspar's bedside table. There, beneath the lantern strewn up with dancing paper dolls, lay a letter.

Cathy, the envelope read – and the word was loaded with all the dread of the journal he used to write, the feeling of his hands on her last night, the strange new silence in the walls.

My own Cathy

By the time you find this letter, I will be gone. I dare not think of your face as you are reading these words. I dare not imagine the moment you tell Martha, my Martha (for she has always been mine, no matter what the particulars of her blood), that she will not see me again. You will not hate me for it, because your heart has always been bigger than hate. But do not think ill of yourself, should you perhaps feel a little *relief.* Because the truth is, I have been gone for many years already. I left you on the day I left the Emporium for those foxholes in the French earth. That I came back at all was down to you. You picked me up and put me back together – and if you could not put me back together whole, that was never your burden, and never your fault.

I have known for too long that I am withering away, but I know now what I must do and, though I do it, I do it with the deepest regret – for I love you as I have only ever loved one thing, and that is the Emporium itself. In my heart and mind, you are bound up with one another and never to be prised apart. But the Emporium is in ruins, and it is me keeping it that way. And, my darling, you are in ruins – and it is me keeping you that way. It is in this letter that I set you free.

Live a long, rich life. Think of me often, but never with regrets. But Papa Jack's Emporium must endure where I cannot, and so must you, my darling. There is a different place for me now. I am going to find it.

Yours for the last time,
Kaspar Godman Esq.

PS. Take care of Emil. He is going to need you now.

Cathy read it once. She read it twice. She forced herself to read it again, each time more agonisingly slowly than the last – but, if she had expected the words to evaporate and change, she was sorely mistaken. There they stayed, imprinted on the page just as they were imprinting themselves on her heart.

An hour passed, maybe more. But the clock had stopped ticking. The motors had wound down. She thought, perhaps, that she herself was winding down – until, with an enormous effort, she got to her feet. She marched to the mirror – and, god, but she looked old. *Dry your eyes, Catherine Wray*, she told herself, and choked when she realised the old name had already come back to her tongue. *No*, she reminded herself. *Whether you're a Godman or a Wray, you're still you. And Cathy, you don't cry.*

Folding the letter neatly to place it in a pocket, she marched out on to the gallery.

He was not in his workshop, but she had known that already. She crossed the silent shopfloor, where no miniature locomotives hurtled along the aisles, no tramping could be heard between floorboards and shelf stack, and into the half-moon hall. She fumbled for a key and opened up the door, staggering out into the whiteness that had encrusted Iron Duke Mews.

The snow had fallen thickly last night. Drifts grew up the walls of the mews, burying the doors of the neighbouring shops. It had fallen too deeply to leave any footprints, but she hastened up the mews all the same: Cathy Godman, still in her nightgown, plunging knee deep with every step.

She had gone halfway when she stumbled. There was a mound in the snow, no doubt belying the cobbles underneath, and she pitched forward as she hit it. The snow cushioned her fall and for a time she lay there, breathing it in: the morning air, the stillness, the very last day of what she'd thought was her life. She watched as a pair of newspapermen crossed the end of the mews, but they did not look in so they did not see her lying there.

Nor did they see the frosted velvet and felt that had been unearthed when she stumbled.

Cathy saw it in the corner of her eye: indigo and tartan; a lolling tongue of darned sock. In an instant the numbness (surely so much more than the snow) to which she was giving herself had been swept away. In its place was fire that thawed every corner of her body. She plunged her forearms into the snow, scrabbled for purchase, shovelled handfuls away where she could not take hold. Then she heaved, until the tartan and felt was lying on top of the snow and she was staring down, down into the lifeless face of Sirius, the patchwork dog.

She brushed crystals of ice away from his cross-stitched nose. She pressed her face to his belly, listened for the whirring of his heart – but the mechanisms that drove him, that had driven him ever since Kaspar was a boy, had stopped. Her fingers fumbled for his belly, but nothing turned within. The key by which Sirius was wound was unnaturally still.

Cathy bore the dog up (how light it was, only cotton wadding and felt!) and carried it back along the mews, through the doors to the half-moon hall. There she spread its legs to see the tiny key protruding from the fabric on its underside. 'Please,' she whispered, and blew on her hands to warm up her fingers. Delicately, she started to turn.

The key caught, and she could feel the touch of the mechanism inside. Something clicked every time it revolved, but soon she came to know she was turning the key in thin air; it was not meshing with whatever contraption lay on the other side. She shifted Sirius around, petting him gently, making yet more promises as she worked. 'It's all right, boy,' she whispered. 'He hasn't gone. He can't have gone. Not now, not after all this. He's coming back. Don't give up, not yet ...'

Something inside Sirius's belly moved; the key had snagged on some tangle of wires. After a moment, the key slipped free once again – but, now that she knew what she was searching for, she knew how to find it again. Soon, the key was driving the motors. She felt them coming to life – and when, at last, the key would turn no tighter, she fell back, collapsed on to the cold shopfloor.

Beside her, Sirius lay still. His motors turned but he did not flicker, not even as if in a dream.

Cathy lay back, defeated. She did not want to sob and so she did not, but something sobbed inside her – for the end of Sirius, for Papa Jack lying cold in the ground, for the idea that she had not lost Kaspar today, but lost him in a thousand tiny moments ever since he returned; for the fact that she had not been able to save him, after all this time.

There was a thunder of footsteps. Somebody else was on the shopfloor. She looked up to see them running to her through a stand of paper trees. Emil crashed through the creeping vines, Mrs Hornung close behind.

'We saw the doors open. The snow coming in. Cathy, is everything all right?'

Before she could answer, the bundle of fabric at her feet started to shift. Cathy looked down and, from between her legs, there rose a cross-stitch nose, two black button eyes. Sirius turned his head, his darned sock tongue lolling out as if desperate for water. Softly, his tail began to beat. He climbed ungainly to his feet.

Cathy gathered him up, clung to him as he lapped at her, leaving dust and dangling thread wherever he touched her face. She dug into her pocket and pressed the note into Emil's waiting hand.

'It's Kaspar,' she said. 'He's gone. He's left us all behind.'

THE GHOST IN THE TOYSHOP

PAPA JACK'S EMPORIUM, 1924–1940

The man's name was Lewis and – or so it seemed to Cathy – he was more interested in the patchwork rabbits proliferating on the shelf than the letter she kept pressing into his hands.

'We're here as a courtesy, Mrs Godman, and because my chief inspector brought his daughters here, once upon a while.' Two other constables were somewhere in the aisles, trying to pull crinkled card berries from the paper trees. 'I'm afraid that what you have there, in your hands, rather disproves your case. Your husband isn't missing, Mrs Godman.' He turned on his heel from the shelf and wiped his hand, in disgust, on his trouser. One of the patchwork rabbits, with precise derision, had deposited a patchwork pellet into his palm. 'He just left. It's there in black and white, and little we can do about it – in a public forum, at least. Listen, you have my sympathies. Before I was a copper I was a soldier, like the lot of us, and … Mr Godman wouldn't be the first to walk out on his wife. If you had my job, why, you'd know some of the terrible things that can happen when a soldier comes home.'

Cathy said, 'You don't know my husband.'

'We done some digging, Mrs Godman. All as a favour, you understand. He was a flamboyant man, your husband. That's what his old soldier pals tell us. Up and down, up and down, that sort of fellow – and that can be the worst. And you knew, of course, what he was doing down at the veterans' home? Down on the Strand with those music boxes of his?'

Cathy stopped herself before she replied. She had thought those music boxes a thing of the past.

'Oh yes, his trips down there seem to have been quite the stir. Music boxes for all the veterans, things to make 'em feel young again. But you knew about that of course.'

The sergeant loped back into the half-moon hall, poked his head out of the door and peered up the snowbound mews.

'And the dog, you say you found it out there?'

'He must have followed Kaspar out, then lain down in the snow ...'

'What, and just froze to death?'

'I wound him back up. He ...'

'I ... see. One of your contraptions then, was it? Not quite real? Mrs Godman, you can understand where I'm coming from. You say the dog followed him out, and yet you still say he's missing. Well, if a man leaves of his own accord ...'

Cathy propped herself against one of the shelves. There was no use in arguing with somebody so blinkered, so instead she just nodded.

'Might I ask you a ... personal question, Mrs Godman? I'm told it has relevance, though Lord knows you'll think I'm a ghoul.'

Cathy said, 'If you think it will help,' and noticed the man could not even look her in the eye.

'When did you and your husband last have … there is no savoury way of saying this … relations?'

'Is that a proper question, sergeant?'

'Not improper, Mrs Godman. It may shed some light.'

Propriety says I ought to be ashamed, thought Cathy, *ashamed to stand here, in front of this man, and even entertain his question.* But, even in that place her mother tried to take her, Cathy had refused to feel ashamed.

'I'll answer, Mr Lewis, this one and nothing more. My husband and I were together on the night that he left.'

The sergeant nodded. 'He was saying goodbye. You can be certain of that. It's a thing with some men. One for the road, as they say. I'm sorry, Mrs Godman. Look, we'll take a picture, if we may. We'll open a file – all in the way of a favour, you understand.'

The sergeant called out for his constables, and idled there while he waited. 'Before I go, I wonder – and this being unprofessional, I know – if I might take a little something? I have a nephew on the coast. His parents have promised him a journey to your Emporium many Christmases now, and yet …' The sergeant shrugged, and in that shrug was all the indifference in the world. 'Just a little trinket. Perhaps … a little toy soldier?'

'I'm afraid we have none.'

The sergeant glowered. 'Papa Jack's Emporium, and not a single toy soldier.'

'It seems my husband took them, each and every one.'

The sergeant nodded, so slowly it seemed he was testing her. 'I suppose you believe they just picked themselves up and marched after him.'

And Cathy, to whom the silence was still so strange, thought: *if only you knew.*

She watched them go from the doorway, knowing in her heart they would not return. As they reached the end of Iron Duke Mews, no doubt already debating the dogs down at Dagenham, Cathy pictured how it might have been seven nights ago, as Kaspar loped the same way. In her mind she saw him turning the corner and Sirius, torn between his loyalty to his master and the Emporium itself, left howling in his wake. Running away, she remembered now, was not like it was in the stories. People did not try and stop you. They did not give chase. The thing people didn't understand was that you had to decide what you were running away from. Most of the time it wasn't husbands or wives or monsters or villains; most of the time you were running away from that little voice inside your head, the one telling you to *stay where you are, that everything will be all right.*

But it would have been, she thought as she slammed the door. She would have gone to the end with him, even if he'd never let her touch him again, even if all he'd wanted to do was to stay in his workshop and make his toys. She had wanted to be the one who was with him on the day that he died, when the century had grown older and the two of them grown older too. But now that hope was gone and, gazing up, the Emporium lay empty before her.

Two weeks since he'd gone and she felt like one of London's vagrants, sitting on a street corner grateful for any crust. There was still snow left in Hyde Park. She came out of St George's on the corner, decorating every lamp post and tree from the Serpentine to the Apsley Gate with the posters she and Martha had laboured over. *Come Home Kaspar* hung from every bough. In the heart of Mayfair, where she had planted one of his paper trees, people gathered for the spectacle and came away with a letter in their hands. *If you see this man, deliver this promise: I still love you, no matter what.*

She went down to the veterans' homes where they said he had taken his music boxes. She dug out the addresses of old soldiers, anyone whose path might have crossed his; she wrote to shop hands past and present, thinking of all the places he might go. She took the train to the estuary, for mightn't Kaspar – deranged, in his way – have thought to find a new life in her old one, just as she had found one in his? But the letters came back – *Dear Cathy, I have seen neither hide nor hair* – and the trips were in vain.

Nineteen hours and fifteen days.

Three hours three weeks.

Spring and summer and autumn and winter again.

Somewhere along the way she stopped going out to hand out pamphlets. The tree in Berkeley Square grew heavy with rain and crumpled to a thick, sticky mulch. Emil said they could hardly afford another full page in *The Times*, not until they began the hard work of repairing the Emporium's reputation. Cathy left the tradesman's door unlocked each night, just in case he returned – until, one day, Mrs Hornung noticed the wet footprints in the windward aisles and deduced, to Emil's horror, that crooks had crept in and stolen a whole crate of magic carpets. After that Cathy just waited, and waiting was the most lonesome thing.

*

She woke in the night, an idea dragging her from dreams. The journal Papa Jack had given her was still in the trunk beneath the bed. She heaved it out, daring not to open it in case this dream was to be shattered. It was almost dawn by the time she opened the journal and, finding no note from Kaspar there, took a pen and scribbled herself. *'Kaspar, my dearest Kaspar. Are you there? Wherever you are, why ever you went, it can be undone.'* But when, three months later (the pages scoured each night), there was no reply, she placed the journal back in the chest beneath the bed and never did open it again.

It was not the silence of her papa that Martha missed in those months, for heaven knows he had been silent long enough. It was the silence in the walls that kept her up at night. Silence, she was starting to realise, could be as oppressive as snow.

Martha put away her *Gulliver's Travels*, her Charles Perrault and *Arabian Nights* on the day the soldiers disappeared. Reading alone was not enough, not when there were once a hundred wooden faces hanging on every word. The books on the shelf spoke of happier times: of Martha on Kaspar's knee, as he told great fables which she later realised he had entirely made up; of the soldiers waiting for every twist and turn, the stories seeping into their sandalwood minds, teaching them, ordering them, programming them with this business of life.

At night the silence weighed on her. The peace frightened her. Seventeen years old, she slept in her mama's bed, in the place where her papa used to lie.

'They can't all have gone, can they?' she said one night, to the impenetrable dark. 'All those hundreds of them, all those thousands, however many lived up and down the walls ... He can't have taken them all, can he?'

All he would have needed, Cathy thought, was one of his bags, like the one he made for me when Martha was born. Open it up and let them all march into its depths, and off they would go, out into the world. But at least that would mean he was alive. At least that might mean he was not rotting at the bottom of the Thames like all the rest of the missing, all the dispossessed.

That first year the shop hands came long before first frost. Emil sent notices out and now, here they were, with new storemen and down-and-out stevedores, all dragged in to set the Emporium to rights.

On the shopfloor the workers were wrenching up the aisles. Nina and the boys were marshalling the patchwork reindeer to heave the shipping containers out of the storerooms so that Emil might make an inventory of all they had left. There were enough toys here of Papa Jack and Kaspar's design to keep the shelves full for the next winter, more still if they rationed them well, and Emil worked hard to supplement them with toys of his own.

In places they tore down the barricades. Mrs Hornung levered up every stretch of railroad track the toy soldiers had lain. The shop hands reconstructed the aisles in such a way that the shopfloor would seem smaller, and yet more packed with excitement than these last winters, when the soldiers had run amok. Foresters were brought in to fell the paper trees, now yellow and sagging with age, while the Wendy House, still boarded up, was loaded up and hauled away. 'We'll refit it next winter,' said Emil, when he saw how Cathy was staring. 'It's not gone for ever, Cathy, I promise.'

But perhaps it ought to be, she thought. Those four walls, so loaded with memory; perhaps what she needed was not to see it sitting there every day, speaking of happier times.

She returned to an aisle where she worked alone, dusting down old dancing bears. At its end, the shelf stacks had been torn up, revealing a great maw in the wall where the masonry had crumbled away. There Martha called out for her mama.

Cathy went down, into the shadows, and crouched at Martha's side. Behind the crumbled wall lay one of the cavities where the soldiers used to march. The light from Martha's lantern spilled over the open face of a doll's house. Tiny paper trees had sprouted in its garden, stunted by the dark.

'Look, Mama …'

Martha had prised up one of the floorboards. Along the piping underneath the toy soldiers had laid out a field, and in that field tiny stones had been arranged.

'Is that …'

'Letters,' Martha realised, for the stones at her feet might, if she squinted just right, spell out the single word:

HELLO

'I was trying to show them,' she said as the men behind her took joy in dragging out six feet of underground railway. 'I'd remembered how Uncle Emil proposed. I thought – why not? If they could understand, they could learn to talk back … If only there was more time, perhaps there could have been a parley, perhaps they might have understood, Uncle Emil isn't a monster, he isn't the tyrant they thought he was. Perhaps we could have understood each other, if only we could have talked ...'

Cathy had been crouching. In the garden of one of the crudely built houses she found a minuscule figure, no bigger then the nail of her little finger. She lay it in her palm and brought it to the light: splinters, trussed up and twisted into the shape of a ballerina.

'They were making their own toys ...'

'Toys for toys,' laughed Martha. 'Maybe one day they'd have learned to wind themselves too. Maybe they'd have woken up, then made toys of their own, even tinier ones, tiny toys out of motes of dust ...'

'Maybe they'd have woken up too.'

'And maybe, just maybe, all we are, every last one of us, is a toy brought to life.'

'You're starting to sound religious.'

'Papa would have liked the idea, wouldn't he, Mama? Well, wouldn't he?'

Cathy lay the tiny ballerina back in the dark, where it surely belonged.

'What are we going to do, Mama?'

Cathy fingered the ruin, the world where the soldiers used to live. 'We're going to wait,' she said, 'and we're going to believe.'

Papa Jack's Emporium
Iron Duke Mews
18th February 1925

Dear Mr Moilliet,

Please find enc. the balance sheets drawn up for the winter season 1924–25. As you will see, the Emporium did not run at profit and will require further hard work to rejuvenate, but rest assured that the work is being undertaken. Next winter will be a triumph!

Yours sincerely
Emil Godman Esq.

Papa Jack's Emporium
Iron Duke Mews
20th January 1926

Dear Mr Moilliet,

Please find enc. the balance sheets drawn up for the winter season 1925–26. Might I impose upon you to extend our credit arrangement in anticipation of next season, when we stalwart Emporium few will return our Emporium to the giddy heights of yore.

Yours sincerely
Emil Godman Esq.

Papa Jack's Emporium
Iron Duke Mews
6th June 1927

Mr Moilliet,

I am sick and tired of the doggerel I receive through my letterbox and the unannounced visits from your associates at the bank. We are late in our annual accounting. Do you not think I have better things to be doing than totting up numbers that don't mean a thing? I was here this winter. I <u>know</u> how the Emporium fares. Please find enc. the balance sheets: BLANK because I have TOYS to make and (lest this be forgotten) my business is in making TOYS and not paying LIP SERVICE to a moneylender.

EG

Papa Jack's Emporium
Iron Duke Mews
18th June 1927

Dear Mr Moilliet,

I received your letter and apologise for mine written in haste. We look forward to your visit and what new arrangements we are able to work out. I remain optimistic that, with a little help, our Emporium will once again be a fixture in London life.

Yours in gratitude,
Emil Godman Esq.

*

The snowdrops blossomed early in the year of 1928 – and thank heavens for small mercies, for Emil could not stand another day, another night, another customer who looked him bare in the face and said: *there used to be such magic.* Now he sat on the floor in his papa's old study, all of the shelves denuded of their books, pages of designs he could barely understand splayed out all around. The chest with a thousand legs had been snapping at him from under the armchair all night, the phoenix (who had refused to leave the room ever since the old man died) was wound down, but watched him nevertheless from its roost in the rafters – but Emil was lost in a world that did not belong to him, searching for a design, an idea, a *something* that might make it all worthwhile.

January became February became March and April. All the ideas of Papa Jack's life came down like an avalanche around Emil. He spent his days braced for the next deluge, holding his breath.

Sometimes he fell asleep there and sometimes he woke there too. He marvelled at the designs for the first patchwork bears, but when he tried to recreate them they were dull, dumb things with barely a character among them. He unearthed plans for the Foldaway Fortress of 1901, the Door Through the Wall of 1898, the Infinity of Russian Dolls of 1911; he lost a month in hewing a new line of runnerless rocking horse, but the brutes were intractable, refused to take a rider, and had – in the end – to be added to a pyre or dismantled for scrap.

Sometimes the only time he spoke to another living soul was when Mrs Hornung arrived with his supper, and sometimes not even then.

He thought it was Mrs Hornung tonight, loitering in the study door with a bowl of pea soup and a hunk of hard bread. That was why, at first, he did not turn around. He was sailing in a sea of books and the blueprint unrolled before him was for a Minotaur, Lost In Its Labyrinth. This one he might even be able to attempt. He was picturing how it might be done when a cough alerted him to the fact that his wife was waiting. She hadn't even brought supper.

'Emil, we have to talk.'

'I can't, not yet, not now. It's in here somewhere, Nina. One of these toys. Something he dreamt up but didn't see through. Well, we'll see it through. Who cares if it isn't mine? Who'll know? We'll find a way to make it, every bit as magical as they would have done, and fill the shopfloor.' He looked up, dewy-eyed. 'There are still six months until Christmas.'

'Four, Emil.'

Emil tore at the blueprint, scything it apart with his hands. *Four. How had he not known it was four?*

Nina swept the papers off his papa's armchair and sat down. 'Do you realise,' she said, 'how long it's been since you read to your boys? How many hours you've been down here? Do you realise,' she went on, punctuating each word with the point of her finger, 'how long it's been since you played with your own sons?'

Emil looked as if he might answer, but Nina quickly cut him off. 'Three weeks. And before that, five. There they are, upstairs, and ... here you are, oblivious.'

'Oblivious? Good God, Nina, what do you think I'm here for? Do you think I *want* to be here every night, poring through this? Every page a reminder of how useless, how ordinary I am? How witless would you have to be to think I'd *want* that. I'm doing it for *them*, Nina. I'm doing it for *you* ...'

'You're not as foolish as that, Emil. Doing it for me? The Emporium in tatters and your names signed on a mortgage deed? No, you're doing it for you. Doing it for us would have been to take that offer from Hamley's. Go and make toys for them and be paid well enough. Staying here? That's for ...' She shook her head. 'You, a toymaker, the best toymaker left in London, and you won't even play with your own boys.'

'Best,' Emil uttered, 'but evidently not good enough.'

She stood. She dusted down her house dress. She said, 'I'm leaving you, Emil.'

There was silence in the study. Emil rose to his feet, with his papa's designs sloughing off him like a skin being shed. 'Nina—'

'No,' she said, and refused to catch his eye as she marched out into the hall, 'we've had this conversation too many times. You're not a father. You're not a husband. You're a little boy, still looking for magic. Well, what about the ordinary magic, Emil? The ordinary magic of simply being a good father. Those boys deserve better. We're to stay with my aunts.'

'That coven? For *my* boys—'

'We'll find our own home, in good course. I have a cousin who has promised his help. It won't be easy, but at least it can be a start. All of this –' and she opened her arms, as if to take in Emil, the study, the whole Emporium itself, '– it's a long, slow end.'

He did not argue with her. He slammed the door and, once his tears were spilled, he marched into his boys' bedroom and spun them the most fantastic tale, of a dumpy little boy who didn't know he was a prince, and a magic sword lying at the bottom of a toybox, and a castle that the prince conquered, a heritage that was rightfully his.

Two weeks later, the boys lined up in the half-moon hall while their mama arranged for their trunks to be ferried to the taxicab waiting outside. They looked smart in their short trousers and blazers, each with a little Gladstone bag at their side. Emil approached each in turn and stiffly shook their hands. To Cathy it looked as if each boy might suddenly bleat out, but whatever they were feeling, they were adept at keeping it in; something, no doubt, they had inherited from their father.

Nina was back in the doorway, summoning them out.

'Be good for your mama,' Emil uttered as they filed out into Iron Duke Mews.

As they left, Cathy put an arm around Emil and he shrunk into her.

'They'll be back, won't they, Cathy? Once the Emporium lives again. Once the Emporium thrives. Then I'll be able to instruct lawyers. I'll bring all the wealth of the Emporium to bear. And then, then, then they'll be here, playing in these aisles, just like it's meant to be . . .'

1929. 1930. 1931.

Pursuant to the Births and Deaths Registration Act 1874

Death in the sub-district of Westminster, London, United Kingdom of England and Wales

~

Kaspar Godman, b. May 24ᵗʰ 1888, foreign national
d. January 12ᵗʰ 1931, in absentia
Male, 43 years, by his own hand

~

Certified to be a True Copy of an entry in the certified copy of
a Register of Deaths in the District Mentioned Above

Cathy was rigid as she folded the paper and pressed it back into the envelope. She thought she might let it flutter down over the Emporium in a tiny thousand pieces, just like that confetti snow they used to be able to afford.

Lurking unshaven behind her, Emil bided his time before he spoke.

'We had to observe it, Cathy. You understand, don't you? If they make the Emporium mine by the deeds, Lloyd's will start lending again. Mr Moilliet's made me a promise. They couldn't possibly lend to a man who's been missing so long – but, now that they can, well, we can get things back to the way they used to be. You and me, Cathy. Together we can do it.'

Cathy handed him the paper.

'I won't believe it, what they've written there.'

'Oh,' said Emil, 'you won't have to! As a matter of fact, I –' he floundered, some memory of his brother no doubt flurrying up '– won't believe it either. But it's only *paper*. It doesn't have to be true. You and me, we can believe what we want to believe, just so long as there are customers at Christmas and the cloud castle's floating on air, just so long as there are festivities on Opening Night ...'

Papa Jack's Emporium
Iron Duke Mews
16th October 1934

Dear Frances (wrote Cathy; and then, on a separate leaf: *Dear Sally-Anne),*

It has come to that time of year again when we look to first frost. Some nights I feel it in the air and I know you will be waking every morning too, looking for that telltale crust of white that has for so long told us our winter has begun.

But I have news, and believe me when I tell you that this is a letter I had hoped never to write. Papa Jack's Emporium will indeed open at first frost, but we will not be inviting our shop hands to return. This winter Emil will labour in his workshop while Martha and I alone work the shopfloor. It is the slow creep of the ages, which you have seen with your own eyes. We have sold the very last paper tree from the storerooms. All of the patchwork animals are gone, and what dogs and cats and sheep and bears Emil makes now are no more magical than the ones they engineer in any other toyshop in London town; and twice as expensive to boot. We have boxes of bric-a-brac and Emil is not short of new designs, but the wherewithal to produce them en masse evades us, and we rely so heavily on credit from Lloyd's that shop hands this winter are a luxury we cannot afford.

Do not think lowly of me, for I have fought the cause and lost. Try not to think unkindly of Emil either, for it is the ledgers that have beaten us, not the man.

Should the stars shine on us this winter, should Emil stumble upon some flight of Imagination so striking that it might draw back the crowds we once had, I will write that same moment. I will tie missives to pipe-cleaner birds and cast them from the terrace into the London skies.

How I will miss you this winter, and for all the winters to come (she crossed out this latter; then, for Sally-Anne alone, she added: *You told me once that I should beware of the Godman boy. I think, now that I stare my middle-age square in the face, that it would not hurt my pride so much to admit you were right! I love you Sally-Anne and hope I will see you again.*)

Yours for ever
Cathy

Cathy set down her inkpen and added the letters to the pile. There was only one more left to write. This she composed with the greatest sinking feeling of all. *'To Whom It May Concern. Please consider this letter as recommendation of Mrs Evelyn Hornung's abilities as nanny, housekeeper, bookkeeper and all else besides.'* She thought to add *'friend'* and *'confidante'*, *'Keeper of Hope in Darkest Times'* and even *'mother, when I had no mother of my own'*, but wanted to spare Mrs Hornung the blushes. She would give it to her at the last moment, when she stepped off through the Emporium doors, and would hope that the guilt lasted no longer than it must.

She was on her way to post the others when she passed by Martha's open door and saw her studying at her desk. Cathy had quite lost track of what this correspondence course might have been, no doubt one of the Latinate languages with which Martha spent the long summers – and, not for the first time, Cathy felt her pride in her daughter like a barb in her side. There wasn't a language on the continent that Martha didn't know (Mr Atlee, God rest his soul, would have been proud), but in these vast, cavernous halls, this latter-day Emporium, there was not a person she might speak to.

Cathy hovered in the doorway, watching her write. Then she stepped nervously within. She had not planned for this, but as she approached she knew that this was right.

'Hard at work, little one?'

Martha had been hunched over her typewriter, an old toy repurposed from the stores. In capital letters across the head of the page were the words THE TRUE HISTORY OF TOYS and, below that: Martha Godman.

'I thought – somebody ought to tell it. Even if there's nobody left who wants to listen, it should be written down somewhere, so it's never forgotten. Not just Papa and Papa Jack, though I've written them too. But … the soldiers, Mama. We shouldn't forget the soldiers.'

If Martha could have recreated them, taken any two toy soldiers and set them to wind each other up, triggered thought and idea and imagination all over again, she would have done it in a second. Sometimes, Cathy thought, that was why she learnt her languages so diligently – for Martha had never been able to do that thing she had dreamed of, and start conversing with the toy soldiers themselves. She had kept the copy of *Gulliver* like it was a totem. It stood, dog-eared, up on the shelf.

'I've written the letters,' Cathy said, sinking to the end of the bed. 'They're not coming back. All of those shop girls, even Mrs Hornung, they'll have to find their own places now. And Martha ...' She hesitated, steeling herself. '... so should you.'

Martha was silent.

'You're twenty-seven years old. Always my little girl, but twenty-seven years old. It's young enough to start again. You, with all your languages, all of that thought. It mustn't go to waste, waiting here with your mama. *You* mustn't go to waste. You might be at the Foreign Office. You might be translating works of great literature. You might be writing your own. You might be ... prime minister, with a mind like yours.'

'A shop girl like me.'

'A shop girl like *you*.'

For a time, Martha returned to THE TRUE HISTORY OF TOYS. 'I won't say I haven't thought of it. But to leave you here, in this ... museum. This ... *mausoleum* ...'

Cathy took her hand. 'Running away isn't like it is in the stories, little one. Most of the time you aren't running away from monsters or villains, not even from memories like the ones we have here. Those things are hardly worth running from, because they'll always catch you up. No, most of the time you're running from that little voice, the one in there, telling you to *stay where you are ...*'

'I'd wanted to wait with you, Mama, to wait for him to come home.'

Cathy whispered in her ear: 'Your father wasted his last years not living. Don't waste yours. *Live*, little one, for us both. It's what Kaspar would have wanted.'

Cathy went out on to the shopfloor and from there out into London town. Regent Street was a bustle. Carriages became ensnared at the Oxford Circus while the sky, so cerulean blue, turned overhead. It would be lonely without Martha. But there would still be Emil. There would always be Emil. And loneliness needed company, even though that was still loneliness of a sort. So when, some time later, Emil came to her with the idea of turning off the power in half of the quarters and, in that way, saving a little money to make the Emporium last a little longer, it did not seem so very strange that they should drag the single beds out of the storerooms and move into Mrs Hornung's old chambers together. It did not seem so very strange that, without Mrs Hornung and with no Martha to care for, Cathy should take to cooking meals for them each night. And if a customer come shopping tipped his hat to 'Mr Godman, Mrs Godman,' as he passed back through the Emporium doors, there was no need to tell him that they were not husband and wife. You did not correct your customers, not if you hoped (not if you *needed*) them to come back.

One year.

Two years.

Three years.

Four.

'We have to find some way to bring back children,' Emil said, locking up the shopfloor on a cold winter night. 'Have you noticed it isn't families who come any more? Now it's just grown men who used to come when *they* were boys. Mothers bringing their children, when it used to be children bringing their mothers ...'

The path of nostalgia, thought Cathy, narrowing into regret.

1937. '38. '39. '40.

The blast woke her. That one had been close. She reached for the nightlamp at her side, thought better of it, and ran with her head bowed low along the hall, up the stair to the place where Kaspar's workshop used to sit. Emil, who had been somewhere on the shopfloor, was not far behind. They crashed into the toybox together and slammed shut the lid.

It was dark in here, the comforting dark, the dark that made the world seem such a faraway, dreamlike place. Cathy waited for the next reverberation.

A voice spoke to her in the darkness. 'Cathy, are you hurt?'

'It was close. Not Iron Duke Mews. Oxford Street? The Circus?'

A succession of smaller conflagrations, somewhere on the other side of the city. The sounds reached out to them through walls of wood, the imaginary air.

'It's an all-night one, isn't it?'

'Yes,' said Cathy, 'I'd imagine it is.'

When the bombardments first came they hadn't known where to hide. Emil spoke of erecting an Anderson shelter in the heart of the shopfloor, but the Emporium had cubbyholes aplenty, cupboards beneath its manifold stairs, hollows in the walls where the toy soldiers had once built their doll's house worlds. Beyond the Emporium doors, London's terrified were flooding into the Underground, but the thought of rushing there, beneath a sky marked with the comet trails of sparring aircraft, was reason enough to stay behind. It was hunkered together in Martha's old closet, the carnival etchings of the Long War all around them, that Cathy first remembered the toybox. Ten years ago they had sold the few Kaspar once made to a collector, and in that way bought themselves a few more months without the fear of Mr Moilliet's letters, but this one had always remained: unpainted, half-finished, propped on its end in the corner of his workshop.

Emil had brought a night light. He fumbled to strike a match and, a moment later, the walls were alive with an incandescent display. Then, as if recognising the solemnity of the occasion, the shadow figures stopped dancing, wrapped their arms around one another and waited out the bombardment.

For a long time they alternated between silences and concern about the other. Emil asked Cathy if she was frightened; Cathy asked the same question of Emil. Emil said he was grateful that Martha was gone, off to the Americas with her husband, because at least she did not have to live through this. Cathy said she was grateful Emil's boys were training as doctors, because at least that meant they might be excused the fighting; at least that meant they might not come back as Kaspar had, all that time ago.

The Emporium shook. The world turned on its axis. Somewhere, somebody's life was opened up; somebody else's, taken away.

Emil said: 'I'm so glad you're here, Cathy.'

And gently she said, 'There's nowhere else I'd be.'

Emil stuttered as he next spoke, forcing his words into the snatches of silence between the falling bombs. 'Perhaps I'm a foolish old man, Cathy, but ... you're the person I've known the longest, in all of my life. After Papa went, after

Kaspar – it's always been you, Cathy, you for more than half of my life. Ever since that summer, when we were young, and everything was good … Do you know, we've been longer like this than we ever were with Kaspar? You and me and our little Emporium.' He stopped. She was staring at him, voiceless, in the dark. 'Aren't *we* married, Cathy? Oh, I know it's not that and I know it's not …' His words came apart. 'But marriage, of a sort. Well, aren't we?'

Another explosion echoed in the Emporium. What the toy soldiers might have made of this, thought Cathy. They would have charged out of the skirting, believing their Long War had returned.

Her eyes were on Emil. He seemed close now, closer than the walls of the toybox compelled him to be. He lifted his hand, dropped it again – and when he found the courage to lift it again, she almost took it in her own. His eyes were cast down but all she would have to do, all it would take, was a word and they would rise up again. She might have reached out to him, touched her fingertips to his, and both of their worlds would have changed.

Instead she curled her fingers into her palm. How long had it been since she felt human arms wrapped around her? Seventeen years since Kaspar, seventeen years since that night he had fallen into her as if for the very first time. And yet, the memory of it remained – just like the memory of how the stars had glittered that night on the seafront, or how the paper trees had risen as he rushed her into the Wendy House walls, or how deranged he had looked as he goaded her through it, pushing Martha out into the world. All of these, a thousand other memories, all of them entwined: the big and the small. The ordinary magic (why was it always those words?) of a husband who loved his wife and was loved in return.

'Sometimes I can still hear him.' She was only really aware she had spoken when Emil looked up; her voice was soft, subsumed in the sirens. 'It's when I'm sleeping, or when I'm lying there, dreaming of sleep. I hear him in the walls, like we used to hear the soldiers – only it isn't him, not really, it's just the memory of him, the ghost of a ghost, refusing to leave. Or I'll wake, even now, and wonder if all my life has been a dream – because what else could it be, me and Kaspar, you and this old Emporium? There are nights I'll hear the things he said to me, or the things I said to him, as if the Emporium captured them, like that old music box of his, ripping me out of the bed where I'm sleeping and casting me back there, where I might be waltzing with him in the paper forest or chasing Martha in those longboats around the cloud castle moat.' One night she had felt his arms close around her but when she opened her eyes she was alone, with only Sirius to keep her warm. In the morning, she thought: I should run now, run away like I ran once before. But his ghost was in the toyshop, and though a heart still beat in her breast, so was hers; both of them haunting the aisles where they first met. 'I can feel him now. Can't you? Crouching here, in his toybox, in space he chipped out of the world himself. That's how I know ...'

Emil mouthed the word, 'Know?', his question turned into a mime by the echoes in the earth.

'Know that he's gone. That Kaspar's dead.'

The shriek of some falling incendiary, the din it made as it made fountains out of some nearby alley, drove them back against the walls.

'Cathy, don't ...'

'It took me an age to see it. Years and years to admit it to myself. But if Kaspar didn't die, if he isn't at the bottom of the Thames or swept out to sea, well, how can he haunt this place like he does? No, Emil. If he didn't die that night, he died the day after. I know that now ...'

Whatever Cathy said next was lost to the sound of brick shearing from brick, of a street opened up to the sewer beneath. The toybox shifted, Emil plunged against Cathy – and then they were toppling, each entangled in the other as the toybox and all the world it contained crashed down, down, down ...

Somehow, even in spite of the ringing in their ears, the sirens sang louder now. Somewhere, there was the smell of smoke.

In the morning, standing upon the ruptured cobbles of Iron Duke Mews, Cathy and Emil looked up at the Emporium edifice, its uppermost storeys open to the world just like the doll's houses that once lined the aisles. Through the shifting reefs of black she could spy the charred timbers where the flames had ebbed away, the terrace where the snowdrops would never flower again. It was a wonder such a place as Papa Jack's Emporium had ever existed; it seemed so tiny from without, so ordinary: just bricks and mortar, like any of the buildings around; and, like any of the buildings around, it was not built to last.

The fire engines were still at the end of the mews. Some of the ARP and fire wardens had shopped at the Emporium once. They had come here as boys to play the Long War or imprint themselves upon patchwork beasts. Now they gazed at it with a kind of despair. This was not just the ruin of a building, Cathy thought, but the ruin of memory itself.

Emil took Sirius into his arms, shivering as he stood.

'How are we going to come back from this, Cathy?'

Cathy said nothing. She too was staring into the open Emporium, at the place where Kaspar's toybox still teetered over the precipice and the wind kept snatching charred pages from the books he had filled with his designs, his ideas, his imagination: the very essence of Kaspar himself. Up they went, up and ever upwards, turning into a thousand blackened fragments as the wind bore them over the rooftops until, at last, they were gone.

1940. '41. '42.

MANY
MORE YEARS
LATER . . .

THIS ORDINARY WORLD

LONDON, AUGUST–NOVEMBER 1953

Consider Catherine Godman: older than you remember her, though you remember her well; greyer, more lined than she was when she first saw the Emporium lights, but still the same girl you followed up from her estuary home, into an upside-down life of mystery, memory and magic. Tonight, if you had crept through the empty Emporium aisles (as so few do these days), you would have found her at the desk in her daughter's old room, and on the scratched surface in front of her two torn letters, salvaged from the bins where her old friend Emil had thrown them away. Three hours of painstaking recreation, of glue, ink and masking tape, was all it took to piece those letters back together. And if you had lurked there on her shoulder, you too might have seen what Cathy herself saw: one letter the notification of Mr Moilliet's retirement from his position at Lloyd's bank, and the appointment of a Mr Greene as his successor; the next, from Mr Greene himself, declaring a full audit of the Emporium records, surprise at the lenience with which his predecessor conducted affairs, an immediate suspension of all credit extended to Papa Jack's Emporium and a demand for all extant payments to be made good, under threat of foreclosure.

If you had been particularly canny (as we know that you are), perhaps you would have seen what Cathy saw last of all, the thing that brought the first tear to her eye – for in the corner of the letters, the date read April and, on the calendar on the wall, the date read August. There had always been secrets aplenty in Papa Jack's Emporium, but perhaps none as devastating as this. Emil had known what was coming all summer long.

Because this is how the world ends: not in the falling incendiaries of an aerial attack, not in a storm of toy soldiers laying waste to the gods who brought them into being, but in the banal letters of a bank. Where once was magic: now only economics.

Yes: consider Catherine Godman. We have followed her all this way. We must follow her a little further yet.

Papa Jack's Emporium closed its doors for the final time on an overcast day in the August of 1953. There was bitterness to the wind that day and, as Cathy left the store by one of its manifold tradesman's exits, she stopped to fasten her overcoat and thought: well, that was a life. Then she toddled off to catch a bus.

It had been some time since she was last alone on London streets. The city was bigger than she remembered. It was more colourful too – and, as she fought for a seat on one of the crowded buses, she got to thinking that here was one of the reasons the Emporium had finally closed its doors; for if there was such extravagance to be found on an everyday London street, what place in the world could there be for a shop grown so drab and ordinary after the glory days of its youth?

The bus took her past the green splendour of Regent's Park, through the elegant porticos of St John's Wood and north, before depositing her upon the Finchley Road – where, finally, she stood outside a simple redbrick terrace, distinguished from its neighbours only by the monkey puzzle standing in the garden. Here she checked the address against the notebook poking out of the top of her day bag. Satisfied, she knocked at the door.

'Mama,' came a voice as the door drew back.

'My little girl.'

'I'm so glad you found us. Lemuel's been berating me all morning for not sending a taxicab – but then, he doesn't know you like I do. I told him: she's my mother, and she doesn't need a fuss. She'd find her way through the Arctic.'

Figures had appeared in the hall behind Martha: three little ones, all lined up, and behind them the beanpole that was Martha's husband. Cathy had seen him so rarely, the rocketeer who had met Martha at the Washington embassy where she worked and allowed himself to be swept off his feet. He had the same figure as Kaspar once had, his hair swept back in the same lovingly bedraggled manner.

'Mrs Godman, it's my pleasure to see you again.' His accent had hardly softened since the last time they met; he still spoke as if he was up on the silver screen. In time, she would learn it was an affectation, meant solely to delight his children; now, it took her by surprise. 'Why, Mrs Godman – is that all you've brought?'

Cathy lifted the day bag on her wrist and nodded. 'I have need for so little, Lemuel.'

'And yet – only this, for an entire life?'

Cathy stepped inside. The house – her new home, she reminded herself – smelled faintly of gingerbread and peppermints. A little bowl on a sideboard was filled with bonbons. 'I should enjoy a pot of tea, Martha dear. It already feels like the longest day.'

It was to get longer. Martha had laid on a spread – with apologies for the haste, for the family had only days before returned from Washington to make their new life – and over sandwiches Cathy was reintroduced to her grandchildren. Bethany was nine and her rose gold hair was either a throwback to some former generation or the inheritance of her father. Lucas (who excavated his nose at the dinner table, despite dire predictions of brain damage from his father) was eight. Cathy had met both when the family made their whirlwind tours of the capital, but for Esther – who, at three years old, had come later into Martha's life than any had expected – it was the very first time. Cathy fed her corners of cake and saw in her a Martha in miniature. Something in this dulled the ache which she had been feeling all day.

The excitement helped too.

'What is it?' Lucas shrieked.

'It's coming to get you!' Bethany cried.

Esther just squalled, but when Lemuel took her in his arms she was the first to touch the new interloper – for Sirius had appeared in the dining-room door, his threadbare tail swishing as he came to meet his new hosts.

'It isn't just a toy,' Bethany insisted. 'It can't be.'

Across the table, Cathy caught Martha's eye. 'Why,' she said and, opening her arms, drew her grandchildren near, as if taking them into a conspiracy, 'there isn't such a thing as *just* a toy. The stories I'm going to tell you, the things you wouldn't believe! Your mother and I grew up in a toyshop, you know, where the most wonderful things happened every day ...'

'But toys are just toys,' grunted Lucas, who had had quite enough of this nonsense.

'Sometimes,' whispered Cathy, and thought: *yes, I can see how this might work. Perhaps there is a place for me here after all.*

Cathy's quarters were on the second storey. They were modest in size, but there were two, one for a bedroom and one for a parlour, and from the parlour there was a balcony on which one might take the sun during summer. As she waited for her dinner-time summons, she set about ordering her new world. She had already arranged all of the trinkets from her bag when she heard the tread on the stairs. The door opened and in crashed the two older children, Esther toddling behind.

They had been coming with shortbread and tea but, now that they saw the room, they were struck dumb. 'Where did it all come from?' Bethany asked, in wide-eyed wonder. For somehow the room had been filled with more items than their grandmother could possibly have carried with her. There were potted plants and bookshelves, a woven sampler on the wall, new bedclothes and blankets. The mantel of the old fireplace was decorated with wedding portraits in grainy black and white.

'Oh,' said Cathy, 'it all came with me, I promise.'

'In that little bag?' Lucas demanded, insisting on an inspection.

'Don't trip now,' grinned Cathy, handing it over. 'You might have a nasty accident.'

'Who's that?' Bethany asked.

She was pointing at the portraits, so Cathy set about explaining: this is me when I was a much younger lady; and this is your mother, hardly as old as your baby sister is now; and this, this is your grandfather. His name was Kaspar, and he was the greatest man I knew.

She was telling them the story when another figure appeared in the door. Lemuel had evidently been hunting his children all over the household, while Martha reacquainted herself with Sirius downstairs.

'Are these monsters hassling you, Mrs Godman?'

'Not for a second,' she said, grappling out to catch Lucas, who was half swallowed inside her bag and threatening to topple further. 'And please, call me Cathy. Or ... Nanny. I should like that. Well ...' With the deepest grimace, she heaved Lucas up and out of the bag, '... I'm to be the children's nanny, aren't I?'

Lucas crashed backwards, landing in the hearth, with a look of such uncertainty: the bewilderment of a baby at being born.

'There are *things* inside. You haven't emptied your bag.'

Cathy flushed red. 'I dare say I'm not the first lady not to have emptied her handbag in half her life.'

'I want to see!' Bethany exclaimed. In a second, Lucas was back on his feet. Esther, prompted by the sound of her siblings' excitement, was shuffling over, determined to join in.

Lemuel swept her up. 'I imagine you're not used to this chaos.'

'Oh, there was chaos, once upon a time.'

Lemuel crossed the room, hovering at the mantel where Kaspar's face peered out.

'This is the man, is it? Martha's father.' Cathy nodded. 'He was a daring fellow, Martha says. I've seen some of the things he made. We never had a place like yours in New York. You must miss home sorely.'

The details of a life, Cathy thought, were too vast to be covered in small talk. But then, she had had her fill of silences too.

'For twenty-nine years ... and yet every day.'

'Did they ...' Lemuel stopped himself, as if what he was about to say had already been outlawed by Martha – but Cathy did not seem as troubled. 'Did they ever find out what happened to him?' 'No,' she went on, 'but, then, a great many men went missing in those days. One among many was hardly enough to stop the world turning. Only in our little Emporium ...'

Sleep did not come easily tonight. First nights, she remembered, were always the worst, but she had been almost fifty years beneath the same roof and the change was going to take some getting used to. For the moment, she was glad of the comforts she had brought with her. Cedar and star anise were Emporium smells, and the fragrance had flurried up all evening from the candles on the ledge, Sirius curled up at the foot of the bed.

Midnight came. Then one o'clock. Then two. At three Esther awoke and an instinct buried for more than forty years drove Cathy up, into her slippers, and out into the hall – but Martha was already at the girl's bedside, shushing her back to sleep. So Cathy sat, instead, on the end of her bed, mindlessly winding Sirius and trying to keep away that inevitable thought: how did the long road of a life come to this?

This is how it ends, she remembered, and Kaspar's face beamed at her from the wedding portrait on the wall.

It was to be another week before Martha's new job at the Ministry, so for a time Cathy had nothing to do but acquaint herself with her grandchildren. There was enough to learn about them, their likes and dislikes, their habits and routines, that it was easy to forget that every passing day was a day closer to the moment the demolition experts would set their charges along Iron Duke Mews, bringing down the Emporium and all its neighbours in the never-ending quest for Post-War Reconstruction. The bus up to Hampstead Heath, Saturday afternoon at the Kilburn theatre, a Technicolor matinee; outside the empty Emporium, the days could easily be filled.

September was the dawn of the new era. There were two schools for the children to attend, a boys' school in St John's Wood for Lucas and a girls' prep for Bethany off Primrose Hill, and the journeys to and fro somehow seemed to dominate the day. In the between times, Esther demanded feeding and bathing and playing, and though some of this could be delegated to Sirius (who seemed to be remembering the tricks he had learned when Martha herself was a girl), Cathy took delight in the small things. When Lucas's teachers were dissatisfied with his attitude in class (for he was more interested in telling the boy in front that he was an American adventurer every bit as famous as

Huckleberry Finn), it was Cathy who sat with him at the end of the day and showed him his fractions, and in that way engaged him with his work. When Bethany slipped in the schoolyard and had to have stitches in her knee, it was Cathy who held her hand in the hospital ward and, afterwards, took her for an Italian ice cream that cured all ills. At bedtime, she plucked the old copy of *Gulliver's Travels* from the shelf and, though they were far too old and grown-up for mere stories, she read to them of Gulliver's adventures in Lilliput and Brobdingnag. And, when that was done (and Esther, too young to understand, was nevertheless demanding to join in), she reached for the only other tome she could find that contained adventures of similar daring, and that was how Martha's THE TRUE HISTORY OF TOYS became a bedtime story for the very first time.

'It can't really have happened that way,' said Lucas, who had embraced the logic of fractions and the certainty of his times tables with a relish Cathy had not expected. 'Toys can't walk and talk …'

'Not the ones you play with, young man. And yet …'

By now, Sirius had taken to sleeping with the grandchildren, and Cathy had instructed them in the solemn duty of winding him up at the end of each night. 'He wound down only once before,' she told them as they fixed a new patch to his hide, 'and who knows if his heart could stand it again.'

'Heart!' Lucas snorted.

'A mechanical heart might still be a heart,' said Cathy, and was delighted to hear them bickering the question through over the days that followed. There was, perhaps, a way the Emporium might live on in hearts and minds, even if its bricks and mortar might soon be obliterated from the London streets.

One afternoon, when half-term holidays came around, Cathy took the children on a bus down to the Oxford Circus and, though both Lucas and Bethany gaped at the garish storefront of Hamley's, finally she lured them away, into that warren of winding Mayfair mews in which the Emporium still waited.

'Is that it?' asked Lucas.

'You said it was as big as Selfridge's inside. Ten times the size!'

'Perhaps it was.'

'Mama said it had its own railway, and a giant dome like at St Paul's.'

'Your mama was right. She should know. She was born through that very door.'

'I think it's all stories,' said Lucas – but that night it was Lucas himself who demanded the honour of winding up Sirius as he lay, basking in the attention, at the foot of the bed. And the next morning, when Cathy woke late, she was not surprised to see that it was Lucas who was chasing Sirius in circles around the garden, throwing him a ball and attaching trowel blades to his paws so that he could dig for bones in the vegetable patch like a real live dog.

Cathy was standing at the window, watching them play, when a neighbour appeared over the back fence and hallooed out. Lucas, his face set in a suspicious mask, summoned Sirius to heel and answered with a respectful (if slightly scornful) nod of the head. It was good to be suspicious of strangers and his school had rightly drilled him in this fact, but on this occasion he need not have worried. Cathy had seen the way the eyes of their neighbour thrilled upon seeing the patchwork dog; a century might pass by, but you would always recognise a fellow who held the Emporium close to his heart.

The following afternoon, Cathy was involved in writing a letter to Emil, when a knock came at the door. Writing to Emil demanded great patience and composure, for leaving the Emporium had laid him lower than it had Cathy herself – and, Cathy was given to believe, he had not truly left, for he still flitted back and forth between the home of one of his estranged sons (much to the horror of their mother), and the barren shopfloor itself. The distraction of the door knocking, while the rest of the family gambolled with Sirius in the back garden, was a deep relief.

The man on the doorstep was the very same who had ogled Sirius with such wonder over the garden fence. He was a rotund little man, evidently given to pastries – and indeed there were the shreds of some sugary foodstuff still sparkling in his whiskers of white and grey – but he had dressed incongruously smartly for a neighbourly visit. In his hands was a paper bag that cast Cathy back half a century in time: brown paper and green ink, with the insignia of Papa Jack's Emporium up and down its sides.

'Forgive me, madam. I'm of the hope you won't reject a little distraction on a Sunday morning. My name is Harold Elderkin. You won't have noticed me, I'm sure, but I couldn't help observe your arrival on our quiet little street. I'm afraid you'll think me a spook, an espionage artist par excellence, but what spying I've done has been quite accidental! I couldn't help it, you see, that ...'

As if on cue, Sirius darted into the hall and let out a series of pillowy barks at the stranger at the door. 'Sirius,' she said, 'do calm down. This is Mr Elderkin, come from …'

'Good Lord,' said Harold, 'I was right! Until yesterday afternoon, I don't believe I'd seen one of these in more than fifty years. We coveted these as lads. I would have cut off half my own arm to open one of these on a Christmas morning. I'm right, aren't I? This is vintage stuff. Vintage Emporium … And you …'

'I worked there,' said Cathy, 'once upon a time.'

'I should say that you did,' said Harold, giving weight to Cathy's first impression that here was a man who would be happy talking to a lamp post, if only he could find a lamp post happy to listen, 'and I remember you, madam. When I was a boy, I was boarded at a little place in Lambeth, a place called Sir Josiah's. A squalid little place, and I dare say you haven't given it a second thought in a generation, but … that was home, to me and my lot. Day in day out, with little to look forward to, until … the visitors from the Emporium.'

Cathy thought back: the summer trips, the carriage over the river, the orphaned boys swarming in the yard.

She stepped back. 'Please Mr Elderkin, come in. I'm delighted you came.'

Harold Elderkin revealed himself a man of the most nervous disposition. Three times he declined tea before, finally, asking plaintively if he might partake of a small cup. Biscuits were proffered twice before he lined them up on a saucer and Cathy could see, in the way his fingers twitched, how eagerly he wanted to cram them into his gullet. Biscuits, he explained, had been in short supply when he was a lad.

'I remember Sir Josiah's,' Cathy began, once Harold was settled, with Sirius up on his lap. 'We would go there every summer, with stock from the winter before. Always my husband and me, and then my daughter. A summer day at Sir Josiah's could rival first frost almost every year for its spectacle. All of those children waiting up against the windows, or spilling out into the yard ...'

'Well, that was me,' Harold replied, with a modicum of pride – for to be remembered by an Emporium Lady was to fulfil the wish of his childhood. 'Yes, Sir Josiah's is a place that's lodged up in this noggin of mine more than most. You know how that feels, I shouldn't wonder. If I might be so bold ... what happened to the Emporium, Mrs Godman? How could a place like that just shut up its doors and ...' He faltered, started wringing his hands. 'I'm sorry. I've spoken out of turn.'

'You haven't. It's only ... I wouldn't know where to begin. A story like that has a thousand beginnings. I should need all night, and my grandchildren ...'

'I've had an inconsequential kind of life, Mrs Godman. I did my bit, I made a few friends, I had a good number of splendid luncheons, and now I spend my time pottering up and down the Finchley Road. I've been to the pictures twice this week already, and neither time for a matinee I cared to see. This Friday, I'm going to a *department store*. But when I think of the Emporium the way it used to be, why ...' Something must have caught in his throat, because suddenly he fell silent. 'Oh, Mrs Godman, I didn't mean to suggest ... Well, it was so long ago, and fortunes can change. What happened to the place, well, who would have predicted? Hard times have fallen on so many in our lives.'

He stopped again, certain he had pursued the conversation into some dreadful quagmire from which he might never extricate himself. 'What I meant to say was … You've lived a remarkable life, Mrs Godman. I should hope I might hear about it some time. And, if you don't mind me saying, I feel … honoured to be sitting here with you. My Maud didn't want me coming, she said I was to make a great fool of myself, but I could hardly stay away, not after I saw this old mutt here. And then, well, there's the real reason I came …' Harold shifted, depositing Sirius back on to the carpet, and brought up the bag he had brought with him.

He was lifting out its contents and placing them on the cushions at his side when the children clattered back into the room, Martha following behind. On seeing Harold they stopped dead – but it was not the sight of the old man that stilled them; for on the cushions beside him were sitting three editions of the Long War, two as pristine as the unopened boxes that had once sat upon the shopfloor, one weathered and worn around the edges. Curiosity had been piqued in Bethany, even in Lucas (who was struggling to project his obligatory indifference), but the colour had drained from Martha's face, even as her eyes dared to believe. In the end, it was Cathy herself who said, 'Mr Elderkin, wherever did you—'

'This dog-eared old thing is my own,' he began. 'You won't remember this but, one summer, you brought boxes down to Sir Josiah's, and I became the proud owner of my very own Long War. When I finally moved on from there, well, I took it with me wherever I hung my hat. The other two, I'm afraid to say, I bought at auction. Maud would say I squandered my savings on them, but I'll have none of that. These pieces are priceless …' He paused. 'And I want you to have them.'

'Me?'

'If not you, Mrs Godman, then the children. I'm afraid I never had children of my own. My Maud and I have been blessed, but not by the patter of tiny feet. I'm an old man now. I'll have need for toys again, I shouldn't wonder, but not for some time ... and perhaps you'll save them for me. Consider it a lifetime's loan. But, for now, they should be played with. They've been wrapped up too long ...' Harold's face broke into the simplest, wildest smile. 'Well, go on then! Get stuck in! Perhaps you wouldn't mind an old man playing a Long War with you, after all ...'

The children needed no further tempting. Lucas and Bethany set about tearing open the sealed copies of the Long War, while Harold lined up the troops of his open box and read to them aloud from the *Rules of Engagement*.

Cathy and Martha watched as battle commenced. The clacking of wind-up soldiers was a familiar sound and if, at first, there was something sinister about the whirring motors, soon the anxiety was gone – and only the thrill of half-forgotten battles remained. Watching them now, Cathy could picture Kaspar and Emil battling across their bedroom floor, or Emil and Nina in the glade that first summer they met. She reached out and clasped her daughter's hand. Sometimes, you had to choose the memories you held dear.

'Wait!' said Lucas, as they set the fronts up for the second time. 'I've an idea ...'

Then he was gone up the stairs, as if toy soldiers were far too old-fashioned a thing with which to waste his time.

While he was gone, Harold and Bethany continued to battle, the old man narrating at length how the older boys of Sir Josiah's had returned, Christmas after Christmas, to wage campaigns with the brothers they had left behind. By the time Lucas returned, grasping something in his fist, Mr Elderkin had noticed the clock on the wall and, to his horror, announced that his poor wife Maud would, even now, have been sitting in front of a Sunday roast, watching the gravy congeal on her plate rather than begin the meal without him.

'I'll be back, if I may,' he began, labouring out into the hall.

Lucas watched as his mother and grandmother saw the old man out. 'Now we can see ...'

'What have you got there, in your fist?'

At first Lucas did not reveal it. 'I knew she had something, up there in her bag. She's full of secrets, isn't she? I thought I saw it that very first day.'

'You sneak thief! You went into her room. Mama will—'

'Not if *you* don't tell.'

Lucas brought out his fist and set down a soldier quite unlike the ones Bethany was lining up out of the box. The first thing she noticed was how much older he was than the rest. He had once had jackboots of sparkling green, a sash of crimson red and rows of tiny brass medals up and down his glistening coat. But his body was a lattice of wounds as well. There was a notch in the wood above his left eye that gave the impression of a scar, but that did not compare to the black char marks that covered his back, as if some brute of a boy had held him too close to the fire. In spite of all that, he had a kind of quiet dignity about him and (or so Bethany thought) there almost seemed an expressiveness in his dark, painted eyes. Wherever she shifted, the soldier's eyes seemed to follow. Later she would think herself so foolish, but fleetingly she wondered what the soldier was *thinking*, to be staring at her with such intensity.

In the corner of the room, Sirius lifted his snout, turned one black button eye on the adults passing out into the hallway and the other on the children settling down across the carpet. It had been so long since he had seen toy soldiers that, at first, he considered it a dream. Then he yapped. When the soldiers did not scatter in fear, he judged them harmless and sank again to his slumber, curled up in a cushiony ball.

'Wind him up then,' said Bethany. 'Let's see how it goes ...'

'He'll knock yours down in a second ...'

Lucas reached down, took hold of the key in the burnt soldier's back and started to turn.

He remembers running. He remembers forcing himself through the bars of his birdcage prison. He remembers hurtling headlong through the heartland, the Skirting Board and Wall Cavities that belonged to his people since the gods gave them life. He remembers what he saw. After that, there is only the terror: the knowledge he must do something, a secret he must tell, if only he could keep the inevitable Wind Down at bay. He remembers climbing up, up and ever up, emerging to bright light, desperate to tell her, desperate to be seen.

Then only blackness, decades long.

Reaching out, tumbling, cursing himself for having no words, for not having the capacity to speak.

All of these things, even now.

The soldier picked itself up. It was, to Lucas's mind, staggering as if drunk. Then, even when it righted, it marched in tiny circles, as if uncertain of its own feet. In the way it lurched there was none of the purpose, none of the bearing, that its expression implied. Probably it was broken. The burnt wood at its back must have stretched as far as its motors, disrupting the way it walked.

'Is that *all*?' Lucas muttered.

'I think he's priceless.'

'I suppose he has a jaunty little strut, but I thought there'd be *more*. Why else would she have squirrelled him away like that? She's such a strange old bird. However did we come from her?'

Lucas turned on his heel, already bored of the game, and as he did the soldier straightened. Bethany watched as it turned on its heel, as if taking in its surroundings. Its eyes met hers – she was not wrong, there was a moment of panic, of terrible realisation – and then it sprang forwards, legs clacking in a way wholly unlike the other solders around, and hurtled into the darkness beneath one of the sofas.

Bethany dropped to her knees, pressed her face to the carpet and peered into the dark.

'It's disappeared ... Lucas! It's disappeared!'

But Lucas was not in the least bit inclined to go hunting, not down there in the dust for anything so peculiarly old-fashioned as a wind-up soldier – and so nobody was there to witness the miracle of a sleeping mind awaking, and nobody heard the first scuttling in the walls.

In the Black Lands beneath the Sofa, in this strange new world of Carpet and Rug, a mind comes back into being.

The fog in which it has been lost takes time to dissipate – but slowly the reefs of grey part and clear. For thirty years the mind of the Imperial Kapitan has been hemmed in. Thirty years of Wind Down. Thirty years: a mind, locked in place, unable to cry out, unable to get help. Thirty years of solitude – that was the real Long War. But now, here he is. He shakes himself out of his stupor, and at last he is alive.

A hand reaches in for him, a giant godly hand made out of blood and bone, and had he not had the instincts to skitter backwards, perhaps its unearthly fingers would have closed around him and dragged him out into the light. The hand comes again, but this time it does not come near – and when, some time after that, the great sonorous voices of the gods echo and fade, the Imperial Kapitan dares to believe he is safe.

He stumbles to the precipice, the edge of the Sofa, where the giant feet of his gods are looming. How the world has changed during his everlasting Wind Down! Out there he sees the children of gods grown, the grandchildren of gods newly cut from their own Workshop Lathe. He sees scores of his wooden brothers lying prone on the Carpet, this forest the gods have raised up to hide the true world of Floorboard underneath, but already he knows they are not like him; what minds reside in those carefully hewn heads have not yet been stirred to idea or imagination; probably these soldiers are yet to wind each other up, yet to march for any other reason than as playthings of the gods. He dares venture out further – and, curled up against the Skirting Board on the far side of the chamber, he sees Sirius, the patchwork dog. That is how he knows for certain that he remains in the same world in which his motors last died. Somehow he knows that Sirius is like him; Sirius *understands*.

Looming above him is the Lady, the one married to the Kaspar God. On seeing her, his wooden heart soars. He wants to run out and take her by the hand, for thirty years has not dulled the urgency of the one idea dominating his thoughts. But the key in his back is not wound to full, he knows that soon it will labour, soon it will slow … And if that happens there is a chance he must wait another thirty years before his chance comes around again. By then, what will the world be? It may already be too late.

There is, he decides, another way.

The gods are crossing the carpet, out into the kitchens beyond. The children of the gods follow after, until all that is left are the toy soldiers lying inert on the carpet fronds and the patchwork dog, lazily sleeping the day away. The Kapitan knows he has only one chance. He darts out of the darkness, grapples with the arms of the nearest toy soldier, and strains to heave him into the shelter from which he ran.

Too late, the patchwork dog sees him. It sets up its wet laundry howl and, seconds later, the grandchildren of the gods hurtle back into the room. But they see nothing – or, if they do, they cannot believe their eyes.

The Kapitan has mere minutes until Wind Down returns. On his knees, he turns over his brother. The contraption in his back is a basic design, sculpted by the daemon-lord himself. But the Kapitan remembers. He opens his brother up, presses his hands into the fine mesh of cogs and gears that drive him. A tweak here, a tweak there, and soon the soldier is up on his feet, his fingers and hands flexing in strange new ways. It is with some joy that the Kapitan feels himself being wound up, the rush of new energy and life to every corner of his frame.

Now that there are two, the work can truly begin. Together we stand; divided, we fall.

Toy soldiers cannot speak (remember, they are only toys). But if they could, the Imperial Kapitan would have taken his new comrade by the hands, turned him around, and shown him the battlefield where the rest of their brothers have been left to die. Look, he would have said. Look at what we are, look at what we were made to do – and look what we can do for ourselves. We have been appointed a task, one that, out of all the toy soldiers in the world, only we are fit to do.

But we are going to need some help.

That night, Cathy put the children to bed with another tale from THE TRUE HISTORY OF TOYS and, on turning out the lights, met Martha on the stair.

'Mama,' she said, 'I was worried about you.'

Mindful that the children might hear, Cathy ushered Martha down the stairs. 'Don't be worried. Don't be afraid. I'm a sturdy old thing, remember?'

'For a moment I thought – what if they were *real*? Real in the way we'd understand it, Mama. But of course, they were only toy soldiers ...' She smiled. 'The Emporium never leaves you, does it? I've been halfway around the world and back, but it doesn't go. Sooner or later, bits of it start appearing.'

'You might as well try and escape your own heart.'

For a time there was silence on the stairs.

'It made me think of him,' said Martha. 'Oh, never a day goes by, of course, when he isn't there – but sometimes he's more there than others. Seeing his soldiers ...'

'Those weren't your father's soldiers, Martha, my love. They were Emil's. Just plain, ordinary Emil's, of the kind we used to rely on, once upon a time. A simpler time.'

Cathy drew close to plant a kiss on her daughter's cheek. 'Sleep tight, my little Martha.'

Martha said nothing until Cathy was halfway back up the stairs. Then, into the silence, she called out: 'I miss him, Mama.'

Cathy stopped.

'Do you ever wish you had one of his music boxes? Remember those dainty old things? You could turn its crank handle and be back there, and there he'd be.'

It was a question to which Cathy had devoted the better part of her life. She tightened her robe against a sudden draught. It was funny how talking about it could play tricks upon your senses. She almost felt as if she could hear the same scuttling in the walls that had disappeared along with her husband.

'Never,' she whispered. 'I loved your father as much as anything else on this earth – but if I had one of his music boxes on my bedside, why, I'd take a hammer to it this very night. If Kaspar was here and in our lives, I'd want him as he is now, every last scar of it, all the things you can see and all the ones you can't. Because the thing your father knew better than any of us, Martha dear, is still true: the past is the past; you can't ever go back.'

The bedroom had a draught too. Cathy checked that the window was closed and watched for a time as the clouds parted, revealing the inky blackness and arcing stars above. A clear night: the kind of November night that might, once upon a time, have heralded first frost.

She was happy for Sirius that he had the children to play with, because there would come a time, soon, when she was gone the same as Kaspar. But toys? Toys lived on.

She woke in the blackness, propelled out of a dream. It was the thought of the soldiers, the visit from Harold Elderkin, those stolen moments with her daughter on the stairs. In her dreams they had been marching again, and she wasn't sure where toy soldier ended and soldier of flesh and blood began.

It was a Kaspar dream, and for decades those dreams had been the worst.

She rolled over, wishing Sirius was here more than ever. She closed her eyes, willing sleep to return, but soon she realised that the dream hadn't ended. She could still hear that terrible scuttling in the wall.

Cathy screwed her eyes tighter. She screwed her eyes tighter still. She drew the covers up and over her head, a little girl afraid of monsters, and still she could hear the scuttling.

All it had taken was one little sight of them. All the walls she had been building, all the ways of keeping the devastation at bay, they were all falling clean away.

Kaspar had once told her that she was brave but she did not feel brave tonight. She felt like the lost little girl she had never been – and, oh, how she hated it …

Kicking off the bedsheets, Cathy got to her feet. The scuttling was louder now, louder than ever, but hot milk would chase it away. Hot milk and hot tea and, yes, she would tempt Sirius to come back through, if only for one night. The children would understand. A patchwork dog's loyalty was an inconstant thing . . .

She was at the door when the scuttling reached its zenith. Then: silence.

It was the silence that stilled her. She had grown used to the nightmare but, now that it was gone, a different kind of dread seeped in. Her body was telling her to turn, but she did not want to turn.

She turned.

For the first time, she realised that the noises had been coming from only one section of the skirting, the gap between the bedside cabinet and the fireplace where her wedding portraits still hung. Down there, the skirting was in shadow. The scuttling had stopped – but now there was movement, movement down there in the gloom.

She crouched, peering downwards. This time she was certain. The skirting board was shifting. It trembled at the edges, a thin seam appeared where two boards had been whitewashed together, and out popped the little tin tacks holding it in place. Then, with the rattling ferocious in the cavity beyond, the skirting board tumbled outwards, landing in the deep pile of the rug.

A myriad of black shapes rushed out of the cavity. Cathy staggered backwards, the candle she had been holding tumbling to her feet.

Out of the skirting, a battalion of wooden soldiers streamed on to the carpet. They came three abreast, until there were twenty, thirty, forty of them all milling on the floor, the keys in their backs slowly winding down. Before

Cathy had caught her breath, long before she had formulated a rational thought, they were swarming towards her.

It couldn't be. The soldiers Harold had brought, they had been wound down, simple, prehistoric things. Not one of them had the knowledge …

As Cathy tried to make sense of what was happening, one of the toy soldiers broke ranks. Advancing beyond the others, it marched to the tip of her slipper, turned on its heel and marched back. By the time it was in front of the battalion, Cathy thought she recognised the uniform and all its golden stripes. 'You,' she whispered, 'but it can't be you …'

The Imperial Kapitan was spinning on the spot, his little bugle pressed to his lips, and at his direction the others were drawing a kaleidoscope across the carpet. When the Imperial Kapitan stopped his pirouette, so did the others come to a halt. Only now did Cathy see what they had been doing. It had been a drill. Now, they were standing in formation – and, as they marched from one formation to another, Cathy could quite clearly see the words being spelled out by the way that they stood:

WE … HAVE … COME

It couldn't be. Not words. Not *language*, not as sophisticated as this. Only hours before, the soldiers had been simple contraptions of wire and wood.

AT LAST WE HAVE COME

Then she remembered the cavities under the shopfloor. The years Martha had spent reading to them. The way story and language seeped into sandalwood and teak, corrupting the grain of the wood, setting it in strange new spirals.

The Imperial Kapitan had been there. The Imperial Kapitan had learned. He had, she thought now, been learning for more than thirty years, trapped inside the confines of his own head ...

He directed the soldiers and, once more, the soldiers swarmed:

HELP HIM!

'Help him?' Cathy whispered. 'Help who?'

The Imperial Kapitan began to spin again, and in response the regiment returned to its dance.

COME WITH US

Cathy must have cried out, for she could hear doors opening underneath her now. Martha was on the stairs and coming up fast. 'Mama?' she called. 'Mama, what's happening up there?'

WE MUST GO BACK

'Go back where?'

HE IS WAITING!

Cathy heard the thunder of footsteps behind her and, moments later, Martha was at her side. In a horror that quickly transformed to delight, she lifted her hand to her mouth.

BACK TO THE ... EMPORIUM!

Wordlessly, Cathy nodded – and at this the soldiers broke into an uncontrolled dance. Only the gesticulations of the Imperial Kapitan seemed to bring them back under control. They twirled in laps around Cathy's feet, and then they lined up, in ranks before her. One after another they raised their arms in salute, until finally only the Kapitan was left.

There would be no salute from him. Instead he marched forward, the key in his back still winding down, and extended his hand. It took a moment for Cathy to recollect, another for her to understand. Then, she crouched down and took his tiny wooden hand in her own. It was only then that she noticed how his wood was charred black, how his varnish had melted and run, leaving those unutterable wounds on his behind.

'Little man, what happened to you?'

Outside, the first frost of winter was hardening across London town – but the Emporium was waiting and there was not far to go.

THE GREAT LONELINESS

PAPA JACK'S EMPORIUM, 30 NOVEMBER 1953

He had salvaged whatever he could. Oh, the removals men had tried, and then the bailiffs, and then the individual creditors (who had, to his opprobrium, been permitted to go into the storerooms and pick out whatever ephemera they wanted, if only to wipe out a little debt), but there were some things Emil was determined to keep. He piled them up behind his workshop door and wrote an inventory of all the things he had: three suitcases of journals, his father's phoenix, a cloth bag lined with cotton and, nestling inside, all of his father's pinecone figurines. This, the sum of a life. He didn't even have ideas any more. He didn't have imagination.

Emil stepped on to the shopfloor, so cavernous and empty that his footsteps echoed like the steps of a giant. There were still crates of bric-a-brac, perhaps even some older toys, in the stores, but across the shopfloor the shelf stacks were gone, the carousel dismantled, the *Midnight Express* taken to pieces for scrap. The cloud castle had been the first to go, sold off at auction to a charitable concern, and now there were only the floorboards (those would go too, before the demolition) and the disconnected pipes underneath.

Strange, but without everything in it, the shopfloor seemed so small. You could see straight through the glade where the Long War used to be played, up past the mezzanines, the corrals and seaport (where once the krakens had lurked beneath crêpe paper waves), over the stumps of the paper forest and the abandoned platforms of the *Midnight Express*. You could see one wall and then the next and, without anything in it, that was all the Emporium was: walls and walls and the space in between. He wondered that he had ever thought it as big as the world.

Emil did not dance across the empty expanse, because he had no feet for dancing. He did not charge around it, hollering into the dark, because even alone he felt foolish. He found a stool (*stupid bailiffs, you could have had this stool!*) and sat in the middle of the dusty expanse and, after a time, he dared to stare upwards, into the vaults where his cloud castle used to be.

Look, he thought, for as he watched ice was forming across the glass in the Emporium dome, a mist that hardened to occlude the night sky beyond. *It's the very last first frost ...*

So there it was: the shuttered-up shop at the end of the alley, lights still dangling from its awnings (but not lit up for a generation or more), sugar frost still in its windows (grown pitted and yellow with age).

Iron Duke Mews was already strung up in notices of demolition, the streetlights torn up or snuffed out. Notices dangled from the other shops along the cobbled row: the gentlemen's tailors had been closed for months already, and the windows of the shoemakers were either boarded up or bare. Service trucks were arrayed in a great horseshoe around the end of the mews, and ribbons forbidding passage made a spiderweb across the entrance.

Sirius was the first to venture through, but the rattling chaos inside Cathy's bag told her there were others demanding to make the march. Parting the ribbons to go into the mews, she knelt down and opened the clasp. First to venture out was the Imperial Kapitan. Turning a circuit across the cobbles, he lifted his bugle for a silent call. Then the wind-up soldiery marched out in procession. Poor creatures, thought Martha; they had not yet learned to think, but their time would come.

The Emporium doors had been boarded already, but the tradesman's entrance was not yet barred. Cathy took out her key and together they peered into the barren blackness within.

It had been a decade and more since Martha came to this place – and, if she had expected fountains of colour and the swooping serpents of old, she was sorely disappointed. All was dark in the half-moon hall. Cathy had opened a cabinet on the wall and was flicking the switches contained within – but no lights sparked high up in the Emporium nave. 'They'd been threatening to do this since 1949,' she said, with an air of resignation. 'I hadn't wanted you to see it like this, Martha. It should have lived in your memory like it does for so many others. But ...'

The tiny footsteps of the toy soldiers echoed lonesomely in the vast expanse – until, at last, the Imperial Kapitan came to a halt, devastated at discovering such dust, such decay. In his mind, his homeland had been scoured, his mother country razed to the ground. Thirty years he had been waiting. Thirty years – and now, *this*.

Cathy crouched down, pressed her finger gently to the finger of the Imperial Kapitan. 'Which way?' she whispered. 'Why are we here?'

The question lifted the Kapitan up and out of his despair. Turning on his heel, he began directing the other soldiers to assemble – and, as he did, Martha lifted a finger to point.

'Mama,' she said, 'we're not alone.'

For there, where the aisles had once tapered to a point, where the shelves had once been stacked in such a spiral as to obscure completely the door on the other side, a lantern was burning. Emil Godman was in his workshop, alone, on this very last first frost.

The Imperial Kapitan led the soldiers in a quick, forced march. Though the aisles had long been torn down, the Kapitan made his way by the charts chipped into his wooden mind, following the lines where the aisles used to be, circling the old carousel, marching in mock triumph across the glade where the Long War had long ago been played. Cathy and Martha hurried in their wake, the light of Emil's workshop fading to a point behind them – until, at last, they stood among the stumps of the old paper forest.

The soldiers amassed across the boards. WHERE? they asked and, with regret, Cathy whispered, 'Felled so many years ago. Paper timber, sold off to schools and children's homes and …'

THE HOUSE …

They formed and then re-formed again.

WENDY'S HOUSE …

The soldiers had not finished drilling their final word, its shape quivering and indistinct, when the Imperial Kapitan startled, wheeled around, and commanded them to line up behind them. Standing at the head of the phalanx, he lifted his wooden rifle, aiming into the darkness behind where Cathy stood. They had been the first to hear the footsteps but Cathy heard them now, tolling with a tread she had known for so many years.

Emil appeared out of the swirling motes of dust, his eyes swollen from lack of sleep, his beard an eruption of untended, wiry tufts. A broom hung at his side, wielded like a weapon.

'Cathy,' he gasped, 'what are you—'

'I might ask you the same thing. I thought you were long gone, Emil. We said goodbye, right there in the half-moon hall.'

'I couldn't go, Cathy, not until ...' It was only then, as his eyes panned down, that he saw the soldiers. In the same moment he recognised them, the Imperial Kapitan sounded the charge. Toy soldiers sallied forth. Wooden bullets flew. The first were drawing tiny balsa sabres to spear Emil's shins when he brought down the broom and scattered them, a titan of the battlefield.

The Imperial Kapitan was scrambling to stop the rout, desperate not to lose his soldiers to Wind Down in the unmapped darkness, when Emil cried out, 'Where did they ... How did they ... Cathy, tell me! Why are you here?'

His voice had risen to a shriek of desperation. 'I don't know, Emil,' she snapped – but something had changed now. She had seen the faltering expression on Emil's face. There was terror here, but it was not just terror of the toy soldiers.

Martha was gone to collect the scattered troops from the darkness, but Sirius remained. 'Emil,' Cathy whispered, 'what's going on?'

At her feet, the remaining soldiers formed up.

TELL HER!

'Tell me what, Emil?' She reached out, grappled with his wrist. 'Tell me what?'

'You've been hiding them,' he stammered. 'All this time, and you'd—'

'The Kapitan stowed away in my bag, Emil. Hidden there, like I was, all those summers ago in our Wendy House. He's been waiting thirty years . . . and for this. Emil, please. What is he trying to say?'

Emil tore his hand away, sank down to his haunches – and there he sat, a grown man with his arms wrapped around his knees like any bullied child. 'He's just a toy,' he breathed. 'He isn't saying a thing. He isn't to be trusted . . .'

'Emil!'

The way she barked dried up any tears he had been threatening to cry. Emil looked plaintively up as the soldiers formed a ring around him. 'I was trying to save us. All this time, and that's all I've been trying to do. But he wouldn't listen. *They* wouldn't listen. They thought I was evil, and all because I wanted to play my Long War. They were going to bring us down. You see that, Cathy, don't you? They were going to bring us down and Nina, she was going to take my boys.'

'She took your boys anyway. The Emporium still came to an end.'

'But I had to try. You see that. I had to ...'

Behind Cathy, Martha reappeared, the remaining soldiers trailing behind.

'Emil,' she uttered, 'what did you do?'

'It was the night we laid Papa to rest. Nina said it had to change, that something had to be done. She was right, wasn't she? Whatever else she was, she was right on this. We couldn't go on ... So I did the only thing I thought I could do.' Emil pointed down. The soldiers had abandoned their watch on him now and, under the Imperial Kapitan's instruction, were drilling another word. 'Parley,' he read. 'I woke my brother in the night and begged him to come to a parley.'

Midnight came too quickly on the night that Kaspar Godman disappeared. As the clocks chimed, Emil prowled up and down the length of his workshop, repeating some petition beneath his breath. Later, the wooden eyes watching him from the skirting would look back and think: if only we'd understood, if only we'd had the capacity to anticipate, to plan. But those things came later, too late to save anyone that night, and instead the painted faces just watched him, wound each other up, and watched him again.

Nina was already in bed. She had taken the boys with her, meaning for Emil to sleep alone in his workshop – but, damn it, Emil didn't care if he never went to bed with her again, just as long as his boys grew up like he did, making their battles up and down the Emporium halls, pouring their every dream, every ounce of imagination, into the toys that would one day populate the shelves.

He held one of his papa's pinecone figurines between his fingers. Every time he touched it, memories breathed themselves back into being in the shadows around him. One moment he was in the Emporium; the next, he was back in that little hovel where he and Kaspar were born, and Kaspar was helping him clean the grazes on his knee. But the memories were too vivid, they played on him in ways he could not abide, and were it not for the thought of his papa being ashamed, he would have crushed the soldier between thumb and forefinger right then. Instead, he set it down. The clocks had finished tolling. It was time.

Besieged by too many memories, he took the long route to the shopfloor. By the time he made it to the paper trees, navigating around the blockaded aisles, he had already stopped twice, each time forcing himself to go on. But through the trees he could hear the whirr of a thousand motors turning. The parley had already begun.

He had taken only one step beneath the branches when he heard the footfall behind him. He knew it was Kaspar by his strange, stilted gait, and turned to meet him.

'Little brother.'

'Kaspar,' Emil breathed, 'thank you for this. Thank you.'

'I've made no promises, remember.'

'It's for the best, you'll see. What's good for the Emporium, it's good for us all. Good for Cathy, Kaspar, and good for Martha too. Don't forget them ...'

Kaspar raised a hand. 'It isn't me you have to convince.'

No, thought Emil, and tried not to bunch his fists, *but I know how to convince them.* 'Shall we?' he said. He would help his brother this last little way under the trees, take his arm or allow his arm to be taken. If this was the end, it was the least he could do.

Above them, the Wendy House seemed more derelict than ever. The slats nailed across its windows gave it the appearance of a blind man, scar tissue crowding its sockets. Emil paused before venturing in, allowing Kaspar to go first.

He counted to ten, then followed.

Inside, the floor was thronged with toy soldiers, every last one who once swarmed in the Emporium walls. Kaspar was already among them, and they spun around him in dizzying array. As Emil approached, they turned and formed ranks.

'Are they all here?'

'All but the Imperial Kapitan. None has seen him.'

'Let us not worry about the Kapitan. Perhaps he's wound down already, somewhere out there. Let us begin.' Emil lifted his hands – but tonight he would not flinch. 'I've come in peace,' he said, and watched as the soldiers turned in circles, each winding its neighbour up.

In the middle of the army, Kaspar stood. 'Tonight, he's here as a friend. So let's hear what he has to say.'

The soldiers bristled, but at least they obeyed. That was good, thought Emil. Their loyalty to Kaspar was the thing he had staked the future of the Emporium upon, the last chance he had for a life with his boys.

'I know what you think of me,' he began. His voice was trembling, but desperation made heroes of mortal men, and he fought it back down. 'You think me a coward ... and you're right. But the war's gone on too long. I concede it.' He looked across the soldiers to address Kaspar alone. 'I beat a retreat, Kaspar. The Long War is over. The triumph is yours. All I ask is that the Emporium goes on.'

Emil was not certain that the soldiers heard – or, if they heard, whether they had the capacity to understand. Perhaps theirs was the primitive intelligence of mice; perhaps they knew only fear. He tried not to startle as a troop of infantrymen made a sally for his shins – and was still holding his ground when a single gunshot popped in the middle of the army, bringing the infantry to a halt.

'They're listening,' said Kaspar.

'Well?'

'It isn't a parley unless you agree terms. So what are the terms ... of your surrender?'

'If we must share the Emporium, then we share it.' Emil hardened himself. 'I'm willing to give them the attics. The burrows in the cellars and the deep layer storerooms too. They can live there and do whatever it is soldiers do in peacetime, build their towns and cities and make toy children of their own. I won't interfere with them, and they won't interfere with us. It will be like night and day. Two states, inside the Emporium, and never the twain shall meet.'

There was uproar on the Wendy House floor. The soldiers swarmed around Kaspar, seeming to squabble for his attention. Others pirouetted and danced.

'The Emporium is their mother country. You ought to know how fiercely a man can fight for his home. What guarantee do they have that you'll stay true to your word? What guarantee that, the moment they're safely tucked away, you don't start making soldiers again – dumb, obedient ones who have to do your every command?'

The chaos stopped. Ranks re-formed. On either flank, the soldiers advanced, as if in a pincer with Emil at its head.

'It is *my* Emporium, Kaspar. I must be allowed to make what toys I can.'

'We have spoken of this, Emil.'

'I don't remember any conversation. All I remember is orders. Orders, ever since I was a little boy. Well, it's my life too, Kaspar. And next winter, when the frost comes, these shelves are going to be full. The Emporium's going to be *alive*. It's what Papa would have wanted. It's what *I* want.'

'They came here tonight to reach an accommodation. What are you giving them, if you mean to just make more—'

Emil hung his head. 'Don't make me do this, Kaspar.'

'You're still a little boy with a puffed-up sense of his own importance. Haven't you—'

As Kaspar had been speaking, the soldiers fanned out. At the foot of the bed where Cathy once slept sat the first toybox Kaspar had made, his earliest, most unrefined design. Now the soldiers had scaled the summit and, working in unison, heaved open its lid. With arms windmilling wildly they drew Kaspar's eye.

Inside were cans of bully beef and seasoned ham, jars of new potatoes in brine, sardines and blackberry preserve. Two of the soldiers descended into the chest and returned smeared in dirt from the terracotta pots underneath. They bore up packets of garden seeds as if they were unearthed treasures.

'Please, Kaspar.'

'What is this?'

'Your provisions,' spat Emil. 'In the event they don't accept my terms.'

Kaspar was still – but somehow the soldiers seemed to understand.

'Because these soldiers can't be trusted,' Emil said, 'because I need a way to be certain this is the end. I'm sorry, Kaspar. I told you I'd do anything, anything at all.' Emil lifted his hand. There dangled the key to the Wendy House door. 'You should have listened to me, Kaspar. You should have listened all along.'

In the same moment that Kaspar understood, the soldiers sprang to life. Emil stepped backwards, making for the exit, but already the soldiers were around him. A dozen infantrymen scythed into his shins and Emil lashed out, sending them sprawling. Too late, he realised another unit was besieging his other foot – and, caught off-balance, he crashed into the Wendy House wall. That was when the first artillery fired. From somewhere on the other side of the Wendy House floor, howitzers rolled into place. Emil took the first volley on the breast, turned against the second, only for the third – coming from some unseen corner of the Wendy House – to catch him full in the face. Stars exploded behind his eyes. Blood exploded from his nose. He reared back, fighting to keep balance as the next wave of infantrymen attacked. It was only five more strides to the exit. He would get there however he could.

They thought him a coward? Well, was this what a coward did? He felt mahogany bullets peppering his back and, propelled by them, staggered through the door. Some of the soldiers were trying to stream out alongside him. He took aim and kicked back, stemming the tide one splintered soldier at a time.

There was blood in his eyes, the taste of fresh meat on his lips. Before he closed the door, he dabbed it away and looked within. In the sea of stampeding soldiers, Kaspar was like an island, a god propped up with walking canes either side.

'I didn't want this,' Emil said, and then he closed the door.

The key was in the lock before the soldiers hit it. Wooden shells sprayed into the other side, but the door only tremored; they would never be enough to break through.

The boards were piled where he had left them, on the ground at his feet. Emil took the first and held it in place against the door. A single nail trembled in his hand.

'They held me to ransom for too long, Kaspar.' His words were punctuated by the pounding of his hammer. Every nail felt like triumph. Every nail felt like guilt. 'Well, now I'll hold them. I'll hold ... *you*.'

The door bucked. Emil fell back, but the board held in place – and, when he heard his brother's voice, it was dull and far away. He got back to his feet, continued his task.

'Don't try and fight it, Kaspar. Nobody will hear you, not through Papa's walls. You can't tear it down. It's stronger than that. Did you ever know a toy Papa made that could possibly break?'

'Emil?'

Emil hammered harder. The second board went up, then a third, and with each one his brother grew more distant. Those Wendy House walls, Emil remembered, designed so children could play inside and never be heard ...

'Emil, you can't mean to ...'

He stopped before lifting the final board. 'I didn't want to,' he said, uncertain if his brother could hear. 'But what else is there when you won't see?'

Emil paused when the last nail was in his hand. Something was pressing on his foot and, unthinking, he kicked it away; it was only when he had driven the last nail into the wood that he looked down and saw it was the Imperial Kapitan. Somehow, the soldier had forced its way out of its birdcage prison, its back still burnt and scarred from his workshop fire. Now it lay by the picket fence, kicking feebly as it tried to stand. Emil left the boarded door behind and loomed above the Kapitan, lifting his boot as if ready to grind it into splinters and tangled wire.

'I ought to,' he said. 'I should, but ... you used to be mine.'

Then, driven by some feeling he did not know, Emil slid his foot away. Lying prostrate on the ground, the Imperial Kapitan stared up. The key in its back was winding down. It turned in circles, desperate to wind itself but unfit for the task.

Slide down, into that sandalwood mind ...

The Imperial Kapitan knows what he has seen. The journey from the birdcage was fraught, but he got here just in time: to know the fate of his creator, the fate of his people. Now there is only him left to face the wrath of the evil one. He thinks: I will kill you now, you daemon, smite you down here in the heart of the paper forest. But new connections have been being made in his mind, chasms of confusion and misunderstanding are being bridged daily, and with this comes deeper, richer ideas. And this time, the Kapitan thinks: I will surely perish if I fight him now. My people might be gone – but there is another way.

So he runs.

Under floorboard and through skirting, up the crevasses in the wall cavities, down the undersides of shelving. These are the homelands of the toy soldier and the Imperial Kapitan knows them better than any. But there is a sword hanging over him now and, the more he exerts himself, the more he feels the touch of its blade: the key in his back is winding down, down, down, and the Kapitan must lift himself up, up, up …

The world and all memory of it is separating, turning into fragments and whirling through the grain of his mind, but finally he reaches his destination. He must conserve energy now so he slows, creeping to that place in the skirting where the monsters who once lived here, creatures of fur and whisker and sharp yellow teeth, once mined their tunnels. Through a tiny portal in the wood he sees the room where she is sleeping: the one who lies with the Kaspar god at night. She is the only one who can save him now, the only one who might lead his people back into the light.

The Imperial Kapitan emerges into the midnight room. It is an ordeal to scale the Bedside (his mind is fraying now, his senses are fading), but somehow he hauls himself up, using the dangling tassels of a blanket as ropes. Then he is there, standing on the sleeping lady's breast. He marches up (his motors almost dead!) and reaches out to open her eyes.

Behind him: the gale of the bedroom door being opened. The Imperial Kapitan turns and sees the great figure stomp into the room.

It is him. The daemon lord. He has come again, by staircase and Secret Door. His feet strike the ground with echoes like earthquakes.

The Imperial Kapitan knows what the daemon is here to do: to capture and imprison the lady, just as he has done the Kaspar god. He will fight him with every iota of tension left in his motors, fight him even though he knows it will do no good. That is his duty, now that he is the only one left. So the Kapitan charges.

When he reaches the end of the bed, ready to launch himself into the black, his motor stops turning. There is life left in his mind, but only the residual echo of energy in his body. He can go no further. He tumbles, tumbles from the bedside, tumbles into the jaws of the lady's bag lying open below. The tumbling seems to last a lifetime. Perhaps it lasts many, for Wind Down has come and his whole existence is flashing before his eyes.

Through the roof of the bag he sees the world turning above him. The darkness is gathering, but in his last moment, before thirty years of sleep come to destroy him, he sees that the daemon lord is not here to steal the lady away at all. Instead, the daemon lord is holding a letter in his hands. He places it gently at the sleeping lady's side and then he himself steals away, out into the Emporium halls.

Never has a blackness been as bitter as this. The Imperial Kapitan has failed his god, failed his people. For thirty years, what parts of his mind survive as knots in the wood, will not let him forget.

Cathy stepped back, in horror, from the Wendy House wall. 'How could you, Emil? It wasn't a parley. It was an ... execution. What am I to find in there? Tell me that, Emil! A husk? Whatever's left of my husband?'

The Wendy House sat in the storeroom where the patchwork beasts had dragged it almost thirty years before. Cathy looked at the boarded windows and crêpe paper ivy, the steepled roof and stoppered-up chimneypot on top. This place that had once been her home, had it also been a ... prison?

'You're the one who wrote that letter,' she breathed.

In reply, there was only stony silence.

'And you're the one who left Sirius out in the snow. Left him to wind down and die. All to make me think Kaspar had walked out, when really ...'

Sirius looked up at the boards and set up a howl.

The toy soldiers were already obeying the Imperial Kapitan, driving wooden bayonets at the boards that sealed the door. But it would take a thousand lifetimes for a toy soldier to break through. Martha crouched down and gathered them near.

'I tried to warn him. I told him I'd do anything, anything to keep our Emporium alive, anything so that it was there for my sons. Well, he didn't listen. It wasn't meant to be like this. It was only meant to be – what did he call it? *A meeting of minds.* But he wouldn't, Cathy, he wouldn't even meet halfway, and I had to make sure ...'

There were other boxes in the storeroom, crates deemed of no value, left behind when the prospectors came. Between them stood an axe, once used to fell the paper trees. Cathy strained to lift it, dragged it to the Wendy House door.

'Mama, you mustn't. You'll break your back.'

'Let me,' said Emil. 'I owe him that. I owe you ...'

But Cathy had already hoisted it high. She brought it up above her shoulders and let its weight carry her forward.

'You owe me thirty years, Emil. You owe me a life. You owe me ...' She stopped herself wheeling around, the axe in her hands. 'You owe me a world. Whatever's through these doors, you ...'

Martha came between them. 'Perhaps you should go, Uncle Emil.'

'Go? But this is mine. My Emporium ...'

The axe bit into the boards, but the door did not buckle. It bit again, and splinters showered down. Three times, four times, five times and more, Cathy threw her body at the axe and the axe into the wood – until, at last, the boards scythed apart. Then, taking to them with fingers and fists, she revealed the little red door.

Its paintwork was tarnished. The brass knocker, its head the shape of a wolf, was thick with grime. Cathy reached out and touched it. She gave Martha a questing look and, when she nodded, she knocked on the door. But the sound was hollow, no answer came, and when she tried again it was in desperation, not belief.

So she returned to the axe.

The door was stronger than the boards, and Cathy remembered, suddenly, the old truth: that Papa Jack had never made a toy that would break and spoil a child's day. Against Papa Jack's invention, an axe was useless. She dropped it at her side, was about to turn and cast invective at Emil – but he was already standing there, drawing a little silver key from a chain that hung around his neck.

The door had grown warped with age, but it gave in to Cathy's touch – and, as it rolled inwards, she saw the Wendy House interior for the first time in half a life.

Inside was only darkness.

By torchlight they crossed the threshold. The sweeping light picked up the corners of the Wendy House, much further away than they had any right to be. Cathy stood in the heart of the room, taking in the bed that had once been hers, the hotplate and cabinets, the old threadbare rug – but, cavernous as it was, the Wendy House was empty. Nothing remained but the dust.

'It can't be,' Martha whispered.

Emil was about to step through when Cathy said, 'No, Emil. This Wendy House isn't for you. It's mine. Mine and Kaspar's, remember? *Ours*. That summer ...'

'Cathy, please.'

'Just go, Emil. Just go.'

For some time, Emil stood on the threshold and stared. He too remembered that summer. He remembered reading books about childbirth and bringing her his designs. He remembered their picnic out in the glade and the way her face had dimpled when she said, *treat yourself more kindly, Emil. That's an order*. He remembered how whole that had made him, how he'd felt capable of doing it all, all because of the girl – and, whether she wanted him or not, how it hardly mattered, because she was here and *she* mattered and she was Cathy Wray. All of those memories, they had lasted a lifetime – and, in an instant, they unravelled.

'Cathy?' he ventured, but the silence was answer enough.

After he was gone, Cathy sat on the edge of the bed and teased her fingers so that Sirius might join her. There he lay, black button eyes as disconsolate as black button eyes could be. Across the floorboards, the toy soldiers came to a halt. The Imperial Kapitan was gesticulating for them to line up in some new formation, but they did not have the words for what they were feeling, and not one of them knew where to stand; sometimes language was such an inconsequential thing.

Martha peered under the bed, and found nothing. She looked behind the broken door, and found nothing still. Dancing in the light of her own torch, she scurried to the little tin sink and squinted down the plughole – but nothing, nothing, nothing, everywhere she looked.

Then she reared up, with an empty can of bully beef in her hands. 'Mama,' she said. 'He *was* here.'

The torch arced over the room, illuminating first her mama, nursing what little hope she had left, then Sirius, still snuggled on her lap. Finally, light spilled upon the toybox at the foot of the bed – that plain, unremarkable thing that Kaspar had brought to her almost fifty years before.

Martha rushed to open it up.

'Mama,' she breathed.

From the lip of the box, into its unseen depths, a stair spiralled down. Where once there had been cans of bully beef and sardines, jars of new potatoes in brine, now there were polished oak steps, a banister rail of glistening bone. Unlit candles were fixed in brackets to a wall that disappeared in the darkness. Balanced in the first was a book of matches.

'Mama?'

'That old fool …' Cathy said. 'Oh Kaspar, what have you done?'

'What *has* he done?'

In the half-light it seemed that Cathy was smiling. She had to try twice before she could speak, for something was clogging her throat – and to Martha it sounded like joy. 'He … got better,' she laughed.

*

It was dull in the Wendy House. The toy soldiers provided some modicum of company, and across the weeks and months Kaspar had grown used to the silence, but no amount of tutoring them, or watching them discover new things, could keep boredom at bay. Sometimes, he let it smother him and lay in bed for days and nights (though he could not tell where one ended and another began, and never would again), and were it not for the memory of the summer Cathy, his Cathy, had spent here, perhaps he would never have got out of bed again. Cathy had thought this place a prison too … at first. But she was carrying Martha inside her, a whole new world, and when Kaspar remembered that, that was when he knew what he had to do. If the world outside was to be denied him, he would have to make the world within.

The toy soldiers stopped their drilling as they watched their demi-god shed his bedclothes and get to his feet. With his canes he shuffled to the toybox and began to empty it of the tins of seasoned ham, the bags of flour and jars of honey that Emil had crammed inside. Beneath were bags of earth and seedling potatoes, onions with shoots and packets of seed. Emil had provisioned him well, and that was both proof of the love his brother still bore him and evidence of how eagerly he had prepared Kaspar's cell.

With the toybox emptied, Kaspar lowered himself inside. The place was more cavernous than he remembered, though scarcely the size of a four-poster bed. He basked in the darkness and remembered: that summer, that first summer with Cathy, I barely made six of these. We painted them in bright colours and put the price tag high, but I never went back to them. It was too slow an endeavour – and back then there were other distractions, the ordinary magic more important than the rest.

But now, he thought, what is time? What else is there? And: I did it once. I could do it again. All it takes is to hold the vision in mind. A little push here, a careful tweak there, and things start changing. You have to remember the textures. You have to cast yourself back, back to when you were eight years old and rooms were bigger, your home was bigger, the world itself bigger than it would ever be again. *Perspectives*, he had told Cathy. It was all about perspectives.

He sat up, at one and the same time at the bottom of the box and peering over its lip. The Wendy House walls were stacked high with other boxes, materials Emil and the shop hands had carted in here that winter they turned it into their secure shopfloor. In there were rolls of felt and bales of wire, reams of crêpe paper and card, pipe cleaners and springs and bags of iron balls: everything a toymaker might need for the greatest creation of his life.

In a crescent around him, the toy soldiers bobbed up and down, as if to ask what he meant to do.

'My wife once told me that, when nobody else can help you, you have to help yourself. And the world, it can be anything we want it to, if only we can hold it in our heads. So, my little friends, what do we want it to be?'

Papa Jack once taught him that a toymaker needed only two commodities: his imagination and his time. Well, now he had both. I'm going to have to get a lot better, he thought, but there was no time like the present – so, with the wind-up soldiers still watching, he got to work.

Cathy took the book of matches, lighting each candle as she came.

There were seventeen steps before she stopped counting. There might have been seventeen more before she felt the crinkling of cardboard creepers underfoot and, looking down, saw crêpe paper flowers in blue and green, a carpet of blossom and berries as in the depths of some summer forest. Behind her, Sirius stopped to sniff at the crinkling foliage.

At the bottom of the steps the paper was thick and entangled, gone to seed for so many years that the way ahead was a wilderness of briars and thorn. Through it, the narrow stairs became a passage and, beyond that, opened out into a room, a cavern, she could not see. That cavern was forested in cardboard larch, evergreens of tinsel, mighty oaks whose paper trunks had hardened and knotted with the passing generations.

'Martha?'

She was at her side now, the axe in her hand. 'I'll give it everything I have,' she said, and together they blazed a path forward.

Under the trees the briars grew less wild. Here there were trails and places where the trees had been coppiced, and in the roots the spoor of some animal. Something startled above them: the goldfinches of pipe cleaners and golden brocade that were roosting above.

A patchwork rabbit darted across Cathy's path. She followed it with her eyes – and there, in the shadows between two cardboard elm, it looked back. Perhaps it was only her imagination, but its eyes seemed to pinch in imitation of a human's surprise, before it turned tail and zigzagged back into the forest.

After that, more rabbits came. One, chewing at the petals of some felt flower, birthed a tiny kit, which took one look at the interlopers and hurtled for cover.

'Mama,' Martha whispered, 'look ...'

Together, their eyes turned upward. Through the lattice of branches, the sky seemed closer than ever. Unable to resist, Martha lifted herself into the nearest elm. There, she reached through a canopy of crinkling green – and felt the touch of the sky, a blue wall against her hand.

By the time she returned to the forest floor, Cathy had already gone on ahead. Somewhere, Sirius yelped in fright – and Cathy barrelled forward, until she chanced upon a clearing. Here was the place the forest met the sky, and surely the outer limit of the toybox. Nestled against the wall stood a cottage of imitation stone, cotton wool smoke billowing out of its chimney.

Cathy was standing outside its picket fence. Patchwork hens clucked around a coop, and in the trees a great wolfhound opened one lazy eye to consider them, then closed it to snooze once again.

'Mama,' Martha ventured, 'mightn't he ...'

Cathy said nothing. She squeezed her daughter's hand, and walked into the cottage.

Inside, there were only boxes – two dozen and more, lined up around the cottage walls, with paper grasses growing up in between. Martha and Cathy opened each one, gazing within. Inside lay new worlds, and nestled in them more worlds still. A great galleon lay beached upon the sand, with patchwork parrots nesting in its sails and troops of patchwork monkeys screeching from the jungles inland. Across icebound taiga, herds of embroidered reindeer outpaced the mountain tigers that stalked them, and beavers made dams out of paper spruce and fir. A miniature railway crossed a lunar landscape, populated by little green men.

'Oh Papa,' said Martha, 'he lived a life …'

So many lives, thought Cathy, but where to begin?

It had taken them some time to catch up, but finally the Imperial Kapitan led the toy soldiers into the cottage. Cathy helped them on to the lips of the toyboxes, so that they might peer into the new worlds within. She was watching them sally in and out, seemingly inspecting each frontier, when she realised that Sirius was whimpering. He had been following a scent in the dirt and now he had risen on his hind paws, scrabbling at the lip of a toybox crammed in behind the others. Cathy moved toward it. The box was of a simple design – and there, on its lid, a single scarlet arrow, in florid design.

'This way,' she smiled.

The way in was a mountain ravine, with the bones of prehistoric patchwork bears littering the way – but soon they emerged into the box's interior, where a rainbow arced across what Cathy took for the sky. On a cliff face above them, words were carved into imitation stone. Cathy read them to herself, each word a prayer. ROBERT KESEY, read the first. ANDREW DUNMORE. DOUGLAS FLOOD. JEKABS GODMAN, PAPA JACK. The names of every other Emporium shop hand lost along the way.

Onwards they went, beneath the memorial stone as high as the sky. Fields of incandescent flowers, like the sparklers of a bonfire night, dropped down toward the shores of a vast lake: streamers of crêpe paper in blue and green, with cross-stitch fish leaping from the waves and gulls, borne up by tiny balloons, hovering above. Cathy stood on the sand and looked across. In the heart of the lake rose an island, and on that island a tower of stone. There was only one window in that tower. Halfway up, firelight crackled, ringing the window in orange and red.

'There's a boat,' Cathy said, and pointed to a coracle moored against a narrow jetty. 'Come on …'

Together, they stood over it. 'There's only room for one, Mama.' Martha looked down. The toy soldiers were already marching aboard. 'And some tiny passengers, perhaps.'

Martha remained only to help her into the boat, Sirius diving into the paper waves alongside, and released her from the mooring. Then, determined to rescue the toybox from ruin, Martha returned to the flowers on fire, the cottage and forests in the world up above.

It was a slow journey over the lake; the paper waves moved sluggishly, and tendrils of satin seaweed seemed to anchor her down, but there was a current to the water and, by accident or design, it was drawing her to the island. Cathy could do nothing more than lie back and whisper in Sirius's ragged ears, while the Imperial Kapitan stood on the coracle's rounded prow and raised his rifle at every leaping fish.

Soon, she felt the quaking of the earth and stepped out of the coracle, on to a new shore of shale and confetti sand. The steps leading to the tower were weatherworn and she took to them carefully, allowing Sirius to venture ahead.

There were no nerves as she reached the tower. The door was nondescript, nothing more than a tradesman's entrance, and up close the white walls seemed scored in lines, as if the paper had been folded, smoothed out and folded again. She stepped into the interior, but all was serene. A stair of ivory white beckoned her on.

She stopped only once as she ventured up. Sirius was eager to continue the climb, but through a door Cathy saw a room much bigger than it had any right to be, and in it a model village of magnificent design. Farmhouses and fields, no bigger than the doll's houses of the Emporium shelves, surrounded a bustling market town of churches and steeples, butchers and grocers and libraries and schools. A model railway ran a circuit through the houses – and, on every street corner, wind-up men and women, no longer painted as the soldiers they used to be, strolled (not marched) up and down.

As she was watching, painted eyes looked up and found her. Soon the whole town was flocking her way. In the fields of paper wheat on the fringes of the farmland, the wind-up host gathered. At Cathy's side, the Imperial Kapitan appeared with his fellows, took one look at the miracle that lay before them, and surged out to meet friends not seen since an age long forgotten. Soon, they were mingling with their brethren. There would, Cathy supposed, be much learning to do; the new arrivals would have to be demobbed. But, for now, they were allowing themselves to be led. A town crier was flinging his arms in circles and the town was falling into formation.

Beneath her, Cathy read out the words.

HE IS WAITING!

Sirius yapped, but Cathy needed no encouragement. Her old bones did not feel young as she returned to the stairs, they still creaked and complained as they had grown used to doing, but there was a new feeling now. Perhaps this was the feeling of being rewound. She took flight. On the next storey, the halls were empty. On the storey above, only old crates and rolls of unused felt. But now she could feel the flickering of the fire she had seen from afar; its heat touched her, luring her on.

She stopped before a wooden door, the only thing of any colour set into the ivory walls. She did not knock, because she did not need to. She pushed it open.

The workshop was small, with a fire and a worktop and a single chair. He was lying back in that wooden throne, a mess of hair and tight white beard, with his head lolling forward. His hands, which had once been so smooth, were mottled in blue, with nails like yellow horns, and they twitched in his sleep, drumming out the pattern of some old dream.

Cathy stuttered forward. She did not know where to stand. Having no such compunctions, Sirius lolloped forward and tasted his fingers with its darned-sock tongue, then lay down to curl at his feet, the thrumming of his motor like a contented purr.

Cathy stood above him. For the longest time, she watched his chest as it rose and fell. She was aware, dimly, that the tower had shifted, the sky through the window seeming askew, and wondered (without really caring) whether Martha was moving the toybox, even now.

He opened his eyes. God, but they were glacial blue. How the years had changed him, and how they had kept him the same. He looked like her Kaspar, inhabiting the body of his father.

His lips came apart. Perhaps it had been decades since he had last spoken, for his voice, when it came, was as coarse as freshly felled wood.

'Miss Wray?' he croaked, scarcely able to believe.

'Kaspar,' she breathed, 'I thought I told you to stop calling me that.'

She fell into his arms.

They demolished Papa Jack's Emporium, Purveyors of Childhood Delights, on a winter's day in the December of 1953. If, like me, you had been there to see it done, you would have stood in the falling snow surrounded by so many others, seen the walls come down and the dust rise up, and thought it the very end of enchantment.

But you would have been wrong.

Come north with me now, past the green splendours of Regent's Park, through the elegant porticos of St John's Wood and north, to a little house off the Finchley Road. Take your shoes off at the door, creep past the kitchen where Martha Godman's children are putting the finishing touches to toys of their very own designs while their patchwork dog watches curiously on, and come up the crooked stairs. Here, in a chamber at the very top, sits an ill-hewn toybox, rescued from the Emporium on that last November night. Inside it are worlds too many to be imagined, and two old lovers making new ones every day.